W9-BYU-611

THE ISLAND OF DOCTOR MOREAU

broadview editions
series editor: L.W. Conolly

THE ISLAND OF DOCTOR MOREAU

H.G. Wells

edited by Mason Harris

broadview editions

Library and Archives Canada Cataloguing in Publication

Wells, H. G. (Herbert George), 1866-1946
    The island of Doctor Moreau / H.G. Wells ; edited by Mason Harris.

Includes bibliographical references.
ISBN 978-1-55111-327-2

    I. Harris, Mason II. Title.

PR5774.I8 2009   823'.912   C2009-902229-X

Broadview Editions

The Broadview Editions series represents the ever-changing canon of literature in English by bringing together texts long regarded as classics with valuable lesser-known works.

Advisory editor for this volume: Denis Johnston

Broadview Press is an independent, international publishing house, incorporated in 1985. Broadview believes in shared ownership, both with its employees and with the general public; since the year 2000 Broadview shares have traded publicly on the Toronto Venture Exchange under the symbol BDP.

We welcome comments and suggestions regarding any aspect of our publications—please feel free to contact us at the addresses below or at broadview@broadviewpress.com.

North America	PO Box 1243, Peterborough, Ontario, Canada K9J 7H5
	2215 Kenmore Ave., Buffalo, New York, USA 14207
	Tel: (705) 743-8990; Fax: (705) 743-8353
	email: customerservice@broadviewpress.com
UK, Ireland,	NBN International, Estover Road, Plymouth, UK PL6 7PY
and continental Europe	Tel: 44 (0) 1752 202300; Fax: 44 (0) 1752 202330
	email: enquiries@nbninternational.com
Australia and New Zealand	UNIREPS, University of New South Wales
	Sydney, NSW, Australia 2052
	Tel: 61 2 9385 0150; Fax: 61 2 9385 0155
	email: info@unireps.com.au

www.broadviewpress.com

Broadview Press acknowledges the financial support of the Government of Canada through the Book Publishing Industry Development Program (BPIDP) for our publishing activities.

PRINTED IN CANADA

For my wife, Aphrodite,
whose patience and understanding
provided vital support through
the many stages of this project.

H.G. Wells, c. 1895–1896
Reproduced with the permission of A.P. Watt Ltd. and
the Rare Book & Manuscript Library of the
University of Illinois at Urbana-Champaign.

Contents

Acknowledgements

I want to acknowledge the kind assistance of Dr. Robert M. Philmus in granting me permission to use the text provided in his variorum edition of *The Island of Doctor Moreau* as the basis for the text of this edition, and also for permission to reprint (Appendix J) a portion of his transcript of Wells's first draft of *Moreau*, published for the first time in his edition. Also, I must gratefully acknowledge my debt to the guidance provided by the commentaries and notes of his exemplary edition, to which my own owes a great deal.

My edition is much indebted to recommendations for revision provided by Dr. Leonard Conolly, Series Editor for Broadview Editions, and to Dr. Denis Johnston's conscientious copy-editing of my text and suggestions for improving it. I also wish to thank Dr. Lee Perry, Librarian of the Rare Books Collection of the Woodward Biomedical Library of the University of British Columbia, for her patience and courtesy in facilitating my study of *La Psychologie Morbide* by Jacques-Joseph Moreau.

Formal acknowledgements are due to the following:

A.P. Watt Ltd. on behalf of The Literary Executors of the Estate of H.G. Wells for permission to reprint excerpts from Wells's first draft of *Moreau* (Appendix J) and to reproduce the photograph of Wells used as the frontispiece for this edition.

The Rare Book and Manuscript Library of the University of Illinois at Urbana-Champaign for generously providing copies of, and permission to reproduce, the photograph of Wells; the title-page of the first American edition of *The Island of Doctor* Moreau; and an illustration that served as the frontispiece of the first British edition.

Manchester University Press for permission to reprint some passages from an article previously published in *Gothic Studies* (Introduction, pp. 44-55).

Dover Press for permission to publish excerpts from their edition of *An Introduction to the Study of Experimental Medicine* by Claude Bernard (Appendix G3).

Patterson Smith for permission to publish extracts from their editions of *Crime: Its Causes and Remedies* by Cesare Lombroso (Appendix F5) and *Criminal Man According to the Classification of Cesare Lombroso* by Gina Lombroso-Ferrero (Appendix F4).

Introduction

The Island of Doctor Moreau has long been recognized as one of the most important but also by far the most disturbing of the science-fiction novellas that made Wells's literary reputation in the 1890s. The pain inflicted by Doctor Moreau's continuous practice of vivisection without anaesthesia enhances but does not fully explain the oppressive emotional atmosphere that envelops his island world. In *Moreau*, Wells achieves not only a major work of science fiction centred on the creation of artificial beings by an overreaching scientist but also a most effective horror story inspired by the renaissance in Gothic literature in the late nineteenth century: Stevenson's *Doctor Jekyll and Mr. Hyde*, published ten years earlier, is an important influence.

Because of its strong emotional impact, its affiliation to more than one genre, and its tendency both to inspire and defeat attempts to find some central allegory manifested in its confused and violent world, *Moreau* has become notorious as a challenge to interpretation. Critics have tended to separate out special aspects of the story, while sometimes expressing uncertainty as to how these relate to the story's motivation as a whole. The story has been approached as a satire of religion (Gorman Beauchamp), of the arrogance of science (R.D. Haynes 1988), and of imperialism (Cyndy Hendershot and Bari J. Gold).

Some critics focus on the way the story seems to be related to several genres but belongs fully to none, or invents a new genre of its own that combines myth with Darwinian biology (Nicoletta Vallorani). Roger Bozzetto notes that Doctor Moreau's relation to the Beast People could be taken as "a metaphor for civil society and its hierarchization"(40) and hence also as a critique of the myths of imperialism. He concludes that the mood of the story could best be characterized paradoxically as "a farcical tragedy" (41).

Both Bozzetto and Roger Bowen emphasize the importance of realistic detail in the island setting, and suggest links to other narratives set on islands. Elaine Showalter sees *Moreau* as a prime example of a special genre invented mainly by male British authors of the late-nineteenth century: the "*fin-de-siècle* male quest romance" that sets fantastic adventure stories in a bachelor world from which women are almost completely excluded. According to Showalter, this genre tends to spin "fantastic plots involving alternative forms of male reproduction and self-replication" ("Apocalyptic Fables" 70-73).

In an article (1981) and in his introduction to his variorum edition of *Moreau*, Robert M. Philmus points out how Wells moved from the style of Stevensonian romance in his first unpublished version of the story to a more hard-edged satiric mode in his final version. Philmus notes the importance of Swift as an influence on the final version, especially Gulliver's adventures in the land of the Houyhnhnms in the last book of *Gulliver's Travels*. Philmus argues that Wells "darwinizes" Swift's Houyhnhnms and Yahoos—which might suggest that at the end Prendick is no more reliable a narrator than Gulliver ("Satiric Ambivalence" 6). J.R. Hammond (1993) also provides a wide-ranging interpretation of the story as "a Swiftian parable."

Critics interested in exploring *Moreau*'s intellectual background tend to see it as a symbolic articulation of the problems of a Darwinian world-view. In his informative book on Wells's science fiction, Frank McConnell gives a general sense of the Darwinian basis of Wells's "evolutionary fables": *The Time Machine*, *The Island of Doctor Moreau*, and *The War of the Worlds*. In an article entitled "Wells's Debt to Huxley," R.D. Haynes sees T.H. Huxley's view of evolution as the launching point for satire of religion in *Moreau*. Patrick Parrinder, in a lucid discussion of the Darwinian implications of *Moreau*, sees the story as a determined attempt at the "dethronement" of the human species from its belief in its superiority to the world of nature, especially its assumption of complete superiority to animals (*Shadows of the Future* 56-64). Recently John Glendening has made a detailed and wide-ranging study of Darwinian ideas in the novel. He sees Doctor Moreau (and Wells) as struggling to disentangle human destiny from the confusion of Darwinian nature and argues that in *Moreau* Wells exposes the "mental flaws" of a scientist to whom he gives some of his favourite ideas. Glendening suggests that in his portrayal of Doctor Moreau, Wells may have gone further than he intended in undermining his own world-view (585).

One problem with approaches that see the story as a play of ideas is that they tend to overlook its atmosphere of horror. Fortunately, some interesting interpretations of *Moreau* have emerged from the recent burgeoning of criticism on Gothic literature. In his now classic history of the Gothic, *The Literature of Terror*, David Punter provides a brief but pithy discussion of *Moreau* (249-56). Punter notes that the pain inflicted by Moreau has an ambiguous role—as well as being a source of horror it is also part of a "'humanizing' process" (251)—and that this ambiguity extends to Moreau's project as a whole (252). Punter observes that in *Moreau* "old Gothic themes of aspiration and dominance" combine with "fears about human status and dignity generated by Darwin" and "images of white imperialism in its decline" (253). More recently, Kelly Hurley, in her discussion of *Moreau* in *Gothic Body*, an important book on the physical and mental disintegration of the self in Gothic literature of the late nineteenth century, links late-Victorian anxieties about biological degeneration and blurring of the boundary between human and animal to the grotesque physicality of the story's Beast People and hidden tendencies of its "human" characters as well (102-13). Hurley shows that anxiety about degeneration provides an important link between the story's Darwinian content and its Gothic effect.

After a brief account of Wells's early life, this Introduction will explore the rich but tangled thicket of the story's Darwinian background, then place Moreau's pursuit of biological research in the context of the late-Victorian controversy over vivisection. The conclusion will ponder the mystery of Moreau's motivation and his deliberate use of pain.

In undertaking to produce a Broadview edition of one of Wells's science-fiction novellas, I am aware of having been preceded by Nicholas Ruddick's impressive Broadview edition of *The Time Machine*, a story closely linked to *Moreau* in its exploration of Darwinian themes. Since Ruddick provides a wide-ranging view of Wells's writing and cultural context, I have tried here to concentrate more narrowly on themes related to *Moreau*, with occasional reference to important material provided in the appendices of Ruddick's edition.

The Early Adventures of H.G. Wells: Science and Fiction

The date of Wells's birth (1866) granted him membership in a generation of imaginative writers who reached maturity towards the end of the nineteenth century, a period of creative innovation in thought and literature. R.L. Stevenson, Oscar Wilde, and Rider Haggard were about ten to fifteen years older than Wells; Conan Doyle, Rudyard Kipling, and J.M. Barrie were near his age. All experimented with fantastic narratives and exotic settings. For a young man who would invent a new genre of imaginative fiction, this was a good time to have appeared on the scene. As Wells made the discovery that he could write for a living, he would be able to take advantage of the broadening interests of a new reading public and a boom in fantasy and shorter forms of fiction in the last decade of the nineteenth century. It would take nearly thirty years, however, for the good fortune of this timing to become evident. Before that, his prospects often looked rather bleak. Wells's early life became an extraordinary struggle against near-catastrophe: the darkness of this experience made its way into his science fiction.

In a brief article that has strongly influenced Wells-criticism, Robert P. Weeks finds a consistent pattern in Wells's fiction, especially clear in his scientific fantasies: the main character makes a desperate revolt against a confining environment—an environment limited both by oppressive social convention and the normal laws of space and time—and achieves a sense of exhilarating liberation, though finally this experience tends to failure and death. In the case of *Moreau*, it is Doctor Moreau himself who attempts a godlike transcendence of the process of evolution and dies as a result (27). Weeks observes that the most likely reason that Wells developed his imaginative world around this pattern was his sense of being in mortal combat with the conventional morality and rigid class-structure of Victorian society (30).

Telling the story of his life and opinions, Wells gives a vivid account of his early struggles against the trap of respectable poverty into which he was born. Both Wells's parents had been upper servants in the world of landed estates—his mother as a lady's maid, his father as a gardener—but upon marrying they purchased a small shop where they sold crockery, hardware, and some equipment for cricket, in Bromley (Kent), a town which was fast becoming a suburb of London. Here they remained trapped for a quarter-century. When they bought the shop from a relative, they were not aware that its business was already in decline because railway travel made it all too easy for potential customers to commute to the new department stores in London. Wells's father, amiable and independent-minded, was away most of the time earning a bit of extra money at professional cricket, leaving Wells's mother to mind the children, the shop, and the "needy shabby home" filled with splinters and bugs.[1]

As a servant on a large estate, Mrs. Wells had early taken on an old-fashioned, hierarchical view of the world (*Experiment* I, 47-49). She also developed a narrow, Puritanical variety of religion. Wells says that in his

---

[1] H.G. Wells, *Experiment in Autobiography*, I; 37. Wells's autobiography is my primary source for his life. Among biographies of Wells, my sense of his development as writer and thinker owes most to *H.G. Wells: A Biography* by Norman and Jeanne MacKenzie. Also, I have benefitted from the careful detail of David C. Smith's biography *H. G Wells: Desperately Mortal*.

childhood he felt obliged to believe in this religion but soon came to hate it, especially its all-seeing, punishing God who condemned sinners to eternal Hellfire. He says that around the age of twelve, after a particularly vivid vision of Hell in a nightmare, "suddenly the light broke through to me and I knew this God was a lie" (*Experiment* I, 45; see Appendix A).

The bitter satire of religion manifested in the cult of the Beast People in *The Island of Doctor Moreau*, with its emphasis on the assumed sinful tendencies of all its members and its detailed prohibitions of physical aspects of life, seems aimed primarily at his mother's Puritanism. Hammond observes that the "whole of *The Island of Doctor Moreau* can be seen ... as a parody of the intensely emotional, Calvinistic view of the universe" to which Wells was subjected from childhood through adolescence ("Swiftian Parable" 35). On the other hand, Wells may also have internalized his mother's Puritan values. A number of commentators have noted that, like his mentor T.H. Huxley, Wells found secular equivalents to the sense of sin, the need for moral regeneration, and the visionary quality characteristic of the British Puritan tradition (MacKenzie 128-30).

His mother's limited and intensely conventional world-view was also shown in her rigid plans for his future. As a boy Wells developed an enthusiastic interest in literature and science, but his mother considered that the draping trade was the height of respectability. After some tantalizingly brief encounters with further education, Wells, at the age of fifteen, was committed by his mother (who had to pay a considerable fee) to a four-year, live-in apprenticeship at a large and prosperous drapery store offering a variety of high-quality textiles, linen, and clothing. Along with his many tasks as a shop-assistant, the young Wells was expected to acquire a complete knowledge of the store's inventory and to cultivate an obsequious manner of presenting its wares to clients. Wells says that it was during this dismal apprenticeship that he first became a conscious rebel against both religion and the social hierarchy, coming to see organized religion as a system of illusions intended to support a society based on class privilege (Appendix A).

After two years apprenticed to the draping trade, Wells announced to the consternation of his family that he could endure it no longer. Thanks to timely assistance from the head of a local boarding school he escaped from his apparently hopeless situation by winning a scholarship to study at a new government-funded school in London devoted to education in science. Leaving rural Sussex in triumph at the age of eighteen, Wells was especially pleased to know that he would be spending his first year as a student in courses in biology and zoology to be taught by the famous Professor Huxley, founder of the school that had given him the scholarship.

Leading spokesman for science, aggressive defender of Darwin, and zealous educator, T.H. Huxley (1825-95) had become concerned at the neglect of science in the rather old-fashioned British educational system and had persuaded the government to endow a school to produce science teachers and industrial managers. This was first named the Normal School of Science (later the Royal College of Science). Placed in the remarkable complex of colleges, museums, and libraries in South Kensington near Hyde Park, this institution provided a central location from which the young Wells could explore the intellectual culture of his time. Huxley became Dean and star teacher of the school.

Ultimately, Wells's career at this institution was not destined for success, but his exposure to Huxley in his first year would be of great importance in focusing his commitment to the Darwinian thought of his time. The young Wells never met Huxley personally except to exchange a "good morning," but he describes his year as Huxley's student as a transformative experience that reordered his way of understanding the world: "That year I spent in Huxley's class, was beyond all question, the most educational year of my life." Wells praises Darwin and Huxley as "very great men" and "mighty intellectual liberators" to be ranked among the leading thinkers of history (*Experiment* I, 201-02; see Appendix A). In later reminiscences of Huxley, Wells tells how he and his fellow students avidly read Huxley's books and clubbed together the money to purchase copies of his latest essays: "I believed then he was the greatest man I was ever likely to meet, and I believe that all the more firmly today." Huxley's courses seemed to the young Wells to provide a comprehensive account of physical life and its development, giving him "a permanent faith in Biology as the basis of all but the most elementary education" (Geoffrey West 49-50).

The extreme, almost religious, value the young Wells placed on Darwinian thought, especially as represented by Huxley, is not surprising for a rebellious young man passionately interested in science in the later nineteenth century. Coiner of the word "agnosticism," Huxley gathered about him some leading scientific minds of his day in a movement of revolt against the religious and educational establishments of Victorian Britain. He proclaimed science, especially the Darwinian kind, as the "New Reformation," a quest for truth that would make religion obsolete. Thus Darwinian ideas as preached by Huxley might indeed seem a glorious liberation for scientifically-minded young people of humble origins, fighting their way to a career outside the Oxford–Cambridge educational system. As Huxley discredited religion in the name of science, he offered his scientific rationalism as a new basis for intellectual certainty. The MacKenzies argue that Huxley's thought gave Wells a meeting ground between the Puritan religion of his childhood and the dedication to science he acquired as Huxley's student and disciple (55–57).

Despite the "irregularity and unsoundness" of his general education, Wells finished his first year at the top of his class—both his courses had been taught by Huxley (*Experiment* I, 163). Unfortunately, at this point Huxley retired because of ill health and Wells's teachers for the next two years had nothing of Huxley's inspirational power. Bored with his science courses, Wells became more aware of his literary interests. In his last two years at the school he took an active role in a debating society organized by the students and began to think of himself as a potential writer rather than a science teacher. Perhaps with this end in view he founded a school magazine, the *Science Schools Journal*, mainly occupied with literature and philosophy. He became the first editor, but the school authorities forced him to quit because he had cut too many classes. He converted to socialism, wore a red tie to advertise the fact, and with like-minded friends attended socialist meetings at the house of William Morris, the leader of the Arts and Crafts Movement now turned ardent Marxist. Here Wells listened to speeches by Morris and also a young Irish writer, George Bernard Shaw.

After failing geology at the end of his third year Wells lost his scholarship and, at the age of twenty, had in effect flunked out.[1] The only teaching job he could find was at a boarding school in Wales that turned out to be appallingly inferior. At this point disaster intervened to deliver him from a miserably ill-paid career in the lower depths of science teaching. (Wells notes that whenever he seemed trapped in a hopeless situation, some catastrophe came along to liberate him [*Experiment* I, 76, 108].) In a game of soccer a student struck him from behind, resulting in a crushed kidney and a severed blood vessel in his lung. When he collapsed and started spitting blood, he was diagnosed as having a case of consumption (tuberculosis) so serious that he would soon expire. The nature of young Wells's physical problems has never been fully explained, but they were real enough. He did not die—he would live to be nearly eighty—but the next twelve years of his life were overshadowed by mysterious kidney and chest problems,

---

1   In a "carefully done" short story, "A Slip Under the Microscope" (1896), Wells describes the difficulties of being a poor student at the school, with a final sense of failure.

the latter sometimes breaking out in lung hemorrhages, and he felt threatened by the possibility of early death or permanent invalidism. This sense of impending doom may have contributed to the apocalyptic mood of his science fiction.

In his autobiography, however, Wells insists that this setback freed him for new opportunities (*Experiment* I, 290-91). His parents' situation had changed. The permanent laming of his father by a gardening accident meant that the family had to survive solely on the income from the shop. After three years of increasing deprivation, his mother had had the luck to find employment as head housekeeper at the mansion of a country estate where she had once served as lady's maid. Here her ailing son took refuge. Since the housekeeper's boy was considered to be on the verge of death he was given the best of everything, including free run of the well-stocked library. Reading copiously in the classics of English literature during his four months of convalescence, Wells gained a new sense of language and style. At last he was discovering the literary values essential to a writer of fiction.

Here he wrote the first, incomplete version of what would eventually become *The Time Machine* and published three instalments of it in the *Science Schools Journal*.[1] After a long visit with friends Wells stated, "I have been dying for nearly two-thirds of a year ... and I have died long enough" and resolved to begin his "second attack on London" (*Experiment* I, 310). After coming near to starvation he had the luck to become science teacher at a first-rate day school, began to contribute articles to magazines associated with the teaching of science, and soon left this school for his last and best position as teacher, an important role in a private "cramming school" organized by an academic entrepreneur and called a "Tutorial College," which offered to prepare undergraduates pursuing a Bachelor of Science degree at the University of London for the University's final examinations in various subjects. Wells became responsible for tutorials in biology and geology. Former students testify to his thorough knowledge of his subjects and his effectiveness as a teacher. Out of the courses he taught, Wells published a textbook on biology, which remained in print for many years, and also, with a friend, a textbook on physiology. He also gave his students practical training in methods of dissecting dead animals, which may have helped later with imagining Doctor Moreau's handiwork on live ones. To further his career he took exams from the College of Preceptors for

---

1   For an account of the many stages though which this narrative eventually became *The Time Machine*, see Nicholas Ruddick's Broadview edition of *The Time Machine*, 22-30.

teaching certificates in several scientific subjects including psychology, and at the age of twenty-four acquired the degree of Bachelor of Science with first-class honours in zoology from the University of London.

On the strength of his teaching career Wells married a pretty cousin who turned out to be afraid of sex, unshakeably conventional in her opinions, and who provided no intellectual companionship. He now could look forward to a respectable life of industrious teaching in the cramming school to support a little house in London and an unhappy marriage. Catastrophe intervened again, this time with a serious hemorrhage of the lungs. After finding himself still alive, Wells decided that he would teach no more. While convalescing at the seashore he discovered from a novel by J.M. Barrie—author of *Peter Pan*—how to turn out amusing essays on incidents in everyday life. He sold enough of these to think that he might make a living by writing, and on the strength of this left his wife for a student from his science class, Amy Catherine Robbins, who would become his permanent wife.

In addition to his light essays, Wells wrote a series of serious essays on speculative aspects of biological science, most of them involving the theory of evolution. Ranging over many subjects, these reveal a detailed knowledge of the most advanced Darwinian thought of his time and sometimes seem to anticipate later developments in Darwinian theory.[1] Also, Wells was persuaded by his editors to do a stint as reviewer of fiction and drama, thus broadening his knowledge of the literary scene.

Encouraged by an editor to use his knowledge of science as a basis for fantastic tales, Wells began his career in science fiction by writing short stories. During the summer of 1894, when the market for his essays and stories seemed to have dried up and financial ruin loomed, Wells decided to follow the advice of the formidable editor W.E. Henley that he should turn some loosely-fictionalized essays on time travel he had published in Henley's magazine a few months earlier into a coherent adventure story (*Experiment* II, 519-19). The result was a novella-length story called *The Time Machine*.

In the novella Wells discovered the right length for a well-plotted story that would also have room for deeper speculations introduced in essay-like

---

1   The most important of these essays have been collected in *H.G. Wells: Early Writings in Science and Science Fiction*, edited by Robert M. Philmus and David Y. Hughes, who also provide a very informative commentary. Hereafter this anthology will be referred to as *Early Writings*.

passages that would arise naturally as the Time Traveller's reflections on the problems and perils he encounters in the far future. (Moreau's long lecture to Prendick on the nature of his project draws on two of Wells's previously published essays [Appendices H1 and H2] but Prendick's angry interventions turn it into a tense dialogue.) *The Time Machine* (1895) and the science-fiction novellas that came after it were widely popular and provided Wells with a splendid launch to his career as writer. (The term "science fiction" had not yet been invented; Wells called his novellas "scientific romances," using "romance" in its traditional sense of a story of fantastic adventure.)

The Island of Doctor Moreau was written under considerable pressure shortly after the completion of the revised version of *The Time Machine*. At the time he was struggling with *Moreau*, Wells was also working on another fantasy novella and a comic novel. Perhaps he took all this on because he was still trying to convince himself that he could make a living through fiction. With *Moreau* he got off to a false start. As Philmus points out (variorum *Moreau*, xx–xxi), the first, incomplete draft of *Moreau*, written in December of 1894, attempts a somewhat whimsical tale in the style of R.L. Stevenson.[1] With his final version, most of which was probably written in the first three months of 1895, Wells broke through into a tough, straightforward prose with no trace of the Victorian tendency to sentimentality and verbal elaboration—an anticipation of the style of Orwell and Hemingway. Many reviewers were appalled by this tale. Perhaps the pressure under which Wells wrote it allowed the emergence of disturbing content of which he was not entirely aware.

Wells's deep involvement with both the scientific and the literary culture of his time makes him a remarkable figure in literature. Ideas associated with Darwin exerted a powerful influence on the mood of the late nineteenth century, and especially on the emergence of new tales in the Gothic tradition, the most popular of which was Stevenson's *Doctor Jekyll and Mr. Hyde* (1886). Most literary authors, however, could not be expected to have anything more than a rather general notion of Darwinian theory. Enriched by his detailed knowledge of the biological science of his time, especially Darwinian, Wells's science fiction provides an intense meditation on the social and psychological implications of Darwinism. This seems especially true of *The Time Machine* and *Moreau*. The first places evolution in the context of class conflict and the fate of Victorian society, while the

---

1   Philmus prints the entire draft of the first version of *Moreau* in his variorum edition; see Appendix J for some short excerpts from this version.

second circles around the animal origin of the human species and its psychological consequences.

The years Wells devoted to teaching and writing about science enabled him to master the discourse suitable to popular, educational summaries of current scientific thought—a genre of expository writing and lecturing much appreciated by the late-Victorian public. As a master of poker-faced fantastic narrative, Wells could start off with a serious discussion of a curious aspect of some contemporary scientific subject—for example, time as the fourth dimension or the habits of deep-sea squid—and then modulate effortlessly into a tale of exciting events that might have seemed rather improbable if the reader had not already been hooked by his sober, well-informed presentation of scientific fact and theory. Also essential to Wells's realism, and related to his scientific background, is his care in surrounding his characters with all the details of everyday life that they would encounter in their situations, particularly evident in his depiction of Prendick's life on Moreau's island.

The Time Machine was the beginning of a series of brilliant science-fiction novellas published over a period of about ten years. This was the creative genre of his youth. Later, in his concern to reshape society, he turned more towards realistic novels with a sociological bias, utopias, and works of popular education, and took a rather condescending view of his early fantasy. While Wells's later work gave him a leading role in the social and political thought of his time, today many readers find his highest literary accomplishment in his science fiction. Wells's literary friends in the 1890s might have agreed with this estimate. Such fastidious artists as Henry James and Joseph Conrad expressed high admiration for the scientific romances.

Darwin and Huxley

The Island of Doctor Moreau focuses relentlessly on a central and, for the Victorians, disturbing aspect of Darwin's theory of evolution: the relationship between animals and the human species. In his first and most famous exposition of his theory, *The Origin of Species* (1859), Darwin avoids discussing human origins but the implications of his argument are obvious. By making "natural selection" the driving force behind change in all living beings, Darwin undermines belief in divine creation, leaving no room for the human species to claim an origin different from that of other animals. The animals that most resemble us are the Great Apes. For those who read Darwin's book attentively, the likelihood that humans are descended from apes could not be missed, although Darwin, anxious about the shock his theory might inflict on the Victorian public, only broaches this subject twelve years later in *The Descent of Man* (1871).

Today, when the idea of the animal ancestry of the human species has found wide acceptance, it may be difficult to imagine how upsetting the idea might have been to a culture still largely dominated by the religious revival that reached its peak in the early nineteenth century. For Victorians still under the emotional influence of Puritanism, the word "animal" might evoke the depravity of the flesh and of physical nature in general, and thus the tendency to sinfulness of unregenerate human nature. To partake of animal nature might suggest giving way to unbridled lust and aggression.

In *Moreau* Wells devotes his skill as storyteller to placing grotesque combinations of animal and human in a Darwinian context. Although Doctor Moreau claims to be engaged in pure research, he is clearly attempting to repeat the process of evolution by turning animals into humans, a project that raises in a peculiarly disturbing way the question of the relationship between the human species and its animal relatives.

As Moreau explains to Prendick in chapter 14, his project depends for its feasibility on the close structural relationship between the anatomy of humans and that of his animal subjects. Also, his claim that once he has improved the brains of his reconstructed animals he can, through training and hypnotism, enable them to think, feel, and talk like humans implies a close relation between animal and human consciousness. This closeness could cut both ways: if the animal mind can be made human, then humans might also revert to the animal emotions from which civilized consciousness has been fashioned, and which it still retains beneath the façade of civilization.

The Beast People, the unsatisfactory results of Moreau's project, could be taken as an extreme representation of the unhappiness and instability of the human condition in a Darwinian universe. As descendants of animals, civilized humans could be seen as still essentially animal, striving like the Beast People to achieve civilized status but never quite succeeding. In this context it should be noted that Prendick always perceives the underlying animality of the Beast People as sinister. The Beast People also feel this way about themselves. They often seem ashamed of their quasi-animal appearance and in their religious rituals represent their animal desires as a kind of Original Sin, which they always struggle against but can never overcome.

Despite their pathetic incompetence we come to feel a potential menace in the Beast People. Prendick assumes that if they were to revert to animal status they would turn ferociously on each other and the three humans who claim to represent civilization on the island. Also, there is an underlying suggestion that the Beast People might resemble human savages who have just emerged from animality.

Moreau's indifference to his creations could represent a cold impersonality and purposelessness in the evolutionary process itself—if there were a god responsible for evolution, he would be like Moreau. The religion the Beast People base on Moreau as an authority figure seems deeply irrational, yet essential to their maintaining some semblance of humanity, thus suggesting the need for religion as a means to enforce civilized morality. As the mood of the story darkens, Prendick makes some of these possibilities explicit.

★ ★ ★

The problems posed by *Moreau* have roots in the thought of Darwin and Huxley, and in the influence of Darwinian ideas on the intellectual culture of the late-Victorian period. Both *Moreau* and Darwin's *The Origin of Species* are permeated not only by the scientific but also by the manufacturing spirit of Britain in the nineteenth century. In her recent biography of Darwin, Janet Browne observes that in *The Origin of Species* Darwin made his theory of natural selection so dependent on competition in nature because he was assisted in working it out by the economic theory of his time, born of industrial competition (Browne 54).

At the beginning of his great book, Darwin launches the concept of change in species with reference to a traditional form of agricultural manufacturing: the breeding of domestic animals. In the first chapter he constructs a vital analogy between selective breeding of animals by British experts and the selection of favourable characteristics by nature (Browne 57). In Darwin's praise of the creative power of the breeder of domestic animals, we seem close to the power and pride of Doctor Moreau (who claims that he can reshape animals at will through surgery), especially when Darwin observes that "breeders habitually speak of an animal's organization as something quite plastic, which they can model almost as they please" (*Origin* 34, ch. 1; see Appendix D2). (The word "plastic" here means easily moulded, like modelling clay.) Moreau explains to Prendick that "these creatures you have seen are animals carven and wrought into new shapes. To that, to the study of the plasticity of living forms, my life has been devoted" (124, ch. 14).

What British experts on animal husbandry accomplish through selective breeding Moreau attempts through reconstructive surgery. He seeks to rival nature by turning one species into another, a feat that eluded even the British breeder. One might wonder about Moreau's motive since, as Prendick indignantly points out, his creations serve no useful purpose. If, however, we consider a crucial difference between artificial and natural selection, a motive might appear. In the first chapter of *The Origin* Darwin emphasizes the power of human intervention in nature, while, starting with his third chapter, "The Struggle for Existence," he describes nature's similar but much greater power to transform species.

It is also true, however, that *natural* selection has no moral object, operates by chance, and blindly sweeps before it all animal life, presumably the human species as well. This contrast between guided and unguided selection might suggest the desirability of human intervention in natural process. A reader of *The Origin of Species* might ask whether humans could acquire some of nature's power over biological destiny by improving their own species through selective breeding, thus rising above the chanciness of nature to produce ever more perfect human beings. An enterprising cousin of Darwin's, Francis Galton (1822-1911), soon invented a new science of "eugenics," devoted to improving the human species through planned intermarriage between superior families to offset the supposedly lowering effect of the high breeding rate of the lower classes. Darwin at first rejected this idea, but came round to cautious agreement with it in *The Descent of Man*. (Galton was too much of a gentleman to recommend elimination of the unfit; that suggestion was made by others.) Huxley rejected the new science because, however useful such a project might be, it would undermine the human sympathy that is the basis of social bonding. Wells criticized Galton as unscientific, but his attitude towards eugenics remained ambivalent; in his *Modern Utopia* and elsewhere he suggested that substandard individuals might be prevented from reproducing.[1]

Some critics have seen an affinity between the goals of the eugenics movement and Moreau's project, which could also be seen as an attempt to purify the human species by redoing the process of evolution.[2] This dream might be the real driving force behind Moreau's research. If his project ever succeeded he would, through his scientific prowess, have established

---

1 For Darwin on eugenics see Appendix F1. For Huxley, see the fable of the eugenicist colonial administrator in Appendix E3. For Wells, see Appendices F2 and F3.

2 David Punter sees Moreau's project as an "attempt to purify the race" (253), while John Glendening sees his goal as "the creation of ultra-rational supermen" (590). Elena Gomel maintains that in Moreau Wells provides "one of the first portrayals of the New Man of eugenics who later evolves into the New Man of fascism" (412). David A. Kirby discusses the theme of eugenics in the film legacy of Moreau.

a control over evolution more effective than selective breeding. As we will see, the possibility of human intervention in the process of evolution, whether through biology or social education, becomes a powerful theme in late-Victorian Darwinism.

Four years after the publication of *The Origin of Species* the young Huxley, soon Darwin's leading disciple and, unlike Darwin, a daring controversialist, undertook in *Man's Place in Nature* (1863) to lay out a succinct case for the descent of the human species from the Great Apes (Appendix D3). This brief and lucid book quickly became a best-seller and has been recognized ever since as a classic of Darwinian science—and must have been familiar reading for students in Huxley's course on zoology at the Normal School of Science.

In *Man's Place in Nature* Huxley's main intent is to explore systematically the affinities of human anatomy with those of other mammals, especially the gorilla and the chimpanzee, a subject bound to seem uncanny to his audience for all his stance of scientific objectivity. In the opening of his central second chapter on the comparative anatomy of humans and apes, Huxley says that when man is "brought face to face with these blurred copies of himself" he will likely find in them "an insulting caricature" of his own image, and may come to question all traditional accounts of human origin. Huxley presents himself as a Dante who will initiate the reader into a new relationship with "the underworld of life" (80-81; see Appendix D3). In *Moreau*, Prendick also explores a jungle "underworld" of disturbingly imperfect and yet recognizable copies of the human form.

Huxley undertakes to show that "no absolute structural line of demarcation ... can be drawn between the animal world and ourselves" (152). His relentless pursuit of comparative anatomy lays the scientific basis for the imagination that conceived *Moreau*. With hardly any fossil record available of types intermediate between ape and human, Huxley had to argue the theory of human origins mainly through detailed observation of similarities between human anatomy and that of animals available for dissection in the laboratory, especially apes. For the young Wells, Huxley's detailed emphasis on similarities in structure between animals and humans as the primary evidence of human origins must have made the idea of recombining animals into human form through surgery seem particularly plausible and fraught with Darwinian implications.

In *Man's Place in Nature* Huxley provides a lesson in anatomy essential to Moreau's quest to transform animal bone and flesh into human form. With frequent reference to Huxley's book, Darwin covers the same ground eight years later in the first two chapters of *The Descent of Man*. In his third and fourth chapters Darwin discusses similarities between animal and human consciousness, arguing that there is nothing unique about human mental processes, which all find precedents in animal behaviour. His conclusions here support the psychological side of Moreau's project: the conversion of animal into human consciousness.

Darwin argues that the qualities that make us human—even those in which we take most pride such as love, sympathy, imagination, the capacity for self-sacrifice, and the use of language—all appear in simpler form in the mental life of animals. He suggests that even in the barking of dogs a rudimentary language can be made out (Appendix D4). In his "explanation" Moreau insists, against Prendick's objections, that animals can be taught to speak after some improvements to the larynx; clearly Moreau knows Darwin's work better than Prendick (125-26; ch. 14). In a recent article Steven McLean shows that by the 1890s the prevailing view that animals do not possess language was being seriously challenged by scientists who had studied the vocalization of monkeys, and that in *Moreau* questions involving the Beast People's use of language have the effect of blurring the boundary between animal and human (43-45).

Darwin's depiction of social behaviour in dogs and monkeys seems far removed from negative associations with animal inheritance, but there may be a double edge in his conviction that social feelings and the basic emotions that constitute religion originate far back in our animal ancestry. Such ancient descent might mean that the attitudes that sustain both religion and the coherence of social groups are irrational and not necessarily moral. Browne observes that Darwin "made no secret of his view that he did not believe religion to have any rational foundations at all. Human beings have a biological need to believe, he suggested" (341). When Darwin cheerfully suggests that a dog's love for his master could be an early manifestation of religion (Appendix D4), he opens the way for Wells to use the Dog-man's veneration for Prendick as a savage satire of religious discipleship. Again, the communal morality that the Beast People enforce in their religion seems disturbingly crude and liable to vicious scapegoating—as in the hunting of the Leopard-man.

Darwin seems to compensate for his somewhat idealized view of animals in *Descent* by attributing demonic qualities to human "barbarians" at the dawn of human history, represented by the shocking state of the Fuegians described at the end of his book (Appendix D4). These are the aboriginal inhabitants (now extinct) of the bleak coast of Tierra del Fuego at the southern tip of South America; Darwin describes his youthful encounter with them in chapter 10 of *The Voyage of the Beagle*. Wells's Beast People also inhabit this uneasy border between animal and civilized human. While their most obvious identity is that of animals barely made human by Moreau's surgery, they could also be seen as very primitive natives kept in order by white Europeans, with Moreau exercising patriarchal authority. Victorian anthropology considered non-European peoples to be less highly evolved than the white race, and hence both childlike and closer to animal status. Some unpleasant comparisons made by Prendick between members of the Beast People and various ethnic groups are characteristic of late-nineteenth-century racial attitudes.

★　★　★

The new evolutionary biology laid out by Darwin and Huxley provides scientific assumptions basic to much of Wells's science fiction. To understand the philosophical aspects of Darwinian thought that most influenced Wells, we must turn to Huxley's later writings. For many years Huxley had been Darwin's main public defender. After Darwin's death (1882) Huxley became the most influential authority on the social and philosophical implications of Darwin's theory and also a leading spokesman of science (and opponent of religion) in late-Victorian Britain. The dark view of the social implications of evolution that Huxley expounded in his later essays had a strong influence on Wells's thought, especially during the period when he was writing his science fiction.

Towards the end of his life Huxley set out to demolish the Victorian equation of evolution with social progress in a series of essays that portray the evolutionary process in nature as the mortal enemy of the development of civilization. Thus Huxley split apart an evolutionary synthesis that had enabled the Victorians to view themselves and their competitive industrial economy as the highest achievement of nature. In his later essays Huxley describes human society as an artificial world, like a cultivated garden, that must oppose and keep out the ferociously competitive process of evolution in nature, which he labels "the cosmic process." He concludes that the unrestrained competition between animals, including human "savages," which drives evolution in nature, is entirely hostile to moral progress in civilized society.

According to Huxley, the garden of civilization is threatened not only by natural forces outside it, but also by the same forces within the civilized individuals who struggle to maintain it. He argues that all humans have inherited an anti-social animal nature, while their civilized nature is the artificial product of social training. Hence we must always struggle against an animal nature within ourselves, a struggle that he sees as the psychological truth behind the Christian doctrine of Original Sin. The incompatibility between our inherited nature and civilization means that as civilized beings we must suffer from a permanent sense of inner conflict. Adrian Desmond notes that Huxley reverses Darwin's view that an instinct for sociability is deeply rooted in our animal past: "Darwin had seen morality develop from the social instincts, but for Huxley the instincts were anti-social, an amoral vestige to be repressed, the primeval lusts" (564).[1]

Despite his hostility to religious belief, Huxley finds an analogue to his opposition between nature and civilization in the spirit of Calvinistic Puritanism (Appendix E2). Desmond notes that Huxley's scientific rationalism has a strong strain of Puritan self-righteousness (280). As we have seen, Wells also had a Puritan element in his religious background. In *Moreau*, Wells parodies Puritan theology in the religion of the Beast People, but it is also possible to find a disgust for the flesh and its animal origin in Prendick's attitude towards the Beast People and Moreau's towards humanity in general, as expressed in his lecture to Prendick.

Huxley gives civilized humans a dual personality when he distinguishes between a "natural" and hence animal personality and a second personality that is the artificial product of social education: "An artificial personality ... is built up beside the natural personality" ("Ethics and Evolution" 30; see Appendix E3). He insists that pain must inevitably result from the renunciation of the "natural man" required by civilization, and that this pain is the price we must pay for human consciousness. Civilization does not grant happiness. The pain of inner conflict becomes more intense as civilization rises higher and produces more sensitive individuals. He concludes with a bracing moral: "Let us understand, once for all, that the ethical progress of society depends, not on imitating the cosmic process, still less in running away from it, but in combating it" (83).

---

1   My discussion of Huxley here owes much to two sources: Adrian Desmond's admirable biography of Huxley, which thoroughly establishes his place in Victorian intellectual culture; and James G. Paradis's long introduction to his edition of Huxley's essay "Evolution and Ethics," especially Paradis's clear discussion of the instability of both society and the individual implicit in Huxley's later thought. Paradis is also the author of an important book on Huxley, *T.H. Huxley: Man's Place in Nature* (Lincoln: Nebraska UP, 1978).

Huxley was primarily concerned with constructing logical arguments in the forum of public debate: one can never be certain whether he fully grasped the psychological implications of the positions he stakes out in his later essays. His opposition between the depraved nature of the inherited animal personality, which can partake of the full energy of "the cosmic process," and the artificial civilized personality, implies that the civilized individual must be permanently racked by inner conflict and, worst of all, must be deeply unstable. The artificial personality must struggle against an inherently irrational component, housed in the same body, and may at any moment revert to the animal level of its ancestors. By the same token, civilization itself becomes unstable and liable to mass reversion.

If Huxley was not entirely aware of these possibilities, they were more fully understood by some of his admirers, Wells and Freud among them.[1] In his introduction to "Evolution and Ethics" (1989), Paradis notes that some psychological problems implicit in Huxley's essay receive a complex elaboration in Freud's psychological thought (39-43), while in the introduction to his edition of *Moreau* Philmus suggests an affinity between *Moreau* and problems later posed by Freud in *The Future of an Illusion* (1927), his critique of religion, and *Civilization and Its Discontents* (1930), a philosophical summary of his ideas about conflict between social morality and the needs of the individual (Philmus xxix). Gorman Beauchamp observes that *Moreau* provides Wells's closest approach to Freud because of the story's insistence on the pain inflicted by renunciation of instinctual needs and its "unrelieved pessimism regarding man's intractably animal nature" (411).

The satire of religion in *Moreau* seems close to Freud's concept of religion, and perhaps civilization in general, as a neurosis. The guilt-ridden religion practised by Moreau's products, the Beast People, could be seen as an anticipation of the conclusion Freud reaches in *Civilization and Its Discontents* that the overwhelming guilt generated by the conflict between animal drives in human nature and the requirements of social morality constitutes the most serious burden that civilization imposes on the individual (Freud 97, ch. 8). If we take the Beast People as a grotesque version of the human condition, their psychological state might imply that civilized humans also pay a high price for civilization.

Moreau was written too early for any of Freud's ideas to have been available to Wells. If this story seems to build up a psychodrama that anticipates

---

1   In his biography of Freud, Ernest Jones says that Freud was "a great admirer of Huxley" (III, 155).

some aspects of Freud's later thought, that may be because both Wells and Freud were influenced by Huxley's version of Darwinism and in different ways made explicit some problems inherent in it. Of all Wells's science fiction, *Moreau* focuses most intensely on the psychological instability of the individual in a Darwinian world.

In what is probably his most important early essay, "Human Evolution, an Artificial Process" (1896), Wells links ideas similar to Huxley's with his own recently published *Island of Doctor Moreau*. Wells published this essay about six months after *Moreau*, but Philmus finds evidence that he was working on a draft of it while writing the final version—the composition of the essay and the novel must have influenced each other (variorum *Moreau* 188).

Taken together, this essay and the novel represent a turning-point in Wells's view of evolution. In the explanatory prefaces to their collection of the early essays and reviews of Wells, Philmus and Hughes give evidence that a decisive and darkening change occurred in Wells's Darwinism as he was working on *Moreau*. This change is especially marked in his renunciation of belief in the theory of inheritance of acquired characteristics, which held that changes that occur to animals or humans during their lifetime could become part of the genetic inheritance they transmit to their offspring. This theory was proposed by Jean Baptiste Lamarck (1744-1829) and became a key idea in Victorian attempts to give an optimistic turn to evolution because it implied that as social progress improves the moral character of individuals, their improved character will in turn become a biological part of human inheritance, which can thus rise ever higher above its animal origins. The evidence of Wells's abandonment of this view lies in his initial rejection and then sudden acceptance of the theories of August Weismann, a German biologist who anticipated modern genetic theory by developing an anti-Lamarckian theory of heredity that maintained that the characteristics an individual can transmit to offspring are fixed at birth.[1]

I would argue that the publication of the complete version of Huxley's most important essay, "Evolution and Ethics," may have played an important role in this change. A short version of Huxley's essay was delivered as a speech and printed as a pamphlet in 1893, but it appeared in its full form, with a long and impressive addition called the "Prolegomena," when published by Macmillan as Volume Nine in Huxley's *Collected Essays* in late August 1894 (Desmond 604). When Wells was working on the final

---

1   See *Early Writings* 9-12 and 182-86; also Appendices E4, E5, and E6.

version of *Moreau*, early in 1895, he would have had time to absorb the full impact of Huxley's culminating essay, which argues with great vigour that human nature has not changed since prehistory and thus remains locked in permanent opposition to civilization. As he pondered the final version of Huxley's essay, Wells must also have realized that Weismann's theory of inheritance was consistent with Huxley's insistence on the fixity of human nature. Just as Wells was giving shape to *Moreau*, Huxley's "Evolution and Ethics" combined with Weismann's biological theory to show that there could be no easy escape from our animal inheritance.

Although Wells does not mention Huxley in "Human Evolution," he takes a series of very Huxleyan positions. He begins with a repudiation of the assumption that evolution can be the basis of moral progress, and argues that biological evolution is opposed to civilization and that inherent human nature has not changed since the Old Stone Age. He asserts that the unchangeable, stubbornly resistant "natural man"—"the culminating ape" (594)—provides an aspect of the self that stretches back over many thousands of years of savagery. The opponent to the savage natural man is the artificial personality created by civilization. Civilized morality attempts to bridge the gap, but faces the impossible task of making a circle into a square: "[W]hat we call morality becomes the padding of suggested emotional habits necessary to keep the round Paleolithic savage in the square hole of the civilized state. And Sin is the conflict of the two factors—as I have tried to convey in my *Island of Dr. Moreau*" (594; see Appendix E5). The primary focus of the sense of sin in *Moreau* would seem to be the obsession with shame and guilt in the religion of the Beast People.

Like Huxley, Wells gives his essay a qualified happy ending. He concludes with the hope that, in the future, social leadership enlightened by an advanced science may construct a society that would be able to achieve a better balance between savage and civilized aspects of the human personality. He repudiates eugenics—"We need not clamour for the Systematic Massacre of the Unfit"—but advocates a strenuous cultural intervention to improve society: "in Education lies the possible salvation of mankind from misery and sin" (595). This last sentence sums up the object of much of Wells's later writing.

Huxley has often been seen as bringing Darwinian thought closer to the modern world-view, but he also seems more Victorian than Darwin in finding demonic implications in the animal ancestry of the human species, thus providing systematic expression of a characteristic Victorian response to the theory of evolution. Both Darwin and Huxley lay the basis for the peculiarly disturbing implications of animalism in *Moreau*. In *The Descent of Man* Darwin argues a close relation between animal and human consciousness, but puts this mostly in positive terms. Moreau's explanation also argues this close relation—his project depends on it—but both his unsuccessful struggle against the animal nature of his creations and Prendick's depiction of the Beast People make their animality seem grotesque, the material for nightmare. Darwin's argument that there is an intimate connection between animal and human nature receives a dark colouration from Huxley's emphasis on animal nature as a threat to civilization.

In *Moreau* Wells directly confronts the problem of the instability of human nature implied in Huxley's later essays while giving little confidence that scientific reason, as represented by Moreau and Prendick, can deal with it. Both Huxley's "Evolution and Ethics" and Wells's "Human Evolution" end on an upbeat note, encouraging the reader to face the problems of a Darwinian world with resolution, and pointing toward social betterment that can be brought about by human effort guided by science. Prendick's unresolved anxiety in the last chapter of *Moreau* provides no such reassurance.

Degeneration, Atavism, and Madness

The tense and sombre version of Darwinism Huxley passed along to Wells was not an outcome of scientific thought alone: it can be seen as one aspect of the intellectual mood of the late-nineteenth century. Among writers and intellectuals, this period was haunted by pessimistic feelings about the present and future state of society, as though the nineteenth century had somehow exhausted itself and the approaching end of the century might initiate a period of decline in Western civilization. In this "end-of-century" mood, alienation from the values of Victorian society seems to have combined with anxiety that the future might bring something worse.[1] Also, such ideas could be motivated by revolt against Victorian convention. Wells made his prophecy of doom in *The Time Machine* with deliberate intent to shock the belief in progress so essential to the world-view of the middle class.

Most disturbing to the public was the notion that mysterious mental and physical processes of degeneration might be undermining the popula-

---

1   In the first chapter of his pioneering book, *The Early H.G. Wells: A Study of the Scientific Romances*, Bernard Bergonzi provides an informative discussion of the end-of-century mood in relation to Wells's science fiction.

tion of the Western world, as though evolutionary advances achieved over millennia could be undone in a few decades.[1] To understand the full impact of the concept of degeneration, we must consider some notions in popular Darwinism that were widely accepted as scientific truth at the time. As we have seen, Galton's science of eugenics recommended selective breeding as the answer to a fear that the population might be declining in quality. On the Continent the mood was more pessimistic. The general tenor of European thinking about degeneracy was set by Benedictin Augustin Morel (1809-73), a French doctor who had devoted his career to the treatment of the mentally-ill.[2] In a very influential work entitled *Treatise on the Degeneration of the Human Species* (1857) Morel set forth his all-embracing theory of the formation and inheritance of brain-lesions as the cause of degeneration, and also the idea that non-European races are the product of degeneracy.

Best known and most influential of all the theorists of degeneration was Cesare Lombroso (1835-1909), an Italian doctor devoted to the study of the supposed Darwinian attributes of the "criminal type"—he named his new science "criminal anthropology." Since he saw his criminal subjects as humans with animal qualities, his theories and his voluminous documentation of them could well have influenced Wells's depiction of the Beast People.

Lombroso updates Morel's all-encompassing theory of degeneration by adding a Darwinian theory of his own. His idea is both simple and easy to represent in graphically physical terms. He says that he began his career as criminal anthropologist with the discovery—with the force of revelation—that a certain type of criminal was a throwback, both in mind and body, to the animal past of the human species. This "born criminal" is incorrigible and liable to commit acts of extreme violence. Dissection of the corpses of such criminals reveals a multiple affinity with the anatomy

---

1   See Kelly Hurley's account of degeneration as evolution in reverse in *The Gothic Body* (66-77), which discusses both *The Time Machine* and *The Island of Doctor Moreau* in this context.

    I have not discussed here the legitimate scientific concept, supported by Huxley and Wells, that natural selection can cause an organism to "degenerate" by evolving towards simplification rather than greater complexity. For Huxley and Wells, this means that evolution has nothing to do with the Victorian ideal of progress. See Ruddick's edition of *The Time Machine*, 30-34 and 157-67.

2   See George Frederick Drinka, *The Birth of Neurosis*, 47-53. Drinka gives a detailed account of psychology and degeneration-theory in the later nineteenth century.

of various animals. Lombroso popularized the word "atavism" to indicate such reversion to an animal past. Today, many of these ideas seem to border on fantasy but in his time Lombroso was widely respected as a scientific thinker.[1] Wells uses the word "atavism" in "Human Evolution," and in another essay relevant to *Moreau*, "The Province of Pain," presents as credible Lombroso's strange speculation that women feel physical pain less than men (Appendix H2).

According to Lombroso, the animality of a "born criminal" is manifested in grossly physical characteristics. Since these represent reversion to non-human anatomy, they stand out as disturbing distortions of the normal human body—Lombroso calls them "stigmata." Typical stigmata of atavism are a low narrow skull, asymmetrical features, high cheekbones, a remarkably large lower face that protrudes forward to approximate the profile of an ape, and a huge jaw with prominent teeth, suggestive of a cannibalistic desire to tear flesh and drink blood. As with an ape, the arms are grotesquely long; the ears stand out from the skull like those of a chimpanzee. The brow-ridges are large and the eyes are abnormally large and deep-set, and have a shifty look. The nose can be flat like an ape's, but in the case of murderers is more likely to be prominent and curved like the beak of a bird of prey. The mouth and lips are particularly distorted, tending to be swollen and protruding (Appendix F4). Lombroso presents tables and charts demonstrating that prostitutes tend to have prehensile feet (Gould 129). Most surprising is his willingness to find physical affinities in his criminals with lower animals remote from the human family tree—rodents, lemurs, birds, snakes, and even insects.

Crime is the biological destiny of the "born criminal." Neither punishment nor attempts at education can result in lasting benefit. To support his theory, Lombroso has to argue that animals are naturally criminal (Gould 124-25). He also finds that the criminal behaviour of his degenerates is closely analogous to the practices of primitive, non-white cultures. "Born criminals" arouse an instinctive dread in the normal person because their stigmata recall memories of cannibalism and oppressive violence from a forgotten prehistoric past.

Fortunately, only about one-third of criminals are "born criminals"; the rest are less aggravated cases, or normal people who have been led astray by passion or need. "Born criminals" have a disproportionate importance,

---

1   Stephen Jay Gould gives a lively critique of Lombroso's use of Darwinian ideas in *The Mismeasure of Man*, 122-45.

however, because of the monstrous nature of their crimes (*Criminal Man* 8). This clear distinction between normal and degenerate helps to explain the popularity of Lombroso's theory. On the one hand, his audience could project anxieties about social change and the lower classes into his vividly described animal-like degenerates, while on the other his audience could be assured that these represent only the lowest dregs of society. His concept of degeneration as something grossly obvious and distinct from normally-evolved humans carries a guarantee of immunity for the respectable reader (Hurley 102). Wells defeats this strategy by evoking in his Beast People the disturbing quality of Lombrosian degenerates while breaking down the supposed barriers between them and the human characters of *Moreau*—and, by implication, the reader as well.

★ ★ ★

The case for an affinity between Wells's Beast People and Lombrosian degeneracy is well argued by Kelly Hurley. In her analysis of the disturbing physicality of the Beast People, she finds a parallel between their quality of being "not quite evolved" and the "atavistic 'criminal types'" of Lombroso (103). I would add that this effect is all the more evident because Prendick at first sees the Beast People as humans distorted by Moreau rather than re-shaped animals. The indications of animalism that will dominate descriptions of the Beast People are laid out in Prendick's first good look at Montgomery's servant, M'ling: the "black face" of this "misshapen man" is profoundly shocking and "singularly deformed"; the large "facial part" projects forward and the mouth reveals "big white teeth" (78; ch. 3). The "prognathous" forward thrust of M'ling's lower face suggests the profile of an ape.

In descriptions of the Beast People alarming teeth are repeatedly emphasized. What appears to be an ordinary savage squatting in front of his hut reveals the mark of the beast when he happens to yawn "showing with startling suddenness scissor-edge incisors and saberlike canines, keen and brilliant as knives" (136; ch. 15). Such dental equipment lends significance to one of the sins emphasized by the Sayer of the Law: "Some want to follow things that move ... and bite, bite deep and rich, sucking the blood" (115; ch. 12). It also suggests that the huge teeth and jaws Lombroso finds in his criminal degenerates, especially the "enormous jaws" of the skull of the bandit Vilella, imply a "desire not only to extinguish the life of the victim, but to mutilate the corpse, tear its flesh and drink its blood" (*Criminal Man* xxv; see Appendix F4).

There is a curious parallel to Lombroso in Prendick's discovery of the animality of the Beast People. In attempting to prove the irrationality and therefore the predisposition to crime of primitive peoples, Lombroso cites their tendency to ecstatic dances that climax in a trancelike state (*Crime* 367; see Appendix F5). In the island's jungle Prendick observes three strange figures working themselves into a frenzy in a rhythmic dance while chanting "some complicated gibberish." It is at this moment that he understands the reason for their strangeness. Each of these creatures has woven into its whole being "a swinish taint, the unmistakable mark of the beast" (100; ch. 9). Gross primitivism could also be found in the "rhythmic fervour" induced by the chanting of the Law (114; ch. 12), which the Pig-people may be attempting to recite.

Setting the story in the context of a late-Victorian controversy over whether animals are capable of speech, Steven McLean observes that the ecstasy induced by verbal repetition of the Law is far removed from the use of language for "abstract reasoning" (45), and may be a satire of religious ritual much as the Big Thinks of the Ape-Man are of philosophy. In recent studies of discourse in *Moreau*, Christine Ferguson and Kimberly Jackson find that the ambiguous speech of the Beast People undermines any belief that the human species acquires a special status through the possession of language.

The grimmest aspect of the affinity of the Beast People with Lombroso's degenerates lies in the certainty of their reversion, a biological destiny from which they cannot escape. Despite Moreau's repeated attempts at surgical improvement and education in the House of Pain, they begin to revert as soon as they leave his hands: "somehow the things drift back again, the stubborn beast flesh grows, day by day, back again" (129; ch. 14). They are all doomed to become throwbacks. Lombroso insists that his atavistic "born criminals" derive little benefit from education and cannot be improved by punishment because of the inevitability of periodic relapse into episodes of violence (*Crime* 438-39, 369).

At this point, however, we should pause to consider a movement counter to Lombroso in Wells's portrayal of the Beast People. Lombroso assumes that regression to animalism involves an increase in vitality and in the physical capacity for a life of criminal violence. He says that the brigand Vilella possessed "extraordinary agility ... he had been known to scale steep mountains bearing a sheep on his shoulders" (*Criminal Man* xxiv). Generally speaking, the monsters of Gothic literature also derive a dangerous but exciting energy from their freedom from moral inhibition. This is, however, not true of most of the Beast People, whose uncanny ugliness arises partly from a pervasive sense of crippling.

A psychological difference between the Beast People and the Lombrosian degenerate appears in their ashamed awareness of their physical appearance. Lombroso finds brazen effrontery a characteristic of the "born criminal" (*Criminal Man* xxiv) while the Beast People are aware of their inhuman ugliness and try to conceal it under voluminous clothing (88; ch. 6; 136; ch. 15). The religious ceremony in which Prendick is forced to participate in chapter 12 reveals that the physical distortions of the Beast People correspond to a deep sense of psychological inhibition. In their repression of animal desire they desperately wish for the fully human status they have not achieved. Being human is the only identity they possess, and they struggle to maintain it; that "upward striving" which Moreau coldly notes in them is a passionate need (131; ch. 14). Their religion seems an absurd parody of Christianity, yet it is the only way they can maintain their ever insecure sense of themselves as human, an uncertainty emphasized by the repeated question in their litany of prohibitions: "Are we not men?" (114; ch. 12).

In his study of oppositions in Wells's science fiction, John Huntington observes that the line between animal and human so emphasized in the religion of the Beast People is also rendered dubious by it, and repeatedly crossed by the human characters (64-65). Along with the commitment of the Beast People to human identity goes a continuous sense of guilt, amounting to a belief in Original Sin—"For everyone the want that is bad" (115; ch. 12)—because adherence to the Law is never fully effective.

Despite their disturbingly animal appearance Wells endows the Beast People with a subjective consciousness. The unashamedly savage Hyena-Swine would indeed be appropriate for one of Lombroso's examples of criminal atavism, but on the whole the anxious, guilt-ridden consciousness of the Beast People seems far removed from the brutal, self-indulgent state of mind Lombroso imagines for his degenerates. The Beast People's subjective world of pervasive guilt, unresolvable inner conflict, and perpetual upward striving suggests the struggle to be a civilized human depicted in Huxley's later essays.

While Lombroso sequesters animality in the criminal class, Huxley sees the struggle against animal inheritance as a problem of civilization in general: each individual must experience it. At the point where we become aware of and possibly able to sympathize with the inner struggle of the Beast People to be human, we enter a realm more appropriate to Huxley's thought than Lombroso's, and perhaps find the Beast People disturbing in a different way. Suspended between Huxley and Lombroso, the Beast People have a double impact: their "upward striving" makes them more human, but Wells's evocation of atavistic degeneracy in their physical appearance and their inevitable slide towards reversion gives a gross, pessimistic physicality to Huxley's universal conflict. After our initial shock at their appearance, the discomfort caused by the Beast People may lie in their being too much like the reader.

★　★　★

The Beast People are so grotesque, however, that we might still be tempted to put them at a safe Lombrosian distance, especially as there are three white British males on the island, all educated and sympathetic to science, who can represent the normal human species. Perhaps the most subtle aspect of this story lies in Wells's undermining of the apparently clear distinction between the three human characters and the Beast People: the more the Beast People seem to converge with the world of Montgomery, Moreau, and Prendick, the closer they come to the reader.

Central to this endeavour is Wells's use of Montgomery to provide a bridge by which the degeneracy of the Beast People can penetrate the white, masculine world of the human characters. As a character Montgomery is coded to correspond to late-Victorian notions of degeneracy. On the other hand, his very fallibility may make him seem more sympathetic than either Moreau, with his obsession with research, or Prendick, with his tendency to self-righteousness. The reviewer of the *Manchester Guardian* found Montgomery "reassuring and quite human in his vulgarity" (Appendix C4).

A number of characteristics link Montgomery with degeneracy theories of the late-nineteenth century. We soon learn that he has a "dropping nether lip" (75; ch.2) and a possibly related speech impediment—a "slobbering articulation" (76; ch. 2) that seems analogous to the thick speech of the Beast People. Most important, he sought refuge in Moreau's island because of a mysterious and possibly criminal offence against morality. Montgomery reveals that he (like Wells) has studied biology at the University of London. His pursuit of a medical degree there, however, was cut short by a mysterious incident serious enough to have sent him into permanent exile: "Why am I here now—an outcast from civilization—instead of being a happy man, enjoying all the pleasures of London? Simply because—eleven years ago—I lost my head for ten minutes on a foggy night" (83; ch. 4).

After Moreau's death he tells Prendick that he can't return to Britain because he is still an "outcast" (153; ch. 19).

This nocturnal indiscretion was probably sexual, and to have such serious results may have been homosexual. There had been a number of prosecutions for homosexuality in late-Victorian Britain, the most famous of which resulted in the ruin of Oscar Wilde in 1895. Even in the enlightened medical opinion of the time, as represented by Richard von Kraft-Ebing's massive study of sexual deviance, *Psychopathia Sexualis* (translated into English in 1894), the homosexual was considered a degenerate, a victim of tainted heredity and a faulty nervous system, and thus akin to more serious Lombrosian-type criminals such as sex-murderers (Drinka 174). By not specifying Montgomery's offence, Wells not only avoids an indecent subject, but also avoids providing the kind of certainty that would put Montgomery in a category separate from the respectable reader.

A decisive aspect of Montgomery's affinity with the Beast People comes out in his response to Moreau's death. We know from their litany that in their struggle to maintain their human status the Beast People have internalized Moreau as a God-figure: "*His* are the stars in the sky" (114; ch. 12). With Moreau gone, they degenerate rapidly. Despite his apparent hostility to Moreau, Montgomery's response to his death reveals that he also has become dependent on Moreau's godlike authority to maintain his sense of self: "He was almost sober, but greatly disturbed in mind. He had been strangely under the influence of Moreau's personality. I do not think it had ever occurred to him that Moreau could die" (153; ch. 19).

Alcoholism, the weakness through which he finally joins the Beast People, figures largely in late-nineteenth-century theories of degeneration (Drinka 49-50). Montgomery's weakness for alcohol has been of long duration: "It was that infernal stuff that led to my coming here. That and a foggy night" (95; ch. 8). The subject of alcohol leads to an interesting argument between Prendick and Montgomery. Turning to drink as consolation for Moreau's death, Montgomery reproaches Prendick for his teetotalism: "Drink.... You logic-chopping, chalky-faced saint of an atheist, drink" (154; ch. 19). One might sympathize with this quip as a revolt against Prendick's moralizing tendency: in particular, the phrase "saint of an atheist" seems a good hit on the Victorian tradition of high-minded agnostic rationalism—the tradition of John Stuart Mill, George Eliot, and T.H. Huxley. On the other hand, Montgomery follows up this remark by the supreme folly of giving brandy to the Beast People, thus justifying

Prendick's dismissal: "You've made a beast of yourself. To the beasts you may go" (154; ch. 19).

After years of lonely alienation Montgomery renounces the problems of being a human individual through alcoholic merging with the Beast People. Unfortunately, he does not reckon with their savage inheritance. During his drunken night on the beach Montgomery openly declares his hostility to civilization by burning the boats to prevent a "return to mankind" (158; ch. 19). Yet he wins back Prendick's sympathy as he expires in a pile of slaughtered Beast People. Montgomery's interest in the Beast People is not entirely to his discredit: he seems to lose his relation to conventional moral categories as he descends into fellowship with them.

★ ★ ★

Moreau presents a more difficult case. While Prendick finds his scientific project disturbing, both Moreau's godlike physique and the strength of character manifested in his dedication to his project would seem to exempt him from the tendencies to degeneration evident in Montgomery. There is, however, an intriguing possibility that Moreau's name might be linked to a medical diagnosis of his case. Philmus (variorum *Moreau* xli-xlii), Hurley (109-10), and Showalter (*Sexual Anarchy* 178) all argue that the most likely source for Moreau's name would be a French psychiatrist of the nineteenth century, Jacques-Joseph Moreau (1804-84).[1]

J.-J. Moreau was particularly interested in combinations of reason and madness. He is best known today as the author of a pioneering book on drug experience, *Hashish and Mental Illness* (1845), in which he compares drug-induced dreams to the hallucinations of the mentally ill. He considered, however, his most important book to be his extensive study of the relation between genius and madness—*La Psychologie Morbide* (1859). (To my knowledge no translation of this book is available; I provide a translation of some passages from it in Appendix F7.) There is little resemblance between J.-J. Moreau's career and that of Doctor Moreau; Wells may have borrowed the name of the real Moreau because his theory of pathological genius would explain the state of mind of his fictional character.

---

1 To give an alternate view: Ian F. Roberts presents a summary of proposals that have been made concerning a source for Moreau's name, and argues that the most likely original for both his name and ideas is "the French scientist and philosopher Pierre Louis Moreau de Maupertuis (1698-1759)" (262). I do not see why we need assume one exclusive source for Doctor Moreau. Both in his name and career, he may well be a composite.

For J.-J. Moreau, genius is a compulsive state. Artists, poets, and scientific discoverers do not choose to create: it is as though an imperious force from outside seizes on the creator (128-29). Excessive excitation of the brain, however, can lead to mental illness, especially monomania, a state that isolates the sufferer from the outside world and traps him in a systematic obsession by which his ideas acquire an unnatural "cohesion" that tends to exclude impressions or ideas not directly related to his obsessive thoughts (500-01). The excessive mental energy characteristic of this kind of disturbance "exaggerates" normal thought processes, introducing subtle distortions (129). Hence the thought of a scientist who has fallen into monomania might follow the lines of accepted scientific theory but with a fervour that drives him to extremes. The great accomplishments of genius, whether in the arts or sciences, could not be attained without an element of obsession, but the intense mental excitation required for genius can always drive one over the edge into self-enclosed monomania.

Moreau's relentless pursuit of his project, his isolation in the laboratory, his refusal to communicate with Prendick except in a lecture devoted entirely to his own ideas, his lack of interest in the Beast People after his dismissal of them as imperfect, all could be taken as a portrait of genius trapped in monomania. In Wells's first version of *Moreau*, Montgomery, who seems a more thoughtful fellow than in the final version, describes Moreau's project in terms that seem close to J.-J. Moreau's diagnosis: "I got interested in a kind of way. But not like he is. This research is only a sane kind of mania. He's driven to make these things, can't help it ..." (variorum *Moreau* 136; see Appendix J).

On the other hand, when we consider that in any case genius is likely to be an obsessive state, can we be quite certain of Moreau's degree of sanity or madness? Enclosure in the laboratory would be typical of the new kind of scientist and research through vivisection was practised relentlessly by major physiologists in this period. Are Montgomery, the failed medical student, and Prendick, the amateur scientist, qualified to judge Moreau's research project?

The theory of the pathology of genius proposed by J.-J. Moreau would enable Wells to place his Doctor Moreau on a border between daring research and degeneration into monomania, thus providing a very subtle portrait of a mad scientist. If indeed Moreau is obsessed to the point of monomania, we might ask two questions: to what extent does his state of mind distort the normal goals of research in physiology; and, most important, what is the nature of his obsession? These questions will be considered in the next section.

We have seen that Wells generates ambiguity in this story by using themes of degeneration and Darwinian inheritance to place all his characters on the borders that define respectable middle-class society and scientific professionalism, thereby calling those borders into question. The Beast People are between animal and human, but also between a grotesque Lombrosian degeneracy that marks them off from normal humanity and a conflicted "upward striving" that from a Huxleyan point of view would be the characteristic situation of the human species. Montgomery is an unlucky fellow who suffers from years of isolation with the obsessed Moreau, but also a degenerate who joins the Beast People and even hastens their regression with alcohol. Moreau is presented as one of the leading physiologists of his time: it may be hard to define exactly what makes him seem so sinister. In the end Prendick, as narrator, is not able to resolve his ambivalence towards the other characters, especially Moreau, or to feel secure in defining the boundaries between human and animal.

Vivisection and the Uses of Pain[1]

We have yet to consider the most disturbing aspect of this story: the repeated suggestion of excruciating pain inflicted by bloody operations, represented primarily by the screaming of the puma.[2] In his history of the Gothic tradition, David Punter finds that the "principal problem" of interpreting *Moreau* "concerns the status of pain in the story" (251). It is Moreau's role as vivisector that makes him so difficult to assess as scientist. Is he a great physiologist devoted to pure research, or a mad scientist driven by the very animal forces he tries to overcome, suspect of taking a sadistic enjoyment in prolonged and exquisitely painful operations? Both images of Moreau—the dedicated researcher and the sadistic torturer of animals—

---

1 Some passages in this section have appeared in a different form in Mason Harris, "Vivisection, the Culture of Science, and Intellectual Uncertainty in *The Island of Doctor Moreau*," *Gothic Studies* 4.2 (2002): 99–115.

2 In the severely masculine world of Moreau's research, the conquest of the female puma may have a special significance. Both Stephen Lehman and Elaine Showalter argue that in creating living beings Moreau attempts to bypass the female role in reproduction. Cyndy Hendershot argues that by altering the puma Moreau will transform both "feminine nature" and the otherness of non-European cultures into "masculine civilization" (13).

would have been familiar to Wells's audience as characteristic of the positions of the opposing sides in the late-Victorian debate over vivisection. It is by playing both sides of this controversy against each other that Wells constructs his double-image of Moreau and also gives some dark twists to Darwinian theory.

Most late-Victorian readers would have been aware of the close relation between Moreau's persecution by the British public and a heated public debate, beginning in the early 1870s, over the increasing use of surgery on living animals for medical research, usually by doctors who had devoted their careers to scientific investigation.[1] The practitioners of this method insisted that the study of processes in living organisms requires experiments on animals still alive rather than the more traditional method of dissecting dead animals. They considered themselves pioneers in a new realm of knowledge known as "experimental medicine," making a decisive break from the abstract physiology inherited from the eighteenth century (Olmstead 16-24). The scientists who supported vivisection, led by Wells's hero T.H. Huxley, were known to be godless Darwinists, while opposition to vivisection was often associated with a religious hostility to science in general.

The most extreme opponents of surgical experiments on living animals asserted that only a scientist who enjoyed inflicting pain could use such a method. Anti-vivisection literature provided hideous descriptions of vivisectors' laboratories and reproduced illustrations of experiments on living animals from manuals on vivisection, with the implication that research through vivisection must be motivated by deliberate cruelty. Frances Power Cobbe, leading spokesperson for the anti-vivisection movement, insisted that vivisection, in its deliberate infliction of pain, would have a degrading effect on public morality (Appendix G7). Cobbe is also hostile to science in general. She argues that the scientific method can be subversive to morality simply by giving objective study of fact precedence over feeling (Ferguson [2002] 468). Vivisection would be the worst-case instance of this problem.

One early reviewer who knew Wells personally suggests a contradiction between Wells's use of vivisection as a source of horror in this story and the position he might have been expected to take in the vivisection

---

1   This account of the anti-vivisection controversy owes much to Richard D. French's detailed history *Antivivisection and Medical Science in Victorian Society*, and to John Vyvyan's *In Pity and in Anger: A Study of the Use of Animals in Science*.

controversy. As a disciple of T.H. Huxley, a teacher of university-level biology, and author of text books on biology and physiology, the young Wells belonged to the scientific, pro-vivisectionist side of the controversy. (Wells makes slighting remarks about the anti-vivisection movement in his early essays [Appendices G8 and H1] and attacks it in detail in a later essay [G9].) Chalmers Mitchell, eminent zoologist and colleague of the young Wells on the staff of *Saturday Review*, twits him in a review of *Moreau* in that journal with having abandoned "a reasoned attitude to life" by producing, in the figure of Doctor Moreau, "a cliché from the pages of an anti-vivisection pamphlet" (Appendix C1). Mitchell complains that in addition to evoking the horrors of the vivisector's laboratory, Wells also follows the conventions of anti-vivisection literature by having Moreau operate entirely without anaesthesia: "Mr. Wells must know that the delicate, prolonged operations of modern surgery became possible only after the introduction of anaesthetics" (369). (Scientists complained that anti-vivisection literature ignored the use of anaesthesia.) On the other side of the controversy, R.H. Hutton, crusader against vivisection and editor of the influential *Spectator*, gives Wells's story one of its few good reviews because he takes it as an attack on vivisection (Appendix C3).

In addition to using Moreau's daily practice of vivisection to generate a pervasive sense of deliberately inflicted pain, the narrative also gives the vivisection controversy a crucial role in his past. While Prendick is struggling with the uncanny feeling that Moreau's strange assistants remind him of something familiar he can't place, he ponders "the unaccountable familiarity" (93) of Moreau's name, also lost in memory. (Memory on this island is always unpleasant, unless falsified. To remember too far back might be to encounter one's animal inheritance.)

A phrase, "the Moreau Horrors," crosses his mind and suddenly he relives his response to a well-publicized incident of ten years ago, when "I had been a mere lad ... and Moreau was ... a prominent and masterful physiologist, well known in scientific circles for his extraordinary imagination and brutal directness in discussion." Moreau's laboratory practices were exposed by an anti-vivisectionist pamphlet "that to read made one shiver and creep," written by a journalist who "obtained access to his laboratory in the capacity of laboratory assistant, with the deliberate intention of making sensational exposures.... It was in a silly season, and a prominent editor ... appealed to the conscience of the nation.... The doctor was simply howled out of the country" (94). This public howling anticipates two hunts on Moreau's island: the Beast People, led by Moreau, hunt first Prendick and then the Leopard Man. Here we also encounter the first of Moreau's vivisected animals. Seemingly by accident, on the day of the publication of the pamphlet, "a wretched dog, flayed and otherwise mutilated, escaped from Moreau's house" (94; ch. 7).

The dating of the story would place Moreau's departure from Britain in a particularly intense period in the vivisection controversy. The "Introduction" provided by Prendick's nephew places the main action of the story in the first half of 1887. In his "explanation" Moreau tells Prendick that he has been on the island for "nearly eleven years" (128; ch. 14). (Montgomery also gives between ten and eleven years as the length of his exile.) This would mean that they left England in or soon after 1876, the year when the vivisection controversy, increasingly vociferous since the early 1870s, came to a climax with the passage of the Cruelty to Animals Act, intended to regulate vivisection.

Due to the British love of animals, the anti-vivisection movement was stronger in Britain than in any other country. The movement gained force in the early 1870s, when British doctors and medical students began to take experimental medicine seriously, using vivisection both in research and to train students in surgery. Prosecutions for cruelty to animals were launched against doctors; none succeeded but conviction was a real possibility.

In 1875 wide public outrage was aroused by a denunciation in the British press of a well-known scientist by a former laboratory assistant. This incident may have suggested the method of Moreau's exposure. The target in this case was the famous French physiologist, Dr. Claude Bernard. A British doctor, George Hoggan, who had worked for four months in Bernard's laboratory, published a long letter in the *Morning Post* describing the suffering inflicted on dogs by experiments conducted by Bernard and his assistants (Appendix G4). R.H. Hutton played the role of the "prominent editor," quickly reprinting the attack in the *Spectator* and keeping the controversy before the public with a series of editorials attacking vivisection. Hutton particularly opposed the idea of using vivisection for pure research, to define new theoretical questions rather than for specific medical benefits (Appendix G5).

Protagonists on both sides and later commentators agree in seeing Hoggan's letter as the most decisive and widely-publicized event in the controversy (Cobbe 263-65; French 68). Bernard was safe in France, but if the object of this attack had been a British scientist, he might well have found it convenient to leave the country. Earlier in his career, the escape of a vivisected dog from his laboratory also caused Bernard some embarrassment, and eventually persecution by neighbours, who accused him of vivisecting children, forced him to move his laboratory (Omlstead 34-35; Tarshis 46-49).

In response to the high level of intensity the public controversy had reached, in 1875 the Home Secretary set up a Royal Commission to conduct hearings on "the practice of subjecting live animals to experiments for scientific purposes" (French 79). These hearings were widely reported in the press. Huxley led the scientists speaking in favour of vivisection, while Hutton led the opposition to it. Huxley defended the use of vivisection for pure research. A majority of the public felt satisfied by the passage of the Cruelty to Animals Act in 1876, which required a government licence for vivisection, but since laboratories were rarely inspected the Act actually did little to limit vivisection.

The anti-vivisection movement felt betrayed by the Act and intensified its campaign but began to lose popular support, partly because of the lurid nature of the material it distributed. Its sensational publications kept the controversy in the public mind, however, and provided a store of gruesome associations for Wells to draw on. In *Moreau* Wells exploits an ambivalence both towards vivisection and the anti-vivisection movement that would be characteristic of the reading public by the 1890s. While Prendick, the narrator of the story, is deeply disturbed by the torment Moreau inflicts on animals, he also suggests that public opposition to vivisection is a kind of lunacy—"it was a silly season." In his argument with Moreau in chapter 14 he oscillates between these positions without fully affirming either.

There is an affinity between the defence of vivisection provided by Claude Bernard (1813-78), the French physiologist attacked by Hoggan, and Wells's Doctor Moreau. Bernard's career seems well suited to provide a focal point for ambivalence towards vivisection. In his single-minded dedication to research in physiology, Bernard made a notoriously ruthless use of animals. On the other hand, his research had a revolutionizing effect on medical science, illuminating, among other subjects, the nature of digestion, the function of the liver, how changes in body temperature affect the circulation of blood, and the action and medicinal value of poisons. Bernard also provided a lucid rationale for the experimental method in research. After his denunciation by Hoggan, the anti-vivisection movement saw Bernard as the arch-vivisectionist. It is in a pamphlet entitled "Bernard's Martyrs" that Cobbe argues that deliberate sadism motivates the vivisecting scientist—quoted at length in her autobiography (290-91; see Appendix G7).

In his most famous book, *An Introduction to the Study of Experimental Science* (1865) (Appendix G3), which earned him membership in the Académie Française, Bernard makes a passionate defence of vivisection that became infamous in anti-vivisection literature: "A physiologist is not a man of fashion, he is a man of science, absorbed by the scientific idea which he pursues: he no longer hears the cry of animals, he no longer sees the blood that flows, he sees only his idea and perceives only organisms concealing problems which he intends to solve" (103). Bernard's view of the animal as an intellectual problem pervades Dr. Moreau's "explanation" (chapter 14). He tells Prendick:

> You see, I went on with this research just the way it led me. That is the only way I ever heard of true research going. I asked a question, devised some method of obtaining an answer, and got—a fresh question. Was this possible or that possible? You can't imagine what this means to an investigator, what an intellectual passion grows upon him! You cannot imagine the strange, colourless delight of these intellectual desires! The thing before you is no longer an animal, a fellow-creature, but a problem! Sympathetic pain—all I know of it I remember as a thing I used to suffer from years ago. (127)[1]

Moreau's defence places him in the great tradition of nineteenth-century physiology, of which Wells strongly approved. Like Moreau, Wells makes a passionate defence of vivisection as pure research in his essay on the anti-vivisection movement (Appendix G9). It is also true, however, that Moreau provides some poetic touches lacking in Bernard's prose. The "strange colourless delight" of "intellectual desires" may be a manifestation of the ecstasy of genius described by J.-J. Moreau. As a comparatively normal prototype of Moreau, Bernard could be seen a genius whose contribution to medical science was enhanced by his obsession with research, while Moreau's excessive enthusiasm for his project has carried him into monomania. Certainly Moreau seems unique in confessing in the next paragraph that "the study of Nature makes a man at last as remorseless as Nature" (128; ch. 14). On the other hand, the affinity between Moreau's defence of his methods and the discourse of his profession may make him

---

1 I am indebted to Thomas Moen, an undergraduate at Simon Fraser University, for calling my attention to the similarity of these two passages and to the single-mindedness with which both Bernard and Moreau pursued their careers in biological research: neither allowed human relationships to stand in their way.

seem closer to the scientific norm of his period, but may also make science itself seem suspect.

★ ★ ★

Understanding Moreau as a colleague of Bernard and refugee from the public uproar over vivisection in the mid-1870s will help to place him in the larger context of the late-Victorian conflict between religion and science, in which the vivisection controversy was a bitterly fought skirmish. As the new priesthood of science, dedicated to the theory of evolution, challenged a more traditional religious and literary leadership, the anti-vivisection movement provided one line of resistance for the traditionalists. The big names of the anti-vivisection movement combined the Church of England (the Archbishop of York), Evangelicalism (Lord Shaftsbury), Catholicism (Cardinal Manning), literature (Browning and Tennyson), and the arts (Landseer and Ruskin).

Both Bernard and Moreau turn defence of vivisection into a battle-cry for the new science, but the rationale of both manifests a mind-body split that might have something in common with the religious attitudes they reject. In his history of the vivisection controversy, French concludes that the tendency of Victorian opponents of vivisection to endow their favourite animals with human characteristics is related to an attempt to deny any dangerous animal element in human nature, an issue made pressing by the Darwinian challenge to religion (384-91). I would add that if the anti-vivisectionists made animal consciousness too human, Bernard and Moreau, in refusing to acknowledge it at all, also divide flesh from spirit. In their case the animal under vivisection becomes mere inert matter, thus freeing the mind of the scientist for a bodiless exercise of pure reason. Bernard contrasts the physicality of vivisection to the purity of scientific theory by likening "the science of life" to "a superb and dazzlingly lighted hall which may be reached only by passing through a long and ghastly kitchen" (15). He declares that "a living organism is nothing but a wonderful machine" that can be taken apart to see how it works (63, 65), while Moreau habitually describes animals as physical substance. Referring to his new shipment of animals, Moreau remarks, "I'm itching to get to work again—with this new stuff" (91; ch. 7).

It is precisely in response to Prendick's question "where is your justification for inflicting all this pain?" that Moreau makes clear his repudiation of the flesh (126; ch. 14). Moreau informs Prendick that anyone who responds to the suffering of animals has hardly risen above animal status: "So long as visible or audible pain turns you sick, so long as your own pain drives you, so long as pain underlies your propositions about sin, so long, I tell you, you are an animal, thinking a little less obscurely what an animal feels..." (126; ch. 14). Moreau reveals an affinity with Puritan hostility to the flesh when he defines both pleasure and pain as bestial inheritance: "This store men and women set on pleasure and pain ... is the mark of the beast upon them, the mark of the beast from which they came!" (127). As the vivisected animals fail to meet Moreau's ideal of the human they lapse into mere physical substance: "the material ... has dripped into the huts yonder" (128).

Moreau's project has a psychological goal far more ambitious than the usual objects of physiological research. Bernard deconstructs living organisms to see how they work, with the end inevitably being the animal's death, while Moreau seeks to reconstruct animals into human form. Along this line he develops an interest in the conversion of animal instinct into the higher feelings, which anticipates Freud's concept of sublimation. Referring to the socializing process in human society, a process he seeks to reproduce through surgery and social conditioning, Moreau informs Prendick that "very much ... of what we call moral education is ... an artificial modification and perversion of instinct; pugnacity is trained into courageous self-sacrifice, and suppressed sexuality into religious emotion" (125).

At this point we might pause to consider Chalmers Mitchell's objections to the painfulness of Moreau's methods. Mitchell points out that only under anaesthesia are the "delicate, prolonged operations of modern surgery" possible. Since Moreau's operations are essentially an elaborate kind of grafting, indeed delicate and prolonged, and, as Mitchell observes, the struggles of an animal in torment would make such operations difficult or impossible, why doesn't Moreau use anaesthesia, so readily available by the 1880s? Had he done so, this story would have far less resemblance to an anti-vivisection tract. The answer reveals a disturbing aspect of Moreau's motivation: he deliberately inflicts prolonged and excruciating pain as part of the humanizing process: "I will conquer yet. Each time I dip a living creature into the bath of burning pain, I say, This time I will burn out all the animal, this time I will make a rational creature of my own" (130; ch. 14). The near-human creatures that result from this process are intended to remember their torment because excruciating pain is part of the civilizing process by which an animal becomes human.

Moreau's "explanation" reveals that Prendick's initial assumption that he is vivisecting humans into animals is the reverse of the truth: he is attempting to vivisect animals into humans, and he uses the pain of vivisection to block memory of their animal past. Like the Christian concept of Hell, memory of torment also becomes a moral disincentive—if they lapse into animality they will go back to the vivisecting table in the "House of Pain." Finally, through inflicting torment Moreau has made himself the punitive father-god of a parodic religion that is essential to preserving the unstable identity of the Beast People, with clear implications for the role of religion in human society. In the trial of the Leopard Man, Moreau reinforces his authority by providing a scapegoat on which the Beast People can project their collective guilt. Considering the well-established rituals with which Moreau opens this assembly, we may suspect that he is not being entirely truthful when he tells Prendick that he had nothing to do with fashioning the religion of the Beast People (130; ch. 14).

Although Moreau presents himself as the supreme rationalist, his ideal of "burning out all the animal" defies the implications of evolution as spelled out in Huxley's famous essay "Evolution and Ethics." Moreau seems, like his author and most of the scientific elite of his time, fully committed to Darwinian theory: his project is a recapitulation of the evolutionary process; he states clearly that the human species comes from "the beast" (127) and has been "a hundred thousand [years] in the making" (130). But from the point of view of evolution as understood by both Huxley and Wells, burning out all the animal is impossible because we are all animals, and will carry an animal inheritance within us no matter how civilized we attempt to become.

Moreau's use of vivisection becomes a metaphor both for biological evolution and the socializing process intended to correct the deficiencies of the human species as the product of evolution. Moreau's claim that pure knowledge is his goal (124) masks an obsession with a more specific object: to purify the human race by perfecting the process of evolution. In his quest to extirpate all the animal he is trying to do evolution one better, to repeat the process this time with no animal inheritance remaining. Impelled by his Puritan longing to "burn out all the animal," Moreau makes a godlike attempt to eliminate the animal inheritance that both Huxley and Wells see as the most enduring problem of human nature.

In his zeal to bring forth a perfected human amid the horrors of his laboratory, Moreau parallels Frankenstein's frenzied labour to produce an ideal being in his "workshop of filthy creation" (Shelley 36). Both Frankenstein and Moreau reject their creations as revoltingly physical and both resist acknowledgement of the conflicted consciousness that their creatures develop, preferring to dismiss them as unacceptable lumps of matter.

Moreau's biological research is as much engaged as the religious opponents of Darwinism in trying to suppress the physicality of the human species and the psychological conflicts arising from our animal inheritance. Ironically, Moreau's Beast People provide the ultimate confounding of the distinction between human and animal.

Moreau denies his own participation in the animality of the flesh, yet the obsessive intensity of his "delight" in his "intellectual desires" suggests a return of the animal nature he denies in the form of unconscious sadism. He speculates on a curiously gothic locale for earlier researchers in his line: "It must have been practised in secret before ... in the vaults of the Inquisition. No doubt their chief aim was artistic torture, but some, at least, of the inquisitors must have had a touch of scientific curiosity" (125; ch. 14).

Moreau's name and career might have been suggested by a French psychiatrist and an eminent French physiologist, respectively, but we have seen that the nature of his project requires no "original": it springs from a need deep in the Darwinian tradition—the need to bring the process of evolution under control through human intervention. Both Huxley and Wells are tempted by but reject the idea of biological intervention to improve the human species; instead they throw their energy into supporting and hopefully improving civilization through social education—a goal clearly spelled out at the end of Wells's essay "Human Evolution, an Artificial Process."

In addition to recommending reproductive curtailment for the lowest class in *A Modern Utopia*, Wells did occasionally pay tribute to the desirability of biological intervention in some form to save the human species, but this never became a major theme in his writing. In his later visions of the future, the temporary destruction of civilization by war seemed a more suitable instrument of transformation. The MacKenzies see the benevolent dictatorship of enlightened scientists after a global war in Wells's prophetic novel *The Shape of Things to Come* (1933) as a more optimistic version of the rule of Doctor Moreau: "Manipulative psychology has taken the place of manipulative surgery as a means of turning beasts into men" (378). Wells's portrait of Moreau can be seen as a satire of a wrong-headed version of his own longing for a world in which our animal inheritance would finally be left behind.

In Moreau's case the tendency to intervene in evolution has gone wrong in a way that may also represent an underlying attitude in both Wells and Huxley: a Puritan horror of the flesh. A story that makes vivisection a metaphor for evolution might well suggest disgust with the idea that we share one flesh with animals. This aversion to our physical inheritance is implicit in Huxley's concept of a war between physical nature and civilization, and goes with his acknowledged affinity with Calvinistic Puritanism. As we have seen, Wells also had a Puritan background. Moreau attacks animal flesh with a Puritan fury as though he could torture it out of existence. If he has fallen into monomania, this would seem to be the obsession that put him there.

As a critique of the eugenicists' proposal to improve the human race by control of breeding, Huxley, in "Evolution and Ethics," presents the fable of a eugenicist colonial administrator who improves the biological nature of his colonists through systematic elimination of the unfit, or at least by preventing mentally or physically inferior colonists from having children. Huxley admits the advantages of such direct intervention but firmly rejects it because it would deny the human sympathy which is essential to social relations and would also undermine the humanity of any administrator who attempted it. David Y. Hughes observes that Moreau plays the same role as Huxley's administrator in attempting to mold the Beast People through scientific intervention. It seems that the centre of Moreau's deficiency, and his failure to rule his created society, may lie in his repeated rejection of "sympathetic pain" and his contempt for the "upward striving" of the Beast People. For Moreau the ultimate object of evolution seems to be rising above sympathy, which he equates with the world of animal emotions.

With the character of Moreau, Wells has done something that seems a remarkable departure from his usual support for the sciences: he has taken typical themes of anti-vivisection literature—the emphasis on the pain of the victim and the supposed sadism of the vivisector—and through his obsessed scientist has expanded these into a coldly arrogant view of human destiny that denies the importance of sympathetic feeling. At least one critic sees in Moreau and his island society an anticipation of dystopian science fiction and of totalitarian politics (McConnell 92). Moreau's methods of exerting authority over the Beast People may well undermine confidence in the rationality of social institutions, especially religion. Wells's use of vivisection for Gothic effect comes close to undermining the authority of science as well.

In addition to its emphasis on pain, the unsettling effect of this story arises from Wells's tendency to challenge interpretation by placing his characters on boundaries between opposites. It is perhaps because of Wells's refusal to establish clear moral identities for his characters that Victorian reviewers tended to denounce the story as immoral. While Bram Stoker's best-selling *Dracula* (1897) provides climactic scenes—the staking of the vampire Lucy by the male vampire-hunters or Dracula's bloody vampirization of Mina—more horrific and suggestive than any specific scene in *Moreau*, Stoker takes care to protect the reader by showing which characters are good and which evil and by providing a divinely-inspired scientist to lead the vampire-hunters, so that we know that goodness will triumph in the end. With characters who are disturbing but do not line up in clear moral polarities, and with Prendick's confused anxieties for a conclusion, Wells allows the reader no moral escape route from the oppressive atmosphere of his story.

Prendick, as representative of a normal point of view, seems outside the story's ambiguities but becomes so threatened by them that he cannot provide a consistent interpretation. Despite his resistance to Moreau, he is too dominated by him to maintain a clear position of his own. Punter observes that Moreau is one of the great Gothic dominators (Count Dracula would be another) and that "Prendick's objections to Moreau's procedures are constantly vitiated by his admiration for Moreau himself, grudging as it is" (251).

Prendick provides an explicit recognition of the Beast People as representing the human condition, yet seems to lose this insight as his response to them lapses into conventional polarities. After the hunt of the Leopard Man, Prendick falls into a grim meditation that gives the pain inflicted by Moreau its widest social meaning, making explicit the story's implied analogy between the plight of the Beast People and the human condition: "A strange persuasion came upon me that ... I had here before me the whole balance of human life in miniature, the whole interplay of instinct, reason, and fate in its simplest form" (145; ch. 16). Prendick concludes that the pain experienced by animals attempting to remain human is far worse than that inflicted by vivisection; the agony inflicted by their creation is followed by the permanent agony of inner conflict: "they stumbled in the shackles of humanity, lived in a fear that never died, fretted by a law they could not understand; their mock-human existence began in an agony, was one long internal struggle, one long dread of Moreau—and for what?" (145; ch. 16).

Prendick cannot accept the implications of this insight, however. In the next chapter he rejects his momentary identification of the Beast People with the human species and dissociates the two entirely, viewing the Beast People with "dislike and abhorrence" from then on (146; ch. 17). As we see in the last chapter, however, he never succeeds in convincing himself that the civilized humans around him are altogether different from the Beast People.

We could find a Darwinian moral in the dark conclusion of the story. None of the characters can come to terms with the fact of animal inheritance: Moreau claims to have risen above it; Prendick despairingly recognizes the Beast People as the human condition but at the same time denies this by maintaining an idealized memory of normal humanity back home—a split which continues to divide his mind after his return to Britain—while neither Montgomery nor the Beast People are consciously aware of their animal past but become hopelessly vulnerable to it. By enabling the reader to understand these fallacies the story can imply the existence of a rational Darwinian perspective that the characters do not possess. In "Human Evolution," the essay Wells published shortly after the novel, he lays out such a perspective—stoical yet not despairing—through which we may hope to deal with our savage inheritance.

This is one way in which the story can be seen. Frank McConnell concludes by finding in *Moreau* a critique of a series of misreadings of Darwin, some of which tend to racism and imperialism (102). I should like to suggest that while Wells undoubtedly does intend a critique of the errors both of Moreau and Prendick in dealing with Darwinian problems, the overall impact of the story may be less clear: a good part of its disturbing effect may lie in depriving the reader of any basis for certainty. This story is focused on biological science, Wells's speciality, yet science does not do well in it. The Time Traveller, hero and main narrator of Wells's first science-fiction novella, maintains a plausible version of the scientific imagination, while here both Moreau and Prendick are unreliable in different ways: Moreau is obsessed by his science, while Prendick seems a rather conventional amateur. Also, Moreau's reliance on vivisection does not present scientific research in a reassuring light, while the symbolic extension of the pain of vivisection to represent the process of evolution itself might raise doubts as to whether any rationality can be found in a Darwinian universe.

Wells may have tackled a problem here that challenged his faith in scientific reason. Through its depiction of the Beast People, this story forces a confrontation in disturbing terms with the psychological problems of human nature posed by a Huxleyan interpretation of Darwin. Moreau seeks to abolish these problems by a purely objective means—corrective surgery—but also exempts himself from them. In his insistence on his own scientific rationality, his dream of a rational species that will no longer be afflicted by sympathy and pain, and his contempt for the "upward striving" of the beings he does create, he not only denies the emotional basis of human relationship but also the individual subjectivity in which inner conflict is experienced.

Moreau's perverse attitudes are part of a larger problem: objective science may not be equipped to deal with the psychological problems posed by evolution. Wells understands Moreau's fallacies but perhaps in his own commitment to science he also feels threatened by the conflicts that emerge in this story. A few years after *Moreau* he would turn to works of futurology and realistic novels with a sociological orientation, both of which would provide a basis for objective vision on the part of the narrator. Soon his utopias would express a hope that human nature could be transformed through social conditioning guided by enlightened scientists. *Moreau* can be seen as a nightmare enactment of problems Wells sought to overcome in his later career.

A Postscript on Genetic Modification: *Oryx and Crake*

To invent new creatures Moreau relies entirely on his scalpel. Writing when genetic theory was just getting started, Wells could not have foreseen that within a century advances in genetics would make *Moreau* the most ominously predictive of all his scientific romances. We now live in a period where genetically-engineered plants are commonplace and the same results clearly can be achieved with animals and humans. Unlike Moreau's products, such invented beings can reproduce effectively, thus perpetuating the altered genes. The long-range results of this tendency can only be imagined—and once more science fiction has risen to the challenge. In a compelling dystopian novel, *Oryx and Crake* (2004), Margaret Atwood dramatizes both the grossly commercial aspects of genetic manipulation and a Moreau-like scientific arrogance lurking behind it.

In the disaster that brings about the final stage of her dystopian world, Atwood seems to provide a deliberate reminder of Wells's story of artificial creation. While the main character of her novel (known as "Snowman" in the novel's present) has been involved in the business side of the genetic distortion of nature, his friend Crake, the brilliant but alienated scientist who finally employs him, turns out to be obsessed with the creation of a supposedly superior version of the human species through manipulation of human genes. The outcome of this project has something in common with Moreau's catastrophe: after Crake's violent death, Snowman provides his invented species of humans with a benevolent parallel to Prendick's attempt to awe the Beast People with a myth of Moreau's resurrection. He assures them that Crake has only gone away for a while and will return, and meanwhile "he'll be watching over you.... To keep you safe" (197). While the "Crakers" happily embrace this belief, Snowman remains as dubious as Prendick about the future.

Wells isolates his invented monsters on a remote island; thanks to the new possibilities of genetic science, Atwood can place hers in our own society, in a convincing vision of the near future. Both worlds are brought into being by a science that assumes its own rationality is superior both to organic nature and to the conflicts and passions of human subjectivity, which partake of nature. In its cold arrogance this science ultimately tears apart the fabric of life by attempting to bring all of nature under human control. Nature, in a distorted form, wins in the end because the results of such an attempt are unforeseeable. Comparison with Atwood's dystopia shows more clearly than ever that the disastrous outcome of Moreau's project has implications far beyond his own personal failure.

H. G. Wells: A Brief Chronology

[This chronology is focused primarily on Wells's evolution as a writer of science fiction and fantasy, and lists most of his publications through the first decade of the early twentieth century. It should be noted, however, that several important essays published by Wells in the 1890s are not mentioned—see *Early Writings*, ed. Hughes and Philmus.

The chronology is much more selective in listing works published after 1910, mentioning those that seem to continue the themes of his earlier writing while also providing samples of other work characteristic of his later period. In assembling this chronology, I am indebted to J.R. Hammond's comprehensive *An H.G. Wells Chronology*, Nicholas Ruddick's chronology of Wells in his Broadview edition of *The Time Machine*, and of course Wells's *Experiment in Autobiography*.

The works listed below are fiction unless otherwise indicated.]

1866   Herbert George Wells born 21 September, the youngest of three brothers (a sister died in childhood). His parents, Joseph and Sarah Wells, have a small and not very successful shop in Bromley, Kent.

1874   Breaks leg and happily devotes his convalescence to reading, including Wood's *Natural History*, a book on all the countries of the world, bound volumes of *Punch*, the works of Washington Irving, the life of the Duke of Wellington, and a book on the American Civil War; soon he will discover Fenimore Cooper and the Wild West. In September, he becomes a pupil at Morley's Academy in Bromley, where he continues for six years, an education intended to provide the accounting and language skills required for office work as a clerk.

1877   Father becomes lame due to a gardening accident and is no longer able to play professional cricket. The family now has only the diminishing income from the shop on which to live.

1880   Mother becomes the housekeeper at Uppark, an estate in West Sussex where she had once been a maid.

1881   Bound apprentice for four years to a draping establishment—a dreary time for him but during visits with his mother he benefits from the excellent library at Uppark. His reading includes the novels of Dickens, some works of Voltaire, Johnson's *Rasselas*,

Tom Paine's *Rights of Man*, an unexpurgated edition of Swift's *Gulliver's Travels*, and Plato's *Republic*. Later he will read Henry George's book *Progress and Poverty* on the injustices of land ownership, and become interested in socialism.

1883   Finally succeeds in escaping from the drapery trade after repeated appeals to his mother and relatives to cancel his apprenticeship so he can continue his education. Fortunately, the headmaster of a local grammar school where he was briefly a student recognizes his ability and employs him as an assistant teacher.

1884   Passes government-set examinations in several subjects with high distinction and wins a scholarship to the Normal School of Science in South Kensington (London). Studies biology and zoology under Professor T.H. Huxley and gains first-class honours in Biology, Zoology, and Mathematics. (Huxley retires at the end of the year.)

1886   Reads papers on the future of the human species and on democratic socialism to the school debating society. Founds and becomes editor of the *Science School Journal*. Reads Carlyle's *French Revolution* and the prophetic works of William Blake. Attends socialist meetings, some at the home of William Morris.

1887   Fails the examination in geology, loses his scholarship, and is unable to continue at the Normal School of Science. Becomes a teacher at a very inferior boarding school in Wales, is seriously injured playing soccer, suffers from lung hemorrhages and is diagnosed as having a fatal case of consumption (tuberculosis). Reads widely in the estate's library during a four-month convalescence at Uppark, including "Shelley, Hume, Lamb, Holmes, Stevenson, Hawthorne, and a number of popular novels" (*Experiment* I, 305). Begins work on "The Chronic Argonauts," a prototype of *The Time Machine*.

1888   Publishes instalments of "The Chronic Argonauts" in the *Science School Journal*. Also works on a novel (never completed) while continuing his convalescence with a three-month visit with friends. Returns to London to continue his struggle to make a living.

1889   Becomes the science teacher at Henley House, a good private grammar school. Takes examinations to earn the Licence of the College of Preceptors (i.e., teacher certification) and wins prizes in mathematics, natural science, theory of education,

1890   Elected a Member of the College of Preceptors. Leaves his grammar school position to become a full-time teacher in biology and geology with the University Tutorial College, a private school that undertakes to prepare students for the graduating examinations of the University of London. Receives a Bachelor of Science degree from the University of London with first-class honours in zoology.

1891   Has a breakdown in health and spends a month convalescing at Uppark, with more health problems later in the year. Publishes "The Rediscovery of the Unique," the first of many articles on contemporary science, mostly on biological themes concerned with evolution. Marries Isabell Mary Wells (a cousin). Becomes a Fellow of the College of Preceptors.

1893   Due to over-work suffers a near-fatal lung hemorrhage. Resolves to give up teaching and make a living solely as a writer; discovers how to write light, amusing essays on incidents in everyday life, which prove quite popular. Publishes *Text-Book of Biology*.

1894   Leaves his wife and goes to live with Amy Catherine Robbins, a former student in his tutorial. Publishes "The Province of Pain," an essay he will make use of in Moreau's explanation in chapter 14 of *The Island of Doctor Moreau*. Also publishes "The Stolen Bacillus," a fantasy on a scientific theme and his first short story to appear with his name on it. Many short stories, mostly fantasy, follow and will continue to flow over the next ten years. Meets the influential editor W.E. Henley, who publishes a hastily-assembled version of *The Time Machine*. Henley urges him to turn this into a coherent piece of fiction. Wells works intensely on this project over July and August, and by September gives Henley a new version of *The Time Machine*, which begins serial publication the next year. Begins but leaves incomplete the first version of *The Island of Doctor Moreau*.

1895   Divorces Isabell Mary Wells and marries Amy Catherine Robbins (known hereafter as Jane Wells). Publishes "The Limits of Individual Plasticity," another essay which closely parallels passages in Moreau's explanation. Completes a thorough revision of *Moreau* between January and March. Also reviews plays by Oscar Wilde and Henry James, and a number of novels. Sends the manuscript of *Moreau* to his agent in April, but makes minor revisions through the summer. *The Time Machine* appears in book form both in Britain and the U.S.; Wells sends a copy to T.H. Huxley. Also publishes *The Stolen Bacillus and Other Incidents* (his first anthology of science-fiction stories), *Select Conversations with an Uncle* (a collection of his humorous essays), and *The Wonderful Visit* (a fantasy-novella about an angel's disastrous visit to an English village).

1896   *The Island of Doctor Moreau* is published in April. Replies to Mitchell's review of *Moreau* in a letter to *The Saturday Review*. Publishes "Human Evolution, an Artificial Process," an essay on themes related to *Moreau*. Also publishes *The Wheels of Chance*, a light-hearted novel recounting a romance conducted through the new recreation of bicycling.

1897   Publishes "Morals and Civilization," a sequel to "Human Evolution." Serial publication begins of both *The War of the Worlds* and *The Invisible Man*; the latter is also published in book form. Also publishes *The Plattner Story and Others*.

1898   *The War of the Worlds* appears in book form. Wells travels in Italy for over two months; visits Rome with George Gissing. After returning to Britain has a serious physical collapse in the course of a bicycle tour and spends two months convalescing. After this his health improves. *Thirty Strange Stories* published in the US.

1899   Publishes *When the Sleeper Wakes: A Story of Years to Come*. (A full-length novel set in a near future in which the population of Britain lives in huge self-enclosed cities. Not as well-known as the other scientific romances, but an important influence on later writers, who learn from Wells that the near future can be useful for social satire.) Also publishes *Tales of Space and Time* and "A Story of the Days to Come," a novella-length tale set in the same near-future world as *When the Sleeper Wakes*.

1900   *Love and Mr. Lewisham*. (A semi-autobiographical novel about the failure of a science student due to an inappropriate marriage.)

1901   Publishes *The First Men in the Moon*, the last of the novella-length scientific romances, and a long story, "A Dream of Armageddon," set in the near future, which broaches the theme of world war, to become important in his later visions of the future. Also publishes *Anticipations of the Reaction of Mechanical and Scientific Progress upon Human Life and Thought*, the first of his attempts at a realistic prediction of the future, (Non-fiction; very popular.

The real message of this book lies in the prophecy that since democracy and nationalism will create ruinous wars, the society of the future will have to be guided towards a world-state by an elite of self-sacrificing, scientifically-educated leaders.)

1903 *Twelve Stories and a Dream*. Joins the Fabian Society, a group of leading intellectuals who undertake to plan a peaceful transition to socialism.

1904 *The Food of the Gods and How It Came to Earth*. (An ambiguous tale about a race of giants who meet resistance to their offer to become benevolent rulers of the human race.)

1905 *A Modern Utopia*. (A carefully thought-out version of Wells's visions of an ideal future.) *Kipps: The Story of a Simple Soul*. (The novel's main character is trapped in the draping trade—as Wells might have been.)

1906 *In the Days of the Comet*. (A mix of realism and prophecy— conflicts arising from class division, sexual jealousy, and war are resolved when gas from a comet turns the earth into a utopia. The novel's conclusion emphasizes Wells's view that free love must be an essential aspect of a utopian society.) While on a lecture tour in the US, he meets President Theodore Roosevelt. Publishes *The Future in America*.

1908 *The War in the Air*. (A full-length novel depicting a war with Germany conducted with fleets of dirigibles, which leads to the collapse of civilization.) *New Worlds for Old*. (Essays on socialism.)

1909 *Tono-Bungay*. (Brilliant satire of the state of British society.) *Ann Veronica* (A defense of free love and gender equality in relationships.)

1910 *The History of Mr. Polly*. (A deeply comic portrayal of the revolt of a shopkeeper against marriage and social convention. *Kipps*, *Tono-Bungay*, *Ann Veronica*, and *Mr. Polly* are generally considered to be Wells's best fiction in a realist vein. After this, he increasingly tends to use fiction as a vehicle for ideas).

1911 *The New Machiavelli*. (The protagonist abandons a career in politics and a stifling marriage for a love affair.) *The Door in the Wall and Other Stories*. *The Country of the Blind and Other Stories*. (The title stories of each of these anthologies are among his very best.)

1914 *The World Set Free*. (Wells foresees nuclear weapons; in the mid-twentieth century a world war conducted with atomic bombs wrecks society. Out of the ruins an ideal World State is constructed, ruled by an enlightened elite.) Visits Russia (pre-revolutionary) for the first time.

1915   *Boon*. (Non-fiction; contains a savage critique of the fiction of Henry James, which alienates his old friend.)

1920   *The Outline of History*. (Non-fiction; becomes a best-seller.) Makes a second visit to Russia; has interview with Lenin. Publishes *Russia in the Shadows*, expressing cautious sympathy with the Soviet Union.

1923   *Men Like Gods*. (A utopia set in the far future, visited accidentally by some British politicians who get everything wrong and a journalist who becomes converted to the cause of utopia.) *The Dream*. (A reversal of the situation in *Men Like Gods*: through a series of dreams a citizen of utopia experiences life in the present—"The Age of Confusion." Some scenes here from Wells's early life and education.)

1924-27 The Atlantic Edition of *The Works of H.G. Wells* with new prefaces by Wells.

1928   *Mr. Blettsworthy on Rampole Island*. (An island adventure which seems descended from *Moreau*. The savage society of the island turns out to be a fantastic projection of the contemporary world.)

1929-30 *The Science of Life*. (Non-fiction; with Julian Huxley and others. A comprehensive textbook on biology intended for the ordinary reader.)

1930   *The Autocracy of Mr. Parham*. (A parody of fascism.)

1932   *The Work, Wealth and Happiness of Mankind*. (Non-fiction; textbook on contemporary society, intended as a companion to *The Science of Life*. These two and *The Outline of History* were intended as a trio of textbooks to provide education for the ordinary reader. They were widely read and appreciated.)

1933   *The Shape of Things to Come*. (Wells's most detailed prophecy of world war destroying civilization, which will gradually be rebuilt under the rule of an austere elite of scientists until a utopian society is achieved.) *The Scientific Romances* with a preface by Wells (an anthology of science fiction from the past); published in 1934 in the U.S. as *Seven Famous Novels*.

1934   *Experiment in Autobiography*. Visits Russia, meets Stalin. Visits U.S., meets President Franklin D. Roosevelt.

1936   *The Croquet Player*. (Uses the atmosphere of a ghost story to emphasize a savage inheritance in human nature as the world moves towards war.) Release of a film version of *The Shape of Things to Come*, over which Wells had considerable influence.

1937   *Star Begotten: A Biological Fantasia*. (Benevolent Martians are improving the genetic inheritance of the human species.)

1939   *The Holy Terror*. (A successful world-leader with Wellsian ideals turns into a repressive dictator; only after his death can utopia be achieved. Wells may be satirizing aspects of his own personality and politics.)

1942   *The Rights of Man*. (Composed by a committee convoked by Wells, this very liberal-minded document spells out what human rights should be after World War II.)

1945   *The Happy Turning: A Dream of Life. Mind at the End of Its Tether*. (Two opposite visions, one optimistic and one despairing; each may equally represent Wells's final state of mind.)

1946   Wells dies on 13 August, at the age of seventy-nine.

A Note on the Text

The text provided here is based on the text of the first American edition of *Moreau*, originally published by the firm of Stone and Kimball in August 1896, and reprinted by Robert M. Philmus in his variorum edition of *The Island of Doctor Moreau*. I have followed Philmus in choosing this text over that of the first British edition published by William Heinemann in April 1896. Philmus discusses the complex problems presented by the various texts of *Moreau* in his variorum edition, xxxii–vi. I here provide a more general summary as to why I have followed his choice.

In assembling this edition I have done my best to recreate the intellectual and literary atmosphere that would have influenced Wells in the mid-1890s. It seems equally important that the text should also be an authentic product of Wells in that period. The texts available today contain a number of minor variants that have been introduced by editors, possibly without Wells's approval. As mentioned in my Introduction, Wells wrote *Moreau* under considerable pressure from other projects. Possibly because of this, there is some raggedness in the style and punctuation of the edition published by Heinemann in 1896. As a result, in later editions Heinemann and other editors have done some tinkering with the text. It is not clear whether Wells had anything to do with these changes.

If Wells was involved in some revision, it is also true that he later tended to lose touch with his early science fiction, and may not have been the most sensitive of editors. In one major alteration, presumably inspired by Wells, the Atlantic Edition of *The Works of H.G. Wells* (1924) leaves out the fictional Introduction by Prendick's nephew, Charles Edward Prendick. Most editors have preferred to retain the Introduction, and I feel that it is an essential part of the story.

The Introduction was restored in the Penguin edition of 1946. Today, in Signet paperback, this is the most widely available version of the text. While the Penguin edition provides a smoother and more stylistically elegant version than the original Heinemann edition of 1896, it has been influenced by later editions and thus has over time been polished by a number of editors, one of whom was likely the English novelist Dorothy Richardson. Wells may have had little or nothing to do with such improvements.

Thus a choice must apparently be made between the undoubtedly authentic but rather rough edition published by Heinemann in 1896, and later editions that may be smoother but not done by Wells. Fortunately,

Philmus has revealed an alternative that mitigates this dilemma. He shows that the first American edition is also based on a typescript from Wells, but one that provides some stylistic improvements over the one used by Heinemann, and hence may contain some revisions Wells made before he sent the typescript to the American publisher. Philmus does not regard the evidence for this possibility as conclusive, but since I find the version he provides better reading than the Heinemann text, I think it very likely that this is indeed a slightly later revision by the author. In any case, with two authentic texts available from 1896, it seems sensible to use the one that is more pleasant to read. I am very grateful to Dr. Philmus for having given me the opportunity to do this. I have followed his text except at very rare instances where a reading from a later text seems to provide word-usage or punctuation more consistent with the general practice of the American edition.

The

Island of Doctor Moreau

A Possibility

By

H. G. Wells

New York
Stone & Kimball
MDCCCXCVI

Title page of the first American Edition
Reproduced with the permission of the Rare Book &
Manuscript Library of the University of Urbana-Champaign.

INTRODUCTION

On February the First, 1887, the *Lady Vain* was lost by collision with a derelict when about the latitude 1° S. and longitude 107° W.

On January the Fifth, 1888—that is, eleven months and four days after—my uncle, Edward Prendick, a private gentleman,[1] who certainly went aboard the *Lady Vain* at Callao,[2] and who had been considered drowned, was picked up in latitude 5° 3′ S. and longitude 101° W. in a small open boat of which the name was illegible, but which is supposed to have belonged to the missing schooner *Ipecacuanha*.[3] He gave such a strange account of himself that he was supposed demented. Subsequently he alleged that his mind was a blank from the moment of his escape from the *Lady Vain*. His case was discussed among psychologists at the time as a curious instance of the lapse of memory consequent upon physical and mental stress. The following narrative was found among his papers by the undersigned, his nephew and heir, but unaccompanied by any definite request for publication.

The only island known to exist in the region in which my uncle was picked up is Noble's Isle, a small volcanic islet and uninhabited. It was visited in 1891 by H.M.S. *Scorpion*.[4] A party of sailors then landed, but found nothing living thereon except certain curious white moths, some hogs and rabbits, and some rather peculiar rats. So that this narrative is without confirmation in its most essential particular. With that understood, there seems no harm in putting this strange story before the public in accordance, as I believe, with my uncle's intentions. There is at least this much in its behalf: my uncle passed out of human knowledge about latitude 5° S. and longitude 105° E., and reappeared in the same part of the ocean after a space of eleven months.[5] In some way he must have lived during the

---

1 Meaning that he lived on a private income and did not have a profession.

2 A port in Peru near Lima.

3 A drug made from the roots of a South American plant of the same name. It is a powerful emetic (i.e., an agent to induce vomiting), especially useful for emptying the stomach in cases of poisoning. This seems an odd name for a ship, perhaps implying that the ship's motion is particularly liable to cause sea-sickness.

4 Possibly a reference to H.M.S. *Rattlesnake*, on which T.H. Huxley served as medical officer and naturalist during an exploration of the South Seas, especially the waters around Australia and New Guinea, that lasted from 1846-50.

5 The location given here is different from that given for the wreck of the *Lady Vain*. Prendick presumably "passed out of human knowledge" at the point where he was abandoned by the captain of the *Ipecacuanha*, and hence these coordinates should

interval. And it seems that a schooner called the *Ipecacuanha* with a drunken captain, John Davies, did start from Arica[1] with a puma and certain other animals aboard in January, 1887, that the vessel was well known at several ports in the South Pacific, and that it finally disappeared from those seas (with a considerable amount of copra aboard), sailing to its unknown fate from Bayna[2] in December, 1887, a date that tallies entirely with my uncle's story.

CHARLES EDWARD PRENDICK.

---

provide the location of Moreau's island. (Prendick's nephew considers it likely that Moreau's island is "Noble's Isle," the location of which would be known—in the world of the novel. Noble's Isle is fictitious.)

The designation of the longitude here as 105° *East* must be a mistake; Wells must have meant 105° *West* (see Philmus, variorum *Moreau*, note 6, p. 89). A longitude of 105° East would put Moreau's island in the same location as Sumatra, on the other side of the Pacific from the wreck of the *Lady Vain*.

Corrected, 5° S. latitude and 105° W. longitude would place Moreau's island in the same general area as the coordinates given for the wreck of the *Lady Vain* and Prendick's final rescue—an area more than 1000 km. (621 miles) west and a bit south of the nearest land, the Galapagos Islands, which in turn are nearly 1000 km. west of the coast of Ecuador. [The coordinates for the Galapagos Islands are 0° latitude, 91° W. longitude; near the Equator, a degree of latitude or longitude represents a distance of about 111 km (69 miles).]

Whatever the problems presented by the coordinates Wells gives here, his intent is clear: to locate Moreau's island in an isolated part of the Pacific with the Galapagos Islands as the nearest land. The Galapagos Islands have a well-known association with Darwin's theory of evolution. The observations Darwin made when he visited them in 1835 during the voyage of H.M.S. *Beagle* laid the basis for his theory that species originate and change through natural selection. Another possible geographic affinity: further south, off the coast of Chile, lie the Juan Fernandez Islands, where Alexander Selkirk, the original of Defoe's *Robinson Crusoe* (1719), was marooned for over four years.

1   A seaport in northern Chile which in the late nineteenth century was devastated by bloody wars.

2   "Banya" in the first English edition. Neither name appears on maps of the South Seas. Philmus thinks that "Banya" may be a misprint for "Banka" (variorum *Moreau*, Note 8, 90). Banka (also spelled Bangka) is an island in Indonesia, off the coast of Sumatra.

The Island of Doctor Moreau
(The Story written by Edward Prendick)

1. IN THE DINGEY OF THE *LADY VAIN*

I do not propose to add anything to what has already been written concerning the loss of the *Lady Vain*. As everyone knows, she collided with a derelict when ten days out from Callao. The long-boat, with seven of the crew, was picked up eighteen days after by H.M. gunboat *Myrtle*, and the story of their terrible privations has become quite as well known as the far more horrible *Medusa* case.[1] But I have to add to the published story of the *Lady Vain* another, possibly as horrible and certainly far stranger. It has hitherto been supposed that the four men who were in the dingey perished, but this is incorrect. I have the best of evidence for this assertion: I was one of the four men.

But in the first place I must state that there never were *four* men in the dingey—the number was three. Constans, who was "seen by the captain to jump into the gig" (*Daily News*, March 17, 1887),[2] luckily for us and unluckily for himself did not reach us. He came down out of the tangle of ropes under the stays of the smashed bowsprit, some small rope caught his heel as he let go, and he hung for a moment head downward, and then fell and struck a block or spar floating in the water. We pulled towards him, but he never came up.

---

1 A French ship that was wrecked off the coast of Africa in 1816 and became a scandal of international repute, because of both the terrible suffering of the survivors and their dramatic representation in a famous painting, *The Raft of the Medusa* (1819) by Théodore Géricault. See Appendix I for selections from an eye-witness account. Wells's mention of the case, without, explanation, suggests that he expected it to be recognized by his readers.

2 Philmus has discovered that though there is no mention of anything like this in the *Daily News* on the date given, an account of a remarkably similar incident did appear in that newspaper less than two years before the composition of *Moreau*. On February 22, 1893, the *Daily News* translated an account from a German newspaper of the trial of three sailors shipwrecked in the North Sea who cannibalized a fourth, selected by drawing lots; Hjalmar was the middle name of one of the sailors (Philmus, variorum *Moreau*, note 11, p. 90). In describing Prendick's experience of shipwreck, Wells might have combined this incident with the lurid atmosphere of the *Medusa* disaster.

I say luckily for us he did not reach us, and I might almost say luckily for himself; for we had only a small breaker[1] of water and some soddened ship's biscuits with us, so sudden had been the alarm, so unprepared the ship for any disaster. We thought the people on the launch would be better provisioned (though it seems they were not), and we tried to hail them. They could not have heard us, and the next morning when the drizzle cleared—which was not until past midday—we could see nothing of them. We could not stand up to look about us, because of the pitching of the boat. The two other men who had escaped so far with me were a man named Helmar, a passenger like myself, and a seaman whose name I don't know—a short sturdy man, with a stammer.

We drifted famishing, and, after our water had come to an end, tormented by an intolerable thirst, for eight days altogether. After the second day the sea subsided slowly to a glassy calm. It is quite impossible for the ordinary reader to imagine those eight days. He has not, luckily for himself, anything in his memory to imagine with. After the first day we said little to one another, and lay in our places in the boat and stared at the horizon, or watched, with eyes that grew larger and more haggard every day, the misery and weakness gaining upon our companions. The sun became pitiless. The water ended on the fourth day, and we were already thinking strange things and saying them with our eyes; but it was, I think, the sixth before Helmar gave voice to the thing we had all been thinking. I remember our voices were dry and thin, so that we bent towards one another and spared our words. I stood out against it with all my might, was rather for scuttling the boat and perishing together among the sharks that followed us; but when Helmar said that if his proposal was accepted we should have drink, the sailor came round to him.

I would not draw lots, however, and in the night the sailor whispered to Helmar again and again, and I sat in the bows with my clasp-knife in my hand, though I doubt if I had the stuff in me to fight; and in the morning I agreed to Helmar's proposal, and we handed halfpence to find the odd man. The lot fell upon the sailor; but he was the strongest of us and would not abide by it, and attacked Helmar with his hands. They grappled together and almost stood up. I crawled along the boat to them, intending to help Helmar by grasping the sailor's leg; but the sailor stumbled with the swaying of the boat, and the two fell upon the gunwale[2] and rolled

---

1   A small cask used to carry water on a boat.
2   The upper edge of the side of a small ship or boat.

overboard together. They sank like stones. I remember laughing at that, and wondering why I laughed. The laugh caught me suddenly like a thing from without.

I lay across one of the thwarts for I know not how long, thinking that if I had the strength I would drink sea-water and madden myself to die quickly. And even as I lay there I saw, with no more interest than if it had been a picture, a sail come up towards me over the sky-line. My mind must have been wandering, and yet I remember all that happened quite distinctly. I remember how my head swayed with the seas, and the horizon with the sail above it danced up and down; but I also remember as distinctly that I had a persuasion that I was dead, and that I thought what a jest it was that they should come too late by such a little to catch me in my body.

For an endless period, as it seemed to me, I lay with my head on the thwart watching the schooner (she was a little ship, schooner-rigged fore and aft) come up out of the sea. She kept tacking to and fro in a widening compass, for she was sailing dead into the wind. It never entered my head to attempt to attract attention, and I do not remember anything distinctly after the sight of her side until I found myself in a little cabin aft. There's a dim half-memory of being lifted up to the gangway, and of a big red countenance covered with freckles and surrounded with red hair staring at me over the bulwarks. I also had a disconnected impression of a dark face, with extraordinary eyes, close to mine; but that I thought was a nightmare, until I met it again. I fancy I recollect some stuff being poured in between my teeth; and that is all.

2. THE MAN WHO WAS GOING NOWHERE

The cabin in which I found myself was small and rather untidy. A youngish man with flaxen hair, a bristly straw-coloured moustache, and a dropping nether lip, was sitting and holding my wrist. For a minute we stared at each other without speaking. He had watery grey eyes, oddly void of expression. Then just overhead came a sound like an iron bedstead being knocked about, and the low angry growling of some large animal. At the same time the man spoke. He repeated his question—

"How do you feel now?"

I think I said I felt all right. I could not recollect how I had got there. He must have seen the question in my face, for my voice was inaccessible to me.

"You were picked up in a boat, starving. The name on the boat was the *Lady Vain*, and there were spots of blood on the gunwale."

At the same time my eye caught my hand, thin so that it looked like a dirty skin-purse full of loose bones, and all the business of the boat came back to me.

"Have some of this," said he, and gave me a dose of some scarlet stuff, iced.

It tasted like blood and made me feel stronger.

"You were in luck," said he, "to get picked up by a ship with a medical man aboard." He spoke with a slobbering articulation, with the ghost of a lisp.

"What ship is this?" I said slowly, hoarse from my long silence.

"It's a little trader from Arica and Callao. I never asked where she came from in the beginning—out of the land of born fools, I guess. I'm a passenger myself, from Arica. The silly ass who owns her—he's captain too, named Davies—he's lost his certificate, or something. You know the kind of man—calls the thing the *Ipecacuanha*, of all silly, infernal names; though when there's much of a sea without any wind, she certainly acts according."

Then the noise overhead began again, a snarling growl and the voice of a human being together. Then another voice, telling some "Heaven-forsaken idiot" to desist.

"You were nearly dead," said my interlocutor. "It was a very near thing, indeed. But I've put some stuff into you now. Notice your arm's sore? Injections. You've been insensible for nearly thirty hours."

I thought slowly. (I was distracted now by the yelping of a number of dogs.) "Am I eligible for solid food?" I asked.

"Thanks to me," he said. "Even now the mutton is boiling."

"Yes," I said with assurance; "I could eat some mutton."

"But," said he with a momentary hesitation, "you know I'm dying to hear of how you came to be alone in that boat. *Damn that howling!*" I thought I detected a certain suspicion in his eyes.

He suddenly left the cabin, and I heard him in violent controversy with some one, who seemed to me to talk gibberish in response to him. The matter sounded as though it ended in blows, but in that I thought my ears were mistaken. Then he shouted at the dogs, and returned to the cabin.

"Well?" said he in the doorway. "You were just beginning to tell me."

I told him my name, Edward Prendick, and how I had taken to Natural History as a relief from the dullness of my comfortable independence.

He seemed interested in this. "I've done some science myself. I did my Biology at University College[1]—getting out the ovary of the earthworm and the radula of the snail, and all that. Lord! It's ten years ago. But go on! go on! tell me about the boat."

He was evidently satisfied with the frankness of my story, which I told in concise sentences enough, for I felt horribly weak; and when it was finished he reverted at once to the topic of Natural History and his own biological studies. He began to question me closely about Tottenham Court Road and Gower Street. "Is Caplatzi[2] still flourishing? What a shop that was!" He had evidently been a very ordinary medical student, and drifted incontinently[3] to the topic of the music halls. He told me some anecdotes. "Left it all," he said, "ten years ago. How jolly it all used to be! But I made a young ass of myself—played myself out before I was twenty-one. I daresay it's all different now. But I must look up that ass of a cook, and see what he's done to your mutton."

The growling overhead was renewed, so suddenly and with so much savage anger that it startled me. "What's that?" I called after him, but the door had closed. He came back again with the boiled mutton, and I was so excited by the appetising smell of it that I forgot the noise of the beast that had troubled me.

After a day of alternate sleep and feeding I was so far recovered as to be able to get from my bunk to the scuttle,[4] and see the green seas trying to keep pace with us. I judged the schooner was running before the wind. Montgomery—that was the name of the flaxen-haired man—came in again as I stood there, and I asked him for some clothes. He lent me some duck[5] things of his own, for those I had worn in the boat had been thrown overboard. They were rather loose for me, for he was large and long in his limbs. He told me casually that the captain was three-parts drunk in

---

1 A college of the University of London. Wells taught "cramming" courses, including practice in dissection, for students preparing for the University of London examination in biology. In 1890 Wells received a Bachelor of Science degree, with first-class honours in zoology, from the University of London.

2 Tottenham Court Road and Gower Street are adjacent to the University College and in this area would provide shops of interest to students. Philmus has discovered that Caplatzi was the proprietor of "an emporium ... selling various sorts of technical equipment and scientific apparatus" (variorum *Moreau*, note 15, p. 91).

3 Immediately or suddenly.

4 A hatch opening on the deck.

5 Clothing made of a strong cotton fabric, like canvas but lighter.

his own cabin. As I assumed the clothes, I began asking him some questions about the destination of the ship. He said the ship was bound to Hawaii, but that it had to land him first.

"Where?" said I.

"It's an island, where I live. So far as I know, it hasn't got a name."

He stared at me with his nether lip dropping, and looked so wilfully stupid of a sudden that it came into my head that he desired to avoid my questions. I had the discretion to ask no more.

3. THE STRANGE FACE

We left the cabin and found a man at the companion[1] obstructing our way. He was standing on the ladder with his back to us, peering over the combing[2] of the hatchway. He was, I could see, a misshapen man, short, broad, and clumsy, with a crooked back, a hairy neck, and a head sunk between his shoulders. He was dressed in dark-blue serge, and had peculiarly thick, coarse, black hair. I heard the unseen dogs growl furiously, and forthwith he ducked back—coming into contact with the hand I put out to fend him off from myself. He turned with animal swiftness.

In some indefinable way the black face thus flashed upon me shocked me profoundly. It was a singularly deformed one. The facial part projected, forming something dimly suggestive of a muzzle, and the huge half-open mouth showed as big white teeth as I had ever seen in a human mouth. His eyes were blood-shot at the edges, with scarcely a rim of white round the hazel pupils. There was a curious glow of excitement in his face.

"Confound you!" said Montgomery. "Why the devil don't you get out of the way?"

The black-faced man started aside without a word. I went on up the companion, staring at him instinctively as I did so. Montgomery stayed at the foot for a moment. "You have no business here, you know," he said in a deliberate tone. "Your place is forward."

The black-faced man cowered. "They—won't have me forward." He spoke slowly, with a queer, hoarse quality in his voice.

"Won't have you forward!" said Montgomery, in a menacing voice. "But I tell you to go!" He was on the brink of saying something further, then looked up at me suddenly and followed me up the ladder.

---

1 Ladder.

2 Raised wooden edge.

I had paused half way through the hatchway, looking back, still aston-ished beyond measure at the grotesque ugliness of this black-faced creature. I had never beheld such a repulsive and extraordinary face before, and yet—if the contradiction is credible—I experienced at the same time an odd feeling that in some way I *had* already encountered exactly the features and gestures that now amazed me. Afterwards it occurred to me that prob-ably I had seen him as I was lifted aboard; and yet that scarcely satisfied my suspicion of a previous acquaintance. Yet how one could have set eyes on so singular a face and have forgotten the precise occasion, passed my imagination.

Montgomery's movement to follow me released my attention, and I turned and looked about me at the flush deck of the little schooner. I was already half prepared by the sounds I had heard for what I saw. Certainly I never beheld a deck so dirty. It was littered with scraps of carrot, shreds of green stuff, and indescribable filth. Fastened by chains to the mainmast were a number of grisly staghounds, who now began leaping and barking at me, and by the mizzen[1] a huge puma was cramped in a little iron cage far too small even to give it turning room. Farther under the starboard bulwark were some big hutches containing a number of rabbits, and a solitary llama was squeezed in a mere box of a cage forward. The dogs were muzzled by leather straps. The only human being on deck was a gaunt and silent sailor at the wheel.

The patched and dirty spankers were tense before the wind, and up aloft the little ship seemed carrying every sail she had. The sky was clear, the sun midway down the western sky; long waves, capped by the breeze with froth, were running with us. We went past the steersman to the taffrail, and saw the water come foaming under the stern and the bubbles go danc-ing and vanishing in her wake. I turned and surveyed the unsavoury length of the ship.

"Is this an ocean menagerie?" said I.

"Looks like it," said Montgomery.

"What are these beasts for? Merchandise, curios? Does the captain think he is going to sell them somewhere in the South Seas?"

"It looks like it, doesn't it?" said Montgomery, and turned towards the wake again.

Suddenly we heard a yelp and a volley of furious blasphemy from the companion hatchway, and the deformed man with the black face clam-

---

1   The mast nearest the stern (the mizzenmast) or a triangular sail set on it.

bered up hurriedly. He was immediately followed by a heavy red-haired man in a white cap. At the sight of the former the staghounds, who had all tired of barking at me by this time, became furiously excited, howling and leaping against their chains. The black hesitated before them, and this gave the red-haired man time to come up with him and deliver a tremendous blow between the shoulder-blades. The poor devil went down like a felled ox, and rolled in the dirt among the furiously excited dogs. It was lucky for him that they were muzzled. The red-haired man gave a yawp of exultation and stood staggering, and as it seemed to me in serious danger of either going backwards down the companion hatchway or forwards upon his victim.

So soon as the second man had appeared, Montgomery had started forward. "Steady on there!" he cried, in a tone of remonstrance. A couple of sailors appeared on the forecastle. The black-faced man, howling in a singular voice, rolled about under the feet of the dogs. No one attempted to help him. The brutes did their best to worry him, butting their muzzles at him. There was a quick dance of their lithe grey-figured bodies over the clumsy, prostrate figure. The sailors forward shouted, as though it was admirable sport. Montgomery gave an angry exclamation, and went striding down the deck, and I followed him. The black-faced man scrambled up and staggered forward, going and leaning over the bulwark by the main shrouds,[1] where he remained, panting and glaring over his shoulder at the dogs. The red-haired man laughed a satisfied laugh.

"Look here, Captain," said Montgomery, with his lisp a little accentuated, gripping the elbows of the red-haired man, "this won't do!"

I stood behind Montgomery. The captain came half round, and regarded him with the dull and solemn eyes of a drunken man. "Wha' won't do?" he said, and added, after looking sleepily into Montgomery's face for a minute, "Blasted Sawbones!"

With a sudden movement he shook his arm free, and after two ineffectual attempts stuck his freckled fists into his side pockets.

"That man's a passenger," said Montgomery. "I'd advise you to keep your hands off him."

"Go to hell!" said the captain, loudly. He suddenly turned and staggered towards the side. "Do what I like on my own ship," he said.

I think Montgomery might have left him then, seeing the brute was drunk; but he only turned a shade paler, and followed the captain to the bulwarks.

---

1 Rigging on the main mast.

"Look you here, Captain," he said; "that man of mine is not to be ill-treated. He has been hazed ever since he came aboard."

For a minute, alcoholic fumes kept the captain speechless. "Blasted Saw-bones!" was all he considered necessary.

I could see that Montgomery had one of those slow, pertinacious tempers that will warm day after day to a white heat, and never again cool to forgiveness; and I saw too that this quarrel had been some time growing. "The man's drunk," said I, perhaps officiously; "you'll do no good."

Montgomery gave an ugly twist to his dropping lip. "He's always drunk. Do you think that excuses his assaulting his passengers?"

"My ship," began the captain, waving his hand unsteadily towards the cages, "was a clean ship. Look at it now!" It was certainly anything but clean. "Crew," continued the captain, "clean, respectable crew."

"You agreed to take the beasts."

"I wish I'd never set eyes on your infernal island. What the devil—want beasts for on an island like that? Then, that man of yours—understood he was a man. He's a lunatic; and he hadn't no business aft. Do you think the whole damned ship belongs to you?"

"Your sailors began to haze the poor devil as soon as he came aboard."

"That's just what he is—he's a devil! an ugly devil! My men can't stand him. *I* can't stand him. None of us can't stand him. Nor *you* either!"

Montgomery turned away. "*You* leave that man alone, anyhow," he said, nodding his head as he spoke.

But the captain meant to quarrel now. He raised his voice. "If he comes this end of the ship again I'll cut his insides out, I tell you. Cut out his blasted insides! Who are *you*, to tell *me* what *I'm* to do? I tell you I'm captain of this ship—captain and owner. I'm the law here, I tell you—the law and the prophets. I bargained to take a man and his attendant to and from Arica, and bring back some animals. I never bargained to carry a mad devil and a silly Sawbones, a—"

Well, never mind what he called Montgomery. I saw the latter take a step forward, and interposed. "He's drunk," said I. The captain began some abuse even fouler than the last. "Shut up!" I said, turning on him sharply, for I had seen danger in Montgomery's white face. With that I brought the downpour on myself.

However, I was glad to avert what was uncommonly near a scuffle, even at the price of the captain's drunken ill-will. I do not think I have ever heard quite so much vile language come in a continuous stream from any man's lips before, though I have frequented eccentric company enough. I found some of it hard to endure, though I am a mild-tempered man; but certainly when I told the captain to "shut up" I had forgotten that I was merely a bit of human flotsam, cut off from my resources and with my fare unpaid; a mere casual dependant on the bounty, or speculative enterprise, of the ship. He reminded me of it with considerable vigour, but at any rate I prevented a fight.

4. AT THE SCHOONER'S RAIL

That night land was sighted after sundown, and the schooner hove to. Montgomery intimated that was his destination. It was too far to see any details; it seemed to me then simply a low-lying patch of dim blue in the uncertain blue-grey sea. An almost vertical streak of smoke went up from it into the sky. The captain was not on deck when it was sighted. After he had vented his wrath on me he had staggered below, and I understand he went to sleep on the floor of his own cabin. The mate practically assumed the command. He was the gaunt, taciturn individual we had seen at the wheel. Apparently he was in an evil temper with Montgomery. He took not the slightest notice of either of us. We dined with him in a sulky silence, after a few ineffectual efforts on my part to talk. It struck me, too, that the men regarded my companion and his animals in a singularly unfriendly manner. I found Montgomery very reticent about his purpose with these creatures, and about his destination; and though I was sensible of a growing curiosity as to both, I did not press him.

We remained talking on the quarter deck until the sky was thick with stars. Except for an occasional sound in the yellow-lit forecastle and a movement of the animals now and then, the night was very still. The puma lay crouched together, watching us with shining eyes, a black heap in the corner of its cage. Montgomery produced some cigars. He talked to me of London in a tone of half-painful reminiscence, asking all kinds of questions about changes that had taken place. He spoke like a man who had loved his life there, and had been suddenly and irrevocably cut off from it. I gossiped as well as I could of this and that. All the time the strangeness of him was shaping itself in my mind; and as I talked I peered at his odd, pallid face in the dim light of the binnacle lantern[1] behind me. Then I looked out at the darkling sea, where in the dimness his little island was hidden.

---

1   The lantern that lights the binnacle (a stand holding the ship's compass) so that the helmsman can see it as he steers.

This man, it seemed to me, had come out of Immensity merely to save my life. To-morrow he would drop over the side, and vanish again out of my existence. Even had it been under commonplace circumstances, it would have made me a trifle thoughtful; but in the first place was the singularity of an educated man living on this unknown little island, and coupled with that the extraordinary nature of his luggage. I found myself repeating the captain's question, What did he want with the beasts? Why, too, had he pretended they were not his when I had remarked about them at first? Then, again, in his personal attendant there was a bizarre quality which had impressed me profoundly. These circumstances threw a haze of mystery round the man. They laid hold of my imagination, and hampered my tongue.

Towards midnight our talk of London died away, and we stood side by side leaning over the bulwarks and staring dreamily over the silent, starlit sea, each pursuing his own thoughts. It was the atmosphere for sentiment, and I began upon my gratitude.

"If I may say it," said I, after a time, "you have saved my life."

"Chance," he answered. "Just chance."

"I prefer to make my thanks to the accessible agent."

"Thank no one. You had the need, and I had the knowledge; and I injected and fed you much as I might have collected a specimen. I was bored, and wanted something to do. If I'd been jaded that day, or hadn't liked your face, well—it's a curious question where you would have been now!"

This damped my mood a little. "At any rate—" I began.

"It's chance, I tell you," he interrupted—"as everything is in a man's life. Only the asses won't see it! Why am I here now, an outcast from civilisation, instead of being a happy man enjoying all the pleasures of London? Simply because—eleven years ago—I lost my head for ten minutes on a foggy night."

He stopped. "Yes?" said I.

"That's all."

We relapsed into silence. Presently he laughed. "There's something in this starlight that loosens one's tongue. I'm an ass, and yet somehow I would like to tell you."

"Whatever you tell me, you may rely upon my keeping to myself—if that's it."

He was on the point of beginning, and then shook his head, doubtfully.

"Don't," said I. "It is all the same to me. After all, it is better to keep your secret. There's nothing gained but a little relief if I respect your confidence. If I don't—well?"

He grunted undecidedly. I felt I had him at a disadvantage, had caught him in the mood of indiscretion; and to tell the truth I was not curious to learn what might have driven a young medical student out of London. I have an imagination. I shrugged my shoulders and turned away. Over the taffrail leant a silent black figure, watching the stars. It was Montgomery's strange attendant. It looked over its shoulder quickly with my movement, then looked away again.

It may seem a little thing to you, perhaps, but it came like a sudden blow to me. The only light near us was a lantern at the wheel. The creature's face was turned for one brief instant out of the dimness of the stern towards this illumination, and I saw that the eyes that glanced at me shone with a pale-green light. I did not know then that a reddish luminosity, at least, is not uncommon in human eyes. The thing came to me as stark inhumanity. That black figure with its eyes of fire struck down through all my adult thoughts and feelings, and for a moment the forgotten horrors of childhood came back to my mind. Then the effect passed as it had come. An uncouth black figure of a man, a figure of no particular import, hung over the taffrail against the starlight, and I found Montgomery was speaking to me.

"I'm thinking of turning in, then," said he, "if you've had enough of this."

I answered him incongruously. We went below, and he wished me good-night at the door of my cabin.

That night I had some very unpleasant dreams. The waning moon rose late. Its light struck a ghostly white beam across my cabin, and made an ominous shape on the planking by my bunk. Then the staghounds woke, and began howling and baying; so that I dreamt fitfully, and scarcely slept until the approach of dawn.

5. THE MAN WHO HAD NOWHERE TO GO

In the early morning (it was the second morning after my recovery, and I believe the fourth after I was picked up), I awoke through an avenue of tumultuous dreams—dreams of guns and howling mobs—and became sensible of a hoarse shouting above me. I rubbed my eyes and lay listening to the noise, doubtful for a little while of my whereabouts. Then came a sudden pattering of bare feet, the sound of heavy objects being thrown about, a violent creaking and the rattling of chains. I heard the swish of the water as the ship was suddenly brought round, and a foamy yellow-green wave flew across the little round window and left it streaming. I jumped into my clothes and went on deck.

As I came up the ladder I saw against the flushed sky—for the sun was just rising—the broad back and red hair of the captain, and over his shoulder the puma spinning from a tackle rigged on to the mizzen spanker-boom.

The poor brute seemed horribly scared, and crouched in the bottom of its little cage.

"Overboard with 'em!" bawled the captain. "Overboard with 'em! We'll have a clean ship soon of the whole bilin' of 'em."

He stood in my way, so that I had perforce to tap his shoulder to come on deck. He came round with a start, and staggered back a few paces to stare at me. It needed no expert eye to tell that the man was still drunk.

"Hullo!" said he, stupidly; and then with a light coming into his eyes, "Why, it's Mister—Mister?"

"Prendick," said I.

"Prendick be damned!" said he. "Shut-up—that's your name. Mister Shut-up."

It was no good answering the brute; but I certainly did not expect his next move. He held out his hand to the gangway by which Montgomery stood talking to a massive white-haired man in dirty-blue flannels, who had apparently just come aboard.

"That way, Mister Blasted Shut-up! that way!" roared the captain.

Montgomery and his companion turned as he spoke.

"What do you mean?" I said.

"That way, Mister Blasted Shut-up—that's what I mean! Overboard, Mister Shut-up—and sharp! We're cleaning the ship out—cleaning the whole blessed ship out; and overboard you go!"

I stared at him dumbfounded. Then it occurred to me that it was exactly the thing I wanted. The lost prospect of a journey as sole passenger with this quarrelsome sot was not one to mourn over. I turned towards Montgomery.

"Can't have you," said Montgomery's companion, concisely.

"You can't have me!" said I, aghast. He had the squarest and most resolute face I ever set eyes upon.

"Look here," I began, turning to the captain.

"Overboard!" said the captain. "This ship ain't for beasts and cannibals and worse than beasts, any more. Overboard you go, Mister Shut-up. If they can't have you, you goes overboard. But, anyhow, you go—with your friends. I've done with this blessed island for evermore, amen! I've had enough of it."

"But, Montgomery," I appealed.

He distorted his lower lip, and nodded his head hopelessly at the white-haired man beside him, to indicate his powerlessness to help me.

"I'll see to you, presently," said the captain.

Then began a curious three-cornered altercation. Alternately I appealed to one and another of the three men—first to the white-haired man to let me land, and then to the drunken captain to keep me aboard. I even bawled entreaties to the sailors. Montgomery said never a word, only shook his head. "You're going overboard, I tell you," was the captain's refrain. "Law be damned! I'm king here." At last I must confess my voice suddenly broke in the middle of a vigorous threat. I felt a gust of hysterical petulance, and went aft and stared dismally at nothing.

Meanwhile the sailors progressed rapidly with the task of unshipping the packages and caged animals. A large launch, with two standing lugs,[1] lay under the lea of the schooner; and into this the strange assortment of goods were swung. I did not then see the hands from the island that were receiving the packages, for the hull off the launch was hidden from me by the side of the schooner. Neither Montgomery nor his companion took the slightest notice of me, but busied themselves in assisting and directing the four or five sailors who were unloading the goods. The captain went forward, interfering rather than assisting. I was alternately despairful and desperate. Once or twice as I stood waiting there for things to accomplish themselves, I could not resist an impulse to laugh at my miserable quandary. I felt all the wretcheder for the lack of a breakfast. Hunger and a lack of blood-corpuscles take all the manhood from a man. I perceived pretty clearly that I had not the stamina either to resist what the captain chose to do to expel me, or to force myself upon Montgomery and his companion. So I waited passively upon fate; and the work of transferring Montgomery's possessions to the launch went on as if I did not exist.

Presently that work was finished, and then came a struggle. I was hauled, resisting weakly enough, to the gangway. Even then I noticed the oddness of the brown faces of the men who were with Montgomery in the launch; but the launch was now fully laden, and was shoved off hastily. A broadening gap of green water appeared under me, and I pushed back with all

---

1   Short for lugsail—a "gaff" rig where the top of the sail is fastened to a yard at an oblique angle to the mast.

my strength to avoid falling headlong. The hands in the launch shouted derisively, and I heard Montgomery curse at them; and then the captain, the mate, and one of the seamen helping him, ran me aft towards the stern.

The dingey of the *Lady Vain* had been towing behind; it was half full of water, had no oars, and was quite unvictualled. I refused to go aboard her, and flung myself full length on the deck. In the end, they swung me into her by a rope (for they had no stern ladder), and then they cut me adrift. I drifted slowly from the schooner. In a kind of stupor I watched all hands take to the rigging, and slowly but surely she came round to the wind; the sails fluttered, and then bellied out as the wind came into them. I stared at her weather-beaten side heeling steeply towards me; and then she passed out of my range of view.

I did not turn my head to follow her. At first I could scarcely believe what had happened. I crouched in the bottom of the dingey, stunned, and staring blankly at the vacant, oily sea. Then I realized that I was in that little hell of mine again, now half swamped; and looking back over the gunwale, I saw the schooner standing away from me, with the red-haired captain mocking at me over the taffrail, and turning towards the island saw the launch growing smaller as she approached the beach.

Abruptly the cruelty of this desertion became clear to me. I had no means of reaching the land unless I should chance to drift there. I was still weak, you must remember, from my exposure in the boat; I was empty and very faint, or I should have had more heart. But as it was I suddenly began to sob and weep, as I had never done since I was a little child. The tears ran down my face. In a passion of despair I struck with my fists at the water in the bottom of the boat, and kicked savagely at the gunwale. I prayed aloud for God to let me die.

6. THE EVIL-LOOKING BOATMEN

But the islanders, seeing that I was really adrift, took pity on me. I drifted very slowly to the eastward, approaching the island slantingly; and presently I saw, with hysterical relief, the launch come round and return towards me. She was heavily laden, and I could make out as she drew nearer Montgomery's white-haired, broad-shouldered companion sitting cramped up with the dogs and several packing-cases in the stern sheets. This individual stared fixedly at me without moving or speaking. The black-faced cripple was glaring at me as fixedly in the bows near the puma. There were three other men besides—three strange brutish-looking fellows, at whom the staghounds were snarling savagely. Montgomery, who was steering, brought the boat by me, and rising, caught and fastened my painter[1] to the tiller to tow me, for there was no room aboard.

I had recovered from my hysterical phase by this time, and answered his hail, as he approached, bravely enough. I told him the dingey was nearly swamped, and he reached me a piggin.[2] I was jerked back as the rope tightened between the boats. For some time I was busy baling.

It was not until I had got the water under (for the water in the dingey had been shipped; the boat was perfectly sound) that I had leisure to look at the people in the launch again.

The white-haired man I found was still regarding me steadfastly, but with an expression, as I now fancied, of some perplexity. When my eyes met his, he looked down at the staghound that sat between his knees. He was a powerfully-built man, as I have said, with a fine forehead and rather heavy features; but his eyes had that odd drooping of the skin above the lids which often comes with advancing years, and the fall of his heavy mouth at the corners gave him an expression of pugnacious resolution. He talked to Montgomery in a tone too low for me to hear.

From him my eyes travelled to his three men; and a strange crew they were. I saw only their faces, yet there was something in their faces—I knew not what—that gave me a queer spasm of disgust. I looked steadily at them, and the impression did not pass, though I failed to see what had occasioned it. They seemed to me then to be brown men; but their limbs were oddly swathed in some thin, dirty, white stuff down even to the fingers and feet: I have never seen men so wrapped up before, and women so only in the East. They wore turbans too, and thereunder peered out their elfin faces at me—faces with protruding lower-jaws and bright eyes. They had lank black hair, almost like horsehair, and seemed as they sat to exceed in stature any race of men I have seen. The white-haired man, who I knew was a good six feet in height, sat a head below any one of the three. I found afterwards that really none were taller than myself; but their bodies were abnormally long, and the thigh-part of the leg short and curiously twisted. At any rate, they were an amazingly ugly gang, and over the heads of them under the forward lug peered the black face of the man whose eyes were luminous in the dark. As I stared at them, they met my gaze; and then first

---

1   A rope attached to the bow of a boat for tying it up.

2   A small container used to bail a boat.

one and then another turned away from my direct stare, and looked at me in an odd, furtive manner. It occurred to me that I was perhaps annoying them, and I turned my attention to the island we were approaching.

It was low, and covered with thick vegetation—chiefly a kind of palm that was new to me. From one point a thin white thread of vapour rose slantingly to an immense height, and then frayed out like a down feather. We were now within the embrace of a broad bay flanked on either hand by a low promontory. The beach was of dull-grey sand, and sloped steeply up to a ridge, perhaps sixty or seventy feet above the sea-level, and irregularly set with trees and undergrowth. Half way up was a square enclosure of some greyish stone, which I found subsequently was built partly of coral and partly of pumiceous lava. Two thatched roofs peeped from within this enclosure. A man stood awaiting us at the water's edge. I fancied while we were still far off that I saw some other and very grotesque-looking creatures scuttle into the bushes upon the slope; but I saw nothing of these as we drew nearer. This man was of a moderate size, and with a black negroid face. He had a large, almost lipless, mouth, extraordinary lank arms, long thin feet, and bow-legs, and stood with his heavy face thrust forward staring at us. He was dressed like Montgomery and his white-haired companion, in jacket and trousers of blue serge. As we came still nearer, this individual began to run to and fro on the beach, making the most grotesque movements.

At a word of command from Montgomery, the four men in the launch sprang up, and with singularly awkward gestures struck the lugs.[1] Montgomery steered us round and into a narrow little dock excavated in the beach. Then the man on the beach hastened towards us. This dock, as I call it, was really a mere ditch just long enough at this phase of the tide to take the longboat. I heard the bows ground in the sand, staved the dingey off the rudder of the big boat with my piggin, and freeing the painter, landed. The three muffled men, with the clumsiest movements, scrambled out upon the sand, and forthwith set to landing the cargo, assisted by the man on the beach. I was struck especially by the curious movements of the legs of the three swathed and bandaged boatmen—not stiff they were, but distorted in some odd way, almost as if they were jointed in the wrong place. The dogs were still snarling, and strained at their chains after these men, as the white-haired man landed with them. The three big fellows spoke to one another in odd guttural tones, and the man who had waited for us on the beach

---

1   Took down the sails.

began chattering to them excitedly—a foreign language, as I fancied—as they laid hands on some bales piled near the stern. Somewhere I had heard such a voice before, and I could not think where. The white-haired man stood, holding in a tumult of six dogs, and bawling orders over their din. Montgomery, having unshipped the rudder, landed likewise, and all set to work at unloading. I was too faint, what with my long fast and the sun beating down on my bare head, to offer any assistance.

Presently the white-haired man seemed to recollect my presence, and came up to me.

"You look," said he, "as though you had scarcely breakfasted." His little eyes were a brilliant black under his heavy brows. "I must apologise for that. Now you are our guest, we must make you comfortable—though you are uninvited, you know." He looked keenly into my face. "Montgomery says you are an educated man, Mr. Prendick; says you know something of science. May I ask what that signifies?"

I told him I had spent some years at the Royal College of Science, and had done some researches in biology under Huxley.[1] He raised his eyebrows slightly at that.

"That alters the case a little, Mr. Prendick," he said, with a trifle more respect in his manner. "As it happens, we are biologists here. This is a biological station—of a sort." His eye rested on the men in white who were busily hauling the puma, on rollers, towards the walled yard. "I and Montgomery, at least," he added. Then, "When you will be able to get away, I can't say. We're off the track to anywhere. We see a ship once in a twelve-month or so."

He left me abruptly, and went up the beach past this group, and I think entered the enclosure. The other two men were with Montgomery, erecting a pile of smaller packages on a low-wheeled truck. The llama was still on the launch with the rabbit hutches; the staghounds were still lashed to the thwarts. The pile of things completed, all three men laid hold of the truck and began shoving the ton-weight or so upon it after the puma. Presently Montgomery left them, and coming back to me held out his hand.

"I'm glad," said he, "for my own part. That captain was a silly ass. He'd have made things lively for you."

"It was you," said I, "that saved me again."

"That depends. You'll find this island an infernally rum place, I promise you. I'd watch my goings carefully, if I were you. He—" He hesitated, and

---

1   Wells spent three years at the same institution. In the first year he took courses taught by Huxley, and considered it a formative experience.

seemed to alter his mind about what was on his lips. "I wish you'd help me with these rabbits," he said.

His procedure with the rabbits was singular. I waded in with him, and helped him lug one of the hutches ashore. No sooner was that done than he opened the door of it, and tilting the thing on one end turned its living contents out on the ground. They fell in a struggling heap one on the top of the other. He clapped his hands, and forthwith they went off with that hopping run of theirs, fifteen or twenty of them I should think, up the beach.

"Increase and multiply, my friends," said Montgomery. "Replenish the island. Hitherto we've had a certain lack of meat here."

As I watched them disappearing, the white-haired man returned with a brandy-flask and some biscuits. "Something to go on with, Prendick," said he, in a far more familiar tone than before. I made no ado, but set to work on the biscuits at once, while the white-haired man helped Montgomery to release about a score more of the rabbits. Three big hutches, however, went up to the house with the puma. The brandy I did not touch, for I have been an abstainer from my birth.

7. THE LOCKED DOOR

The reader will perhaps understand that at first everything was so strange about me, and my position was the outcome of such unexpected adventures, that I had no discernment of the relative strangeness of this or that thing. I followed the llama up the beach, and was overtaken by Montgomery, who asked me not to enter the stone enclosure. I noticed then that the puma in its cage and the pile of packages had been placed outside the entrance to this quadrangle.

I turned and saw that the launch had now been unloaded, run out again, and was being beached, and the white-haired man was walking towards us. He addressed Montgomery.

"And now comes the problem of this uninvited guest. What are we to do with him?"

"He knows something of science," said Montgomery.

"I'm itching to get to work again—with this new stuff," said the white-haired man, nodding towards the enclosure. His eyes grew brighter.

"I daresay you are," said Montgomery, in anything but a cordial tone.

"We can't send him over there, and we can't spare the time to build him a new shanty; and we certainly can't take him into our confidence just yet."

"I'm in your hands," said I. I had no idea of what he meant by "over there."

"I've been thinking of the same things," Montgomery answered. "There's my room with the outer door—"

"That's it," said the elder man, promptly, looking at Montgomery; and all three of us went towards the enclosure. "I'm sorry to make a mystery, Mr. Prendick; but you'll remember you're uninvited. Our little establishment here contains a secret or so, is a kind of Blue-Beard's chamber, in fact. Nothing very dreadful, really, to a sane man; but just now, as we don't know you—"

"Decidedly," said I, "I should be a fool to take offence at any want of confidence."

He twisted his heavy mouth into a faint smile—he was one of those saturnine people who smile with the corners of the mouth down—and bowed his acknowledgment of my complaisance. The main entrance to the enclosure we passed; it was a heavy wooden gate, framed in iron and locked, with the cargo of the launch piled outside it, and at the corner we came to a small doorway I had not previously observed. The white-haired man produced a bundle of keys from the pocket of his greasy blue jacket, opened this door, and entered. His keys, and the elaborate locking-up of the place even while it was still under his eye, struck me as peculiar. I followed him, and found myself in a small apartment, plainly but not uncomfortably furnished, and with its inner door, which was slightly ajar, opening into a paved courtyard. This inner door Montgomery at once closed. A hammock was slung across the darker corner of the room, and a small unglazed window defended by an iron bar looked out towards the sea.

This, the white-haired man told me, was to be my apartment; and the inner door, which "for fear of accidents," he said, he would lock on the other side, was my limit inward. He called my attention to a convenient deck-chair before the window, and to an array of old books—chiefly, I found, surgical works and editions of the Latin and Greek classics (languages I cannot read with any comfort), on a shelf near the hammock. He left the room by the outer door, as if to avoid opening the inner one again.

"We usually have our meals in here," said Montgomery, and then, as if in doubt, went out after the other. "Moreau!" I heard him call, and for the moment I do not think I noticed. Then as I handled the books on the shelf it came up in consciousness: Where had I heard the name of Moreau before? I sat down before the window, took out the biscuits that still remained to me, and ate them with an excellent appetite. Moreau!

Through the window I saw one of those unaccountable men in white, lugging a packing-case along the beach. Presently the window-frame hid him. Then I heard a key inserted and turned in the lock behind me. After a little while I heard through the locked door the noise of the staghounds, that had now been brought up from the beach. They were not barking, but sniffing and growling in a curious fashion. I could hear the rapid patter of their feet and Montgomery's voice soothing them.

I was very much impressed by the elaborate secrecy of these two men regarding the contents of the place, and for some time I was thinking of that and of the unaccountable familiarity of the name of Moreau; but so odd is the human memory that I could not then recall that well-known name in its proper connection. From that my thoughts went to the inde-finable queerness of the deformed man on the beach. I never saw such a gait, such odd motions as he pulled at the box. I recalled that none of these men had spoken to me, though most of them I had found looking at me at one time or another in a peculiarly furtive manner, quite unlike the frank stare of your unsophisticated savage. Indeed, they had all seemed remarka-bly taciturn, and when they did speak, endowed with very uncanny voices. What was wrong with them? Then I recalled the eyes of Montgomery's ungainly attendant.

Just as I was thinking of him he came in. He was now dressed in white, and carried a little tray with some coffee and boiled vegetables thereon. I could hardly repress a shuddering recoil as he came, bending amiably, and placed the tray before me on the table. Then astonishment paralysed me. Under his stringy black locks I saw his ear; it jumped upon me suddenly close to my face. The man had pointed ears, covered with a fine brown fur!

"Your breakfast, sair," he said.

I stared at his face without attempting to answer him. He turned and went towards the door, regarding me oddly over his shoulder. I followed him out with my eyes and as I did so, by some odd trick of unconscious cerebration, there came surging into my head the phrase, "The Moreau Hollows"—was it? "The Moreau—"Ah! It sent my memory back ten years. "The Moreau Horrors!" The phrase drifted loose in my mind for a moment, and then I saw it in red lettering on a little buff-coloured pamphlet, to read which made one shiver and creep. Then I remembered distinctly all about it. That long-forgotten pamphlet came back with startling vividness to my mind. I had been a mere lad then, and Moreau was, I suppose, about fifty—a prominent and masterful physiologist, well-known in scientific circles for his extraordinary imagination and his brutal directness in discussion.

Was this the same Moreau? He had published some very astonishing facts in connection with the transfusion of blood, and in addition was known to be doing valuable work on morbid[1] growths. Then suddenly his career was closed. He had to leave England. A journalist obtained access to his laboratory in the capacity of laboratory assistant, with the deliberate intention of making sensational exposures; and by the help of a shocking accident (if it was an accident), his gruesome pamphlet became notorious. On the day of its publication a wretched dog, flayed and otherwise mutilated, escaped from Moreau's house. It was in the silly season, and a prominent editor, a cousin of the temporary laboratory assistant, appealed to the conscience of the nation.[2] It was not the first time that conscience has turned against the methods of research. The doctor was simply howled out of the country. It may be that he deserved to be; but I still think that the tepid support of his fellow-investigators and his desertion by the great body of scientific workers was a shameful thing. Yet some of his experiments, by the journalist's account, were wantonly cruel. He might perhaps have purchased his social peace by abandoning his investigations; but he apparently preferred the latter, as most men would who have once fallen under the overmastering spell of research. He was unmarried, and had indeed nothing but his own interest to consider.

I felt convinced that this must be the same man. Everything pointed to it. It dawned upon me to what end the puma and the other animals—which had now been brought with other luggage into the enclosure behind the house—were destined; and a curious faint odour, the halitus[3] of something familiar, an odour that had been in the background of my consciousness hitherto, suddenly came forward into the forefront of my thoughts. It was the antiseptic odour of the dissecting-room. I heard the puma growling through the wall, and one of the dogs yelped as though it had been struck.

---

1 Diseased.

2 As noted in the Introduction (47), the manner of Moreau's exposure has something in common with an influential letter published in 1875 by Dr. George Hoggan, a former lab. assistant to Bernard. The controversy over vivisection was particularly intense in the mid-1870s, about the time Moreau left England.

3 An old-fashioned scientific word meaning breath, exhalation, or vapour. It is manifested in this case by a faint odour with a disturbing implication, as also in *The Time Machine* in which the Time Traveller detects in the dark underground hall of the Morlocks "the faint halitus of freshly-shed blood" (Broadview Edition, 116; ch. 9).

Yet surely, and especially to another scientific man, there was nothing so horrible in vivisection as to account for this secrecy; and by some odd leap in my thoughts the pointed ears and luminous eyes of Montgomery's attendant came back again before me with the sharpest definition. I stared before me out at the green sea, frothing under a freshening breeze, and let these and other strange memories of the last few days chase one another through my mind.

What could it all mean? A locked enclosure on a lonely island, a notorious vivisector, and these crippled and distorted men?...

8. THE CRYING OF THE PUMA

Montgomery interrupted my tangle of mystification and suspicion about one o'clock, and his grotesque attendant followed him with a tray bearing bread, some herbs and other eatables, a flask of whiskey, a jug of water, and three glasses and knives. I glanced askance at this strange creature, and found him watching me with his queer, restless eyes. Montgomery said he would lunch with me, but that Moreau was too preoccupied with some work to come.

"Moreau!" said I. "I know that name."

"The devil you do!" said he. "What an ass I was to mention it to you! I might have thought. Anyhow, it will give you an inkling of our—mysteries. Whiskey?"

"No, thanks; I'm an abstainer."

"I wish I'd been. But it's no use locking the door after the steed is stolen. It was that infernal stuff which led to my coming here—that, and a foggy night. I thought myself in luck at the time, when Moreau offered to get me off. It's queer—"

"Montgomery," said I, suddenly, as the outer door closed, "why has your man pointed ears?"

"Damn!" he said, over his first mouthful of food. He stared at me for a moment, and then repeated, "Pointed ears?"

"Little points to them," said I, as calmly as possible, with a catch in my breath; "and a fine black fur at the edges?"

He helped himself to whiskey and water with great deliberation. "I was under the impression—that his hair covered his ears."

"I saw them as he stooped by me to put that coffee you sent to me on the table. And his eyes shine in the dark."

By this time Montgomery had recovered from the surprise of my question. "I always thought," he said deliberately, with a certain accentuation of his flavouring of lisp, "that there *was* something the matter with his ears, from the way he covered them. What were they like?"

I was persuaded from his manner that this ignorance was a pretence. Still, I could hardly tell the man that I thought him a liar. "Pointed," I said; "rather small and furry—distinctly furry. But the whole man is one of the strangest beings I ever set eyes on."

A sharp, hoarse cry of animal pain came from the enclosure behind us. Its depth and volume testified to the puma. I saw Montgomery wince.

"Yes?" he said.

"Where did you pick up the creature?"

"San Francisco. He's an ugly brute, I admit. Half-witted, you know. Can't remember where he came from. But I'm used to him, you know. We both are. How does he strike you?"

"He's unnatural," I said. "There's something about him—don't think me fanciful, but it gives me a nasty little sensation, a tightening of my muscles, when he comes near me. It's a touch—of the diabolical, in fact."

Montgomery had stopped eating while I told him this. "Rum!" he said. "*I* can't see it." He resumed his meal. "I had no idea of it," he said, and masticated. "The crew of the schooner must have felt it the same. Made a dead set at the poor devil. You saw the captain?"

Suddenly the puma howled again, this time more painfully. Montgomery swore under his breath. I had half a mind to attack him about the men on the beach. Then the poor brute within gave vent to a series of short, sharp cries.

"Your men on the beach," said I; "what race are they?"

"Excellent fellows, aren't they?" said he, absentmindedly, knitting his brows as the animal yelled out sharply.

I said no more. There was another outcry worse than the former. He looked at me with his dull grey eyes, and then took some more whiskey. He tried to draw me into a discussion about alcohol, professing to have saved my life with it. He seemed anxious to lay stress on the fact that I owed my life to him. I answered him distractedly.

Presently our meal came to an end; the misshapen monster with the pointed ears cleared the remains away, and Montgomery left me alone in the room again. All the time he had been in a state of ill-concealed irritation at the noise of the vivisected puma. He had spoken of his odd want of nerve, and left me to the obvious application.

I found myself that the cries were singularly irritating, and they grew in depth and intensity as the afternoon wore on. They were painful at first, but their constant resurgence at last altogether upset my balance. I flung aside a crib of Horace[1] I had been reading, and began to clench my fists, to bite my lips, and to pace the room. Presently I got to stopping my ears with my fingers.

The emotional appeal of those yells grew upon me steadily, grew at last to such an exquisite expression of suffering that I could stand it in that confined room no longer. I stepped out of the door into the slumberous heat of the late afternoon, and walking past the main entrance—locked again, I noticed—turned the corner of the wall.

The crying sounded even louder out of doors. It was as if all the pain in the world had found a voice. Yet had I known such pain was in the next room, and had it been dumb, I believe—I have thought since—I could have stood it well enough. It is when suffering finds a voice and sets our nerves quivering that this pity comes troubling us. But in spite of the brilliant sunlight and the green fans of the trees waving in the soothing sea-breeze, the world was a confusion, blurred with drifting black and red phantasms, until I was out of earshot of the house in the chequered wall.

9. THE THING IN THE FOREST

I strode through the undergrowth that clothed the ridge behind the house, scarcely heeding whither I went; passed on through the shadow of a thick cluster of straight-stemmed trees beyond it, and so presently found myself some way on the other side of the ridge, and descending towards a streamlet that ran through a narrow valley. I paused and listened. The distance I had come, or the intervening masses of thicket, deadened any sound that might be coming from the enclosure. The air was still. Then with a rustle a rabbit emerged, and went scampering up the slope before me. I hesitated, and sat down in the edge of the shade.

The place was a pleasant one. The rivulet was hidden by the luxuriant vegetation of the banks save at one point, where I caught a triangular patch

---

1 An edition with the Latin text and a translation in English printed opposite each other. As a classical Roman poet noted for humane rationality and balance, and a favourite poet of the Enlightenment, Horace might present an ironic contrast to the problems Prendick will encounter on Moreau's island.

of its glittering water. On the farther side I saw through a bluish haze a tangle of trees and creepers, and above these again the luminous blue of the sky. Here and there a splash of white or crimson marked the blooming of some trailing epiphyte.[1] I let my eyes wander over this scene for a while, and then began to turn over in my mind again the strange peculiarities of Montgomery's man. But it was too hot to think elaborately, and presently I fell into a tranquil state midway between dozing and waking.

From this I was aroused, after I know not how long, by a rustling amidst the greenery on the other side of the stream. For a moment I could see nothing but the waving summits of the ferns and reeds. Then suddenly upon the bank of the stream appeared Something—at first I could not distinguish what it was. It bowed its round head to the water, and began to drink. Then I saw it was a man, going on all-fours like a beast. He was clothed in bluish cloth, and was of a copper-coloured hue, with black hair. It seemed that grotesque ugliness was an invariable character of these islanders. I could hear the suck of the water at his lips as he drank.

I leant forward to see him better and a piece of lava, detached by my hand, went pattering down the slope. He looked up guiltily, and his eyes met mine. Forthwith he scrambled to his feet, and stood wiping his clumsy hand across his mouth and regarding me. His legs were scarcely half the length of his body. So, staring one another out of countenance, we remained for perhaps the space of a minute. Then, stopping to look back once or twice, he slunk off among the bushes to the right of me, and I heard the swish of the fronds grow faint in the distance and die away. Long after he had disappeared, I remained sitting up staring in the direction of his retreat. My drowsy tranquillity had gone.

I was startled by a noise behind me, and turning suddenly saw the flapping white tail of a rabbit vanishing up the slope. I jumped to my feet. The apparition of this grotesque, half-bestial creature had suddenly populated the stillness of the afternoon for me. I looked around me rather nervously, and regretted that I was unarmed. Then I thought that the man I had just seen had been clothed in bluish cloth, had not been naked as a savage would have been; and I tried to persuade myself from that fact that he was after all probably a peaceful character, that the dull ferocity of his countenance belied him.

---

1 A plant that grows nonparasitically on another plant, deriving its nutrients and water from rain and material in the air.

Yet I was greatly disturbed at the apparition. I walked to the left along the slope, turning my head about, and peering this way and that among the straight stems of the trees. Why should a man go on all-fours and drink with his lips? Presently I heard an animal wailing again, and taking it to be the puma, I turned about and walked in a direction diametrically opposite to the sound. This led me down to the stream, across which I stepped and pushed my way up through the undergrowth beyond.

I was startled by a great patch of vivid scarlet on the ground, and going up to it found it to be a peculiar fungus, branched and corrugated like a foliaceous lichen, but deliquescing into slime at the touch. And then in the shadow of some luxuriant ferns I came upon an unpleasant thing—the dead body of a rabbit covered with shining flies, but still warm and with the head torn off. I stopped aghast at the sight of the scattered blood. Here at least was one visitor to the island disposed of! There were no traces of other violence about it. It looked as though it had been suddenly snatched up and killed; and as I stared at the little furry body came the difficulty of how the thing had been done. The vague dread that had been in my mind since I had seen the inhuman face of the man at the stream grew distincter as I stood there. I began to realise the hardihood of my expedition among these unknown people. The thicket about me became altered to my imagination. Every shadow became something more than a shadow—became an ambush; every rustle became a threat. Invisible things seemed watching me. I resolved to go back to the enclosure on the beach. I suddenly turned away and thrust myself violently, possibly even frantically, through the bushes, anxious to get a clear space about me again.

I stopped just in time to prevent myself emerging upon an open space. It was a kind of glade in the forest, made by a fall; seedlings were already starting up to struggle for the vacant space; and beyond, the dense growth of stems and twining vines and splashes of fungus and flowers closed in again.[1] Before me, squatting together upon the fungoid ruins of a huge fallen tree and still unaware of my approach, were three grotesque human figures. One was evidently a female; the other two were men. They were naked, save for swathings of scarlet cloth about the middle; and their

---

1   This "struggle" recalls Darwin's account, in the third chapter of *The Origin of Species*, of the "war" by which plants gradually establish supremacy in a clearing in a forest (Appendix D2). Wells's description of the island's tropical forest combines a Romantic sense of the beauty of nature with undertones of a Darwinian nature pervaded by struggle and mysterious dangers.

skins were of a dull pinkish-drab colour, such as I had seen in no savages before. They had fat, heavy, chinless faces, retreating foreheads, and a scant bristly hair upon their heads. Never before had I seen such bestial-looking creatures.

They were talking, or at least one of the men was talking to the other two, and all three had been too closely interested to heed the rustling of my approach. They swayed their heads and shoulders from side to side. The speaker's words came thick and sloppy, and though I could hear them distinctly I could not distinguish what he said. He seemed to me to be reciting some complicated gibberish. Presently his articulation became shriller, and spreading his hands he rose to his feet. At that the others began to gibber in unison, also rising to their feet, spreading their hands and swaying their bodies in rhythm with their chant. I noticed then the abnormal shortness of their legs, and their lank, clumsy feet. All three began slowly to circle round, raising and stamping their feet and waving their arms; a kind of tune crept into their rhythmic recitation, and a refrain—"Aloola," or "Balloola," it sounded like. Their eyes began to sparkle, and their ugly faces to brighten, with an expression of strange pleasure. Saliva dripped from their lipless mouths.[1]

Suddenly, as I watched their grotesque and unaccountable gestures, I perceived clearly for the first time what it was that had offended me, what had given me the two inconsistent and conflicting impressions of utter strangeness and yet of the strangest familiarity. The three creatures engaged in this mysterious rite were human in shape, and yet human beings with the strangest air about them of some familiar animal. Each of these creatures, despite its human form, its rag of clothing, and the rough humanity of its bodily form, had woven into it—into its movements, into the expression of its countenance, into its whole presence—some now irresistible suggestion of a hog, a swinish taint, the unmistakable mark of the beast.

I stood overcome by this amazing realisation; and then the most horrible questionings came rushing into my mind. They began leaping in the air, first one and then the other, whooping and grunting. Then one slipped,

---

1   The ecstatic mood induced by this mixture of dance and chant suggests that it has a religious significance, yet the fact that the words cannot be made out, combined with Wells's use of animal imagery, also suggests that the performance has nothing to do with the use of language for rational purposes. The same could be suspected of the litany of the Law recited in chapter 12. For a prejudicial view that ecstatic dance is an irrational aspect of primitive religion, see Appendix F4.

and for a moment was on all-fours—to recover, indeed, forthwith. But that transitory gleam of the true animalism of these monsters was enough.

I moved as noiselessly as possible, and becoming every now and then rigid with the fear of being discovered, as a branch cracked or a leaf rustled, I pushed back into the bushes. It was long before I grew bolder, and dared to move freely. My only idea for the moment was to get away from these foul beings, and I scarcely noticed that I had emerged upon a faint pathway amidst the trees. Then, suddenly traversing a little glade, I saw with an unpleasant start two clumsy legs among the trees, walking with noiseless footsteps parallel with my course, and perhaps thirty yards away from me. The head and upper part of the body were hidden by a tangle of creeper. I stopped abruptly, hoping the creature did not see me. The feet stopped as I did. So nervous was I that I controlled an impulse to headlong flight with the utmost difficulty. Then, looking hard, I distinguished through the interlacing network the head and body of the brute I had seen drinking. He moved his head. There was an emerald flash in his eyes as he glanced at me from the shadow of the trees, a half-luminous colour that vanished as he turned his head again. He was motionless for a moment, and then with a noiseless tread began running through the green confusion. In another moment he had vanished behind some bushes. I could not see him, but I felt that he had stopped and was watching me again.

What on earth was he—man or beast? What did he want with me? I had no weapon, not even a stick. Flight would be madness. At any rate the Thing, whatever it was, lacked the courage to attack me. Setting my teeth hard, I walked straight towards him. I was anxious not to show the fear that seemed chilling my backbone. I pushed through a tangle of tall, white-flowered bushes, and saw him twenty paces beyond, looking over his shoulder at me and hesitating. I advanced a step or two, looking steadfastly into his eyes.

"Who are you?" said I.

He tried to meet my gaze. "*No!*" he said suddenly, and turning went bounding away from me through the undergrowth. Then he turned and stared at me again. His eyes shone brightly out of the dusk under the trees.

My heart was in my mouth; but I felt my only chance was bluff, and walked steadily towards him. He turned again, and vanished into the dusk. Once more I thought I caught the glint of his eyes, and that was all.

For the first time I realised how the lateness of the hour might affect me. The sun had set some minutes since, the swift dusk of the tropics was already fading out of the eastern sky, and a pioneer moth fluttered silently by my head. Unless I would spend the night among the unknown dangers of the mysterious forest, I must hasten back to the enclosure. The thought of a return to that pain-haunted refuge was extremely disagreeable, but still more so was the idea of being overtaken in the open by darkness and all that darkness might conceal. I gave one more look into the blue shadows that had swallowed up this odd creature, and then retraced my way down the slope towards the stream, going as I judged in the direction from which I had come.

I walked eagerly, my mind confused with many things, and presently found myself in a level place among scattered trees. The colourless clearness that comes after the sunset flush was darkling; the blue sky above grew momentarily deeper, and the little stars one by one pierced the attenuated light; the interspaces of the trees, the gaps in the further vegetation, that had been hazy blue in the daylight, grew black and mysterious. I pushed on. The colour vanished from the world. The tree-tops rose against the luminous blue sky in inky silhouette, and all below that outline melted into one formless blackness. Presently the trees grew thinner, and the shrubby undergrowth more abundant. Then there was a desolate space covered with a white sand, and then another expanse of tangled bushes. I did not remember crossing the sand-opening before. I began to be tormented by a faint rustling upon my right hand. I thought at first it was fancy, for whenever I stopped there was silence, save for the evening breeze in the tree-tops. Then when I turned to hurry on again there was an echo to my footsteps.

I moved away from the thickets, keeping to the more open ground, and endeavouring by sudden turns now and then to surprise something in the act of creeping upon me. I saw nothing, and nevertheless my sense of another presence grew steadily. I increased my pace, and after some time came to a slight ridge, crossed it, and turned sharply, regarding it steadfastly from the further side. It came out black and clear-cut against the darkling sky; and presently a shapeless lump heaved up momentarily against the sky-line and vanished again. I felt assured now that my tawny-faced antagonist was stalking me once more; and coupled with that was another unpleasant realisation, that I had lost my way.

For a time I hurried on hopelessly perplexed, and pursued by that stealthy approach. Whatever it was, the Thing either lacked the courage to attack me, or it was waiting to take me at some disadvantage. I kept studiously to the open. At times I would turn and listen; and presently I had half persuaded myself that my pursuer had abandoned the chase, or was a mere creation of my disordered imagination. Then I heard the sound of the sea. I quickened my footsteps almost to a run, and immediately there was a stumble in my rear.

I turned suddenly, and stared at the uncertain trees behind me. One black shadow seemed to leap into another. I listened, rigid, and heard nothing but the creep of the blood in my ears. I thought that my nerves were unstrung, and that my imagination was tricking me, and turned resolutely towards the sound of the sea again.

In a minute or so the trees grew thinner, and I emerged upon a bare, low headland running out into the sombre water. The night was calm and clear, and the reflection of the growing multitude of the stars shivered in the tranquil heaving of the sea. Some way out, the wash upon an irregular band of reef shone with a pallid light of its own. Westward I saw the zodiacal light[1] mingling with the yellow brilliance of the evening star. The coast fell away from me to the east, and westward it was hidden by the shoulder of the cape. Then I recalled the fact that Moreau's beach lay to the west.

A twig snapped behind me, and there was a rustle. I turned, and stood facing the dark trees. I could see nothing—or else I could see too much. Every dark form in the dimness had its ominous quality, its peculiar suggestion of alert watchfulness. So I stood for perhaps a minute, and then, with an eye to the trees still, turned westward to cross the headland; and as I moved, one among the lurking shadows moved to follow me.

My heart beat quickly. Presently the broad sweep of a bay to the westward became visible, and I halted again. The noiseless shadow halted a dozen yards from me. A little point of light shone on the further bend of the curve, and the grey sweep of the sandy beach lay faint under the starlight. Perhaps two miles away was that little point of light. To get to the beach I should have to go through the trees where the shadows lurked, and down a bushy slope.

I could see the Thing rather more distinctly now. It was no animal, for it stood erect. At that I opened my mouth to speak, and found a hoarse phlegm choked my voice. I tried again, and shouted, "Who is there?" There was no answer. I advanced a step. The Thing did not move, only gathered itself together. My foot struck a stone. That gave me an idea. Without taking my eyes off the black form before me, I stooped and picked up this lump of rock; but at my motion the Thing turned abruptly as a dog might

---

1 A glow of light after sunset extending up from the horizon, especially visible in the tropics.

have done, and slunk obliquely into the further darkness. Then I recalled a schoolboy expedient against big dogs, and twisted the rock into my hand-kerchief, and gave this a turn round my wrist. I heard a movement further off among the shadows, as if the Thing was in retreat. Then suddenly my tense excitement gave way; I broke into a profuse perspiration and fell a-trembling, with my adversary routed and this weapon in my hand.

It was some time before I could summon resolution to go down through the trees and bushes upon the flank of the headland to the beach. At last I did it at a run; and as I emerged from the thicket upon the sand, I heard some other body come crashing after me. At that I completely lost my head with fear, and began running along the sand. Forthwith there came the swift patter of soft feet in pursuit. I gave a wild cry, and redoubled my pace. Some dim, black things about three or four times the size of rabbits went running or hopping up from the beach towards the bushes as I passed.

So long as I live, I shall remember the terror of that chase. I ran near the water's edge, and heard every now and then the splash of the feet that gained upon me. Far away, hopelessly far, was the yellow light. All the night about us was black and still. Splash, splash, came the pursuing feet, nearer and nearer. I felt my breath going, for I was quite out of training; it whooped as I drew it, and I felt a pain like a knife in my side. I perceived the Thing would come up with me long before I reached the enclosure, and, desperate and sobbing for my breath, I wheeled round upon it and struck at it as it came up to me—struck with all my strength. The stone came out of the sling of the handkerchief as I did so. As I turned, the Thing, which had been running on all-fours, rose to its feet, and the mis-sile fell fair on its left temple. The skull rang loud, and the animal-man blundered into me, thrust me back with its hands, and went staggering past me to fall headlong upon the sand with its face in the water; and there it lay still.

I could not bring myself to approach that black heap. I left it there, with the water rippling round it, under the still stars, and giving it a wide berth pursued my way towards the yellow glow of the house; and presently, with a positive effect of relief, came the pitiful moaning of the puma, the sound that had originally driven me out to explore this mysterious island. At that, though I was faint and horribly fatigued, I gathered together all my strength, and began running again towards the light. I thought I heard a voice calling me.

10. THE CRYING OF THE MAN

As I drew near the house I saw that the light shone from the open door of my room; and then I heard coming from out of the darkness at the side of that orange oblong of light, the voice of Montgomery shouting, "Prendick!" I continued running. Presently I heard him again. I replied by a feeble "Hullo!" and in another moment had staggered up to him.

"Where have you been?" said he, holding me at arm's length, so that the light from the door fell on my face. "We have both been so busy that we forgot you until about half an hour ago." He led me into the room and set me down in the deck chair. For awhile I was blinded by the light. "We did not think you would start to explore this island of ours without telling us," he said; and then, "I was afraid—But—what—Hullo!"

My last remaining strength slipped from me, and my head fell forward on my chest. I think he found a certain satisfaction in giving me brandy.

"For God's sake," said I, "fasten that door."

"You've been meeting some of our curiosities, eh?" said he.

He locked the door and turned to me again. He asked me no questions, but gave me some more brandy and water and pressed me to eat. I was in a state of collapse. He said something vague about his forgetting to warn me, and asked me briefly when I left the house and what I had seen.

I answered him as briefly, in fragmentary sentences. "Tell me what it all means," said I, in a state bordering on hysterics.

"It's nothing so very dreadful," said he. "But I think you have had about enough for one day." The puma suddenly gave a sharp yell of pain. At that he swore under his breath. "I'm damned," said he, "if this place is not as bad as Gower Street, with its cats."[1]

"Montgomery," said I, "what was that thing that came after me? Was it a beast or was it a man?"

"If you don't sleep to-night," he said, "you'll be off your head to-morrow."

I stood up in front of him. "What was that thing that came after me?" I asked.

---

1   University College, and its medical school, is located on Gower Street. Philmus suggests that Montgomery is here referring to the cats used by medical students for dissection and vivisection (variorum *Moreau*, p. 94, n. 36).

He looked me squarely in the eyes, and twisted his mouth askew. His eyes, which had seemed animated a minute before, went dull. "From your account," said he, "I'm thinking it was a bogle."[1]

I felt a gust of intense irritation, which passed as quickly as it came. I flung myself into the chair again, and pressed my hands on my forehead. The puma began once more.

Montgomery came round behind me and put his hand on my shoulder. "Look here, Prendick," he said, "I had no business to let you drift out into this silly island of ours. But it's not so bad as you feel, man. Your nerves are worked to rags. Let me give you something that will make you sleep. That—will keep on for hours yet. You must simply get to sleep, or I won't answer for it."

I did not reply. I bowed forward, and covered my face with my hands. Presently he returned with a small measure containing a dark liquid. This he gave me. I took it unresistingly, and he helped me into the hammock.

When I awoke, it was broad day. For a little while I lay flat, staring at the roof above me. The rafters, I observed, were made out of the timbers of a ship. Then I turned my head, and saw a meal prepared for me on the table. I perceived that I was hungry, and prepared to clamber out of the hammock, which, very politely anticipating my intention, twisted round and deposited me upon all-fours on the floor.

I got up and sat down before the food. I had a heavy feeling in my head, and only the vaguest memory at first of the things that had happened overnight. The morning breeze blew very pleasantly through the unglazed window, and that and the food contributed to the sense of animal comfort which I experienced. Presently the door behind me—the door inward towards the yard of the enclosure—opened. I turned and saw Montgomery's face.

"All right," said he. "I'm frightfully busy." And he shut the door.

Afterwards I discovered that he forgot to relock it. Then I recalled the expression of his face the previous night, and with that the memory of all I had experienced reconstructed itself before me. Even as that fear came back to me came a cry from within; but this time it was not the cry of a puma. I put down the mouthful that hesitated upon my lips, and listened. Silence, save for the whisper of the morning breeze. I began to think my ears had deceived me.

---

1   A minor evil spirit inclined to haunting. Montgomery's use of this word implies that the stalker was a product of Prendick's imagination.

After a long pause I resumed my meal, but with my ears still vigilant. Presently I heard something else, very faint and low. I sat as if frozen in my attitude. Though it was faint and low, it moved me more profoundly than all that I had hitherto heard of the abominations behind the wall. There was no mistake this time in the quality of the dim, broken sounds; no doubt at all of their source. For it was groaning, broken by sobs and gasps of anguish. It was no brute this time; it was a human being in torment!

As I realised this I rose, and in three steps had crossed the room, seized the handle of the door into the yard, and flung it open before me.

"Prendick, man! Stop!" cried Montgomery, intervening.

A startled deerhound yelped and snarled. There was blood, I saw, in the sink—brown, and some scarlet—and I smelled the peculiar smell of carbolic acid.[1] Then through an open doorway beyond, in the dim light of the shadow, I saw something bound painfully upon a framework, scarred, red, and bandaged; and then blotting this out appeared the face of old Moreau, white and terrible. In a moment he had gripped me by the shoulder with a hand that was smeared red, had twisted me off my feet, and flung me headlong back into my own room. He lifted me as though I was a little child. I fell at full length upon the floor, and the door slammed and shut out the passionate intensity of his face. Then I heard the key turn in the lock, and Montgomery's voice in expostulation.

"Ruin the work of a lifetime," I heard Moreau say.

"He does not understand," said Montgomery, and other things that were inaudible.

"I can't spare the time yet," said Moreau.

The rest I did not hear. I picked myself up and stood trembling, my mind a chaos of the most horrible misgivings. Could it be possible, I thought, that such a thing as the vivisection of men was carried on here? The question shot like lightning across a tumultuous sky; and suddenly the clouded horror of my mind condensed into a vivid realisation of my own danger.

---

1 Following the practice of Joseph Lister (1827-1912), carbolic acid (phenol) was widely used to disinfect surgical instruments and dressings, and was also sprayed in the air of the operating room. If Moreau is up-to-date with disinfection, one might wonder why he doesn't use anaesthesia as well.

It came before my mind with an unreasonable hope of escape that the outer door of my room was still open to me. I was convinced now, absolutely assured, that Moreau had been vivisecting a human being. All the time since I had heard his name, I had been trying to link in my mind in some way the grotesque animalism of the islanders with his abominations; and now I thought I saw it all. The memory of his work on the transfusion of blood recurred to me. These creatures I had seen were the victims of some hideous experiment. These sickening scoundrels had merely intended to keep me back, to fool me with their display of confidence, and presently to fall upon me with a fate more horrible than death—with torture; and after torture the most hideous degradation it was possible to conceive—to send me off a lost soul, a beast, to the rest of their Comus rout.[1]

I looked round for some weapon. Nothing. Then with an inspiration I turned over the deck chair, put my foot on the side of it, and tore away the side rail. It happened that a nail came away with the wood, and projecting, gave a touch of danger to an otherwise petty weapon. I heard a step outside, and incontinently flung open the door and found Montgomery within a yard of it. He meant to lock the outer door! I raised this nailed stick of mine and cut at his face; but he sprang back. I hesitated a moment, then turned and fled, round the corner of the house. "Prendick, man!" I heard his astonished cry, "don't be a silly ass, man!"

Another minute, thought I, and he would have had me locked in, and as ready as a hospital rabbit for my fate. He emerged behind the corner, for I heard him shout, "Prendick!" Then he began to run after me, shouting things as he ran. This time, running blindly, I went northeastward in a direction at right angles to my previous expedition. Once, as I went running headlong up the beach, I glanced over my shoulder and saw his attendant with him. I ran furiously up the slope, over it, then turning eastward along a rocky valley fringed on either side with jungle I ran for perhaps a mile altogether, my chest straining, my heart beating in my ears; and then hearing nothing of Montgomery or his man, and feeling upon the verge

---

1 A reference to a poetic drama, *Comus* (1634), by John Milton (1608-74), which presents a version of the classical myth of Circe, an enchantress who transforms humans into animals. Milton's Comus, son of Circe, accomplishes this transformation by evoking animal aspects of human nature, assisted by drunkenness. See Philmus, variorum *Moreau*, Note 38, p. 94.

of exhaustion, I doubled sharply back towards the beach, as I judged, and lay down in the shelter of a canebrake.[1] There I remained for a long time, too fearful to move, and indeed too fearful even to plan a course of action. The wild scene about me lay sleeping silently under the sun, and the only sound near me was the thin hum of some small gnats that had discovered me. Presently I became aware of a drowsy breathing sound, the soughing[2] of the sea upon the beach.

After about an hour I heard Montgomery shouting my name, far away to the north. That set me thinking of my plan of action. As I interpreted it then, this island was inhabited only by these two vivisectors and their animalised victims. Some of these no doubt they could press into their service against me if need arose. I knew both Moreau and Montgomery carried revolvers; and, save for a feeble bar of deal[3] spiked with a small nail, the merest mockery of a mace, I was unarmed.

So I lay still there, until I began to think of food and drink; and at that thought the real hopelessness of my position came home to me. I knew no way of getting anything to eat. I was too ignorant of botany to discover any resort of root or fruit that might lie about me; I had no means of trapping the few rabbits upon the island. It grew blanker the more I turned the prospect over. At last in the desperation of my position, my mind turned to the animal-men I had encountered. I tried to find some hope in what I remembered of them. In turn I recalled each one I had seen, and tried to draw some augury of assistance from my memory.

Then suddenly I heard a staghound bay, and at that realised a new danger. I took little time to think, or they would have caught me then, but snatching up my nailed stick, rushed headlong from my hiding-place towards the sound of the sea. I remember a growth of thorny plants, with spines that stabbed like penknives. I emerged bleeding and with torn clothes upon the lip of a long creek opening northward. I went straight into the water without a minute's hesitation, wading up the creek, and presently finding myself kneedeep in a little stream. I scrambled out at last on the westward bank, and with my heart beating loudly in my ears, crept into a tangle of ferns to await the issue. I heard the dog (there was only one) draw nearer, and yelp when it came to the thorns. Then I heard no more, and presently began to think I had escaped.

---

1 A thicket of canes (possibly bamboo).
2 Rushing or murmuring.
3 Inexpensive sawn wood, usually pine or fir.

The minutes passed; the silence lengthened out, and at last after an hour of security my courage began to return to me. By this time I was no longer very much terrified or very miserable. I had, as it were, passed the limit of terror and despair. I felt now that my life was practically lost, and that persuasion made me capable of daring anything. I had even a certain wish to encounter Moreau face to face; and as I had waded into the water, I remembered that if I were too hard pressed at least one path of escape from torment still lay open to me—they could not very well prevent my drowning myself. I had half a mind to drown myself then; but an odd wish to see the whole adventure out, a queer, impersonal, spectacular interest in myself,[1] restrained me. I stretched my limbs, sore and painful from the pricks of the spiny plants, and stared around me at the trees; and, so suddenly that it seemed to jump out of the green tracery about it, my eyes lit upon a black face watching me. I saw that it was the simian creature who had met the launch upon the beach. He was clinging to the oblique stem of a palm-tree. I gripped my stick, and stood up facing him. He began chattering. "You, you, you," was all I could distinguish at first. Suddenly he dropped from the tree, and in another moment was holding the fronds apart and staring curiously at me.

I did not feel the same repugnance towards this creature which I had experienced in my encounters with the other Beast Men. "You," he said, "in the boat." He was a man, then—at least as much of a man as Montgomery's attendant—for he could talk.

"Yes," I said, "I came in the boat. From the ship."

"Oh!" he said, and his bright, restless eyes travelled over me, to my hands, to the stick I carried, to my feet, to the tattered places in my coat, and the cuts and scratches I had received from the thorns. He seemed puzzled at something. His eyes came back to my hands. He held his own hand out and counted his digits slowly, "One, two, three, four, five—eigh?"

I did not grasp his meaning then; afterwards I was to find that a great proportion of these Beast People had malformed hands, lacking sometimes even three digits. But guessing this was in some way a greeting, I did the same thing by way of reply. He grinned with immense satisfaction. Then his swift roving glance went round again; he made a swift movement—and vanished. The fern fronds he had stood between came swishing together.

I pushed out of the brake after him, and was astonished to find him swinging cheerfully by one lank arm from a rope of creepers that looped down from the foliage overhead. His back was to me.

---

1 Seeing himself objectively, in a detached way.

"Hullo!" said I.

He came down with a twisting jump, and stood facing me.

"I say," said I, "where can I get something to eat?"

"Eat!" he said. "Eat Man's food, now." And his eye went back to the swing of ropes. "At the huts."

"But where are the huts?"

"Oh!"

"I'm new, you know."

At that he swung round, and set off at a quick walk. All his motions were curiously rapid. "Come along," said he.

I went with him to see the adventure out. I guessed the huts were some rough shelter where he and some more of these Beast People lived. I might perhaps find them friendly, find some handle in their minds to take hold of. I did not know how far they had forgotten their human heritage.

My ape-like companion trotted along by my side, with his hands hanging down and his jaw thrust forward. I wondered what memory he might have in him. "How long have you been on this island?" said I.

"How long?" he asked; and after having the question repeated, he held up three fingers.

The creature was little better than an idiot. I tried to make out what he meant by that, and it seems I bored him. After another question or two he suddenly left my side and went leaping at some fruit that hung from a tree. He pulled down a handful of prickly husks and went on eating the contents. I noted this with satisfaction, for here at least was a hint for feeding. I tried him with some other questions, but his chattering, prompt responses were as often as not quite at cross purposes with my question. Some few were appropriate, others quite parrot-like.

I was so intent upon these peculiarities that I scarcely noticed the path we followed. Presently we came to trees, all charred and brown, and so to a bare place covered with a yellow-white incrustation, across which went a drifting smoke, pungent in whiffs to nose and eyes. On our right, over a shoulder of bare rock, I saw the level blue of the sea. The path coiled down abruptly into a narrow ravine between two tumbled and knotty masses of blackish scoriae.[1] Into this we plunged.

It was extremely dark, this passage, after the blinding sunlight reflected from the sulphurous ground. Its walls grew steep, and approached each other. Blotches of green and crimson drifted across my eyes. My conductor

---

1   Rock formations left by the cooling of a lava-flow.

stopped suddenly. "Home!" said he, and I stood in a floor of a chasm that was at first absolutely dark to me. I heard some strange noises, and thrust the knuckles of my left hand into my eyes. I became aware of a disagreeable odor, like that of a monkey's cage ill-cleaned. Beyond, the rock opened again upon a gradual slope of sunlit greenery, and on either hand the light smote down through narrow ways into the central gloom.

12. THE SAYERS OF THE LAW

Then something cold touched my hand. I started violently, and saw close to me a dim pinkish thing, looking more like a flayed child than anything else in the world. The creature had exactly the mild but repulsive features of a sloth, the same low forehead and slow gestures.

As the first shock of the change of light passed, I saw about me more distinctly. The little sloth-like creature was standing and staring at me. My conductor had vanished. The place was a narrow passage between high walls of lava, a crack in the knotted rock, and on either side interwoven heaps of sea-mat, palm-fans, and reeds leaning against the rock formed rough and impenetrably dark dens. The winding way up the ravine between these was scarcely three yards wide, and was disfigured by lumps of decaying fruit-pulp and other refuse, which accounted for the disagreeable stench of the place.

The little pink sloth-creature was still blinking at me when my Ape-man reappeared at the aperture of the nearest of these dens, and beckoned me in. As he did so, a slouching monster wriggled out of one of the places, further up this strange street, and stood up in featureless silhouette against the bright green beyond, staring at me. I hesitated, having half a mind to bolt the way I had come; and then, determined to go through with the adventure, I gripped my nailed stick about the middle and crawled into the little evil-smelling lean-to after my conductor.

It was a semi-circular space, shaped like the half of a bee-hive; and against the rocky wall that formed the inner side of it was a pile of variegated fruits, cocoa-nuts among others. Some rough vessels of lava and wood stood about the floor, and one on a rough stool. There was no fire. In the darkest corner of the hut sat a shapeless mass of darkness that grunted "Hey!" as I came in, and my Ape-man stood in the dim light of the doorway and held out a split cocoa-nut to me as I crawled into the other corner and squatted down. I took it, and began gnawing it, as serenely as possible, in spite of a certain trepidation and the nearly intolerable closeness of the den. The little pink sloth-creature stood in the aperture of the hut, and something else with a drab face and bright eyes came staring over its shoulder.

"Hey!" came out of the lump of mystery opposite. "It is a man."

"It is a man," gabbled my conductor, "a man, a man, a five-man, like me."

"Shut up!" said the voice from the dark, and grunted. I gnawed my cocoa-nut amid an impressive stillness.

I peered hard into the blackness, but could distinguish nothing.

"It is a man," the voice repeated. "He comes to live with us?"

It was a thick voice, with something in it—a kind of whistling over-tone—that struck me as peculiar; but the English accent was strangely good.

The Ape-man looked at me as though he expected something. I perceived the pause was interrogative. "He comes to live with you," I said.

"It is a man. He must learn the Law."[1]

I began to distinguish now a deeper blackness in the black, a vague outline of a hunched-up figure. Then I noticed the opening of the place was darkened by two more black heads. My hand tightened on my stick.

The thing in the dark repeated in a louder tone, "Say the words." I had missed its last remark. "Not to go on all-fours; that is the Law," it repeated in a kind of sing-song.

I was puzzled.

"Say the words," said the Ape-man, repeating, and the figures in the doorway echoed this, with a threat in the tone of their voices.

I realised that I had to repeat this idiotic formula; and then began the insanest ceremony. The voice in the dark began intoning a mad litany, line by line, and I and the rest to repeat it. As they did so, they swayed from side to side in the oddest way, and beat their hands upon their knees; and I followed their example. I could have imagined I was already dead and in another world. That dark hut, these grotesque dim figures, just flecked

---

1   Both Bernard Bergonzi and Robert L. Platzner suggest that the Law of the Jungle obeyed by the animals in Kipling's *Jungle Book* and *Second Jungle Book* (1894/95) may have given Wells the idea of the Law of the Beast People in *Moreau*. If so, Kipling's Law of the Jungle, a rational and gentlemanly code of fair play, is, as Platzner observes, very different in spirit. If Wells was influenced by Kipling's Law, he seems to have parodied it. In any case, the Law of the Beast People certainly parodies the Ten Commandments.

here and there by a glimmer of light, and all of them swaying in unison and chanting,

"Not to go on all-fours; *that* is the Law. Are we not Men?
"Not to suck up Drink; *that* is the Law. Are we not Men?
"Not to eat Flesh or Fish; *that* is the Law. Are we not Men?
"Not to claw the Bark of Trees; *that* is the Law. Are we not Men?
"Not to chase other Men; *that* is the Law. Are we not Men?"

And so from the prohibition of these acts of folly, on to the prohibition of what I thought then were the maddest, most impossible, and most indecent things one could well imagine. A kind of rhythmic fervour fell on all of us; we gabbled and swayed faster and faster, repeating this amazing Law. Superficially the contagion of these brute men was upon me, but deep down within me laughter and disgust struggled together. We ran through a long list of prohibitions, and then the chant swung round to a new formula:

"*His* is the House of Pain.
"*His* is the Hand that makes.
"*His* is the Hand that wounds.
"*His* is the Hand that heals."

And so on for another long series, mostly quite incomprehensible gibberish to me about *Him*, whoever he might be. I could have fancied it was a dream, but never before have I heard chanting in a dream.

"*His* is the lightning flash," we sang. "*His* is the deep, salt sea."

A horrible fancy came into my head that Moreau, after animalising these men, had infected their dwarfed brains with a kind of deification of himself. However, I was too keenly aware of white teeth and strong claws about me to stop my chanting on that account.

"*His* are the stars in the sky."

At last that song ended. I saw the Ape-man's face shining with perspiration; and my eyes being now accustomed to the darkness, I saw more distinctly the figure in the corner from which the voice came. It was the size of a man, but it seemed covered with a dull grey hair almost like a Skyeterrier. What was it? What were they all? Imagine yourself surrounded by all the most horrible cripples and maniacs it is possible to conceive, and you may understand a little of my feelings with these grotesque caricatures of humanity about me.

"He is a five-man, a five-man, a five-man—like me," said the Ape-man. I held out my hands. The grey creature in the corner leant forward.

"Not to run on all-fours; that is the Law. Are we not Men?" he said.

He put out a strangely distorted talon and gripped my fingers. The thing was almost like the hoof of a deer produced into claws. I could have yelled with surprise and pain. His face came forward and peered at my nails, came forward into the light of the opening of the hut; and I saw with a quivering disgust that it was like the face of neither man nor beast, but a mere shock of grey hair, with three shadowy overarchings to mark the eyes and mouth.

"He has little nails," said this grisly creature in his hairy beard. "It is well."

He threw my hand down, and instinctively I gripped my stick.

"Eat roots and herbs; it is His will," said the Ape-man.

"I am the Sayer of the Law," said the grey figure. "Here come all that be new to learn the Law. I sit in the darkness and say the Law."

"It is even so," said one of the beasts in the doorway.

"Evil are the punishments of those who break the Law. None escape."

"None escape," said the Beast Folk, glancing furtively at one another.

"None, none," said the Ape-man, "none escape. See! I did a little thing, a wrong thing, once. I jabbered, jabbered, stopped talking. None could understand. I am burnt, branded in the hand. He is great. He is good!"

"None escape," said the grey creature in the corner.

"None escape," said the Beast People, looking askance at one another.

"For every one the want that is bad,"[1] said the grey Sayer of the Law. "What you will want we do not know; we shall know. Some want to follow things that move, to watch and slink and wait and spring; to kill and bite, bite deep and rich, sucking the blood. It is bad. 'Not to chase other Men; that is the Law. *Are we not Men?* Not to eat Flesh or Fish; that is the Law. *Are we not Men?*'"

"None escape," said a dappled brute standing in the doorway.

---

1 This universal "want that is bad" sounds like an equivalent to the Christian doctrine of Original Sin.

"For every one the want is bad," said the grey Sayer of the Law. "Some want to go tearing with teeth and hands into the roots of things, snuffing into the earth. It is bad."

"None escape," said the men in the door.

"Some go clawing trees; some go scratching at the graves of the dead; some go fighting with foreheads or feet or claws; some bite suddenly, none giving occasion; some love uncleanness."

"None escape," said the Ape-man, scratching his calf.

"None escape," said the little pink sloth-creature.

"Punishment is sharp and sure. Therefore learn the Law. Say the words."

And incontinently he began again the strange litany of the Law, and again I and all these creatures began singing and swaying. My head reeled with this jabbering and the close stench of the place; but I kept on, trusting to find presently some chance of a new development.

"Not to go on all-fours; that is the Law. *Are we not Men?*"

We were making such a noise that I noticed nothing of a tumult outside, until some one, who I think was one of the two Swine Men I had seen, thrust his head over the little pink sloth-creature and shouted something excitedly, something that I did not catch. Incontinently those at the opening of the hut vanished; my Ape-man rushed out; the thing that had sat in the dark followed him (I only observed that it was big and clumsy, and covered with silvery hair), and I was left alone. Then before I reached the aperture I heard the yelp of a staghound.

In another moment I was standing outside the hovel, my chair-rail in my hand, every muscle of me quivering. Before me were the clumsy backs of perhaps a score of these Beast People, their misshapen heads half hidden by their shoulder-blades. They were gesticulating excitedly. Other half-animal faces glared interrogation out of the hovels. Looking in the direction in which they faced, I saw coming through the haze under the trees beyond the end of the passage of dens the dark figure and awful white face of Moreau. He was holding the leaping staghound back, and close behind him came Montgomery; revolver in hand.

For a moment I stood horror-struck. I turned and saw the passage behind me blocked by another heavy brute, with a huge grey face and twinkling little eyes, advancing towards me. I looked round and saw to the right of me and a half-dozen yards in front of me a narrow gap in the wall of rock through which a ray of light slanted into the shadows.

"Stop!" cried Moreau as I strode towards this, and then, "Hold him!"

At that, first one face turned towards me and then others. Their bestial minds were happily slow. I dashed my shoulder into a clumsy monster who was turning to see what Moreau meant, and flung him forward into another. I felt his hands fly round, clutching at me and missing me. The little pink sloth-creature dashed at me, and I gashed down its ugly face with the nail in my stick, and in another minute was scrambling up a steep side pathway, a kind of sloping chimney, out of the ravine. I heard a howl behind me, and cries of "Catch him!" "Hold him!" and the grey-faced creature appeared behind me and jammed his huge bulk into the cleft. "Go on! go on!" they howled. I clambered up the narrow cleft in the rock and came out upon the sulphur on the westward side of the village of the Beast Men.

That gap was altogether fortunate for me, for the narrow chimney, slanting obliquely upward, must have impeded the nearer pursuers. I ran over the white space and down a steep slope, through a scattered growth of trees, and came to a low-lying stretch of tall reeds, through which I pushed into a dark, thick undergrowth that was black and succulent under foot. As I plunged into the reeds, my foremost pursuers emerged from the gap. I broke my way through this undergrowth for some minutes. The air behind me and about me was soon full of threatening cries. I heard the tumult of my pursuers in the gap up the slope, then the crashing of the reeds, and every now and then the crackling crash of a branch. Some of the creatures roared like excited beasts of prey. The staghound yelped to the left. I heard Moreau and Montgomery shouting in the same direction. I turned sharply to the right. It seemed to me even then that I heard Montgomery shouting for me to run for my life.

Presently the ground gave, rich and oozy under my feet; but I was desperate and went headlong into it, struggled through knee-deep, and so came to a winding path among tall canes. The noise of my pursuers passed away to my left. In one place three strange, pink, hopping animals, about the size of cats, bolted before my footsteps. This pathway ran up hill, across another open space covered with white incrustation, and plunged into a canebrake again. Then suddenly it turned parallel with the edge of a steep-walled gap, which came without warning, like the ha-ha[1] of an English park—turned with an unexpected abruptness. I was still running with all

---

1   A sunken fence on the grounds of a large estate, intended to restrain livestock without appearing in view; the name is supposed to represent one's exclamation of surprise at coming upon it. This reference to elaborate artificial landscaping on great estates in the eighteenth century presents an ironic contrast to Prendick's situation.

my might, and I never saw this drop until I was flying headlong through the air.

I fell on my forearms and head, among thorns, and rose with a torn ear and bleeding face. I had fallen into a precipitous ravine, rocky and thorny, full of a hazy mist which drifted about me in wisps, and with a narrow streamlet, from which this mist came, meandering down the centre. I was astonished at this thin fog in the full blaze of daylight; but I had no time to stand wondering then. I turned to my right, down-stream, hoping to come to the sea in that direction, and so have my way open to drown myself. It was only later I found that I had dropped my nailed stick in my fall.

Presently the ravine grew narrower for a space, and carelessly I stepped into the stream. I jumped out again pretty quickly, for the water was almost boiling. I noticed too there was a thin sulphurous scum drifting upon its coiling water.[1] Almost immediately came a turn in the ravine, and the indistinct blue horizon. The nearer sea was flashing the sun from a myriad facets. I saw my death before me; but I was hot and panting, with the warm blood oozing out on my face and running pleasantly through my veins. I felt more than a touch of exultation, too, at having distanced my pursuers. It was not in me then to go out and drown myself yet. I stared back the way I had come.

I listened. Save for the hum of the gnats and the chirp of some small insects that hopped among the thorns, the air was absolutely still. Then came the yelp of a dog, very faint, and a chattering and gibbering, the snap of a whip, and voices. They grew louder, then fainter again. The noise receded up the stream and faded away. For a while the chase was over; but I knew now how much hope of help for me lay in the Beast People.

13. A PARLEY

I turned again and went on down towards the sea. I found the hot stream broadened out to a shallow, weedy sand, in which an abundance of crabs and long-bodied, many-legged creatures started from my footfall. I walked

---

1   This scalding stream seems the climax of Prendick's observations of sulphurous encrustations and lava formations, reminding us that this island, volcanic in origin, has a still-smoking volcano. The volcanic nature of the island reinforces the story's theme of threatening animal forces under the surface of personality, and also suggests impermanence. In chapter 20 of *The Voyage of the Beagle*, Darwin describes how volcanic islands may shrink into atolls, and may finally disappear altogether.

to the very edge of the salt water, and then I felt I was safe. I turned and stared, arms akimbo, at the thick green behind me, into which the steamy ravine cut like a smoking gash. But, as I say, I was too full of excitement and (a true saying, though those who have never known danger may doubt it) too desperate to die.

Then it came into my head that there was one chance before me yet. While Moreau and Montgomery and their bestial rabble chased me through the island, might I not go round the beach until I came to their enclosure—make a flank march upon them, in fact, and then with a rock lugged out of their loosely-built wall, perhaps, smash in the lock of the smaller door and see what I could find (knife, pistol, or what not) to fight them with when they returned? It was at any rate something to try.

So I turned to the westward and walked along by the water's edge. The setting sun flashed his blinding heat into my eyes. The slight Pacific tide was running in with a gentle ripple. Presently the shore fell away southward, and the sun came round upon my right hand. Then suddenly, far in front of me, I saw first one and then several figures emerging from the bushes—Moreau, with his grey staghound, then Montgomery, and two others. At that I stopped.

They saw me, and began gesticulating and advancing. I stood watching them approach. The two Beast Men came running forward to cut me off from the undergrowth, inland. Montgomery came running also, but straight towards me. Moreau followed slower with the dog.

At last I roused myself from my inaction, and turning seaward walked straight into the water. The water was very shallow at first. I was thirty yards out before the waves reached to my waist. Dimly I could see the intertidal creatures darting away from my feet.

"What are you doing, man?" cried Montgomery.

I turned, standing waist deep, and stared at them. Montgomery stood panting at the margin of the water. His face was bright-red with exertion, his long flaxen hair blown about his head, and his dropping nether lip showed his irregular teeth. Moreau was just coming up, his face pale and firm, and the dog at his hand barked at me. Both men had heavy whips. Farther up the beach stared the Beast Men.

"What am I doing? I am going to drown myself," said I.

Montgomery and Moreau looked at each other. "Why?" asked Moreau.

"Because that is better than being tortured by you."

"I told you so," said Montgomery, and Moreau said something in a low tone.

"What makes you think I shall torture you?" asked Moreau.

"What I saw," I said. "And those—yonder."

"Hush!" said Moreau, and held up his hand.

"I will not," said I. "They were men: what are they now? I at least will not be like them."

I looked past my interlocutors. Up the beach were M'ling, Montgomery's attendant, and one of the white-swathed brutes from the boat. Farther up, in the shadow of the trees, I saw my little Ape-man, and behind him some other dim figures.

"Who are these creatures?" said I, pointing to them and raising my voice more and more that it might reach them. "They were men, men like yourselves, whom you have infected with some bestial taint—men whom you have enslaved, and whom you still fear. You who listen," I cried, pointing now to Moreau and shouting past him to the Beast Men, "You who listen! Do you not see these men still fear you, go in dread of you? Why, then, do you fear them? You are many—"

"For God's sake," cried Montgomery, "stop that, Prendick!"

"Prendick!" cried Moreau.

They both shouted together, as if to drown my voice; and behind them lowered the staring faces of the Beast Men, wondering, their deformed hands hanging down, their shoulders hunched up. They seemed, as I fancied, to be trying to understand me, to remember, I thought, something of their human past.

I went on shouting, I scarcely remember what—that Moreau and Montgomery could be killed, that they were not to be feared: that was the burden of what I put into the heads of the Beast People. I saw the green-eyed man in the dark rags, who had met me on the evening of my arrival, come out from among the trees, and others followed him, to hear me better. At last for want of breath I paused.

"Listen to me for a moment," said the steady voice of Moreau; "and then say what you will."

"Well?" said I.

He coughed, thought, then shouted: "Latin, Prendick! bad Latin, schoolboy Latin; but try and understand. *Hi non sunt homines; sunt animalia qui nos habemus*[1]—vivisected. A humanising process. I will explain. Come ashore."

I laughed. "A pretty story," said I. "They talk, build houses. They were men. It's likely I'll come ashore."

---

[1] "These are not men; they are animals whom we have—".

"The water just beyond where you stand is deep—and full of sharks."

"That's my way," said I. "Short and sharp. Presently."

"Wait a minute." He took something out of his pocket that flashed back the sun, and dropped the object at his feet. "That's a loaded revolver," said he. "Montgomery here will do the same. Now we are going up the beach until you are satisfied the distance is safe. Then come and take the revolvers."

"Not I! You have a third between you."

"I want you to think over things, Prendick. In the first place, I never asked you to come upon this island. If we vivisected men, we should import men, not beasts. In the next, we had you drugged last night, had we wanted to work you any mischief; and in the next, now your first panic is over and you can think a little, is Montgomery here quite up to the character you give him? We have chased you for your good. Because this island is full of—inimical phenomena. Besides, why should we want to shoot you when you have just offered to drown yourself?"

"Why did you set—your people onto me when I was in the hut?"

"We felt sure of catching you, and bringing you out of danger. Afterwards we drew away from the scent, for your good."

I mused. It seemed just possible. Then I remembered something again. "But I saw," said I, "in the enclosure—"

"That was the puma."

"Look here, Prendick," said Montgomery, "you're a silly ass! Come out of the water and take these revolvers, and talk. We can't do anything more than we could do now."

I will confess that then, and indeed always, I distrusted and dreaded Moreau; but Montgomery was a man I felt I understood.

"Go up the beach," said I, after thinking, and added, "holding your hands up."

"Can't do that," said Montgomery, with an explanatory nod over his shoulder. "Undignified."

"Go up to the trees, then," said I, "as you please."

"It's a damned silly ceremony," said Montgomery.

Both turned and faced the six or seven grotesque creatures, who stood there in the sunlight, solid, casting shadows, moving, and yet so incredibly unreal. Montgomery cracked his whip at them, and forthwith they all turned and fled helter-skelter into the trees; and when Montgomery and Moreau were at a distance I judged sufficient, I waded ashore, and picked up and examined the revolvers. To satisfy myself against the subtlest trickery, I discharged one at a round lump of lava, and had the satisfaction of seeing the stone pulverised and the beach splashed with lead. Still I hesitated for a moment.

"I'll take the risk," said I, at last; and with a revolver in each hand I walked up the beach towards them.

"That's better," said Moreau, without affectation. "As it is, you have wasted the best part of my day with your confounded imagination." And with a touch of contempt which humiliated me, he and Montgomery turned and went on in silence before me.

The knot of Beast Men, still wondering, stood back among the trees. I passed them as serenely as possible. One started to follow me, but retreated again when Montgomery cracked his whip. The rest stood silent—watching. They may once have been animals; but I never before saw an animal trying to think.

14. DOCTOR MOREAU EXPLAINS[1]

"And now, Prendick, I will explain," said Doctor Moreau, so soon as we had eaten and drunk. "I must confess that you are the most dictatorial guest I ever entertained. I warn you that this is the last I shall do to oblige you. The next thing you threaten to commit suicide about, I shan't do—even at some personal inconvenience."

He sat in my deck chair, a cigar half consumed in his white, dexterous-looking fingers. The light of the swinging lamp fell on his white hair; he stared through the little window out at the starlight. I sat as far away from him as possible, the table between us and the revolvers to hand. Montgomery was not present. I did not care to be with the two of them in such a little room.

"You admit that the vivisected human being, as you called it, is, after all, only the puma?" said Moreau. He had made me visit that horror in the inner room, to assure myself of its inhumanity.

"It is the puma," I said, "still alive, but so cut and mutilated as I pray I may never see living flesh again. Of all vile—"

"Never mind that," said Moreau; "at least, spare me those youthful horrors. Montgomery used to be just the same. You admit that it is the puma. Now be quiet, while I reel off my physiological lecture to you."

---

1   The aspects of the biological science expounded by Moreau in this chapter are closely related to two essays by Wells—see Appendix H.

And forthwith, beginning in the tone of a man supremely bored, but presently warming a little, he explained his work to me. He was very simple and convincing. Now and then there was a touch of sarcasm in his voice. Presently I found myself hot with shame at our mutual positions.

The creatures I had seen were not men, had never been men. They were animals—humanised animals—triumphs of vivisection.

"You forget all that a skilled vivisector can do with living things," said Moreau. "For my own part, I'm puzzled why the things I have done here have not been done before. Small efforts, of course, have been made—amputation, tongue-cutting, excisions. Of course you know a squint may be induced or cured by surgery? Then in the case of excisions[1] you have all kinds of secondary changes, pigmentary disturbances, modifications of the passions, alterations in the secretion of fatty tissue. I have no doubt you have heard of these things?"

"Of course," said I. "But these foul creatures of yours—"

"All in good time," said he, waving his hand at me; "I am only beginning. Those are trivial cases of alteration. Surgery can do better things than that. There is building up as well as breaking down and changing. You have heard, perhaps, of a common surgical operation resorted to in cases where the nose has been destroyed: a flap of skin is cut from the forehead, turned down on the nose, and heals in the new position. This is a kind of grafting in a new position of part of an animal upon itself. Grafting of freshly obtained material from another animal is also possible—the case of teeth, for example. The grafting of skin and bone is done to facilitate healing: the surgeon places in the middle of the wound pieces of skin snipped from another animal, or fragments of bone from a victim freshly killed. Hunter's cock-spur[2]—possibly you have heard of that—flourished on the bull's neck; and the rhinoceros rats of the Algerian zouaves[3] are also to be thought of—monsters manufactured by transferring a slip from the tail of an ordinary rat to its snout, and allowing it to heal in that position."[4]

"Monsters manufactured!" said I. "Then you mean to tell me—"

---

1 Surgical removals of tissue, organ, or bone by cutting it away with a sharp knife.

2 John Hunter (1728-93), one of the most famous of English anatomists, also made important contributions to the scientific practice of surgery. Later in life he maintained a small menagerie of animals on whom he performed experiments, among which were a number of successful transplants of tissue from one species to another.

3 Algerian infantry in the French army.

4 The first draft of *Moreau* provides a more detailed account of the operation (Philmus, variorum *Moreau*, note 45, p. 95).

"Yes. These creatures you have seen are animals carven and wrought into new shapes. To that, to the study of the plasticity of living forms, my life has been devoted. I have studied for years, gaining in knowledge as I go. I see you look horrified, and yet I am telling you nothing new. It all lay in the surface of practical anatomy years ago, but no one had the temerity to touch it. It's not simply the outward form of an animal which I can change. The physiology, the chemical rhythm of the creature, may also be made to undergo an enduring modification, of which vaccination and other methods of inoculation with living or dead matter are examples that will, no doubt, be familiar to you. A similar operation is the transfusion of blood, with which subject, indeed, I began. These are all familiar cases. Less so, and probably far more extensive, were the operations of those mediaeval practitioners who made dwarfs and beggar-cripples, show-monsters— some vestiges of whose art still remain in the preliminary manipulation of the young mountebank or contortionist. Victor Hugo gives an account of them in *L'Homme qui Rit*....[1] But perhaps my meaning grows plain now. You begin to see that it is a possible thing to transplant tissue from one part of an animal to another, or from one animal to another; to alter its chemical reactions and methods of growth; to modify the articulations of its limbs; and, indeed, to change it in its most intimate structure.

"And yet this extraordinary branch of knowledge has never been sought as an end, and systematically, by modern investigators until I took it up! Some such things have been hit upon in the last resort of surgery; most of the kindred evidence that will recur to your mind has been demonstrated, as it were by accident—by tyrants, by criminals, by the breeders of horses and dogs, by all kinds of untrained clumsy-handed men working for their own immediate ends. I was the first man to take up this question armed with antiseptic surgery, and with a really scientific knowledge of the laws of growth. Yet one would imagine it must have been practised in secret

---

1   Victor Hugo's novel *The Man Who Laughs* (1869), especially its third and fourth chapters, describes a sinister group, the "Comprachios," who in the seventeenth and eighteenth centuries used surgical techniques, now supposedly lost, to distort the growth, alter the appearance, and even limit the minds of children in order to produce monsters for display. He also mentions a supposedly Chinese practice of forcing children to grow up in jars so that the resulting body would have the same shape as the container. In *The First Men in the Moon* (1901) Wells describes an insect-like species living under the surface of the moon which uses a similar method to produce workers whose bodies are ideally shaped to their tasks.

before. Such creatures as the Siamese Twins....[1]And in the vaults of the Inquisition. No doubt their chief aim was artistic torture, but some at least of the inquisitors must have had a touch of scientific curiosity...."

"But," said I, "these things—these animals *talk*!"

He said that was so, and proceeded to point out that the possibility of vivisection does not stop at a mere physical metamorphosis. A pig may be educated. The mental structure is even less determinate than the bodily. In our growing science of hypnotism[2] we find the promise of a possibility of superseding old inherent instincts by new suggestions, grafting upon or replacing the inherited fixed ideas. Very much indeed of what we call moral education, he said, is such an artificial modification and perversion of instinct; pugnacity is trained into courageous self-sacrifice, and suppressed sexuality into religious emotion.[3] And the great difference between man and monkey is in the larynx,[4] he continued—in the incapacity to frame delicately different sound-symbols by which thought could be sustained. In this I failed to agree with him, but with a certain incivility he declined

---

1   Moreau speculates that Siamese Twins might have been manufactured surgically by joining together identical twins.

2   Hypnotism has been known since antiquity, but was usually associated with sorcery. In the late eighteenth century it was brought part-way into medical science by a Viennese physician, Franz Mesmer (1734-1815), but Mesmer still maintained a mystical aura around his methods: he claimed to work through an occult power called "animal magnetism." By the mid-nineteenth century hypnotism had begun to gain a respectable place in Victorian medicine. Belief in its power to lessen pain and cure physical and mental disease reached a high point in the late nineteenth century. It is still acknowledged to have medical value today, but less is expected of it. In literature, however, hypnotism kept its older, sinister associations, often being represented as a means by which a dominating personality can take complete control of another's mind, as with the villainous Svengali's hypnotic control of a young woman through which he transforms her into a famous singer, in George du Maurier's popular novel *Trilby* (1895).

3   The passage from "In our growing science of hypnotism" to "religious emotion" appears almost word-for-word in "The Limits of Individual Plasticity," in which Wells presents as his own this view of morality and religion as "the perversion of instinct." See Appendix H2.

4   A structure in the throat housing the vocal cords. In humans the larynx (or "voice box") is located lower in the throat than in apes and other mammals, thus leaving a larger open space above it—essential to making the variety of sounds necessary for language (Leakey 130-32). Moreau implies that only the structure of the throat prevents an ape from talking. In rejecting this idea Prendick would be arguing for a greater human superiority to apes. Stephen McLean places problems presented by the language of the Beast People in the context of a controversy of that time as to whether apes were mentally capable of using language.

to notice my objection. He repeated that the thing was so, and continued his account of his work.

I asked him why he had taken the human form as a model. There seemed to me then, and there still seems to me now, a strange wickedness in that choice.[1]

He confessed that he had chosen that form by chance. "I might just as well have worked to form sheep into llamas and llamas into sheep. I suppose there is something in the human form that appeals to the artistic turn more powerfully than any animal shape can. But I've not confined myself to man-making. Once or twice—" He was silent, for a minute perhaps. "These years! How they have slipped by! And here I have wasted a day saving your life, and am now wasting an hour explaining myself!"

"But," said I, "I still do not understand. Where is your justification for inflicting all this pain? The only thing that could excuse vivisection to me would be some application—"

"Precisely," said he. "But, you see, I am differently constituted. We are on different platforms. You are a materialist."

"I am *not* a materialist," I began hotly.

"In my view—in my view. For it is just this question of pain that parts us. So long as visible or audible pain turns you sick; so long as your own pains drive you; so long as pain underlies your propositions about sin—so long, I tell you, you are an animal, thinking a little less obscurely what an animal feels. This pain—"

I gave an impatient shrug at such sophistry.

"Oh, but it is such a little thing! A mind truly opened to what science has to teach must see that it is a little thing. It may be that save in this little planet, this speck of cosmic dust, invisible long before the nearest star could be attained—it may be, I say, that nowhere else does this thing called *pain* occur. But the laws we feel our way towards.... Why, even on this earth, even among living things, what pain is there?"

As he spoke he drew a little penknife from his pocket, opened the smaller blade, and moved his chair so that I could see his thigh. Then, choosing the place deliberately, he drove the blade into his leg and withdrew it.

"No doubt," he said, "you have seen that before. It does not hurt a pin-prick. But what does it show? The capacity for pain is not needed in

---

1 Philmus, following the first American edition, has "for that choice." Later editions change "for" to "in," as given here.

the muscle, and it is not placed there, is but little needed in the skin, and only here and there over the thigh is a spot capable of feeling pain. Pain is simply our intrinsic medical adviser to warn us and stimulate us. Not all living flesh is painful; nor is all nerve, not even all sensory nerve. There's no tint of pain, real pain, in the sensations of the optic nerve. If you wound the optic nerve, you merely see flashes of light—just as disease of the auditory nerve merely means a humming in our ears. Plants do not feel pain, nor the lower animals; it's possible that such animals as the starfish and crayfish do not feel pain at all. Then with men, the more intelligent they become, the more intelligently they will see after their own welfare, and the less they will need the goad to keep them out of danger. I never yet heard of a useless thing that was not ground out of existence by evolution sooner or later. Did you? And pain gets needless.

"Then I am a religious man, Prendick, as every sane man must be. It may be, I fancy, that I have seen more of the ways of this world's Maker than you—for I have sought his laws, in *my* way, all my life, while you, I understand, have been collecting butterflies. And I tell you, pleasure and pain have nothing to do with heaven or hell. Pleasure and pain—bah! What is your theologian's ecstasy but Mahomet's houri[1] in the dark? This store which men and women set on pleasure and pain, Prendick, is the mark of the beast upon them—the mark of the beast from which they came! Pain, pain and pleasure, they are for us only so long as we wriggle in the dust.

"You see, I went on with this research just the way it led me. That is the only way I ever heard of true research going. I asked a question, devised some method of obtaining an answer, and got—a fresh question. Was this possible or that possible? You cannot imagine what this means to an investigator, what an intellectual passion grows upon him! You cannot imagine the strange, colourless delight of these intellectual desires! The thing before you is no longer an animal, a fellow-creature, but a problem! Sympathetic pain—all I know of it I remember as a thing I used to suffer from years ago. I wanted—it was the one thing I wanted—to find out the extreme limit of plasticity in a living shape."[2]

---

1   In Islamic tradition, beautiful maidens who will wait upon and marry the faithful in paradise. Moreau implies here that mystical aspects of Christian theology are sensuality in disguise.

2   Moreau here claims that his goal is pure research. The use of vivisection for research not bound to a practical purpose was supported by Huxley and Wells. Many who wanted to impose limits on vivisection argued that it could only be justified if directed toward some specific medical goal of obvious benefit. In his demand earlier in the

"But," said I, "the thing is an abomination—"

"To this day I have never troubled about the ethics of the matter," he continued. "The study of Nature makes a man at last as remorseless as Nature. I have gone on, not heeding anything but the question I was pursuing; and the material has—dripped into the huts yonder. It is nearly eleven years since we came here, I and Montgomery and six Kanakas.[1] I remember the green stillness of the island and the empty ocean about us, as though it was yesterday. The place seemed waiting for me.

"The stores were landed and the house was built. The Kanakas founded some huts near the ravine. I went to work here upon what I had brought with me. There were some disagreeable things happened at first. I began with a sheep, and killed it after a day and a half by a slip of the scalpel. I took another sheep, and made a thing of pain and fear and left it bound up to heal. It looked quite human to me when I had finished it; but when I went to it I was discontented with it. It remembered me, and was terrified beyond imagination; and it had no more than the wits of a sheep. The more I looked at it the clumsier it seemed, until at last I put the monster out of its misery. These animals without courage, these fear-haunted, pain-driven things, without a spark of pugnacious energy to face torment—they are no good for man-making.

"Then I took a gorilla I had; and upon that, working with infinite care and mastering difficulty after difficulty, I made my first man. All the week, night and day, I moulded him. With him it was chiefly the brain that needed moulding; much had to be added, much changed. I thought him a fair specimen of the negroid type when I had finished him, and he lay bandaged, bound, and motionless before me. It was only when his life was assured that I left him and came into this room again, and found Montgomery much as you are. He had heard some of the cries as the thing grew human—cries like those that disturbed *you* so. I didn't take him completely into my confidence at first. And the Kanakas too, had realised something of it. They were scared out of their wits by the sight of me. I got Montgomery over to me—in a way; but I and he had the hardest job to prevent the Kanakas deserting. Finally they did; and so we lost the yacht. I spent many days edu-

---

conversation for "some application" to "excuse vivisection," Prendick seems to take this view. (For Huxley's place in this controversy, see French 99–108 and Desmond 461-62. For Wells's defense of vivisection in the cause of pure science, see the concluding paragraph of his essay "Popular Feeling," Appendix G9.)

1   Natives of South Sea Islands.

cating the brute—altogether I had him for three or four months. I taught him the rudiments of English; gave him ideas of counting; even made the thing read the alphabet. But at that he was slow, though I've met with idiots slower. He began with a clean sheet, mentally; had no memories left in his mind of what he had been. When his scars were quite healed, and he was no longer anything but painful and stiff, and able to converse a little, I took him yonder and introduced him to the Kanakas as an interesting stowaway.

"They were horribly afraid of him at first, somehow—which offended me rather, for I was conceited about him; but his ways seemed so mild, and he was so abject, that after a time they received him and took his education in hand. He was quick to learn, very imitative and adaptive, and built himself a hovel rather better, it seemed to me, than their own shanties. There was one among the boys a bit of a missionary, and he taught the thing to read, or at least to pick out letters, and gave him some rudimentary ideas of morality; but it seems the beast's habits were not all that is desirable.

"I rested from work for some days after this, and was in a mind to write an account of the whole affair to wake up English physiology. Then I came upon the creature squatting up in a tree and gibbering at two of the Kanakas who had been teasing him. I threatened him, told him the inhumanity of such a proceeding, aroused his sense of shame, and came home resolved to do better before I took my work back to England. I *have* been doing better. But somehow the things drift back again: the stubborn beast-flesh grows day by day back again. But I mean to do better things still. I mean to conquer that. This puma—

"But that's the story. All the Kanaka boys are dead now; one fell overboard of the launch, and one died of a wounded heel that he poisoned in some way with plant-juice. Three went away in the yacht, and I suppose and hope were drowned. The other one—was killed. Well, I have replaced them. Montgomery went on much as you are disposed to do at first, and then—"

"What became of the other one?" said I, sharply, "the other Kanaka who was killed?"

"The fact is, after I had made a number of human creatures I made a Thing." He hesitated.

"Yes," said I.

"It was killed."

"I don't understand," said I; "do you mean to say—"

"It killed the Kanaka—yes. It killed several other things that it caught. We chased it for a couple of days. It only got loose by accident—I never meant it to get away. It wasn't finished. It was purely an experiment. It was a limbless thing, with a horrible face, that writhed along the ground in a serpentine fashion. It was immensely strong, and in infuriating pain. It lurked in the woods for some days, until we hunted it; and then it wriggled into the northern part of the island, and we divided the party to close in upon it. Montgomery insisted upon coming with me. The man had a rifle; and when his body was found, one of the barrels was curved into the shape of an S and very nearly bitten through. Montgomery shot the thing. After that I stuck to the ideal of humanity—except for little things."

He became silent. I sat in silence watching his face.

"So for twenty years altogether—counting nine years in England—I have been going on; and there is still something in everything I do that defeats me, makes me dissatisfied, challenges me to further effort. Sometimes I rise above my level, sometimes I fall below it; but always I fall short of the things I dream. The human shape I can get now, almost with ease, so that it is lithe and graceful, or thick and strong; but often there is trouble with the hands and the claws—painful things, that I dare not shape too freely. But it is in the subtle grafting and reshaping one must needs do to the brain that my trouble lies. The intelligence is often oddly low, with unaccountable blank ends, unexpected gaps. And least satisfactory of all is something that I cannot touch, somewhere—I cannot determine where—in the seat of the emotions. Cravings, instincts, desires that harm humanity, a strange hidden reservoir to burst forth suddenly and inundate the whole being of the creature with anger, hate, or fear. These creatures of mine seemed strange and uncanny to you so soon as you began to observe them; but to me, just after I make them, they seem to be indisputably human beings. It's afterwards, as I observe them, that the persuasion fades. First one animal trait, then another, creeps to the surface and stares out at me. But I will conquer yet! Each time I dip a living creature into the bath of burning pain I say, 'This time I will burn out all the animal; this time I will make a rational creature of my own!' After all, what is ten years? Man has been a hundred thousand in the making." He thought darkly. "But I am drawing near the fastness. This puma of mine—" After a silence, "And they revert. As soon as my hand is taken from them the beast begins to creep back, begins to assert itself again." Another long silence.

"Then you take the things you make into those dens?" said I.

"They go. I turn them out when I begin to feel the beast in them, and presently they wander there. They all dread this house and me. There is a kind of travesty of humanity over there. Montgomery knows about it, for he interferes in their affairs. He has trained one or two of them to our service. He's ashamed of it, but I believe he half likes some of those beasts. It's his business, not mine. They only sicken me with a sense of failure. I take no interest in them. I fancy they follow in the lines the Kanaka missionary marked out, and have a kind of mockery of a rational life, poor beasts! There's something they call the Law. Sing hymns about 'all thine.'[1] They build themselves their dens, gather fruit, and pull herbs—marry even. But I can see through it all, see into their very souls, and see there nothing but the souls of beasts, beasts that perish, anger and the lusts to live and gratify themselves.—Yet they're odd; complex, like everything else alive. There is a kind of upward striving in them, part vanity, part waste sexual emotion, part waste curiosity. It only mocks me. I have some hope of that puma. I have worked hard at her head and brain—

"And now," said he, standing up after a long gap of silence, during which we had each pursued our own thoughts, "what do you think? Are you in fear of me still?"

I looked at him, and saw but a white-faced, white-haired man, with calm eyes. Save for his serenity, the touch almost of beauty that resulted from his set tranquillity and his magnificent build, he might have passed muster among a hundred other comfortable old gentlemen. Then I shivered. By way of answer to his second question, I handed him a revolver with either hand.

"Keep them," he said, and snatched at a yawn. He stood up, stared at me for a moment, and smiled. "You have had two eventful days," said he. "I should advise some sleep. I'm glad it's all clear. Good-night." He thought me over for a moment, then went out by the inner door.

I immediately turned the key in the outer one. I sat down again; sat for a time in a kind of stagnant mood, so weary, emotionally, mentally, and physically, that I could not think beyond the point at which he had left me. The black window stared at me like an eye. At last with an effort I put out the light and got into the hammock. Very soon I was asleep.

---

1 Later, Moreau's use of the Law in the gathering of the Beast People in chapter 16 reveals a more detailed knowledge of their religion that he admits to here. Can we entirely believe him when he says that this religion was all the work of a Kanaka missionary, implying that he had nothing to do with fashioning it?

15. CONCERNING THE BEAST FOLK

I woke early. Moreau's explanation stood before my mind, clear and definite, from the moment of my awakening. I got out of the hammock and went to the door to assure myself that the key was turned. Then I tried the window-bar, and found it firmly fixed. That these man-like creatures were in truth only bestial monsters, mere grotesque travesties of men, filled me with a vague uncertainty of their possibilities which was far worse than any definite fear.

A tapping came at the door, and I heard the glutinous accents of M'ling speaking. I pocketed one of the revolvers (keeping one hand upon it), and opened to him.

"Good-morning, sair," he said, bringing in, in addition to the customary herb-breakfast, an ill-cooked rabbit. Montgomery followed him. His roving eye caught the position of my arm and he smiled askew.

The puma was resting to heal that day; but Moreau, who was singularly solitary in his habits, did not join us. I talked with Montgomery to clear my ideas of the way in which the Beast Folk lived. In particular, I was urgent to know how these inhuman monsters were kept from falling upon Moreau and Montgomery and from rending one another. He explained to me that the comparative safety of Moreau and himself was due to the limited mental scope of these monsters. In spite of their increased intelligence and the tendency of their animal instincts to reawaken, they had certain *fixed ideas* implanted by Moreau in their minds, which absolutely bounded their imaginations. They were really hypnotised; had been told that certain things were impossible, and that certain things were not to be done, and these prohibitions were woven into the texture of their minds beyond any possibility of disobedience or dispute.

Certain matters, however, in which old instinct was at war with Moreau's convenience, were in a less stable condition.[1] A series of propositions called the Law (I had already heard them recited) battled in their minds with the deep-seated, ever-rebellious cravings of their animal natures. This Law they were ever repeating, I found, and ever breaking. Both Montgomery

---

1   One might question whether this distinction between the permanently fixed and "less stable" aspects of the personalities of the Beast People is fully borne out by their behaviour, starting with the Leopard Man's pursuit of Prendick in chapter 9. In chapter 14 Moreau admits a constant tendency to reversion—"the things drift back again"—and that he has no influence over "a strange hidden reservoir" of anti-social impulse.

and Moreau displayed particular solicitude to keep them ignorant of the taste of blood; they feared the inevitable suggestions of that flavour. Montgomery told me that the Law, especially among the feline Beast People, became oddly weakened about nightfall; that then the animal was at its strongest; that a spirit of adventure sprang up in them at the dusk, when they would dare things they never seemed to dream about by day. To that I owed my stalking by the Leopard-man, on the night of my arrival. But during these earlier days of my stay they broke the Law only furtively and after dark; in the daylight there was a general atmosphere of respect for its multifarious prohibitions.

And here perhaps I may give a few general facts about the island and the Beast People. The island, which was of irregular outline and lay low upon the wide sea, had a total area, I suppose, of seven or eight square miles. It was volcanic in origin, and was now fringed on three sides by coral reefs; some fumaroles[1] to the northward, and a hot spring, were the only vestiges of the forces that had long since originated it. Now and then a faint quiver of earthquake would be sensible, and sometimes the ascent of the spire of smoke would be rendered tumultuous by gusts of steam; but that was all. The population of the island, Montgomery informed me, now numbered rather more than sixty of these strange creations of Moreau's art, not counting the smaller monstrosities which lived in the undergrowth and were without human form. Altogether he had made nearly a hundred and twenty; but many had died, and others—like the writhing Footless Thing of which he had told me—had come by violent ends. In answer to my question, Montgomery said that they actually bore offspring, but that these generally died. When they lived, Moreau took them and stamped the human form upon them. There was no evidence of the inheritance of their acquired human characteristics.[2] The females were less numerous than the males, and liable to much furtive persecution in spite of the monogamy the Law enjoined.

It would be impossible for me to describe these Beast People in detail; my eye has had no training in details, and unhappily I cannot sketch. Most

---

1 Small holes that vent volcanic gases. Prendick has already encountered the scalding spring in chapter 12.

2 Philmus says that Wells added this sentence to the final draft of *Moreau*, and notes that it signals his abandonment of the Larmarckian belief that characteristics acquired during an animal's lifetime could be inherited by its offspring (variorum *Moreau*, note 57, p. 97). Wells's change of opinion on this point would have given a grim twist to his Darwinism as he was working on *Moreau*.

striking, perhaps, in their general appearance was the disproportion between the legs of these creatures and the length of their bodies; and yet—so
relative is our idea of grace—my eye became habituated to their forms, and
at last I even fell in with their persuasion that my own long thighs were ungainly. Another point was the forward carriage of the head and the clumsy
and inhuman curvature of the spine. Even the Ape-man lacked that inward
sinuous curve of the back which makes the human figure so graceful.[1]
Most had their shoulders hunched clumsily, and their short forearms hung
weakly at their sides. Few of them were conspicuously hairy—at least, until
the end of my time upon the island.

The next most obvious deformity was in their faces, almost all of which
were prognathous,[2] malformed about the ears, with large and protuber-
ant noses, very furry or very bristly hair, and often strangely-coloured or
strangely-placed eyes.[3] None could laugh, though the Ape-man had a
chattering titter. Beyond these general characters their heads had little in
common; each preserved the quality of its particular species: the human
mark distorted but did not hide the leopard, the ox, or the sow, or other
animal or animals, from which the creature had been moulded. The voices,
too, varied exceedingly. The hands were always malformed; and though
some surprised me by their unexpected human appearance, almost all were
deficient in the number of the digits, clumsy about the finger-nails, and
lacking any tactile sensibility.

The two most formidable Animal Men were my Leopard-man and a
creature made of hyena and swine. Larger than these were the three bull-
creatures who pulled in the boat. Then came the silvery-hairy-man, who
was also the Sayer of the Law, M'ling, and a satyr-like creature of ape and
goat. There were three Swine-men and a Swine-woman, a mare-rhinoc-
eros-creature, and several other females whose sources I did not ascertain.
There were several wolf-creatures, a bear-bull, and a Saint-Bernard-man.
I have already described the Ape-man, and there was a particularly hateful
(and evil-smelling) old woman made of vixen and bear, whom I hated

---

1 Another suggestion that the Beast People seem at least partially crippled by conversion to human status. Richard Leakey observes that the change from the pot-bellied,
   waistless physique of the ape, to the bone structure that provides the lithe waist of the
   human was essential for effective running on two feet (56-57). When the Leopard-man
   pursues Prendick or is hunted himself, he runs on four feet.
2 Having protruding jaws, like the profile of an ape.
3 These details resemble Lombroso's description of the "atavistic" degenerate—see Appendix F4.

from the beginning. She was said to be a passionate votary of the Law. Smaller creatures were certain dappled youths and my little sloth-creature. But enough of this catalogue.

At first I had a shivering horror of the brutes, felt all too keenly that they were still brutes; but insensibly I became a little habituated to the idea of them, and moreover I was affected by Montgomery's attitude towards them. He had been with them so long that he had come to regard them as almost normal human beings. His London days seemed a glorious, impossible past to him. Only once in a year or so did he go to Arica to deal with Moreau's agent, a trader in animals there. He hardly met the finest type of mankind in that seafaring village of Spanish mongrels. The men aboardship, he told me, seemed at first just as strange to him as the Beast Men seemed to me—unnaturally long in the leg, flat in the face, prominent in the forehead, suspicious, dangerous, and cold-hearted. In fact, he did not like men: his heart had warmed to me, he thought, because he had saved my life. I fancied even then that he had a sneaking kindness for some of these metamorphosed brutes, a vicious sympathy with some of their ways, but that he attempted to veil it from me at first.

M'ling, the black-faced man, Montgomery's attendant, the first of the Beast Folk I had encountered, did not live with the others across the island, but in a small kennel at the back of the enclosure. The creature was scarcely so intelligent as the Ape-man, but far more docile, and the most human-looking of all the Beast Folk; and Montgomery had trained it to prepare food, and indeed to discharge all the trivial domestic offices that were required. It was a complex trophy of Moreau's horrible skill—a bear, tainted with dog and ox, and one of the most elaborately made of all his creatures. It treated Montgomery with a strange tenderness and devotion. Sometimes he would notice it, pat it, call it half-mocking, half-jocular names, and so make it caper with extraordinary delight; sometimes he would ill-treat it, especially after he had been at the whiskey, kicking it, beating it, pelting it with stones or lighted fusees.[1] But whether he treated it well or ill, it loved nothing so much as to be near him.

I say I became habituated to the Beast People, that a thousand things which had seemed unnatural and repulsive speedily became natural and ordinary to me. I suppose everything in existence takes its colour from the average hue of our surroundings. Montgomery and Moreau were too peculiar and individual to keep my general impressions of humanity well

---

1 Large matches.

defined. I would see one of the clumsy bovine-creatures who worked the launch, treading heavily through the undergrowth, and find myself asking, trying hard to recall, how he differed from some really human yokel trudging home from his mechanical labours; or I would meet the Fox-bear woman's vulpine, shifty face, strangely human in its speculative cunning, and even imagine I had met it before in some city byway.

Yet every now and then the beast would flash out upon me beyond doubt or denial. An ugly-looking man, a hunch-backed human savage to all appearance, squatting in the aperture of one of the dens, would stretch his arms and yawn, showing with startling suddenness scissor-edged incisors and sabre-like canines, keen and brilliant as knives. Or in some narrow pathway, glancing with a transitory daring into the eyes of some lithe, white-swathed female figure, I would suddenly see (with a spasmodic revulsion) that she had slit-like pupils, or glancing down note the curving nail with which she held her shapeless wrap about her. It is a curious thing, by the bye, for which I am quite unable to account, that these weird creatures—the females, I mean—had in the earlier days of my stay an instinctive sense of their own repulsive clumsiness, and displayed in consequence a more than human regard for the decency and decorum of extensive costume.

16. HOW THE BEAST FOLK TASTED BLOOD

My inexperience as a writer betrays me, and I wander from the thread of my story.

After I had breakfasted with Montgomery, he took me across the island to see the fumarole and the source of the hot spring into whose scalding waters I had blundered on the previous day. Both of us carried whips and loaded revolvers. While going through a leafy jungle on our road thither, we heard a rabbit squealing. We stopped and listened, but we heard no more; and presently we went on our way, and the incident dropped out of our minds. Montgomery called my attention to certain little pink animals with long hind-legs, that went leaping through the undergrowth. He told me they were creatures made of the offspring of the Beast People, that Moreau had invented. He had fancied they might serve for meat, but a rabbit-like habit of devouring their young had defeated this intention. I had already encountered some of these creatures—once during my moonlight flight from the Leopard-man, and once during my pursuit by Moreau on the previous day. By chance, one hopping to avoid us leapt into the hole caused by the uprooting of a wind-blown tree; before it could extricate itself we managed to catch it. It spat like a cat, scratched and kicked vigorously with its hind-legs, and made an attempt to bite; but its teeth were too feeble to inflict more than a painless pinch. It seemed to me rather a pretty little creature; and as Montgomery stated that it never destroyed the turf by burrowing, and was very cleanly in its habits, I should imagine it might prove a convenient substitute for the common rabbit in gentlemen's parks.

We also saw on our way the trunk of a tree barked in long strips and splintered deeply. Montgomery called my attention to this. "Not to claw bark of trees, *that* is the Law," he said. "Much some of them care for it!" It was after this, I think, that we met the Satyr and the Ape-man. The Satyr was a gleam of classical memory on the part of Moreau—his face ovine in expression, like the coarser Hebrew type; his voice a harsh bleat, his nether extremities Satanic.[1] He was gnawing the husk of a pod-like fruit as he passed us. Both of them saluted Montgomery.

"Hail," said they, "to the Other with the Whip!"

"There's a Third with a Whip now," said Montgomery. "So you'd better mind!"

"Was he not made?" said the Ape-man. "He said—he said he was made." The Satyr-man looked curiously at me.

"The Third with the Whip, he that walks weeping into the sea, has a thin white face."

"He has a thin long whip," said Montgomery.

"Yesterday he bled and wept," said the Satyr. "You never bleed nor weep. The Master does not bleed or weep."

"Ollendorffian beggar!"[2] said Montgomery, "you'll bleed and weep if you don't look out!"

---

1 At the beginning of the first chapter of *Man's Place in Nature*, T.H. Huxley cites the Centaur and the Satyr, two half-human and half-animal creatures of classical myth, as foreshadowings of the Darwinian problems posed by the "Man-like Apes." According to myth, the Satyr was a goat below the waist. The Satanic quality Prendick finds in his "nether extremities" refers to the belief that Satan has cloven hooves for feet, but also reflects the view a Puritan culture might take of the Satyr's reputation for lust. Prendick's reference to "the coarser Hebrew type," suggestive of anti-Semitism, would be typical of theories of racial types in the late nineteenth century.

2 Philmus says that here Montgomery probably refers to Heinrich Ollendorf (1803-65), who produced many books intended to facilitate the learning of foreign languages (variorum *Moreau*, note 60, p. 97). The repetitions in the Satyr's previous statement could suggest an exercise in beginner's English. "Beggar" is a slang term implying that the Satyr is a disreputable rogue.

"He has five fingers, he is a five-man like me," said the Ape-man.

"Come along, Prendick," said Montgomery, taking my arm; and I went on with him.

The Satyr and the Ape-man stood watching us and making other remarks to each other.

"He says nothing," said the Satyr. "Men have voices."

"Yesterday he asked me of things to eat," said the Ape-man. "He did not know."

Then they spoke inaudible things, and I heard the Satyr laughing.

It was on our way back that we came upon the dead rabbit. The red body of the wretched little beast was rent to pieces, many of the ribs stripped white, and the backbone indisputably gnawed.

At that Montgomery stopped. "Good God!" said he, stooping down, and picking up some of the crushed vertebrae to examine them more closely. "Good God!" he repeated, "what can this mean?"

"Some carnivore of yours has remembered its old habits," I said after a pause. "This backbone has been bitten through."

He stood staring, with his face white and his lip pulled askew. "I don't like this," he said slowly.

"I saw something of the same kind," said I, "the first day I came here."

"The devil you did! What was it?"

"A rabbit with its head twisted off."

"The day you came here?"

"The day I came here. In the undergrowth at the back of the enclosure, when I went out in the evening. The head was completely wrung off."

He gave a long, low whistle.

"And what is more, I have an idea which of your brutes did the thing. It's only a suspicion, you know. Before I came on the rabbit I saw one of your monsters drinking in the stream."

"Sucking his drink?"

"Yes."

"'Not to suck your drink; *that* is the Law.' Much the brutes care for the Law, eh? when Moreau's not about!"

"It was the brute who chased me."

"Of course," said Montgomery; "it's just the way with carnivores. After a kill, they drink. It's the taste of blood, you know.—What was the brute like?" he continued. "Would you know him again?" He glanced about us, standing astride over the mess of dead rabbit, his eyes roving among the shadows and screens of greenery, the lurking-places and ambuscades of the forest that bounded us in. "The taste of blood," he said again.

He took out his revolver, examined the cartridges in it, and replaced it. Then he began to pull at his dropping lip.

"I think I should know the brute again," I said. "I stunned him. He ought to have a handsome bruise on the forehead of him."

"But then we have to *prove* that he killed the rabbit," said Montgomery. "I wish I'd never brought the things here."

I should have gone on, but he stayed there thinking over the mangled rabbit in a puzzle-headed way. As it was, I went to such a distance that the rabbit's remains were hidden.

"Come on!" I said.

Presently he woke up and came towards me. "You see," he said, almost in a whisper, "they are all supposed to have a fixed idea against eating anything that runs on land.[1] If some brute has by any accident tasted blood—" He went on some way in silence. "I wonder what can have happened," he said to himself. Then, after a pause again: "I did a foolish thing the other day. That servant of mine—I showed him how to skin and cook a rabbit. It's odd—I saw him licking his hands—It never .occurred to me." Then: ".We must put a stop to this. I must tell Moreau."

He could think of nothing else on our homeward journey.

Moreau took the matter even more seriously than Montgomery, and I need scarcely say that I was affected by their evident consternation.

"We must make an example," said Moreau. "I've no doubt in my own mind that the Leopard-man was the sinner. But how can we prove it? I wish, Montgomery, you had kept your taste for meat in hand, and gone without these exciting novelties. We may find ourselves in a mess yet, through it."

"I was a silly ass," said Montgomery. "But the thing's done now; and you said I might have them, you know."

"We must see to the thing at once," said Moreau. "I suppose if anything should turn up, M'ling can take care of himself?"

"I'm not so sure of M'ling," said Montgomery. "I think I *ought* to know him."

In the afternoon, Moreau, Montgomery, myself, and M'ling went across the island to the huts in the ravine. We three were armed; M'ling carried the little hatchet he used in chopping firewood, and some coils of wire. Moreau had a huge cowherd's horn slung over his shoulder.

---

1 The Leopard-man may have been inspired to hunt Prendick by the taste of blood, but if so he must first have violated this "fixed idea" by killing a rabbit.

"You will see a gathering of the Beast People," said Montgomery. "It is a pretty sight!"

Moreau said not a word on the way, but the expression of his heavy, white-fringed face was grimly set.

We crossed the ravine down which smoked the stream of hot water, and followed the winding pathway through the canebrakes until we reached a wide area covered over with a thick, powdery yellow substance which I believe was sulphur. Above the shoulder of a weedy bank the sea glittered. We came to a kind of shallow natural amphitheatre, and here the four of us halted. Then Moreau sounded the horn, and broke the sleeping stillness of the tropical afternoon.[1] He must have had strong lungs. The hooting note rose and rose amidst its echoes, to last an ear-penetrating intensity.

"Ah!" said Moreau, letting the curved instrument fall to his side again.

Immediately there was a crashing through the yellow canes, and a sound of voices from the dense green jungle that marked the morass through which I had run on the previous day. Then at three or four points on the edge of the sulphurous area appeared the grotesque forms of the Beast People, hurrying towards us. I could not help a creeping horror as I perceived first one and then another trot out from the trees or reeds and come shambling along over the hot dust. But Moreau and Montgomery stood calmly enough; and, perforce, I stuck beside them.

First to arrive was the Satyr, strangely unreal for all that he cast a shadow and tossed the dust with his hoofs. After him from the brake came a monstrous lout, a thing of horse and rhinoceros, chewing a straw as it came; then appeared the Swine-woman and two Wolf-women; then the Fox-bear witch, with her red eyes in her peaked red face, and then others—all hurrying eagerly. As they came forward they began to cringe towards Moreau and chant, quite regardless of one another, fragments of the latter half of the litany of the Law: "*His* is the Hand that wounds; *His* is the Hand that heals," and so forth. As soon as they had approached within a distance of perhaps thirty yards they halted, and bowing on knees and elbows began flinging the white dust upon their heads.

Imagine the scene if you can! We three blue-clad men, with our misshapen black-faced attendant, standing in a wide expanse of sunlit yellow dust under the blazing blue sky, and surrounded by this circle of crouching

---

1   The readiness with which the Beast People respond to this summons and participate in the ritual that follows shows that such gatherings have become habitual to them and that Moreau is well acquainted with their Law.

and gesticulating monstrosities—some almost human save in their subtle expression and gestures, some like cripples, some so strangely distorted as to resemble nothing but the denizens of our wildest dreams; and, beyond, the reedy lines of a canebrake in one direction, a dense tangle of palm-trees on the other, separating us from the ravine with the huts, and to the north the hazy horizon of the Pacific Ocean.

"Sixty-two, sixty-three," counted Moreau. "There are four more."

"I do not see the Leopard-man," said I.

Presently Moreau sounded the great horn again, and at the sound of it all the Beast People writhed and grovelled in the dust. Then, slinking out of the canebrake, stooping near the ground and trying to join the dust-throwing circle behind Moreau's back, came the Leopard-man. The last of the Beast People to arrive was the little Ape-man. The earlier animals, hot and weary with their grovelling, shot vicious glances at him.

"Cease!" said Moreau, in his firm, loud voice; and the Beast People sat back upon their hams and rested from their worshipping.

"Where is the Sayer of the Law?" said Moreau, and the Hairy Grey Monster bowed his face in the dust.

"Say the words!" said Moreau.

Forthwith all in the kneeling assembly, swaying from side to side and dashing up the sulphur with their hands—first the right hand and a puff of dust, and then the left—began once more to chant their strange litany. When they reached "Not to eat Flesh or Fowl, *that* is the Law," Moreau held up his lank white hand.

"*Stop!*" he cried, and there fell absolute silence upon them all.

I think they all knew and dreaded what was coming. I looked round at their strange faces. When I saw their wincing attitudes and the furtive dread in their bright eyes, I wondered that I had ever believed them to be men.

"That Law has been broken!" said Moreau.

"None escape," from the faceless creature with the silvery hair. "None escape," repeated the kneeling circle of Beast People.

"Who is he?" cried Moreau, and looked round at their faces, cracking his whip. I fancied the Hyena-swine looked dejected, so too did the Leopard-man. Moreau stopped, facing this creature, who cringed towards him with the memory and dread of infinite torment. "Who is he?" repeated Moreau, in a voice of thunder.

"Evil is he who breaks the Law," chanted the Sayer of the Law.

Moreau looked into the eyes of the Leopard-man, and seemed to be dragging the very soul out of the creature.

"Who breaks the Law—" said Moreau, taking his eyes off his victim, and turning towards us (it seemed to me there was a touch of exultation in his voice).

"Goes back to the House of Pain," they all clamoured—"goes back to the House of Pain, O Master!"

"Back to the House of Pain, back to the House of Pain," gabbled the Ape-man, as though the idea was sweet to him.

"Do you hear?" said Moreau, turning back to the criminal, "my friend—Hullo!"

For the Leopard-man, released from Moreau's eye, had risen straight from his knees, and now, with eyes aflame and his huge feline tusks flashing out from under his curling lips, leapt towards his tormentor. I am convinced that only the madness of unendurable fear could have prompted this attack. The whole circle of threescore monsters seemed to rise about us. I drew my revolver. The two figures collided. I saw Moreau reeling back from the Leopard-man's blow. There was a furious yelling and howling all about us. Every one was moving rapidly. For a moment I thought it was a general revolt. The furious face of the Leopard-man flashed by mine, with M'ling close in pursuit. I saw the yellow eyes of the Hyena-swine blazing with excitement, his attitude as if he were half resolved to attack me. The Satyr, too, glared at me over the Hyena-swine's hunched shoulders. I heard the crack of Moreau's pistol, and saw the pink flash dart across the tumult. The whole crowd seemed to swing round in the direction of the glint of fire, and I too was swung round by the magnetism of the movement. In another second I was running, one of a tumultuous shouting crowd, in pursuit of the escaping Leopard-man.

That is all I can tell definitely. I saw the Leopard-man strike Moreau, and then everything spun about me until I was running headlong. M'ling was ahead, close in pursuit of the fugitive. Behind, their tongues already lolling out, ran the Wolf-women in great leaping strides. The Swine-folk followed, squealing with excitement, and the two Bull-men in their swathings of white. Then came Moreau in a cluster of the Beast People, his wide-brimmed straw hat blown off, his revolver in hand, and his lank white hair streaming out. The Hyena-swine ran beside me, keeping pace with me and glancing furtively at me out of his feline eyes, and the others came pattering and shouting behind us.

The Leopard-man went bursting his way through the long canes, which sprang back as he passed, and rattled in M'ling's face. We others in the rear found a trampled path for us when we reached the brake. The chase lay through the brake for perhaps a quarter of a mile, and then plunged into a dense thicket, which retarded our movements exceedingly, though we went through it in a crowd together—fronds flicking into our faces, ropy creepers catching us under the chin or gripping our ankles, thorny plants hooking into and tearing cloth and flesh together.

"He has gone on all-fours through this," panted Moreau, now just ahead of me.

"None escape," said the Wolf-bear, laughing into my face with the exultation of hunting.

We burst out again among rocks, and saw the quarry ahead running lightly on all-fours and snarling at us over his shoulder. At that the Wolf Folk howled with delight. The Thing was still clothed, and at a distance its face still seemed human; but the carriage of its four limbs was feline, and the furtive droop of its shoulder was distinctly that of a hunted animal. It leapt over some thorny yellow-flowering bushes, and was hidden. M'ling was halfway across the space.

Most of us now had lost the first speed of the chase, and had fallen into a longer and steadier stride. I saw as we traversed the open that the pursuit was now spreading from a column into a line. The Hyena-swine still ran close to me, watching me as it ran, every now and then puckering its muzzle with a snarling laugh. At the edge of the rocks the Leopard-man, realising that he was making for the projecting cape upon which he had stalked me on the night of my arrival, had doubled in the undergrowth; but Montgomery had seen the manoeuvre, and turned him again. So, panting, tumbling against rocks, torn by brambles, impeded by ferns and reeds, I helped to pursue the Leopard-man, who had broken the Law, and the Hyena-swine ran, laughing savagely, by my side. I staggered on, my head reeling and my heart beating against my ribs, tired almost to death, and yet not daring to lose sight of the chase lest I should be left alone with this horrible companion. I staggered on in spite of infinite fatigue and the dense heat of the tropical afternoon.

At last the fury of the hunt slackened. We had pinned the wretched brute into a corner of the island. Moreau, whip in hand, marshalled us all into an irregular line, and we advanced now slowly, shouting to one another as we advanced and tightening the cordon about our victim. He lurked noiseless and invisible in the bushes through which I had run from him during that midnight pursuit.

"Steady!" cried Moreau, "steady!" as the ends of the line crept round the tangle of undergrowth and hemmed the brute in.

"Ware a rush!" came the voice of Montgomery from beyond the thicket.

I was on the slope above the bushes; Montgomery and Moreau beat along the beach beneath. Slowly we pushed in among the fretted network of branches and leaves. The quarry was silent.

"Back to the House of Pain, the House of Pain, the House of Pain!" yelped the voice of the Ape-man, some twenty yards to the right.

When I heard that, I forgave the poor wretch all the fear he had inspired in me. I heard the twigs snap and the boughs swish aside before the heavy tread of the Horse-rhinoceros upon my right. Then suddenly through a polygon of green, in the half darkness under the luxuriant growth, I saw the creature we were hunting. I halted. He was crouched together into the smallest possible compass, his luminous green eyes turned over his shoulder regarding me.

It may seem a strange contradiction in me—I cannot explain the fact—but now, seeing the creature there in a perfectly animal attitude, with the light gleaming in its eyes and its imperfectly human face distorted with terror, I realised again the fact of its humanity. In another moment other of its pursuers would see it, and it would be overpowered and captured, to experience once more the horrible tortures of the enclosure. Abruptly I whipped out my revolver, aimed between its terror-struck eyes, and fired. As I did so, the Hyena-swine saw the Thing, and flung itself upon it with an eager cry, thrusting thirsty teeth into its neck. All about me the green masses of the thicket were swaying and cracking as the Beast People came rushing together. One face and then another appeared.

"Don't kill it, Prendick!" cried Moreau. "Don't kill it!" And I saw him stooping as he pushed through under the fronds of the big ferns.

In another moment he had beaten off the Hyena-swine with the handle of his whip, and he and Montgomery were keeping away the excited carnivorous Beast People, and particularly M'ling, from the still quivering body. The Hairy Grey Thing came sniffing at the corpse under my arm. The other animals, in their animal ardour, jostled me to get a nearer view.

"Confound you, Prendick!" said Moreau. "I wanted him."

"I'm sorry," said I, though I was not. "It was the impulse of the moment." I felt sick with exertion and excitement. Turning, I pushed my way out of the crowding Beast People and went on alone up the slope towards the higher part of the headland. Under the shouted directions of Moreau, I heard the three white-swathed Bull-men begin dragging the victim down towards the water.

It was easy now for me to be alone. The Beast People manifested a quite human curiosity about the dead body, and followed it in a thick knot, sniffing and growling at it as the Bull-men dragged it down the beach. I went to the headland and watched the Bull-men, black against the evening sky, as they carried the weighted dead body out to sea; and like a wave across my mind came the realisation of the unspeakable aimlessness of things upon the island. Upon the beach among the rocks beneath me were the Ape-man, the Hyena-swine, and several other of the Beast People, standing about Montgomery and Moreau. They were all still intensely excited, and all overflowing with noisy expressions of their loyalty to the Law; yet I felt an absolute assurance in my own mind that the Hyena-swine was implicated in the rabbit-killing. A strange persuasion came upon me, that, save for the grossness of the line, the grotesqueness of the forms, I had here before me the whole balance of human life in miniature, the whole interplay of instinct, reason, and fate in its simplest form. The Leopard-man had happened to go under: that was all the difference. Poor brute!

Poor brutes! I began to see the viler aspect of Moreau's cruelty. I had not thought before of the pain and trouble that came to these poor victims after they had passed from Moreau's hands. I had shivered only at the days of actual torment in the enclosure. But now that seemed to me the lesser part. Before, they had been beasts, their instincts fitly adapted to their surroundings, and happy as living things may be. Now they stumbled in the shackles of humanity, lived in a fear that never died, fretted by a law they could not understand; their mock-human existence, begun in an agony, was one long internal struggle, one long dread of Moreau—and for what? It was the wantonness of it that stirred me.

Had Moreau had any intelligible object, I could have sympathised at least a little with him. I am not so squeamish about pain as that. I could have forgiven him a little even had his motive been only hate. But he was so irresponsible, so utterly careless! His curiosity, his mad, aimless investigations, drove him on; and the Things were thrown out to live a year or so, to struggle and blunder and suffer, and at last to die painfully. They were wretched in themselves; the old animal hate moved them to trouble one another; the Law held them back from a brief hot struggle and a decisive end to their natural animosities.

In those days my fear of the Beast People went the way of my personal fear of Moreau. I fell indeed into a morbid state, deep and enduring, and alien to fear, which has left permanent scars upon my mind. I must confess that I lost faith in the sanity of the world when I saw it suffering the painful disorder of this island. A blind Fate, a vast pitiless Mechanism, seemed to cut and shape the fabric of existence and I, Moreau (by his passion for research), Montgomery (by his passion for drink), the Beast People with their instincts and mental restrictions, were torn and crushed, ruthlessly, inevitably, amid the infinite complexity of its incessant wheels.[1] But this condition did not come all at once: I think indeed that I anticipate a little in speaking of it now.

17. A CATASTROPHE

Scarcely six weeks passed before I had lost every feeling but dislike and abhorrence for this infamous experiment of Moreau's. My one idea was to get away from these horrible caricatures of my Maker's image, back to the sweet and wholesome intercourse of men. My fellow-creatures, from whom I was thus separated, began to assume idyllic virtue and beauty in my memory. My first friendship with Montgomery did not increase. His long separation from humanity, his secret vice of drunkenness, his evident sympathy with the Beast People, tainted him to me. Several times I let him go alone among them. I avoided intercourse with them in every possible way. I spent an increasing proportion of my time upon the beach, looking for some liberating sail that never appeared—until one day there fell upon us an appalling disaster, which put an altogether different aspect upon my strange surroundings.

It was about seven or eight weeks after my landing—rather more, I think, though I had not troubled to keep account of the time—when this catastrophe occurred. It happened in the early morning—I should think about six. I had risen and breakfasted early, having been aroused by the noise of three Beast Men carrying wood into the enclosure.

After breakfast I went to the open gateway of the enclosure, and stood there smoking a cigarette and enjoying the freshness of the early morning. Moreau presently came round the corner of the enclosure and greeted me. He passed by me, and I heard him behind me unlock and enter his laboratory. So indurated was I at that time to the abomination of the place, that I heard without a touch of emotion the puma victim begin another day of torture. It met its persecutor with a shriek almost exactly like that of an angry virago.[2]

Then suddenly something happened—I do not know what, to this day. I heard a short, sharp cry behind me, a fall, and turning saw an awful face

---

1   The intellectual culture of the later nineteenth century was haunted by the possibility that the entire natural world, including all of human behaviour, might be governed by a blind determinism. Here Prendick suffers from a Darwinian version of this anxiety.
2   A loud-voiced, ill-tempered, scolding woman.

rushing upon me—not human, not animal, but hellish, brown, seamed with red branching scars, red drops starting out upon it, and the lidless eyes ablaze. I threw up my arm to defend myself from the blow that flung me headlong with a broken forearm; and the great monster, swathed in lint[1] and with red-stained bandages fluttering about it, leapt over me and passed. I rolled over and over down the beach, tried to sit up, and collapsed upon my broken arm. Then Moreau appeared, his massive white face all the more terrible for the blood that trickled from his forehead. He carried a revolver in one hand. He scarcely glanced at me, but rushed off at once in pursuit of the puma.

I tried the other arm and sat up. The muffled figure in front ran in great striding leaps along the beach, and Moreau followed her. She turned her head and saw him, then doubling abruptly made for the bushes. She gained upon him at every stride. I saw her plunge into them, and Moreau, running slantingly to intercept her, fired and missed as she disappeared. Then he too vanished in the green confusion.[2]

I stared after them, and then the pain in my arm flamed up, and with a groan I staggered to my feet. Montgomery appeared in the doorway, dressed, and with his revolver in his hand.

"Great God, Prendick!" he said, not noticing that I was hurt, "that brute's loose! Tore the fetter out of the wall! Have you seen them?" Then sharply, seeing I gripped my arm, "What's the matter?"

"I was standing in the doorway," said I.

He came forward and took my arm. "Blood on the sleeve," said he, and rolled back the flannel. He pocketed his weapon, felt my arm about painfully, and led me inside. "Your arm is broken," he said, and then, "Tell me exactly how it happened—what happened?"

I told him what I had seen; told him in broken sentences, with gasps of pain between them, and very dexterously and swiftly he bound my arm meanwhile. He slung it from my shoulder, stood back and looked at me.

"You'll do," he said. "And now?"

He thought. Then he went out and locked the gates of the enclosure. He was absent some time.

I was chiefly concerned about my arm. The incident seemed merely one more of many horrible things. I sat down in the deck chair, and, I must

---

1   A soft material made from linen for dressing wounds.
2   This is the second use of the phrase "green confusion." The first occurs during Prendick's encounter with the Leopard-man in chapter 9 (101). It could be taken as implying that Darwinian nature defies human reason.

admit, swore heartily at the island. The first dull feeling of injury in my arm had already given way to a burning pain when Montgomery reappeared. His face was rather pale, and he showed more of his lower gums than ever.

"I can neither see nor hear anything of him," he said. "I've been thinking he may want my help." He stared at me with his expressionless eyes. "That was a strong brute," he said. "It simply wrenched its fetter out of the wall." He went to the window, then to the door, and there turned to me. "I shall go after him," he said. "There's another revolver I can leave with you. To tell you the truth, I feel anxious somehow."

He obtained the weapon, and put it ready to my hand on the table; then went out, leaving a restless contagion in the air. I did not sit long after he left, but took the revolver in hand and went to the doorway.

The morning was as still as death. Not a whisper of wind was stirring; the sea was like polished glass, the sky empty, the beach desolate. In my half-excited, half-feverish state, this stillness of things oppressed me. I tried to whistle, and the tune died away. I swore again—the second time that morning. Then I went to the corner of the enclosure and stared inland at the green bush that had swallowed up Moreau and Montgomery. When would they return, and how? Then far away up the beach a little grey Beast Man appeared, ran down to the water's edge and began splashing about. I strolled back to the doorway, then to the corner again, and so began pacing to and fro like a sentinel upon duty. Once I was arrested by the distant voice of Montgomery bawling, "Coo-ee—Mor-eau!" My arm became less painful, but very hot. I got feverish and thirsty. My shadow grew shorter. I watched the distant figure until it went away again. Would Moreau and Montgomery never return? Three sea-birds began fighting for some stranded treasure.

Then from far away behind the enclosure I heard a pistol-shot. A long silence, and then came another. Then a yelling cry nearer, and another dismal gap of silence. My unfortunate imagination set to work to torment me. Then suddenly a shot close by. I went to the corner, startled, and saw Montgomery, his face scarlet, his hair disordered, and the knee of his trousers torn. His face expressed profound consternation. Behind him slouched the Beast Man, M'ling, and round M'ling's jaws were some queer dark stains.

"Has he come?" said Montgomery.

"Moreau?" said I. "No."

"My God!" The man was panting, almost sobbing. "Go back in," he said, taking my arm. "They're mad. They're all rushing about mad. What can have happened? I don't know. I'll tell you, when my breath comes. Where's some brandy?"

Montgomery limped before me into the room and sat down in the deck chair. M'ling flung himself down just outside the doorway and began panting like a dog. I got Montgomery some brandy-and-water. He sat staring in front of him at nothing, recovering his breath. After some minutes he began to tell me what had happened.

He had followed their track for some way. It was plain enough at first on account of the crushed and broken bushes, white rags torn from the puma's bandages, and occasional smears of blood on the leaves of the shrubs and undergrowth. He lost the track, however, on the stony ground beyond the stream where I had seen the Beast Man drinking, and went wandering aimlessly westward shouting Moreau's name. Then M'ling had come to him carrying a light hatchet. M'ling had seen nothing of the puma affair; had been felling wood, and heard him calling. They went on shouting together. Two Beast Men came crouching and peering at them through the undergrowth, with gestures and a furtive carriage that alarmed Montgomery by their strangeness. He hailed them, and they fled guiltily. He stopped shouting after that, and after wandering some time farther in an undecided way, determined to visit the huts.

He found the ravine deserted.

Growing more alarmed every minute, he began to retrace his steps. Then it was he encountered the two Swine-men I had seen dancing on the night of my arrival; blood-stained they were about the mouth, and intensely excited. They came crashing through the ferns, and stopped with fierce faces when they saw him. He cracked his whip in some trepidation, and forthwith they rushed at him. Never before had a Beast Man dared to do that. One he shot through the head; M'ling flung himself upon the other, and the two rolled grappling. M'ling got his brute under and with his teeth in its throat, and Montgomery shot that too as it struggled in M'ling's grip. He had some difficulty in inducing M'ling to come on with him. Thence they had hurried back to me. On the way, M'ling had suddenly rushed into a thicket and driven out an undersized Ocelot-man, also blood-stained, and lame through a wound in the foot. This brute had run a little way and then turned savagely at bay, and Montgomery—with a certain wantonness, I thought—had shot him.

"What does it all mean?" said I.

He shook his head, and turned once more to the brandy.

18. THE FINDING OF MOREAU

When I saw Montgomery swallow a third dose of brandy, I took it upon myself to interfere. He was already more than half fuddled. I told him that some serious thing must have happened to Moreau by this time, or he would have returned before this, and that it behoved us to ascertain what that catastrophe was. Montgomery raised some feeble objections, and at last agreed. We had some food, and then all three of us started.

It is possibly due to the tension of my mind at the time, but even now that start into the hot stillness of the tropical afternoon is a singularly vivid impression. M'ling went first, his shoulder hunched, his strange black head moving with quick starts as he peered first on this side of the way and then on that. He was unarmed; his axe he had dropped when he encountered the Swine-man. Teeth were *his* weapons, when it came to fighting. Montgomery followed with stumbling footsteps, his hands in his pockets, his face downcast; he was in a state of muddled sullenness with me on account of the brandy. My left arm was in a sling (it was lucky it was my left), and I carried my revolver in my right. Soon we traced a narrow path through the wild luxuriance of the island, going northwestward; and presently M'ling stopped and became rigid with watchfulness. Montgomery almost staggered into him, and then stopped too. Then, listening intently, we heard coming through the trees the sound of voices and footsteps approaching us.

"He is dead," said a deep, vibrating voice.

"He is not dead; he is not dead," jabbered another.

"We saw, we saw," said several voices.

"*Hul*-lo!" suddenly shouted Montgomery, "Hul-lo, there!"

"Confound you!" said I, and gripped my pistol.

There was a silence, then a crashing among the interlacing vegetation, first here, then there, and then half-a-dozen faces appeared—strange faces, lit by a strange light. M'ling made a growling noise in his throat. I recognised the Ape-man—I had indeed already identified his voice—and two of the white-swathed brown-featured creatures I had seen in Montgomery's boat. With these were the two dappled brutes and that grey, horribly crooked creature who said the Law, with grey hair streaming down its cheeks, heavy grey eyebrows, and grey locks pouring off from a central parting upon its sloping forehead—a heavy, faceless thing, with strange red eyes, looking at us curiously from amidst the green.

For a space no one spoke. Then Montgomery hiccoughed, "Who—said he was dead?"

The Ape-man looked guiltily at the Hairy Grey Thing. "He is dead," said this monster. "They saw."

There was nothing threatening about this detachment, at any rate. They seemed awestricken and puzzled.

"Where is he?" said Montgomery.

"Beyond," and the grey creature pointed.

"Is there a Law now?" asked the Ape-man. "Is it still to be this and that? Is he dead indeed?"

"Is there a Law?" repeated the man in white. "Is there a Law, thou Other with the Whip?"

"He is dead," said the Hairy Grey Thing. And they all stood watching us.

"Prendick," said Montgomery, turning his dull eyes to me. "He's dead, evidently."

I had been standing behind him during this colloquy. I began to see how things lay with them. I suddenly stepped in front of Montgomery and lifted up my voice:—

"Children of the Law," I said, "he is *not* dead!" M'ling turned his sharp eyes on me. "He has changed his shape; he has changed his body," I went on. "For a time you will not see him.[1] He is—there," I pointed upward, "where he can watch you. You cannot see him, but he can see you. Fear the Law!"

I looked at them squarely. They flinched.

"He is great, he is good," said the Ape-man, peering fearfully upward among the dense trees.

"And the other Thing?" I demanded.

"The Thing that bled, and ran screaming and sobbing—that is dead too," said the Grey Thing, still regarding me.

"That's well," grunted Montgomery.

"The Other with the Whip—" began the Grey Thing.

"Well?" said I.

"Said he was dead."

---

1   In his hasty attempt to add Moreau's resurrection to the religion of the Beast People, Prendick borrows a phrase that Jesus repeatedly emphasizes when, in the Gospel of John, he attempts to prepare his disciples for his death and Resurrection: "A little while, and ye shall not see me; and again, a little while, and ye shall see me...." The outcome for the disciples, however, will be quite different from the mood of Prendick's theology. Jesus concludes: "ye shall be sorrowful, but your sorrow shall be turned to joy". (John 16:16-22, King James Version). Since Prendick's motive is to re-establish the Law of the Beast People with Moreau's punitive authority behind it, there is no hint of forgiveness of sins or divine grace in his parody of the Resurrection.

But Montgomery was still sober enough to understand my motive in denying Moreau's death. "He is not dead," he said slowly, "not dead at all. No more dead than I am."

"Some," said I, "have broken the Law: they will die. Some have died. Show us now where his old body lies—the body he cast away because he had no more need of it."

"It is this way, Man who walked in the Sea,"[1] said the Grey Thing.

And with these six creatures guiding us, we went through the tumult of ferns and creepers and tree-stems towards the northwest. Then came a yelling, a crashing among the branches, and a little pink homunculus rushed by us shrieking. Immediately after appeared a feral monster in headlong pursuit, blood-bedabbled, who was amongst us almost before he could stop his career. The Grey Thing leapt aside. M'ling, with a snarl, flew at it, and was struck aside. Montgomery fired and missed, bowed his head, threw up his arm, and turned to run. I fired, and the Thing still came on; fired again, point-blank, into its ugly face. I saw its features vanish in a flash: its face was driven in. Yet it passed me, gripped Montgomery, and holding him, fell headlong beside him and pulled him sprawling upon itself in its death-agony.

I found myself alone with M'ling, the dead brute, and the prostrate man. Montgomery raised himself slowly and stared in a muddled way at the shattered Beast Man beside him. It more than half sobered him. He scrambled to his feet. Then I saw the Grey Thing returning cautiously through the trees.

"See," said I, pointing to the dead brute, "is the Law not alive? This came of breaking the Law."

He peered at the body. "He sends the Fire that kills," said he, in his deep voice, repeating part of the Ritual.[2] The others gathered round and stared for a space.

At last we drew near the westward extremity of the island. We came upon the gnawed and mutilated body of the puma, its shoulder-bone smashed by a bullet, and perhaps twenty yards farther found at last what we sought. Moreau lay face downward in a trampled space in a canebrake. One hand was almost severed at the wrist, and his silvery hair was dab-

---

1 This sounds like a parodic evocation of one of the best-known of Jesus's miracles. In chapter 21 Prendick's disciple, the Dog-man, addresses him as "Walker in the Sea" (163).

2 Apparently a line, not given in chapter 12, from the litany deifying Moreau that follows the Beast People's recitation of the Law. Fire might suggest the Day of Judgment, but the reference is probably to the lethal effect of Moreau's revolver.

bled in blood. His head had been battered in by the fetters of the puma. The broken canes beneath him were smeared with blood. His revolver we could not find. Montgomery turned him over.

Resting at intervals, and with the help of the seven Beast People (for he was a heavy man), we carried Moreau back to the enclosure. The night was darkling. Twice we heard unseen creatures howling and shrieking past our little band, and once the little pink sloth-creature appeared and stared at us, and vanished again. But we were not attacked again. At the gates of the enclosure our company of Beast People left us, M'ling going with the rest. We locked ourselves in, and then took Moreau's mangled body into the yard and laid it upon a pile of brushwood. Then we went into the laboratory and put an end to all we found living there.

19. MONTGOMERY'S "BANK HOLIDAY"[1]

When this was accomplished, and we had washed and eaten, Montgomery and I went into my little room and seriously discussed our position for the first time. It was then near midnight. He was almost sober, but greatly disturbed in his mind. He had been strangely under the influence of Moreau's personality: I do not think it had ever occurred to him that Moreau could die. This disaster was the sudden collapse of the habits that had become part of his nature in the ten or more monotonous years he had spent on the island. He talked vaguely, answered my questions crookedly, wandered into general questions.

"This silly ass of a world," he said; "what a muddle it all is! I haven't had any life. I wonder when it's going to begin. Sixteen years being bullied by nurses and schoolmasters at their own sweet will; five in London grinding hard at medicine, bad food, shabby lodgings, shabby clothes, shabby vice,[2] a blunder—I didn't know any better—and hustled off to this beastly island. Ten years here! What's it all for, Prendick? Are we bubbles blown by a baby?"

It was hard to deal with such ravings. "The thing we have to think of now," said I, "is how to get away from this island."

"What's the good of getting away? I'm an outcast. Where am I to join on? It's all very well for you, Prendick. Poor old Moreau! We can't leave

---

1   In Britain, a statutory holiday on which banks are closed.

2   Except for the "shabby vice," this resembles the account Wells gives of the results of trying to live in London on a scholarship of one pound a week for three years while studying biology at the Normal School (later Royal Academy) of Science (*Experiment* I, Ch. 5, Section 7, pp. 280-84).

him here to have his bones picked. As it is— And besides, what will become of the decent part of the Beast Folk?"

"Well," said I, "that will do to-morrow. I've been thinking we might make that brushwood into a pyre and burn his body—and those other things. Then what will happen with the Beast Folk?"

"*I* don't know. I suppose those that were made of beasts of prey will make silly asses of themselves sooner or later. We can't massacre the lot— can we? I suppose that's what *your* humanity would suggest? But they'll change. They are sure to change."

He talked thus inconclusively until at last I felt my temper going.

"Damnation!" he exclaimed at some petulance of mine; "can't you see I'm in a worse hole than you are?" And he got up, and went for the brandy. "Drink!" he said returning, "you logic-chopping, chalky-faced saint of an atheist,[1] drink!"

"Not I," said I, and sat grimly watching his face under the yellow paraffine flare, as he drank himself into a garrulous misery.

I have a memory of infinite tedium. He wandered into a maudlin defence of the Beast People and of M'ling. M'ling, he said, was the only thing that had ever really cared for him. And suddenly an idea came to him.

"I'm damned!" said he, staggering to his feet and clutching the brandy bottle.

By some flash of intuition I knew what it was he intended. "You don't give drink to that beast!" I said, rising and facing him.[2]

"Beast!" said he. "You're the beast. He takes his liquor like a Christian. Come out of the way, Prendick!"

"For God's sake," said I.

"*Get*—out of the way!" he roared, and suddenly whipped out his revolver.

"Very well," said I, and stood aside, half-minded to fall upon him as he put his hand upon the latch, but deterred by the thought of my useless arm. "You've made a beast of yourself—to the beasts you may go."

---

1 This insult associates Prendick with Huxley's high-minded agnosticism; Montgomery knows that Prendick has studied under Huxley.

2 Evidently an echo of a comic sub-plot in *The Tempest,* Shakespeare's play of island adventure, in which Stephano, a drunken cook, gives liquor to Caliban, a part-human and part-animal monster. Under the influence of alcohol, both construct grandiose fantasies of killing Prospero and becoming rulers of the island. In giving brandy to the Beast-People, Montgomery also seems motivated by a drunken fantasy of revolt against civilized morality, but here it quickly turns tragic.

He flung the doorway open, and stood half facing me between the yellow lamp-light and the pallid glare of the moon; his eye-sockets were blotches of black under his stubbly eyebrows.

"You're a solemn prig, Prendick, a silly ass! You're always fearing and fancying. We're on the edge of things. I'm bound to cut my throat to-morrow. I'm going to have a damned Bank Holiday to-night." He turned and went out into the moonlight. "M'ling!" he cried; "M'ling, old friend!"

Three dim creatures in the silvery light came along the edge of the wan beach—one a white-wrapped creature, the other two blotches of blackness following it. They halted, staring. Then I saw M'ling's hunched shoulders as he came round the corner of the house.

"Drink!" cried Montgomery, "drink, you brutes! Drink and be men! Damme, I'm the cleverest. Moreau forgot this; this is the last touch. Drink, I tell you!" And waving the bottle in his hand, he started off at a kind of quick trot to the westward, M'ling ranging himself between him and the three dim creatures who followed.

I went to the doorway. They were already indistinct in the mist of the moonlight before Montgomery halted. I saw him administer a dose of the raw brandy to M'ling, and saw the five figures melt into one vague patch.

"Sing!" I heard Montgomery shout; "sing all together, 'Confound old Prendick!' That's right; now again, 'Confound old Prendick!'"

The black group broke up into five separate figures, and wound slowly away from me along the band of shining beach. Each went howling at his own sweet will, yelping insults at me, or giving whatever other vent this new inspiration of brandy demanded. Presently I heard Montgomery's voice shouting, "Right turn!" and they passed with their shouts and howls into the blackness of the landward trees. Slowly, very slowly, they receded into silence.

The peaceful splendour of the night healed again. The moon was now past the meridian and travelling down the west. It was at its full, and very bright riding through the empty blue sky. The shadow of the wall lay, a yard wide and of inky blackness, at my feet. The eastward sea was a featureless grey, dark and mysterious; and between the sea and the shadow the grey sands (of volcanic glass and crystals) flashed and shone like a beach of diamonds. Behind me the paraffin lamp flared hot and ruddy.

Then I shut the door, locked it, and went into the enclosure where Moreau lay beside his latest victims—the staghounds and the llama and some other wretched brutes—with his massive face calm even after his terrible death, and with the hard eyes open, staring at the dead white moon above. I sat down upon the edge of the sink, and with my eyes upon that ghastly pile of silvery light and ominous shadows began to turn over my plans. In the morning I would gather some provisions in the dingey, and after setting fire to the pyre before me, push out into the desolation of the high sea once more. I felt that for Montgomery there was no help; that he was, in truth, half akin to these Beast Folk, unfitted for human kindred.

I do not know how long I sat there scheming. It must have been an hour or so. Then my planning was interrupted by the return of Montgomery to my neighbourhood. I heard a yelling from many throats, a tumult of exultant cries passing down towards the beach, whooping and howling, and excited shrieks that seemed to come to a stop near the water's edge. The riot rose and fell; I heard heavy blows and the splintering smash of wood, but it did not trouble me then. A discordant chanting began.

My thoughts went back to my means of escape. I got up, brought the lamp, and went into a shed to look at some kegs I had seen there. Then I became interested in the contents of some biscuit-tins, and opened one. I saw something out of the tail of my eye—a red flicker—and turned sharply.

Behind me lay the yard, vividly black-and-white in the moonlight, and the pile of wood and faggots on which Moreau and his mutilated victims lay, one over another. They seemed to be gripping one another in one last revengeful grapple. His wounds gaped, black as night, and the blood that had dripped lay in black patches upon the sand. Then I saw, without understanding, the cause of my phantom, a ruddy glow that came and danced and went upon the wall opposite. I misinterpreted this, fancied it was a reflection of my flickering lamp, and turned again to the stores in the shed. I went on rummaging among them, as well as a one-armed man could, finding this convenient thing and that, and putting them aside for to-morrow's launch. My movements were slow, and the time passed quickly. Insensibly the daylight crept upon me.

The chanting died down, giving place to a clamour; then it began again, and suddenly broke into a tumult. I heard cries of, "More! more!" a sound like quarrelling, and a sudden wild shriek. The quality of the sounds changed so greatly that it arrested my attention. I went out into the yard and listened. Then, cutting like a knife across the confusion, came the crack of a revolver.

I rushed at once through my room to the little doorway. As I did so I heard some of the packing-cases behind me go sliding down and smash together with a clatter of glass on the floor of the shed. But I did not heed these. I flung the door open and looked out.

Up the beach by the boathouse a bonfire was burning, raining up sparks into the indistinctness of the dawn. Around this struggled a mass of black figures. I heard Montgomery call my name. I began to run at once towards this fire, revolver in hand. I saw the pink tongue of Montgomery's pistol lick out once, close to the ground. He was down. I shouted with all my strength and fired into the air. I heard some one cry, "The Master!" The knotted black struggle broke into scattering units, the fire leapt and sank down. The crowd of Beast People fled in sudden panic before me, up the beach. In my excitement I fired at their retreating backs as they disappeared among the bushes. Then I turned to the black heaps upon the ground.

Montgomery lay on his back, with the Hairy Grey Beast-man sprawling across his body. The brute was dead, but still gripping Montgomery's throat with its curving claws. Near by lay M'ling on his face and quite still, his neck bitten open and the upper part of the smashed brandy bottle in his hand. Two other figures lay near the fire, the one motionless, the other groaning fitfully, every now and then raising its head slowly, then dropping it again.

I caught hold of the Grey Man and pulled him off Montgomery's body; his claws drew down the torn coat reluctantly as I dragged him away. Montgomery was dark in the face and scarcely breathing. I splashed sea-water on his face and pillowed his head on my rolled-up coat. M'ling was dead. The wounded creature by the fire—it was a Wolf-brute with a bearded grey face—lay, I found, with the fore part of its body upon the still glowing timber. The wretched thing was injured so dreadfully that in mercy I blew its brains out at once. The other brute was one of the Bull-men swathed in white. He too was dead. The rest of the Beast People had vanished from the beach.

I went to Montgomery again and knelt beside him, cursing my ignorance of medicine. The fire beside me had sunk down, and only charred beams of timber glowing at the central ends and mixed with a grey ash of brushwood remained. I wondered casually where Montgomery had got his wood. Then I saw that the dawn was upon us. The sky had grown brighter, the setting moon was becoming pale and opaque in the luminous blue of the day. The sky to the eastward was rimmed with red.

Suddenly I heard a thud and a hissing behind me, and, looking round, sprang to my feet with a cry of horror. Against the warm dawn great tumultuous masses of black smoke were boiling up out of the enclosure, and through their stormy darkness shot flickering threads of blood-red flame. Then the thatched roof caught. I saw the curving charge of the flames across the sloping straw. A spurt of fire jetted from the window of my room.

I knew at once what had happened. I remembered the crash I had heard. When I had rushed out to Montgomery's assistance, I had overturned the lamp.

The hopelessness of saving any of the contents of the enclosure stared me in the face. My mind came back to my plan of flight, and turning swiftly I looked to see where the two boats lay upon the beach. They were gone! Two axes lay upon the sands beside me; chips and splinters were scattered broadcast, and the ashes of the bonfire were blackening and smoking under the dawn. Montgomery had burned the boats to revenge himself upon me and prevent our return to mankind!

A sudden convulsion of rage shook me. I was almost moved to batter his foolish head in as he lay there helpless at my feet. Then suddenly his hand moved, so feebly, so pitifully, that my wrath vanished. He groaned, and opened his eyes for a minute. I knelt down beside him and raised his head. He opened his eyes again, staring silently at the dawn, and then they met mine. The lids fell.

"Sorry," he said presently, with an effort. He seemed trying to think. "The last," he murmured, "the last of this silly universe. What a mess—"

I listened. His head fell helplessly to one side. I thought some drink might revive him, but there was neither drink nor vessel in which to bring drink at hand. He seemed suddenly heavier. My heart went cold. I bent down to his face, put my hand through the rent in his blouse. He was dead; and even as he died a line of white heat, the limb[1] of the sun, rose eastward beyond the projection of the bay, splashing its radiance across the sky and turning the dark sea into a weltering tumult of dazzling light. It fell like a glory upon his death-shrunken face.

I let his head fall gently upon the rough pillow I had made for him, and stood up. Before me was the glittering desolation of the sea, the awful solitude upon which I had already suffered so much; behind me the island, hushed under the dawn, its Beast People silent and unseen. The enclosure, with all its provisions and ammunition, burnt noisily, with sudden gusts of flame, a fitful crackling, and now and then a crash. The heavy smoke drove up the beach away from me, rolling low over the distant tree-tops towards the huts in the ravine. Beside me were the charred vestiges of the boats and these five dead bodies.[2]

Then out of the bushes came three Beast People, with hunched shoulders, protruding heads, misshapen hands awkwardly held, and inquisitive, unfriendly eyes, and advanced towards me with hesitating gestures.

---

1 A term from astronomy meaning the edge of the disk of the sun, moon, or a planet.
2 The American edition, on which Philmus's is based, has "four dead bodies." However, Philmus changes the number to five (variorum *Moreau*, p. 98, n. 66), pointing out that there have been five casualties: Montgomery, M'ling, the grey-haired Sayer of the Law, a Wolf-man, and a Bull-man.

I faced these people, facing my fate in them, single-handed now—literally single-handed, for I had a broken arm. In my pocket was a revolver with two empty chambers. Among the chips scattered about the beach lay the two axes that had been used to chop up the boats. The tide was creeping in behind me. There was nothing for it but courage. I looked squarely into the faces of the advancing monsters. They avoided my eyes, and their quivering nostrils investigated the bodies that lay beyond me on the beach. I took half-a-dozen steps, picked up the blood-stained whip that lay beneath the body of the Wolf-man, and cracked it. They stopped and stared at me.

"Salute!" said I. "Bow down!"

They hesitated. One bent his knees. I repeated my command, with my heart in my mouth, and advanced upon them. One knelt, then the other two.

I turned and walked towards the dead bodies, keeping my face towards the three kneeling Beast Men, very much as an actor passing up the stage faces the audience.

"They broke the Law," said I, putting my foot on the Sayer of the Law, "they have been slain—even the Sayer of the Law; even the Other with the Whip. Great is the Law! Come and see."

"None escape," said one of them, advancing and peering.

"None escape," said I. "Therefore hear and do as I command." They stood up, looking questioningly at one another.

"Stand there," said I.

I picked up the hatchets and swung them by their heads from the sling of my arm; turned Montgomery over; picked up his revolver still loaded in two chambers, and bending down to rummage, found half-a-dozen cartridges in his pocket.

"Take him," said I, standing up again and pointing with the whip; "take him, and carry him out and cast him into the sea."

They came forward, evidently still afraid of Montgomery, but still more afraid of my cracking red whip-lash; and after some fumbling and hesitation, some whip-cracking and shouting, they lifted him gingerly, carried him down to the beach, and went splashing into the dazzling welter of the sea.

"On!" said I, "on! Carry him far."

They went in up to their armpits and stood regarding me.

"Let go," said I; and the body of Montgomery vanished with a splash. Something seemed to tighten across my chest.

"Good!" said I, with a break in my voice; and they came back, hurrying and fearful, to the margin of the water, leaving long wakes of black in the silver. At the water's edge they stopped, turning and glaring into the sea as though they presently expected Montgomery to arise therefrom and exact vengeance.

"Now these," said I, pointing to the other bodies.

They took care not to approach the place where they had thrown Montgomery into the water, but instead, carried the four dead Beast People slantingly along the beach for perhaps a hundred yards before they waded out and cast them away.

As I watched them disposing of the mangled remains of M'ling, I heard a light footfall behind me, and turning quickly saw the big Hyena-swine perhaps a dozen yards away. His head was bent down, his bright eyes were fixed upon me, his stumpy hands clenched and held close by his side. He stopped in this crouching attitude when I turned, his eyes a little averted.

For a moment we stood eye to eye. I dropped the whip and snatched at the pistol in my pocket; for I meant to kill this brute, the most formidable of any left now upon the island, at the first excuse. It may seem treacherous, but so I was resolved. I was far more afraid of him than of any other two of the Beast Folk. His continued life was, I knew, a threat against mine.

I was perhaps a dozen seconds collecting myself. Then cried I, "Salute! Bow down!"

His teeth flashed upon me in a snarl. "Who are *you* that I should—"

Perhaps a little too spasmodically I drew my revolver, aimed quickly and fired. I heard him yelp, saw him run sideways and turn, knew I had missed, and clicked back the cock with my thumb for the next shot. But he was already running headlong, jumping from side to side, and I dared not risk another miss. Every now and then he looked back at me over his shoulder. He went slanting along the beach, and vanished beneath the driving masses of dense smoke that were still pouring out from the burning enclosure. For some time I stood staring after him. I turned to my three obedient Beast Folk again and signalled them to drop the body they still carried. Then I went back to the place by the fire where the bodies had fallen, and kicked the sand until all the brown blood-stains were absorbed and hidden.

I dismissed my three serfs with a wave of the hand, and went up the beach into the thickets. I carried my pistol in my hand, my whip thrust with the hatchets in the sling of my arm. I was anxious to be alone, to think out the position in which I was now placed. A dreadful thing that I was only beginning to realise was, that over all this island there was now no safe place where I could be alone and secure to rest or sleep. I had recovered strength amazingly since my landing, but I was still inclined to be nervous and to break down under any great stress. I felt that I ought to cross the island and establish myself with the Beast People, and make myself secure in their confidence. But my heart failed me. I went back to the beach, and turning eastward past the burning enclosure, made for a point where a shallow spit of coral sand ran out towards the reef. Here I could sit down and think, my back to the sea and my face against any surprise. And there I sat, chin on knees, the sun beating down upon my head and unspeakable dread in my mind, plotting how I could live on against the hour of my rescue (if ever rescue came). I tried to review the whole situation as calmly as I could, but it was difficult to clear the thing of emotion.

I began turning over in my mind the reason of Montgomery's despair. "They will change," he said; "they are sure to change." And Moreau—what was it that Moreau had said? "The stubborn beast-flesh grows day by day back again." Then I came round to the Hyena-swine. I felt sure that if I did not kill that brute, he would kill me. The Sayer of the Law was dead: worse luck. They knew now that we of the Whips could be killed even as they themselves were killed. Were they peering at me already out of the green masses of ferns and palms over yonder, watching until I came within their spring? Were they plotting against me? What was the Hyena-swine telling them? My imagination was running away with me into a morass of unsubstantial fears.

My thoughts were disturbed by a crying of sea-birds hurrying towards some black object that had been stranded by the waves on the beach near the enclosure. I knew what that object was, but I had not the heart to go back and drive them off. I began walking along the beach in the opposite direction, designing to come round the eastward corner of the island and so approach the ravine of the huts, without traversing the possible ambuscades of the thickets.

Perhaps half a mile along the beach I became aware of one of my three Beast Folk advancing out of the landward bushes towards me. I was now so nervous with my own imaginings that I immediately drew my revolver. Even the propitiatory gestures of the creature failed to disarm me. He hesitated as he approached.

"Go away!" cried I.

There was something very suggestive of a dog in the cringing attitude of the creature. It retreated a little way, very like a dog being sent home, and stopped, looking at me imploringly with canine brown eyes.

"Go away," said I. "Do not come near me."

"May I not come near you?" it said.

"No; go away," I insisted, and snapped my whip. Then putting my whip in my teeth, I stooped for a stone, and with that threat drove the creature away.

So in solitude I came round by the ravine of the Beast People, and hiding among the weeds and reeds that separated this crevice from the sea I watched such of them as appeared, trying to judge from their gestures and appearance how the death of Moreau and Montgomery and the destruction of the House of Pain had affected them. I know now the folly of my cowardice. Had I kept my courage up to the level of the dawn, had I not allowed it to ebb away in solitary thought, I might have grasped the vacant sceptre of Moreau and ruled over the Beast People. As it was I lost the opportunity, and sank to the position of a mere leader among my fellows.

Towards noon certain of them came and squatted basking in the hot sand. The imperious voices of hunger and thirst prevailed over my dread. I came out of the bushes, and, revolver in hand, walked down towards these seated figures. One, a Wolf-woman, turned her head and stared at me, and then the others. None attempted to rise or salute me. I felt too faint and weary to insist, and I let the moment pass.

"I want food," said I, almost apologetically, and drawing near.

"There is food in the huts," said an Ox-boar-man, drowsily, and looking away from me.

I passed them, and went down into the shadow and odours of the almost deserted ravine. In an empty hut I feasted on some specked and half-decayed fruit; and then after I had propped some branches and sticks about the opening, and placed myself with my face towards it and my hand upon my revolver, the exhaustion of the last thirty hours claimed its own, and I fell into a light slumber, hoping that the flimsy barricade I had erected would cause sufficient noise in its removal to save me from surprise.

21. THE REVERSION OF THE BEAST FOLK

In this way I became one among the Beast People in the Island of Doctor Moreau. When I awoke, it was dark about me. My arm ached in its bandages. I sat up, wondering at first where I might be. I heard coarse voices talking outside. Then I saw that my barricade had gone, and that the opening of the hut stood clear. My revolver was still in my hand.

I heard something breathing, saw something crouched together close beside me. I held my breath, trying to see what it was. It began to move slowly, interminably. Then something soft and warm and moist passed across my hand. All my muscles contracted. I snatched my hand away. A cry of alarm began and was stifled in my throat. Then I just realised what had happened sufficiently to stay my fingers on the revolver.

"Who is that?" I said in a hoarse whisper, the revolver still pointed.

"*I*, Master."

"Who are *you*?"

"They say there is no Master now. But I know, I know. I carried the bodies into the sea, O Walker in the Sea! the bodies of those you slew. I am your slave, Master."

"Are you the one I met on the beach?" I asked.

"The same, Master."

The Thing was evidently faithful enough, for it might have fallen upon me as I slept. "It is well," I said, extending my hand for another licking kiss. I began to realise what its presence meant, and the tide of my courage flowed. "Where are the others?" I asked.

"They are mad; they are fools," said the Dog-man. "Even now they talk together beyond there. They say, 'The Master is dead. The Other with the Whip is dead. That Other who walked in the Sea is as we are. We have no Master, no Whips, no House of Pain, any more. There is an end. We love the Law, and will keep it; but there is no Pain, no Master, no Whips for ever again.'[1] So they say. But I know, Master, I know."

I felt in the darkness, and patted the Dog-man's head. "It is well," I said again.

"Presently you will slay them all," said the Dog-man.

"Presently," I answered, "I will slay them all—after certain days and certain things have come to pass. Every one of them save those you spare, every one of them shall be slain."

"What the Master wishes to kill, the Master kills," said the Dog-man with a certain satisfaction in his voice.

---

[1] The sentences quoted by the Dog-man sum up the characteristic attitude towards religion of intellectual sceptics of the late nineteenth century such as J.S. Mill, George Eliot, Thomas Hardy, and T.H. Huxley. They sought to dispense with belief in God and the prospects of heavenly reward and eternal torment as incentives for morality, but also to re-establish the best in Christian ethics on a secular foundation of reason and sympathetic feeling. In using a fraudulent superstition to subvert the attempt of the Beast People to establish a secular basis for morality, Prendick violates the highest ideal of agnostic culture. To Wells in the mid-1890s, the respect that agnostic intellectuals held for Christian morality may have seemed a bit old fashioned.

"And that their sins may grow," I said, "let them live in their folly until their time is ripe. Let them not know that I am the Master."

"The Master's will is sweet," said the Dog-man, with the ready tact of his canine blood.[1]

"But one has sinned," said I. "Him I will kill, whenever I may meet him. When I say to you, 'That is he,' see that you fall upon him. And now I will go to the men and women who are assembled together."

For a moment the opening of the hut was blackened by the exit of the Dog-man. Then I followed and stood up, almost in the exact spot where I had been when I had heard Moreau and his staghound pursuing me. But now it was night, and all the miasmatic ravine about me was black; and beyond, instead of a green, sunlit slope, I saw a red fire, before which hunched, grotesque figures moved to and fro. Farther were the thick trees, a bank of darkness, fringed above with the black lace of the upper branches. The moon was just riding up on the edge of the ravine, and like a bar across its face drove the spire of vapour that was for ever streaming from the fumaroles of the island.

"Walk by me," said I, nerving myself; and side by side we walked down the narrow way, taking little heed of the dim Things that peered at us out of the huts.

None about the fire attempted to salute me. Most of them disregarded me, ostentatiously. I looked round for the Hyena-swine, but he was not there. Altogether, perhaps twenty of the Beast Folk squatted, staring into the fire or talking to one another.

"He is dead, he is dead! the Master is dead!" said the voice of the Ape-man to the right of me. "The House of Pain—there *is* no House of Pain!"

"He is not dead," said I, in a loud voice. "Even now he watches us!"

This startled them. Twenty pairs of eyes regarded me.

"The House of Pain is gone," said I. "It will come again. The Master you cannot see; yet even now he listens among you."

"True, true!" said the Dog-man.

They were staggered at my assurance. An animal may be ferocious and cunning enough, but it takes a real man to tell a lie.

"The Man with the Bandaged Arm speaks a strange thing," said one of the Beast Folk.

"I tell you it is so," I said. "The Master and the House of Pain will come again. Woe be to him who breaks the Law!"

---

1 In *The Descent of Man*, Darwin suggests that a dog's devotion to his master may be a primitive version of religious feeling—see Appendix D4.

They looked curiously at one another. With an affectation of indifference I began to chop idly at the ground in front of me with my hatchet. They looked, I noticed, at the deep cuts I made in the turf.

Then the Satyr raised a doubt. I answered him. Then one of the dappled things objected, and an animated discussion sprang up round the fire. Every moment I began to feel more convinced of my present security. I talked now without the catching in my breath, due to the intensity of my excitement, that had troubled me at first. In the course of about an hour I had really convinced several of the Beast Folk of the truth of my assertions, and talked most of the others into a dubious state. I kept a sharp eye for my enemy the Hyena-swine, but he never appeared. Every now and then a suspicious movement would startle me, but my confidence grew rapidly. Then as the moon crept down from the zenith, one by one the listeners began to yawn (showing the oddest teeth in the light of the sinking fire), and first one and then another retired towards the dens in the ravine; and I, dreading the silence and darkness, went with them, knowing I was safer with several of them than with one alone.

In this manner began the longer part of my sojourn upon this Island of Doctor Moreau. But from that night until the end came, there was but one thing happened to tell save a series of innumerable small unpleasant details and the fretting of an incessant uneasiness. So that I prefer to make no chronicle for that gap of time, to tell only one cardinal incident of the ten months I spent as an intimate of these half-humanised brutes. There is much that sticks in my memory that I could write, things that I would cheerfully give my right hand to forget; but they do not help the telling of the story.

In the retrospect it is strange to remember how soon I fell in with these monsters' ways, and gained my confidence again. I had my quarrels with them of course, and could show some of their teeth-marks still; but they soon gained a wholesome respect for my trick of throwing stones and for the bite of my hatchet. And my Saint-Bernard-man's loyalty was of infinite service to me. I found their simple scale of honour was based mainly on the capacity for inflicting trenchant wounds. Indeed, I may say—without vanity, I hope—that I held something like pre-eminence among them. One or two, whom in a rare access of high spirits I had scarred rather badly, bore me a grudge; but it vented itself chiefly behind my back, and at a safe distance from my missiles, in grimaces.

The Hyena-swine avoided me, and I was always on the alert for him. My inseparable Dog-man hated and dreaded him intensely. I really believe that was at the root of the brute's attachment to me. It was soon evident to me that the former monster had tasted blood, and gone the way of the Leopard-man. He formed a lair somewhere in the forest, and became solitary. Once I tried to induce the Beast Folk to hunt him, but I lacked the authority to make them co-operate for one end. Again and again I tried to approach his den and come upon him unaware; but always he was too acute for me, and saw or winded me and got away. He too made every forest pathway dangerous to me and my ally with his lurking ambuscades. The Dog-man scarcely dared to leave my side.

In the first month or so the Beast Folk, compared with their latter condition, were human enough, and for one or two besides my canine friend I even conceived a friendly tolerance. The little pink sloth-creature displayed an odd affection for me, and took to following me about. The Ape-man bored me, however; he assumed, on the strength of his five digits, that he was my equal, and was for ever jabbering at me—jabbering the most arrant nonsense. One thing about him entertained me a little: he had a fantastic trick of coining new words. He had an idea, I believe, that to gabble about names that meant nothing was the proper use of speech. He called it "Big Thinks" to distinguish it from "Little Thinks," the sane everyday interests of life. If ever I made a remark he did not understand, he would praise it very much, ask me to say it again, learn it by heart, and go off repeating it, with a word wrong here or there, to all the milder of the Beast People. He thought nothing of what was plain and comprehensible. I invented some very curious "Big Thinks" for his especial use. I think now that he was the silliest creature I ever met; he had developed in the most wonderful way the distinctive silliness of man without losing one jot of the natural folly of a monkey.

This, I say, was in the earlier weeks of my solitude among these brutes. During that time they respected the usage established by the Law, and behaved with general decorum. Once I found another rabbit torn to pieces—by the Hyena-swine, I am assured—but that was all. It was about May when I first distinctly perceived a growing difference in their speech and carriage, a growing coarseness of articulation, a growing disinclination to talk. My Ape-man's jabber multiplied in volume, but grew less and less comprehensible, more and more simian. Some of the others seemed altogether slipping their hold upon speech, though they still understood what I said to them at that time. (Can you imagine language, once clear-cut and exact, softening and guttering, losing shape and import, becoming mere lumps of sound again?) And they walked erect with an increasing difficulty. Though they evidently felt ashamed of themselves, every now and then I would come upon one or another running on toes and finger-tips, and quite unable to recover the vertical attitude. They held things more clumsily; drinking by suction, feeding by gnawing, grew commoner every day. I realised more keenly than ever what Moreau had told me about the "stubborn beast-flesh." They were reverting, and reverting very rapidly.

Some of them—the pioneers in this, I noticed with some surprise, were all females—began to disregard the injunction of decency, deliberately for the most part. Others even attempted public outrages upon the institution of monogamy. The tradition of the Law was clearly losing its force. I cannot pursue this disagreeable subject.

My Dog-man imperceptibly slipped back to the dog again; day by day he became dumb, quadrupedal, hairy. I scarcely noticed the transition from the companion on my right hand to the lurching dog at my side.

As the carelessness and disorganisation increased from day to day, the lane of dwelling places, at no time very sweet, became so loathsome that I left it, and going across the island made myself a hovel of boughs amid the black ruins of Moreau's enclosure. Some memory of pain, I found, still made that place the safest from the Beast Folk.

It would be impossible to detail every step of the lapsing of these monsters—to tell how, day by day, the human semblance left them; how they gave up bandagings and wrappings, abandoned at last every stitch of clothing; how the hair began to spread over the exposed limbs; how their foreheads fell away and their faces projected; how the quasi-human intimacy I had permitted myself with some of them in the first month of my loneliness became a shuddering horror to recall.

The change was slow and inevitable. For them and for me it came without any definite shock. I still went among them in safety, because no jolt in the downward glide had released the increasing charge of explosive animalism that ousted the human day by day. But I began to fear that soon now that shock must come. My Saint-Bernard-brute followed me to the enclosure every night, and his vigilance enabled me to sleep at times in something like peace. The little pink sloth-thing became shy and left me, to crawl back to its natural life once more among the tree-branches. We were in just the state of equilibrium that would remain in one of those "Happy Family" cages which animal-tamers exhibit, if the tamer were to leave it for ever.

Of course these creatures did not decline into such beasts as the reader has seen in zoological gardens—into ordinary bears, wolves, tigers, oxen, swine, and apes. There was still something strange about each; in each Moreau had blended this animal with that. One perhaps was ursine chiefly, another feline chiefly, another bovine chiefly; but each was tainted with other creatures—a kind of generalised animalism appearing through the specific dispositions. And the dwindling shreds of the humanity still startled me every now and then—a momentary recrudescence of speech perhaps, an unexpected dexterity of the fore-feet, a pitiful attempt to walk erect.

I too must have undergone strange changes. My clothes hung about me as yellow rags, through whose rents showed the tanned skin. My hair grew long, and became matted together. I am told that even now my eyes have a strange brightness, a swift alertness of movement.

At first I spent the daylight hours on the southward beach watching for a ship, hoping and praying for a ship. I counted on the *Ipecacuanha* returning as the year wore on; but she never came. Five times I saw sails, and thrice smoke; but nothing ever touched the island. I always had a bonfire ready, but no doubt the volcanic reputation of the island was taken to account for that.

It was only about September or October that I began to think of making a raft. By that time my arm had healed, and both my hands were at my service again. At first, I found my helplessness appalling. I had never done any carpentry or such-like work in my life, and I spent day after day in experimental chopping and binding among the trees. I had no ropes, and could hit on nothing wherewith to make ropes; none of the abundant creepers seemed limber or strong enough, and with all my litter of scientific education I could not devise any way of making them so. I spent more than a fortnight grubbing among the black ruins of the enclosure and on the beach where the boats had been burnt, looking for nails and other stray pieces of metal that might prove of service. Now and then some Beast-creature would watch me, and go leaping off when I called to it. There came a season of thunder-storms and heavy rain, which greatly retarded my work; but at last the raft was completed.

I was delighted with it. But with a certain lack of practical sense which has always been my bane, I had made it a mile or more from the sea; and before I had dragged it down to the beach the thing had fallen to pieces. Perhaps it is as well that I was saved from launching it; but at the time my misery at my failure was so acute that for some days I simply moped on the beach, and stared at the water and thought of death.[1]

I did not, however, mean to die, and an incident occurred that warned me unmistakably of the folly of letting the days pass so—for each fresh day was fraught with increasing danger from the Beast People.

---

1   Robinson Crusoe has a similar disappointment: he expends much labour on building a large dugout canoe but finds that he cannot drag it to the water.

I was lying in the shade of the enclosure wall, staring out to sea, when I was startled by something cold touching the skin of my heel, and starting round found the little pink sloth-creature blinking into my face. He had long since lost speech and active movement, and the lank hair of the little brute grew thicker every day and his stumpy claws more askew. He made a moaning noise when he saw he had attracted my attention, went a little way towards the bushes and looked back at me.

At first I did not understand, but presently it occurred to me that he wished me to follow him; and this I did at last—slowly, for the day was hot. When we reached the trees he clambered into them, for he could travel better among their swinging creepers than on the ground. And suddenly in a trampled space I came upon a ghastly group. My Saint-Bernard-creature lay on the ground, dead; and near his body crouched the Hyena-swine, gripping the quivering flesh with its misshapen claws, gnawing at it, and snarling with delight. As I approached, the monster lifted its glaring eyes to mine, its lips went trembling back from its red-stained teeth, and it growled menacingly. It was not afraid and not ashamed; the last vestige of the human taint had vanished. I advanced a step farther, stopped, and pulled out my revolver. At last I had him face to face.

The brute made no sign of retreat; but its ears went back, its hair bristled, and its body crouched together. I aimed between the eyes and fired. As I did so, the Thing rose straight at me in a leap, and I was knocked over like a ninepin. It clutched at me with its crippled hand, and struck me in the face. Its spring carried it over me. I fell under the hind part of its body; but luckily I had hit as I meant, and it had died even as it leapt. I crawled out from under its unclean weight and stood up trembling, staring at its quivering body. That danger at least was over; but this, I knew, was only the first of the series of relapses that must come.

I burned both of the bodies on a pyre of brushwood; but after that I saw that unless I left the island my death was only a question of time. The Beast People by that time had, with one or two exceptions, left the ravine and made themselves lairs according to their taste among the thickets of the island. Few prowled by day, most of them slept, and the island might have seemed deserted to a new-comer; but at night the air was hideous with their calls and howling. I had half a mind to make a massacre of them; to build traps, or fight them with my knife. Had I possessed sufficient cartridges, I should not have hesitated to begin the killing. There could now be scarcely a score left of the dangerous carnivores; the braver of these were already dead. After the death of this poor dog of mine, my last friend, I too adopted to some extent the practice of slumbering in the daytime in order to be on my guard at night. I rebuilt my den in the walls of the enclosure, with such a narrow opening that anything attempting to enter must necessarily make a considerable noise. The creatures had lost the art of fire too, and recovered their fear of it. I turned once more, almost passionately now, to hammering together stakes and branches to form a raft for my escape.

I found a thousand difficulties. I am an extremely unhandy man (my schooling was over before the days of Slöjd);[1] but most of the requirements of a raft I met at last in some clumsy, circuitous way or other, and this time I took care of the strength. The only insurmountable obstacle was that I had no vessel to contain the water I should need if I floated forth upon these untravelled seas. I would have even tried pottery, but the island contained no clay. I used to go moping about the island trying with all my might to solve this one last difficulty. Sometimes I would give way to wild outbursts of rage, and hack and splinter some unlucky tree in my intolerable vexation. But I could think of nothing.

And then came a day, a wonderful day, which I spent in ecstasy. I saw a sail to the southwest, a small sail like that of a little schooner; and forthwith I lit a great pile of brushwood, and stood by it in the heat of it, and the heat of the midday sun, watching. All day I watched that sail, eating or drinking nothing, so that my head reeled; and the Beasts came and glared at me, and seemed to wonder, and went away. It was still distant when night came and swallowed it up; and all night I toiled to keep my blaze bright and high, and the eyes of the Beasts shone out of the darkness, marvelling. In the dawn, the sail was nearer, and I saw it was the dirty lug-sail of a small boat. But it sailed strangely. My eyes were weary with watching, and I peered and could not believe them. Two men were in the boat, sitting low down—one by the bows, the other at the rudder. The head was not kept to the wind; it yawed and fell away.

As the day grew brighter, I began waving the last rag of my jacket to them; but they did not notice me, and sat still, facing each other. I went to the lowest point of the low headland, and gesticulated and shouted. There was no response, and the boat kept on her aimless course, making slowly, very slowly, for the bay. Suddenly a great white bird flew up out of the boat,

---

1 A system for teaching handicrafts created by the Swedish educator Otto Salomon (1849-1907), a pioneer in establishing manual training as a regular part of elementary and secondary school curriculum. Intended to teach self-reliance and respect for work as well as manual dexterity, this system (often spelled Sloyd in English) attracted attention world-wide, and became especially popular in Britain and North America in the 1890s—see "Otto Salomon," Hans Thorbjörnsson, *Prospects: the Quarterly Review of Comparative Education*, 24, no. 3/4 (1994) 371-85.

and neither of the men stirred nor noticed it; it circled round, and then came sweeping overhead with its strong wings outspread.

Then I stopped shouting, and sat down on the headland and rested my chin on my hands and stared. Slowly, slowly, the boat drove past towards the west. I would have swum out to it, but something—a cold, vague fear—kept me back. In the afternoon the tide stranded the boat, and left it a hundred yards or so to the westward of the ruins of the enclosure. The men in it were dead, had been dead so long that they fell to pieces when I tilted the boat on its side and dragged them out. One had a shock of red hair, like the captain of the *Ipecacuanha*, and a dirty white cap lay in the bottom of the boat.

As I stood beside the boat, three of the Beasts came slinking out of the bushes and sniffing towards me. One of my spasms of disgust came upon me. I thrust the little boat down the beach and clambered on board her. Two of the brutes were Wolf-beasts, and came forward with quivering nostrils and glittering eyes; the third was the horrible nondescript of bear and bull. When I saw them approaching those wretched remains, heard them snarling at one another and caught the gleam of their teeth, a frantic horror succeeded my repulsion. I turned my back upon them, struck the lug[1] and began paddling out to sea. I could not bring myself to look behind me.

I lay, however, between the reef and the island that night, and the next morning went round to the stream and filled the empty keg aboard with water. Then, with such patience as I could command, I collected a quantity of fruit, and waylaid and killed two rabbits with my last three cartridges. While I was doing this I left the boat moored to an inward projection of the reef, for fear of the Beast People.

22. THE MAN ALONE

In the evening I started, and drove out to sea before a gentle wind from the southwest, slowly, steadily; and the island grew smaller and smaller, and the lank spire of smoke dwindled to a finer and finer line against the hot sunset. The ocean rose up around me, hiding that low, dark patch from my eyes. The daylight, the trailing glory of the sun, went streaming out of the sky, was drawn aside like some luminous curtain, and at last I looked into the blue gulf of immensity which the sunshine hides, and saw the floating

---

1 Lowered the sail. Presumably, Prendick does not want to take the risk of sailing inside the coral reef.

hosts of the stars. The sea was silent, the sky was silent. I was alone with the night and silence.

So I drifted for three days, eating and drinking sparingly, and meditating upon all that had happened to me—not desiring very greatly then to see men again. One unclean rag was about me, my hair a black tangle: no doubt my discoverers thought me a madman.

It is strange, but I felt no desire to return to mankind. I was only glad to be quit of the foulness of the Beast People. And on the third day I was picked up by a brig from Apia[1] to San Francisco. Neither the captain nor the mate would believe my story, judging that solitude and danger had made me mad; and fearing their opinion might be that of others, I refrained from telling my adventure further, and professed to recall nothing that had happened to me between the loss of the *Lady Vain* and the time when I was picked up again—the space of a year.

I had to act with the utmost circumspection to save myself from the suspicion of insanity. My memory of the Law, of the two dead sailors, of the ambuscades of the darkness, of the body in the canebrake, haunted me; and, unnatural as it seems, with my return to mankind came, instead of that confidence and sympathy I had expected, a strange enhancement of the uncertainty and dread I had experienced during my stay upon the island. No one would believe me; I was almost as queer to men as I had been to the Beast People. I may have caught something of the natural wildness of my companions. They say that terror is a disease, and anyhow I can witness that for several years now a restless fear has dwelt in my mind—such a restless fear as a half-tamed lion cub may feel.

My trouble took the strangest form. I could not persuade myself that the men and women I met were not also another Beast People, animals half wrought into the outward image of human souls, and that they would presently begin to revert, to show first this bestial mark and then that. But I have confided my case to a strangely able man—a man who had known Moreau, and seemed half to credit my story; a mental specialist—and he has helped me mightily, though I do not expect that the terror of that island will ever altogether leave me. At most times it lies far in the back of my mind, a mere distant cloud, a memory, and a faint distrust; but there are times when the little cloud spreads until it obscures the whole sky. Then I look about me at my fellow-men; and I go in fear. I see faces keen

---

1 A port on the island of Upolu in Western Samoa. Philmus says that the course usually followed by sailing ships heading across the Pacific to San Francisco would likely have passed through the area in which Prendick is sailing (variorum *Moreau*, note 72, p. 99).

and bright; others dull or dangerous; others, unsteady, insincere—none that have the calm authority of a reasonable soul. I feel as though the animal was surging up through them; that presently the degradation of the Island-ers will be played over again on a larger scale. I know this is an illusion; that these seeming men and women about me are indeed men and women, men and women for ever, perfectly reasonable creatures, full of human desires and tender solicitude, emancipated from instinct and the slaves of no fantastic Law—beings altogether different from the Beast Folk. Yet I shrink from them, from their curious glances, their inquiries and assistance, and long to be away from them and alone.[1] For that reason I live near the broad free downland,[2] and can escape thither when this shadow is over my soul; and very sweet is the empty downland then, under the wind-swept sky.

When I lived in London the horror was well-nigh insupportable. I could not get away from men: their voices came through windows; locked doors were flimsy safeguards. I would go out into the streets to fight with my delusion, and prowling women would mew after me; furtive, craving men glance jealously at me; weary, pale workers go coughing by me with tired eyes and eager paces, like wounded deer dripping blood; old people, bent and dull, pass murmuring to themselves; and, all unheeding, a ragged tail of gibing children. Then I would turn aside into some chapel—and even there, such was my disturbance, it seemed that the preacher gibbered "Big Thinks," even as the Ape-man had done; or into some library, and there the intent faces over the books seemed but patient creatures wait-ing for prey. Particularly nauseous were the blank, expressionless faces of people in trains and omnibuses; they seemed no more my fellow-creatures than dead bodies would be, so that I did not dare to travel unless I was assured of being alone. And even it seemed that I too was not a reasonable creature, but only an animal tormented with some strange disorder in its brain which sent it to wander alone, like a sheep stricken with gid.[3]

This is a mood, however, that comes to me now, I thank God, more rarely. I have withdrawn myself from the confusion of cities and multitudes, and spend my days surrounded by wise books—bright windows in this life

---

1 This state of mind resembles Gulliver's identification of humans with the Yahoos when he returns from his final voyage in *Gulliver's Travels*, though Gulliver admits the identi-fication while Prendick resists it.

2 High, open rolling country, especially in southern England, usually covered with grass and sometimes used as pasture. Also called the Downs.

3 A brain disease of sheep that causes them to stagger and walk in circles.

of ours, lit by the shining souls of men. I see few strangers, and have but a small household. My days I devote to reading and to experiments in chemistry, and I spend many of the clear nights in the study of astronomy. There is—though I do not know how there is or why there is—a sense of infinite peace and protection in the glittering hosts of heaven.[1] There it must be, I think, in the vast and eternal laws of matter, and not in the daily cares and sins and troubles of men, that whatever is more than animal within us must find its solace and its hope. I *hope*, or I could not live.

And so, in hope and solitude, my story ends.

EDWARD PRENDICK

Note[2] [by H.G. Wells]

The substance of the chapter entitled "Dr. Moreau Explains," which contains the essential idea of the story, appeared as a middle article in the *Saturday Review* in January 1895. This is the only portion of this story that has been previously published, and it has been entirely recast to adapt it to the narrative form. Strange as it may seem to the unscientific reader, there can be no denying that, whatever amount of credibility attaches to the detail of this story, the manufacture of monsters—and perhaps even of quasi-human monsters—is within the possibilities of vivisection.

---

1   In *The Time Machine*, the Time Traveller also finds consolation in the eternal recurrence suggested by the stars in the night sky (chapter 10).

2   Wells here refers to an essay on the possibilities of vivisection, entitled "The Limits of Individual Plasticity." He also gives Moreau a number of ideas from an essay he published in 1894, entitled "The Province of Pain"—see Appendix H.

Appendix A: Wells on Wells

From H.G. Wells, *Experiment in Autobiography: Discoveries and Conclusions of a Very Ordinary Brain (Since 1866)*. 2 Vols. London: Gollancz and Cresset Press, 1934

[Wells's autobiography, written in his late sixties, focuses on the development of his political ideas but also gives an informative account of his childhood, educational activities, and development as a writer, especially up to the publication of *The Time Machine*.

Some of Wells's responses to his early reading in Natural History may indicate a childhood fear of animals, and of apes in particular, that later lurked beneath his enthusiasm for the theory of evolution. Prendick says that when he saw Montgomery's servant M'ling against the night sky, "that black figure, with its eyes of fire, struck down through all my adult thoughts and feelings, and for a moment the forgotten horrors of childhood came back to my mind" (84; ch. 4).

Since the religion of the Beast People in *Moreau* seems a satire on Christian theology—Wells himself called the story a "theological grotesque" and "an exercise in youthful blasphemy" (see Appendices B2 and B3)—some passages selected here describe Well's early hostility towards religion. While the religion of the Beast People seems mainly an attack on the Puritan side of Protestantism, Wells's criticism of Catholicism in his autobiography may be reflected in the hypnotic use of group ritual in the recitation of the Law—perhaps Catholicism seen from a Protestant bias.

Wells gives a glowing account of his encounter with T.H. Huxley in the "Normal School of Science." The final selection on his experience there reveals, however, that for all his enthusiasm for science and praise for Darwin and Huxley, he preferred reading the prophetic books of William Blake to the study of geology. Wells ended his career at the School by failing the exam in geology.]

[A lucky break and some early reading in Natural History]

My leg was broken for me when I was between seven and eight. Probably I am alive today and writing this autobiography instead of being a worn-out, dismissed and already dead shop-assistant, because my leg was broken....

I had just taken to reading.... [Among the many books I read in convalescence] was Wood's *Natural History* ... copiously illustrated and full of exciting and terrifying facts. I conceived a profound fear of the gorilla, of which there was a fearsome picture, which came out of the book at times after dark and followed me noiselessly about the house. The half landing was a favourite lurking place for this terror. I passed it whistling, but wary and then ran for my life up the next flight.... (I: 76-77)

[Early hostility to religion]

I was indeed a prodigy of Early Impiety. I was scared by Hell, I did not at first question the existence of Our Father, but no fear nor terror could prevent my feeling that his All Seeing Eye was that of an Old Sneak and that the Atonement for which I had to be so grateful was either an imposture, a trick of sham self-immolation, or a crazy nightmare. I felt the unsoundness of these things before I dared to think it....

I feared Hell dreadfully for some time. Hell was indeed good enough to scare me and prevent me calling either of my brothers fools, until I was eleven or twelve. But one night I had a dream of Hell so preposterous that it blasted that undesirable resort out of my mind for ever. In an old number of *Chambers Journal*[1] I had read of the punishment of breaking a man on the wheel. The horror of it got into my dreams and there was Our Father in a particularly malignant phase, busy basting a poor broken sinner rotating slowly over a fire built under the wheel. I saw no Devil in the vision; my mind in its simplicity went straight to the responsible fountain head. That dream pursued me into the day time. Never had I hated God so intensely.

And then suddenly the light broke through to me and I knew this God was a lie.... (I: 66-67)

[During his apprenticeship at a drapery establishment, Wells began to develop the idea that organized religion plays an important role in maintaining an oppressive social system.]

Somewhen during my stay at Portsmouth my mother wrote to me about my confirmation as a Member of the Church of England ... and that I was to go to the Vicar of Portsmouth to be prepared.... I told the Vicar that I believed in Evolution and that I could not understand upon that hypothesis, when it was that the Fall had occurred. The vicar did not meet my objections but warned me against the sin of presumption....

One picture of this last phase of critical suspense about the quality and significance of Christianity still stands out in my mind. It is a memory of a popular preacher preaching one Sunday evening in the Portsmouth Roman Catholic cathedral.... The theme was the extraordinary merit of Our Saviour's sacrifice and the horror and torment of hell from which he had

---

1 *Chambers Journal of Popular Literature, Science, and Art* was an inexpensive magazine with wide popular readership.

saved the elect. The Preacher ... was enjoying himself thoroughly. He spared us nothing of hell's dreadfulness. All the pain and anguish of life as we knew it, every suffering we had ever experienced or imagined, or read about, was as nothing to one moment in the unending black despair of hell. And so on. For a little while his accomplished volubility carried me with him and then my mind broke into amazement and contempt. This was my old childish nightmare of God and the flaming wheel; this was the sort of thing to scare ten year olds.... A real fear of Christianity assailed me.... (I: 162-64)

It marks a new phase in mental development when one faces ideas not simply as ideas but as ideas embodied in architecture and usage and every-day material fact, and still resists. Hitherto I had taken churches and cathedrals as being as much a part of indisputable reality as my hands and feet. They had imposed themselves upon me as a necessary part of urban scenery just as I had taken Windsor Castle and Eton College as natural growths of the Thames valley.[1] But somehow this Portsmouth Cathedral, perhaps because it had been newly built and so seemed more active than a time-worn building, took on the quality of an engine rather than an edifice. It was a big disseminator; it was one of that preacher's gestures tempered and made into a permanent implement; it was there to put hell and fear and submission into people's minds. And from this starting apprehension, my realization that all religious buildings are in reality kinetic,[2] spread out more and more widely to all the other visible things of human life. They were all, I began to see dimly, ideas,—ideas clothed and armed with substance. It was impossible just to say that there was no hell and no divine Trinity and no atonement, and then leave these things alone, as to declare myself republican[3] or claim a right to an equal education with everyone else, without moving towards a clash with Windsor and Eton. These things existed and there was no denying it. If I denied the ideas they substantiated then I proposed to push them off my earth; no less. (I: 166-67)

[Education in science]

The day when I walked from my lodging in Westbourne Park across Kensington Gardens to the Normal School of Science,[4] signed on at the entrance to that burly red-brick and terra-cotta building and went up by the

---

1 Windsor Castle is a residence of the royal family; Eton is an exclusive boarding school with a special relation to Oxford University. Both are near the river Thames.
2 A term from physics: energy becomes kinetic rather than potential when it causes objects to move.
3 Opposed to monarchy as a form of government.
4 Later named the Royal College of Science.

lift to the biological laboratory was one of the great days of my life. All my science hitherto had been second hand—or third or fourth hand ... Here I was under the shadow of Huxley, the acutest observer, the ablest generalizer, the great teacher, the most lucid and valiant of controversialists. I had been assigned to his course in Elementary Biology and afterwards I was to go on with Zoology under him....

The study of zoology ... was an acute, delicate, rigorous and sweepingly magnificent series of exercises. It was a grammar of form and a criticism of fact. That year I spent in Huxley's class, was beyond all question, the most educational year of my life. It left me under that urgency for coherence and consistency, that repugnance from haphazard assumptions and arbitrary statements, which is the essential distinction of the educated from the uneducated mind.

I worked very hard indeed throughout that first year....

[Darwin and Huxley] were two very great men. They thought boldly, carefully and simply, they spoke and wrote fearlessly and plainly, they lived modestly and decently; they were mighty intellectual liberators.... Darwin and Huxley, in their place and measure, belong to the same aristocracy as Plato, and Aristotle and Galileo, and they will ultimately dominate the priestly and orthodox mind as surely, because there is a response, however reluctant, masked and stifled, in every human soul to rightness and a firmly stated truth. (I: 199-203)

[In his third and final year at the School, Wells neglects his studies in Geology for other reading.]

I had just discovered the heady brew of Carlyle's *French Revolution* and the prophetic works of William Blake. Every day I went off with my notebooks and textbooks to either the Dyce and Foster Reading Room or the Art Library. I would work hard, I decided, for two hours, abstracting notes, getting the stuff in order—and then as a treat it should be (let us say) half an hour of Carlyle (whose work I kept at my disposal in the Dyce and Foster) or Blake (in the Art Reading Room).... But long before the two hours were up a frightful lassitude, a sort of petrographic nausea, a surfeit of minerals, would supervene....There, ready to hand on the table, was a folder of Blake's strange tinted designs; his lank-haired rugose gods, his upward whirling spirits, his strained, contorted powers of light and darkness. What exactly was Blake getting at in this stuff about "Albion"? He seemed to have everything to say and Judd [Professor of Geology] seemed to have nothing to say. Almost subconsciously, the note-books and textbooks drew themselves apart into a shocked little heap and the riddles of Blake opened of their own accord before me. (I: 241)

Appendix B: Wells on Moreau and Science Fiction

1. From Arthur H. Lawrence. "The Romance of the Scientist: An Interview with Mr. H.G. Wells." *The Young Man*, No. 128 (London, August 1897): 254-57

[This brief comment is of special interest because it comes from the period when Wells was writing his science fiction; the interview took place only a year after *Moreau* was published. The other comments by Wells on *Moreau* provided here come from prefaces written much later.

At this time, being asked which of his books "represents his best work," Wells had published only three other works of fiction: *The Time Machine*, *The Wonderful Visit* (a romance in which an angel visits an English village), and *The Wheels of Chance* (a humorous novel about a draper's assistant on a cycling holiday). The last two are slighter works than *Moreau*. On the other hand, Wells's placing *Moreau* above *The Time Machine*, a very popular story with a serious philosophical intent, shows that in 1897 he took *Moreau* very seriously indeed.

Wells's mention of "The *Guardian* critic" likely refers to the detailed and sympathetic review of *Moreau* printed in the *Manchester Guardian*, rather than the one in *The Guardian*, a lesser-known Anglican weekly whose reviewer complained of the story's blasphemous intent. See excerpts from both reviews in Appendix C.]

[The interviewer asks Wells which of his published works he considers the best.] "If I must return a true answer to your searching question, I should say that *The Island of Dr. Moreau*, although it was written in a great hurry and is marred by many faults, is the best work I have done. It has been stupidly dealt with—as a mere shocker—by people who ought to have known better. The *Guardian* critic seemed to be the only one who read it aright, and who therefore succeeded in giving a really intelligent notice of it." (256)

2. From H.G. Wells, "Preface." *The Works of H.G. Wells*. Vol. 2. *The Island of Doctor Moreau, The Sleeper Awakes*. New York: Charles Scribner's Sons, 1924. ix-xiii

[Later in his career Wells tended to a condescending and rather distant attitude towards his science fiction. His later comments, however interesting, may not be entirely accurate. His characterization here of *Moreau* as a "theological grotesque" seems a clear indication of an intent to satirize religion in the tale. On the other hand, his implication that the story was inspired by the fall of Oscar Wilde—"the graceless and pitiful downfall of a man of genius"—seems rather puzzling as Wilde's writing seems quite different from Moreau's science. Philmus argues that by the time of Wilde's trials for homosexuality—April and May of 1895—Wells was well into writing the final version of Moreau. I would add that a complete account of Moreau's public exposure as a vivisectionist is given in Wells's first draft of Moreau, written late in 1894 (variorum Moreau xviii, xliii, 114). Perhaps in Wilde's ruin Wells found not the original inspiration for his story but confirmation of its Darwinian view of human nature, and nearly thirty years later was not quite accurate in remembering which came first.]

"The Island of Doctor Moreau" was written in 1895, and it was begun while "The Wonderful Visit" was still in hand. It is a theological grotesque, and the influence of Swift is very apparent in it. There was a scandalous trial about that time, the graceless and pitiful downfall of a man of genius, and this story was the response of an imaginative mind to the reminder that humanity is but animal rough-hewn to a reasonable shape and in perpetual internal conflict between instinct and injunction.[1] This story embodies this ideal, but apart from this embodiment it has no allegorical quality. It was written just to give the utmost possible vividness to that conception of men as hewn and confused and tormented beasts. When the reader comes to read the writings upon history in this collection, he will find the same idea of man as a re-shaped animal no longer in flaming caricature, but as a weighed and settled conviction. (ix)

3. From H.G. Wells, "Preface." *The Scientific Romances of H.G. Wells*. London: Gollancz, 1933. vii–x. (Published in America in 1934 as *Seven Famous Novels*)

[This preface provides an important statement of Wells's method of establishing the reality of his science fiction, and his sense of its relation to a literary tradition. The distinction from the predictive fantasy of Jules Verne, the use of the techniques of fictional realism once the "impossible hypothesis" of the story has been established, the substitution of scientific discourse for supernatural terror, and the tendency to Swiftian social criticism, are all important to the emergence of science fiction as a modern genre. On the other hand, his reference to "scientific patter" does not do justice to the philosophical themes evoked by the use of science in his stories. Also, as we see in Wells's letter in Appendix C2, he wanted the scientific basis of Doctor Moreau's experiments to be taken seriously.

---

1   "Injunction" here means the rules of morality. This view of human nature seems very Huxleyan.

In the second paragraph Wells gives a list of fantastic narratives, ranging from ancient Rome to the nineteenth century, as precedents for his kind of fantasy. All the listed authors are interested in social reality and most have a satiric tendency. As a writer of science fiction, Wells saw himself as working within a definable genre with roots in classical antiquity. This type of narrative has sometimes been called "Menippean satire"—a genre originating in ancient Greece which parodies and produces fantastic versions of traditional literary genres.]

Mr. Gollancz has asked me to write a preface to this collection of my fantastic stories. They are put in chronological order, but let me say here right at the beginning of the book, that for anyone who does not as yet know anything of my work it will probably be more agreeable to begin with *The Invisible Man* or *The War of the Worlds*. *The Time Machine* is a little bit stiff about the fourth dimension and *The Island of Dr. Moreau* rather painful.

These tales have been compared with the work of Jules Verne and there was a disposition on the part of literary journalists at one time to call me the English Jules Verne. As a matter of fact there is no literary resemblance whatever between the anticipatory inventions of the great Frenchman and these fantasies. His work dealt almost always with actual possibilities of invention and discovery, and he made some remarkable forecasts. The interest he invoked was a practical one; he wrote and believed and told that this or that thing could be done, which was not at that time done. He helped his reader to imagine it done and to realize what fun, excitement or mischief would ensue. Many of his inventions have "come true." But these stories of mine collected here do not pretend to deal with possible things; they are exercises of the imagination in a quite different field. They belong to a class of writing which includes the *Golden Ass of Apuleius*,[1] the *True Histories of Lucian*,[2] *Peter Schlemil*[3] and the story of *Frankenstein*.[4] It includes too some admirable

---

1   Also known as *Metamorphoses*, a comic novel by by Lucius Apuleius (fl. ca. 155 AD). Its central theme is transformation from human to animal and back again: the narrator is turned into a donkey by accident during an amateur foray into magic and undergoes a series of degrading (and very amusing) adventures before he can regain human form.

2   A fantastic journey, parodying travellers' tales, that begins with a warning that its adventures are not true and could not possibly have happened. A contemporary of Apuleius, Lucian was a famous satirist who parodied classical genres.

3   *Peter Schlemihl's Remarkable Story* (1814) by German poet and botanist Adalbert von Chamisso (1781-1838). Its hero is a young man who sells his shadow to the devil and then finds that without his shadow he becomes a social outcast.

4   Mary Shelley's famous story, published in 1818, of an overreaching scientist who creates an artificial monster and then rejects him. It has important affinities with *Moreau*.

inventions by Mr. David Garnett, *Lady into Fox*[1] for instance. They are all fantasies; they do not aim to project a serious possibility; they aim indeed only at the same amount of conviction as one gets in a good gripping dream. They have to hold the reader to the end by art and illusion and not by proof and argument, and the moment he closes the cover and reflects he wakes up to their impossibility....

In all this type of story the living interest lies in their non-fantastic elements and not in the invention itself. They are appeals for human sympathy quite as much as any "sympathetic" novel, and the fantastic element, the strange property or the strange world, is used only to throw up and intensify our natural reactions of wonder, fear, or perplexity.... The thing that makes such imaginations interesting is their translation into commonplace terms and a rigid exclusion of other marvels from the story. Then it becomes human....

For the writer of fantastic stories to help the reader to play the game properly, he must help him in every possible unobtrusive way to *domesticate* [Wells's emphasis] the impossible hypothesis. He must trick him into an unwary concession to some plausible assumption and get on with his story while the illusion holds. And that is where there was a certain slight novelty in my stories when they first appeared. Hitherto, except in exploration fantasies, the fantastic element was brought in by magic. Frankenstein even, used some jiggery-pokery magic to animate his artificial monster. There was trouble about the thing's soul. But by the end of the last century it had become difficult to squeeze even a momentary belief out of magic any longer. It occurred to me that instead of the usual interview with the devil or a magician, an ingenious use of scientific patter might with advantage be substituted. That was no great discovery. I simply brought the fetish stuff up to date, and made it as near actual theory as possible....

My early, profound and lifelong admiration for Swift, appears again and again in this collection, and it is particularly evident in a predisposition to make the stories reflect upon contemporary political and social discussions....

For some years I produced one or more of these "scientific fantasies," as they were called, every year. In my student days we were much exercised by talk about a possible fourth dimension of space; the fairly obvious idea that events could be presented in a rigid four dimensional space time framework had occurred to me, and this is used as the magic trick for a glimpse of the future [in *The Time Machine*] that ran counter to the placid assumption of that time that Evolution was a pro-human force making

---

1 The 1922 story of irreversible transformation of human into animal, much admired by Wells but published far too late to have influenced *Moreau*.

things better and better for mankind. *The Island of Dr. Moreau* is an exercise in youthful blasphemy. Now and then, though I rarely admit it, the universe projects itself towards me in a hideous grimace. It grimaced that time, and I did my best to express my vision of the aimless torture in creation. *The War of the Worlds*, like *The Time Machine* was another assault on human self-satisfaction.

All these three books are consciously grim, under the influence of Swift's tradition.... (vii–ix)

Appendix C: Contemporary Reviews

1. Chalmers Mitchell, *The Saturday Review of Politics, Literature, Science and Art* (11 April 1896), lxxxi. 368-69

[Despite the conventional literary taste manifested in his disapproval of the horrors of the story, the reviewer's scientific perspective and interest in Wells as a writer may make this the most thought-provoking of the early reviews of *Moreau*. Sir Peter Chalmers Mitchell (1864-1945) became a well-known zoologist and also wrote a biography of Huxley. When he wrote this review he was a colleague of Wells on the staff of *The Saturday Review*. Writing as a scientist as well as a literary critic, Mitchell expresses surprise at Wells's gruesome presentation of vivisection, as though Wells were writing on the anti-scientific side of the debate over vivisection. Mitchell also notes the problematic role of pain in the story, asks why Doctor Moreau doesn't use anaesthesia, and questions the validity of the science behind Moreau's project. Wells's letter replying to the last point follows Mitchell's review.]

Those who have delighted in the singular talent of Mr. Wells will read *The Island of Doctor Moreau* with dismay. We have all been saying that here is an author with the emotions of an artist and the intellectual imagination of a scientific investigator. He has given us in *The Time Machine* a diorama of prophetic visions of the dying earth, imagined with a pitiless logic, and yet filled with a rare beauty, sometimes sombre and majestic, sometimes shining with fantastic grace.... Behind these high gifts, behind the simple delight of his story-telling, there has seemed to lie a reasoned attitude to life, a fine seriousness that one at least conjectures to be the background of the greater novelists. When the prenatal whispers of "The Island of Doctor Moreau" reached me, I rejoiced at the promise of another novel with a scientific basis, and I accepted gladly the opportunity given me to say something of it, from the scientific point of view, as well as from that of a devoted novel-reader. But, instead of being able to lay my little wreath at the feet of Mr. Wells, I have to confess the frankest dismay.

For Mr. Wells has put out his talent to the most flagitious usury.[1] His central idea is a modelling of the human frame and endowment of it with some semblance of humanity, by plastic operations upon living animals. The possibilities of grafting and moulding, of shaping the limbs and larynx and

---

1   Literally, lending money at a criminally high rate of interest. Mitchell implies that Wells has abused his literary talent by investing it entirely in the production of sensational effects.

brain, of transfusing blood, of changing physiological rhythm, and vague suggestions of hypnotizing dawning intelligence with the elemental rules of human society—these would seem to offer a rich vein to be worked by Mr. Wells's logical fancy. They are, indeed, finely imagined, and the story of the hero, suddenly brought into an island peopled with such nightmare creatures, is vivid and exciting to the last degree. To realize them, you must read of the bewilderment and horror of the hero, while he thinks the creatures are men outraged and distorted: of his fear for his own fate at the hands of the artificer of the unnatural: of his gradual acquaintance with the real nature of the monsters: of his new horror at the travesties of human form and mind: of the perils that begin when the 'stubborn beast-flesh' has overcome the engrafted humanity, and the population risen in rebellion against its creator. All this is excellent; but the author, during the inception of his story, like his own creatures, has tasted blood. The usurious interest began when the author, not content with the horror inevitable in his idea, and yet congruous with the fine work he has given us hitherto, sought out revolting details with the zeal of a sanitary inspector probing a crowded graveyard.[1]

You begin with a chromolithographic[2] shipwreck, and three starving survivors playing odd-man-out for a cannibal feast. The odd man breaks faith, and, in the resulting struggle, the hero is left alone in a blood-bespattered boat. When he is rescued, a drunken doctor, no doubt disinclined to change the supposed diet,[3] restores him with a draught of iced blood. When the island is reached he is not allowed by Mr. Wells to land until, refused hospitality by Dr. Moreau and cast adrift by the drunken captain, he has again meditated upon starvation, this time without any mates for whose blood he may pass halfpence. Dr. Moreau himself is a *cliché* from the pages of an anti-vivisection pamphlet. He has been hounded out of London because a flayed dog (you hear the shuddering ladies handing over their guineas) has been liberated from his laboratory by a spying reporter.[4] It is the blood that Mr. Wells insists

---

1   In cities of Victorian England, especially London, the practice of stuffing bodies into overcrowded graveyards became a serious problem. Reports describing the gruesome consequences and the resulting threat to public health inspired wide controversy. Charles Dickens uses this material as a background to *Bleak House*.

2   Popular method of printing multi-colour illustrations. Unless applied with great technical expertise, the colours might seem somewhat unnatural, as for instance in illustrations for an adventure story in a cheap popular magazine.

3   Apparently referring to the cannibalism proposed in the boat.

4   Mitchell refers disapprovingly to the sale of pamphlets describing the horrors of the vivisector's laboratory to raise money for the anti-vivisection cause. As a scientist he is contemptuous of the anti-vivisection movement. Hence he feels that Wells, also an ally of science, is betraying the cause of science in using Moreau's surgery on living animals to generate horror.

upon forcing on us; blood in the sink 'brown and red,' on the floor, on the hands of the operators, on the bandages that swathe the creatures or that they have left hanging on the bushes—physically disgusting details inevitable in the most conservative surgery;[1] but still more unworthy of restrained art, and, in this case, of scientific *vraisemblance*,[2] is the insistence upon the terror and pains of the animals, on their screams under the knife, and on Dr. Moreau's indifference to the 'bath of pain' in which his victims were moulded and re-cast. Mr. Wells must know that the delicate, prolonged operations of modern surgery became possible only after the introduction of anaesthetics.[3] Equally wrong is the semi-psychological suggestion that pain could be a humanizing agency. It may be that the conscious subjection to pain for a purpose has a desirable mental effect; pain in itself, and above all continuous pain inflicted on a struggling, protesting creature, would produce only madness and death. Mr. Wells will not even get his hero out of the island decently. When Dr. Moreau has been killed by his latest victim—a puma become in the labora-tory 'not human, not animal, but hellish, brown, seamed with red branching scars, red drops starting out upon it'—Mr. Wells must needs bring in an alien horror. The 'boat from the machine'[4] drifts ashore with two dead men in it—men 'dead so long that they fell in pieces' when the hero dumped them out for the last of the island monsters to snarl over.

It may be that a constant familiarity with the ways and work of labora-tories has dulled my sense of the aesthetic possibilities of blood—anatomists, for the most part, wash their hands before they leave their work—and that a public attuned to Mr. Rider Haggard's view of the romantic may demand the insertion of details physically unpleasant;[5] but, for my own part, I feel that Mr. Wells has spoiled a fine conception by greed of cheap horrors. I beg of him, in the name of many, a return to his sane transmutations of the dull conceptions of science into the living and magical beauty he has already

---

1   Can mean either the operation or the room in which it is performed.

2   Convincingness; appearing to be true to life.

3   Anaesthesia became widely used in British hospitals after James Y. Simpson introduced the use of chloroform in 1847. By the end of the century anaesthesia was used routinely and with increasing sophistication.

4   An ironic twist of the phrase "a god from a machine," a literary term meaning an arbi-trary contrivance from beyond the main action. The term comes from the occasional use of a god who descends from heaven--lowered onto the stage by a "machine"--to arrange the ending of the play in ancient Greek drama; Mitchell suggests that Wells has contrived this ending for further gruesome effect.

5   H. Rider Haggard (1856-1925) wrote many popular stories of fantastic adventure, in-cluding *King Solomon's Mines* (1885) and *She* (1887). *She* provides some particularly grotesque effects, involving themes of cultural regression and degeneracy.

given us. We that have read his earlier stories will read all he chooses to write; but must he choose the spell of Circe?[1]

There remains to be said a word about the scientific conceptions underlying Dr. Moreau's experiments. I quite agree that there is scientific basis enough to form the plot of a story. But in an appended note, Mr. Wells is scaring the public unduly. He declares:—'There can be no denying that whatever amount of specific credibility attaches to the detail of this story, the manufacture of monsters—and perhaps even of *quasi*-human monsters—is within the possibilities of vivisection.' The most recent discussion of grafting and transfusion experiments is to be found in a treatise by Oscar Hertwig,[2] a translation of which Mr. Heinemann announces. Later investigators have failed to repeat the grafting experiments of Hunter,[3] and a multitude of experiments on skin and bone grafting and on transfusion of blood shows that animal-hybrids cannot be produced in these fashions. You can transfuse blood or graft skin from one man to another; but attempts to combine living material from different creatures fail.

2. Letter from H.G. Wells to Chalmers Mitchell, the Editor of *The Saturday Review of Politics, Literature, Science and Art* (1 November 1896), 497

[Seven months after the publication of Mitchell's review, Wells wrote this letter refuting the argument in its last paragraph that the science in the story was invalid because recent research had shown grafts of skin or tissue between species to be impossible. As Wells explains, he delayed in replying until he had found scientific evidence to counter Mitchell's assertion. Mitchell conceded Wells's point in an apology published a week later in the same journal.

This letter shows that Wells regarded the science in his fantasies as something more than just a means to make the story seem plausible to the reader. In an essay entitled "The Limits of Individual Plasticity," written at the same time as *Moreau*, Wells suggests that surgical grafting may grant freedom from the limits of physical evolution, an idea that he seems to share with his Doctor Moreau—see Appendix H2.]

---

1   In Greek mythology, an enchantress and seductive temptress who turns men into animals. Circe lives on an island inhabited by her victims, who become tame pets. In Book Ten of *The Odyssey* she turns Odysseus's sailors into swine; immune to her magic, Odysseus forces her to turn them back into men.
2   A German embryologist (1849-1922) who studied the interaction of cells in living tissue.
3   A reference to John Hunter (1728-93), a famous English surgeon who raised surgery to the level of a scientific discipline, and who also conducted many experiments on living animals, including grafts of tissue from one species to another. Doctor Moreau cites him as a predecessor in his explanation to Prendick in chapter 14.

Sir, In a special article in the "Saturday Review" of 11 April, 1896, reviewing my "Island of Dr. Moreau", Mr. Chalmers Mitchell, in addition to certain literary criticisms, which rest upon their merits, gave the lie direct to a statement of mine that the grafting of tissues between animals of different species is possible. This was repeated more elaborately in "Natural Science", and from these centres of distribution passed into the provincial press, where it was amplified to my discredit in various, animated, but to me, invariably painful phrasing. And the contradiction, with implication of headlong ignorance it conveys, is now traversing the continent of America (where phrasing is often very vivid indeed)....

I was aware at the time that Mr. Chalmers Mitchell was mistaken in relying upon Oscar Hertwig as his final authority upon this business, that he was making the rash assertion and not I, but for a while I was unable to replace the stigma of ignorance he had given me, for the simple reason that I knew of no published results of the kind I needed. But the "British Medical Journal" for 31 October, 1896, contains the report of a successful graft, by Mr. Mayo Robson, not merely of connective tissue between rabbit and man. I trust, therefore, that "Natural Science" will now modify its statement concerning my book, and the gentlemen of the provincial press who waxed scornful, and even abusive, on Mr. Chalmers Mitchell's authority, will now wax apologetic. There is quite enough to misunderstand and abuse in the story without any further application of this little mistake of Mr. Chalmers Mitchell's.

Yours, very truly,
H. G. Wells

3. [R.H. Hutton], *Spectator* (11 April 1896), lxxvi, 519-20

[This review bears out Mitchell's charge that *The Island of Doctor Moreau* could be taken as an anti-vivisection pamphlet. The reviewer provides one of the few favourable reviews of *Moreau* and excuses all its horrors because he takes it for an attack on vivisection. Richard Holt Hutton (1826-97), theologian, intellectual journalist, and editor of the *Spectator*, wielded considerable influence in British intellectual culture. A passionate anti-vivisectionist, he did much to keep the issue of vivisection before the public through the late nineteenth century. As a member of the Royal Commission on vivisection (1875-76) Hutton became a vocal opponent of T.H. Huxley (the most forceful representative of science on the Commission), especially over the question of using vivisection for pure research. Hutton opposed the scientific, agnostic rationalism represented by Huxley, as well as his stand on vivisection. There is some irony in Hutton taking Huxley's disciple, the young Wells, as a writer on the anti-science side of the controversy.]

The ingenious author of *The Time Machine* has found in this little book a subject exactly suited to his rather peculiar type of imagination.... [T]he impossibility is of a less unworkable order [than that of *The Time Machine*], though it is also much more gruesome. He has taken a few of the leading methods of the modern surgery and exaggerated them in the hands of an accomplished vivisector into a new physiological calculus that enables its professor to transmute various animals into the semblance of man.... (519)

Of course, the real value for literary purposes of this ghastly conception depends on the power of the author to make his readers realize the half-way stages between the brute and the rational creature, with which he has to deal. And we must admit that Mr. Wells succeeds in this little story in giving a most fearful vividness to his picture of half-created monsters endowed with a little speech, a little human curiosity, a little sense of shame, and an overgrown dread of the pain and terror which the scientific dabbler in creative processes had inflicted. There is nothing in Swift's grim conceptions of animalized man and rationalized animals[1] more powerfully conceived than Mr. Wells's description of these deformed and malformed creations of Dr. Moreau, repeating the litany in which they abase themselves before the psychological demigod by whom they have been endowed with their new powers of speech, their new servility to a human master, and their profound dread of that 'house of pain' in which they have been made and fashioned into half-baked men.... (519)

It is, of course, a very ingenious caricature of what has been done in certain exceptional efforts of human surgery,—a caricature inspired by the fanaticism of a foul ambition to remake God's creatures by confusing and transfusing and remoulding human and animal organs so as to extinguish so far as possible the chasm which divides man from brute. Mr. Wells has had the prudence, too, not to dwell on the impossibilities of his subject too long. He gives us a very slight, though a very powerful and ghastly, picture, and may, we hope, have done more to render vivisection unpopular, and that contempt for animal pain, which enthusiastic physiologists seem to feel, hideous, than all the efforts of the societies which have been organized for that wholesome and beneficent end. Dr. Moreau is a figure to make an impression on the imagination, and his tragic death under the attack of the puma which he has been torturing so long, has a kind of poetic justice in it which satisfies the mind of the reader. Again, the picture of a rapid reversion to the brute, of the victims which Dr. Moreau had so painfully fashioned, so soon as

---

1 A reference to the species of rational horses (the Houyhnhnms) and the degraded but human-like Yahoos in Part IV of *Gulliver's Travels*—an important source for *Moreau*.

the terrors of his 'house of pain' are withdrawn, is very impressively painted. Altogether, though we do not recommend *The Island of Doctor Moreau* to readers of sensitive nerves, as it might well haunt them only too powerfully, we believe that Mr. Wells has almost rivalled Swift in the power of his very gruesome, but very salutary as well as impressive, conception. (520)

4. *Manchester Guardian* (14 April 1896), 4

[This is probably the review mentioned in Wells's interview with Arthur Lawrence (Appendix B1) where he praises "the *Guardian* critic ... who seemed to be the only one to read [the story] aright, and who therefore succeeded in giving a really intelligent notice of it."]

In *The Island of Doctor Moreau* Mr. H.G. Wells gains our attention at once by the closeness and vigour of his narrative style and by his terse and natural dialogue. His realism of detail is, in fact, the sign of imagination. It is full of skilful and subtle touches, and, harrowing as is the whole effect, he cannot be accused of forcing the note beyond the limits of his conception by any irrelevant accumulation of horrors. But this curious fantasy, with its quasi-scientific foundation, in which a doctor upon a remote island practises vivisection in the spirit of a modern and unsentimental Frankenstein, is intrinsically horrible. The impressions should not be put to the test of analysis or reflection. As it is, they grip the mind with a painful interest and a fearful curiosity. The mysteries of the forbidden enclosure; the cries of the tortured puma; the pursuit through the dark wood by the leopard man; the strange litany of the beast folk; Prendick's flight and frantic apprehensions; the revolt of the beast folk—such scenes and incidents crowd upon us with a persistent fascination. Absolute success in such a narrative is impossible; to play these curious tricks with science is not the highest art; it might even be contended that this is no legitimate subject for art at all; but in its kind Mr. Wells has achieved a success unquestionable and extraordinary. There must be, of course, a weak place where science and fantasy join. To obscure this plausibly is the great difficulty, and we think that here, as too in *Dr. Jekyll and Mr. Hyde*, there is some little creaking of the machinery. But if the chapter 'Dr. Moreau Explains' brings us dangerously near a too critical habit of mind, it is full of striking things—the masterful, overbearing manner of the Doctor, his dreadful plausibility in maintaining his impossible position, his perfect devotion to investigation, the fine contempt for both pleasure and pain which enables him to make the effective counterstroke of accusing his opponent of materialism. 'The study of nature makes a man at last as remorseless as nature,' he says, and with Prendick we are thrown on our resources to combat this appalling inversion....

But though the reader of this book must sup full of horrors, it must not be supposed that there are no mitigations and no relief. There is a grotesque pathos about the beast folk which redeems them, and Montgomery, a character very much in Mr. Stevenson's manner, is reassuring and quite human in his vulgarity. The effect of the final chapter, 'The Man Alone', is admirable, and that he should find solace and a 'sense of infinite peace and protection' in the study of the stars is one of the many points that differentiate Mr. Wells from the mere sensational story-spinner. Yet, great as is the ability and pronounced as is the success of this book, we are convinced that Mr. Wells is too strong and original a writer to devote himself exclusively to fantastic themes.

5. *The Guardian* (3 June 1896), 871

[This *Guardian* is an Anglican weekly. The reviewer is impressed by the book without liking it, and sees that it can be taken as an attack on religion. Of all reviewers, this one has the clearest sense of the story as a "theological grotesque," as Wells later called it.]

The Island of Doctor Moreau is an exceedingly ghastly book; of which it is not altogether easy to divine the intention. Dr. Moreau is a vivisectionist who has the strange and horrible ambition to manufacture men out of animals by means of hideous operations He lives on an island with an entirely human confederate and a rout of semi-human attendants and subjects of his own manufacturing, until accident throws in his way a ship-wrecked man, who very much against his own will finds himself obliged to stay also on the island. This man is supposed to write the story of the horrors he is compelled to witness, and very repulsive much of his story is. Sometimes one is inclined to think the intention of the author has been to satirise and rebuke the presumption of science; at other times his object seems to be to parody the work of the Creator of the human race, and cast contempt upon the dealings of God with His creatures. This is the suggestion of the exceedingly clever and realistic scenes in which the humanized beasts recite the Law their human maker has given them, and show very plainly how impossible it is to them to keep that law. The inevitable reversion of these creatures to bestiality is very well described; but it ought to have been shown that they revert inevitably because they are only man-made creatures. The book is one no one could have the courage to recommend, and we are not inclined to commend it either. It is certainly unpleasant and painful, and we cannot find it profitable. But it is undoubtedly a clever, original, and very powerful effort of the imagination.

6. The Times (17 June 1896), 17

[The review in The Times is typical of a number of reviews which con-demned the story without any acknowledgement of its intellectual content. In accusing the story of representing a perverse sensationalism in contem-porary literature from which the public must be protected, the Times review seems to classify it among "decadent" literature. This would be typical of the attitude of the conventional middle-class public after the fall of Oscar Wilde.]

We hesitate as to whether we ought to notice The Island of Dr. Moreau at all. We know that sending a book to the Index Expurgatorius[1] is a sure means of giving it a certain advertisement. Yet we feel bound to expostulate against a new departure which may lead we know not whither, and to give a word of warning to the unsuspecting who would shrink from the loathsome and repulsive. This novel is the strongest example we have met of the perverse quest after anything in any shape that is freshly sensational. Suffice it to say that the most cold-blooded of vivisectors, who years before, as he confesses, has lost all sense of sympathetic pain, makes a torture-hell of one of the love-liest isles in the Pacific. His vile experiments are doubly diabolical inasmuch as he imparts to his mangled victims so much of humanity as gives them the fullest sense of their sufferings and degradation. The ghastly fancies are likely to haunt and cling, and so the book should be kept out of the way of young people and avoided by all who have good taste, good feeling, or feeble nerves. It is simple sacrilege to steep fair nature in the blood and antiseptics of the vivisecting anatomical theatre.

7. The Review of Reviews. Ed. W.T. Stead. 13 (July–December 1895): 374

[This review finds a disturbing sexual implication in the confusion between human and animal manifested in the "hybrid monsters" of the story. W.T. Stead (1849-1912) was a controversial crusading journalist, best known as the author of a series of articles, entitled the "Maiden Tribute of Modern Babylon" (1885), exposing exploitation of children and young women in the prostitution trade in London. No name is given for the authorship of the review section of Stead's journal—the "Monthly Parcel of Books" suppos-edly being sent to a friend—but this response to Moreau partakes of Stead's characteristic combination of strong Puritan morality, fascination with sexual vice, and reforming zeal. All emphases are those of the author.]

---

1 "The List of Prohibited Books" that the faithful were forbidden to read. This was published by the Roman Catholic Church beginning in the sixteenth century.

[The "frontispiece" (an illustration facing the title page) is a depiction of Prendick watching the Pig People (chapter nine) which appeared in the first English edition of *Moreau*.]

" I could not distinguish what he said."

Frontispiece of the first British edition.
Reproduced with the permission of the Rare Book &
Manuscript Library of the University of Urbana-Champaign.

To turn now to some of the novels I send—although I will first mention one that I do *not* send—Mr. H.G. Wells's "The Island of Dr. Moreau" (Heinemann, 6s). No one admires the peculiar genius of Mr. Wells more than I. He is a born psychic, with a marvellous gift of realistically rendering his psychic experiences. But the frontispiece alone of his new story is enough to keep it out of circulation. The law against sex [*sic*] intercourse with animals may be, and is, unduly severe, but it is an offense against humanity to represent the result of the intermingling of man and beast. In Mr. Wells's story the hybrid monsters are not begotten: they are represented as the possible outcome of vivisectional experiment. But the result in the picture is exactly that which would follow as the result of the engendering of human and animal. It is loathsome.

Appendix D: Evolution and Struggle I: Classical Darwinism

1. From Alfred Tennyson, *In Memoriam*. London: Edward Moxon, 1850

[*In Memoriam* is a series of lyric poems, written between 1833 and 1849, describing Tennyson's grief for the death of a close friend, Arthur Hallam, and a crisis in faith resulting from this experience. Both sets of stanzas given here provide a remarkable foreshadowing of ideas and moods that would later be associated with Darwin's theory of evolution. Tennyson probably wrote sections 55 and 56 in the late 1830s, about twenty years before Darwin presented the concept of "natural selection" as the basic principle of evolution in *The Origin of Species* (1859). Here Tennyson is responding not to Darwin but to Charles Lyell's *Principles of Geology* (1830-33), which argues the antiquity of the earth and replaces Divine Creation with a physical process of evolution less specific than Darwin's. Section 118 was probably written several years later.

Sections 55 and 56 describe a mood of deep depression in response to the incongruity between human aspirations and nature as the product of evolution. This could well correspond to Prendick's mood in the later chapters of *Moreau*. In section 118, however, Tennyson offers a way out which anticipates a characteristic Victorian response to evolution: the idea that evolution in nature will bring about a moral evolution in the human species, gradually purging it of its animal inheritance. In his most important essay, "Evolution and Ethics," T.H. Huxley repudiates any belief that human nature can divest itself of that animal inheritance Tennyson represents as the "ape and tiger" (Appendix E3). Wells agrees with this position: in an early essay, "Human Evolution, an Artificial Process," he maintains that human nature has remained fixed since the Stone Age and will continue to be so for a long period (Appendix E5).]

55
The wish, that of the living whole
   No life may fail beyond the grave,
   Derives it not from what we have
The likest God within the soul?

Are God and Nature then at strife,
   That Nature sends such evil dreams?

So careful of the type[1] she seems,
So careless of the single life,

That I, considering everywhere
   Her secret meaning in her deeds,
   And finding that of fifty seeds
She often brings but one to bear,

I falter where I firmly trod,
   And falling with my weight of cares
   Upon the great world's altar-stairs
That slope through darkness up to God,

I stretch lame hands of faith, and grope,
   And gather dust and chaff, and call
   To what I feel is Lord of all,
And faintly trust the larger hope.

56

"So careful of the type?" but no.
   From scarped[2] cliff and quarried stone
   She[3] cries, "A thousand types are gone:
I care for nothing, all shall go.

"Thou makest thine appeal to me:
   I bring to life, I bring to death;
   The spirit does but mean the breath:
I know no more." And he, shall he,

Man, her last work, who seemed so fair,
   Such splendid purpose in his eyes,
   Who rolled the psalm to wintry skies,
Who built him fanes[4] of fruitless prayer,

Who trusted God was love indeed
   And love Creation's final law—
   Though Nature, red in tooth and claw
With ravine, shrieked against his creed—

---

1 Species.
2 Broken open so that the different strata are visible.
3 Nature.
4 Temples or churches.

Who loved, who suffered countless ills,
    Who battled for the True, the Just,
    Be blown about the desert dust,
Or sealed within the iron hills?

No more? A monster then, a dream,
    A discord. Dragons of the prime,[1]
    That tare[2] each other in their slime,
Were mellow music matched with him.

O life as futile, then, as frail!
    O for thy voice[3] to soothe and bless!
    What hope of answer, or redress?
Behind the veil, behind the veil?...

118

Contemplate all this work of Time,
    The giant labouring in his youth;
    Nor dream of human love and truth,
As dying Nature's earth and lime;[4]

But trust that those we call the dead
    Are breathers of an ampler day
    For ever nobler ends. They say,
The solid earth whereon we tread

In tracts of fluent heat began,[5]
    And grew to seeming-random forms,
    The seeming prey of cyclic storms,
Till at the last arose the man;

Who throve and branched from clime to clime,
    The herald of a higher race.
    And of himself in higher place,
If so he type this work of time

---

1 Monstrous creatures of an early period in geological time. These lines were probably inspired by the fossil remains of the animals we now classify as dinosaurs.

2 Tore.

3 I.e., the voice of Arthur Hallam.

4 Representative of the materials out of which living organisms are composed.

5 Reference to the theory that the solar system began as a gaseous nebula which gradually condensed into the sun and planets.

Within himself, from more to more;
    Or, crowned with attributes of woe
    Like glories, move his course, and show
That life is not as idle ore,

But iron dug from central gloom,
    And heated hot with burning fears,
    And dipped in baths of hissing tears,
And battered with the shocks of doom

To shape and use.[1] Arise and fly
    The reeling Faun,[2] the sensual feast;
    Move upward, working out the beast,
And let the ape and tiger die.[3]

2. From Charles Darwin, *The Origin of Species*. New York: D. Appleton and Co., 1859, 1872

[The first version of *The Origin of Species* was published in 1859. These selections are from the text of the Sixth Edition (1872), the last edition published by Darwin and the one which Wells would likely have read. In the first selection Darwin praises a human power of altering animals through selective breeding which might have some affinity to Moreau's project. The other selections illustrate Darwin's insistence on a ferocious struggle in nature.]

From Chapter One, "Variation Under Domestication"
Let us now briefly consider the steps by which domestic races [of animals] have been produced.... We cannot suppose that all breeds [of domestic animals] were suddenly produced as perfect and as useful as we now see them; indeed, in several cases, we know that this has not been their history. The key is man's power of accumulative selection: nature gives successive variations; man adds them up in certain directions useful to him. In this sense he may be said to have made for himself useful breeds.

    The great power of this principle of selection is not hypothetical. It is certain that several of our eminent breeders have, even within a single lifetime,

---

1 Through experience the individual can internalize the process of evolution as moral progress in his own consciousness. Thus suffering can lead to deeper moral insight.

2 A mythical being, half human and half animal. See Huxley's comparison of apes to satyrs in the first paragraph of *Man's Place in Nature*, Appendix D3.

3 The ape and tiger represent different aspects of an inherited animality in human nature: perhaps crude self-interest and animal ferocity.

modified to a large extent their breeds of cattle and sheep.... Breeders habitually speak of an animal's organisation as something quite plastic,[1] which
they can model almost as they please.... Youatt, who was probably better
acquainted with the works of agriculturists than almost any other individual,
and who was himself a very good judge of animals, speaks of the principle
of selection as "that which enables the agriculturist, not only to modify the
character of his flock, but to change it altogether. It is the magician's wand,
by means of which he may summon into life whatever form and mould he
pleases." Lord Somerville, speaking of what breeders have done for sheep,
says:—"It would seem as if they had chalked out upon a wall a form perfect
in itself, and then had given it existence." [That most skilful breeder, Sir John
Sebright, used to say, with regard to pigeons, that "he would produce any
given feather in three years, but it would take him six to obtain head and
beak."][2]

What English breeders have actually effected is proved by the enormous
prices given for animals with a good pedigree; and these have been exported
to almost every corner of the world.... If selection consisted merely in separating some very distinct variety, and breeding from it, the principle would
be so obvious as to be hardly worth notice; but its importance consists in
the great effect produced by the accumulation in one direction, during successive generations, of differences absolutely inappreciable by an uneducated
eye—differences which I for one have vainly attempted to appreciate. Not
one man in a thousand has accuracy of eye and judgment sufficient to become an eminent breeder. If gifted with these qualities, and he studies his
subject for years, and devotes his lifetime to it with indomitable perseverance,
he will succeed, and may make great improvements; if he wants any of these
qualities, he will assuredly fail. Few would readily believe in the natural capacity and years of practice requisite to become even a skilful pigeon-fancier.
(34-37)

From Chapter Three, "Struggle for Existence"
[I]t may be asked, how is it that varieties, which I have called incipient species, become ultimately converted into good and distinct species, which in
most cases obviously differ from each other far more than do the varieties

---

1   Easily moulded, like modelling clay. Moreau uses this word to describe the object of
    his research: "to the plasticity of living forms ... my life has been devoted." (124; ch. 13).
    This meaning persists in the phrase "plastic surgery."

2   The sentence in brackets is from the first edition of the *Origin*—Facsimile Edition,
    Harvard 1964, p. 31. Sebright's boast was dropped from later editions. In "Evolution and
    Ethics" Huxley accuses the eugenics movement of wanting to use Sebright's methods
    to turn society into "a pigeon fancier's polity"—see Appendix E3.

of the same species?... All these results ... follow from the struggle for life. Owing to this struggle, variations, however slight and from whatever cause proceeding, if they be in any degree profitable to the individuals of a species ... will tend to the preservation of such individuals, and will generally be inherited by the offspring. The offspring, also, will thus have a better chance of surviving, for, of the many individuals of any species which are periodically born, but a small number can survive. I have called this principle, by which each slight variation, if useful, is preserved, by the term Natural Selection, in order to mark its relation to man's power of selection [through selective breeding of domestic animals]. But the expression often used by Mr. Herbert Spencer[1] of the Survival of the Fittest is more accurate, and is sometimes equally convenient. We have seen that man by selection can certainly produce great results, and can adapt organic beings to his own uses, through the accumulation of slight but useful variations, given to him by the hand of Nature. But Natural Selection, as we shall hereafter see, is a power incessantly ready for action, and is as immeasurably superior to man's feeble efforts, as the works of Nature are to those of Art. (76-77)

A struggle for existence inevitably follows from the high rate at which all organic beings tend to increase. Every being, which during its natural lifetime produces several eggs or seeds, must suffer destruction during some period of its life ... otherwise ... its numbers would quickly become so inordinately great that no country could support the product. Hence, as more individuals are produced than can possibly survive, there must in every case be a struggle for existence, either one individual with another of the same species, or with the individuals of distinct species, or with the physical conditions of life. It is the doctrine of Malthus[2] applied with manifold force to the whole animal and vegetable kingdoms; for in this case there can be no artificial increase of food, and no prudential restraint from marriage. Although some species may be increasing, more or less rapidly, in numbers, all cannot do so, or the world would not hold them. (79)

---

1   A very influential Victorian philosopher (1820-1903) who supported the idea that social progress would result from unrestricted competition, an argument later rejected by Huxley. Spencer coined the phrase "survival of the fittest," adopted by Darwin in the second edition of *The Origin of Species*.

2   T.R. Malthus (1766-1834), a British thinker in the realm of economics and population theory. His most influential book, *An Essay on the Principle of Population*, first published in 1798, played a central role in British economic theory in the nineteenth century. Malthus argued that human population growth always tends to outstrip the food supply. Darwin argues that this is even more true with animals, who lack the moral restraints imposed on reproduction by society.

When we look at the plants and bushes clothing an entangled bank, we are tempted to attribute their proportional number and kinds to what we call chance. But how false a view is this! Every one has heard that when an American forest is cut down, a very different vegetation springs up; but it has been observed that ancient Indian ruins in the Southern United States, which must formerly have been cleared of trees, now display the same beautiful diversity and proportion of kinds as in the surrounding virgin forest. What a struggle must have gone on during long centuries between the several kinds of trees, each annually scattering its seeds by the thousand; what war between insect and insect—between insects, snails, and other animals with birds and beasts of prey—all striving to increase, all feeding on each other, or on the trees, their seeds and seedlings, or on the other plants which first clothed the ground and thus checked the growth of the trees![1] (91)

From Chapter Four, "Natural Selection; or the Survival of the Fittest"
Though Nature grants long periods of time for the work of natural selection, she does not grant an indefinite period; for as all organic beings are striving to seize on each place in the economy of nature, if any one species does not become modified and improved in a corresponding degree with its competitors, it will be exterminated. (125)

3. From Thomas H. Huxley, *Man's Place in Nature*. First published in 1863. Published as Vol. 7 of *Collected Essays*. New York: D. Appleton and Co., 1902

[*Man's Place in Nature* excited much controversy when it was first published. In a clear, straightforward way Huxley presents the first detailed argument that the human species is descended from apes, a subject not mentioned in Darwin's *Origin* but implicit in his theory of evolution. In the absence of a satisfactory fossil record of human descent, Huxley bases his argument on structural affinities between humans and mammals in general and the great apes in particular. Huxley's book blazed the way for Darwin's *The Descent of Man*.]

From Chapter One, "On the Natural History of the Man-like Apes"
Ancient traditions, when tested by the severe processes of modern investigation, commonly enough fade away into mere dreams: but it is singular how often the dream turns out to have been a half-waking one, presaging a reality. Ovid foreshadowed the discoveries of the geologist: the Atlantis was an

---

1 Aspects of this passage are echoed in Wells's descriptions of the tropical forest on Moreau's island, especially in chapter nine.

imagination, but Columbus found a western world: and though the quaint forms of Centaurs and Satyrs have an existence only in the realms of art, creatures[1] approaching man more nearly than they in essential structure, and yet as thoroughly brutal as the goat's or horse's half of the mythical compound, are now not only known, but notorious.[2] (1)

From Chapter Two, "On the Relations of Man to the Lower Animals"

[I]t will be admitted that some knowledge of man's position in the animate world is an indispensable preliminary to the proper understanding of his relations to the universe—and this again resolves itself, in the long run, into an inquiry into the nature and the closeness of the ties which connect him with those singular creatures whose history has been sketched in the preceding pages.

The importance of such an inquiry is indeed intuitively manifest. Brought face to face with these blurred copies of himself, the least thoughtful of men is conscious of a certain shock, due, perhaps, not so much to disgust at the aspect of what looks like an insulting caricature, as to the awakening of a sudden and profound mistrust of time-honoured theories and strongly-rooted prejudices regarding his own position in nature, and his relations to the underworld of life; while that which remains a dim suspicion for the unthinking, becomes a vast argument, fraught with the deepest consequences, for all who are acquainted with the recent progress of the anatomical and physiological sciences. (80–81)

Without question, the mode of origin and the early stages of the development [before birth] of man are identical with those of the animals immediately below him on the scale.... Indeed, it is very long before the body [foetus] of the young human being can be readily discriminated from that of the young puppy.... But, exactly in those respects in which the developing Man differs from the Dog, he resembles the Ape.... So that it is only quite in the later stages of development [as a foetus] that the young human being presents marked differences from the young ape, while the latter departs as much from the dog in its development as the man does.

---

1   I.e., man-like apes.

2   Huxley compares the "man-like apes" to two hybrid creatures from Greek mythology who were half human and half animal: below the waist the Centaur was a horse, the Satyr a goat. In Greek mythology both stand for lust and the predominance of animal passions over human reason. When Wells makes one of Moreau's creations a Satyr "his voice a harsh bleat, his nether extremities Satanic" (137; ch. 16)—he may be alluding to this paragraph.

Startling as the last assertion may appear to be, it is demonstrably true, and it alone appears to me sufficient to place beyond all doubt the structural unity of man with the rest of the animal world, and more particularly and closely with the apes.

Thus, identical in the physical processes by which he originates, identical in the early stages of his formation—identical in the mode of his nutrition before and after birth, with the animals which lie immediately below him in the scale—Man, if his adult and perfect structure be compared with theirs, exhibits, as might be expected, a marvellous likeness of organization. (89-93)

There would remain then, but one order [of mammals] for comparison, that of the Apes (using that word in its broadest sense), and the question for discussion would narrow itself to this—is Man so different from any of these Apes that he must form an order by himself? Or does he differ less from them than they differ from one another, and hence must take his place in the same order with them? (96)

It is quite certain that the Ape which most nearly approaches man, in the totality of its organization, is either the Chimpanzee or the Gorilla.... I shall select the latter (so far as its organization is known)—as a brute now so celebrated in prose and verse, that all must have heard of him, and have formed some conception of his appearance. (97)

Whatever part of the animal fabric—whatever series of muscles, whatever viscera might be selected for comparison—the result would be the same— the lower Apes and the Gorilla would differ more than the Gorilla and the Man. (116)

[L]et us now turn to the limbs of the Gorilla. The terminal division of the fore limb presents no difficulty—bone for bone and muscle for muscle, are found to be arranged essentially as in man, or with such minor differences as are found as varieties in man. The Gorilla's hand is clumsier, heavier, and has a thumb somewhat shorter in proportion than that of man; but no one has ever doubted its being a true hand.

At first sight, the termination of the hind limb of the Gorilla looks very hand-like.... But the most cursory anatomical investigation at once proves that the resemblance of the so-called "hind hand" to a true hand, is only skin deep, and that, in all essential respects, the hind limb of the Gorilla is as truly terminated by a foot as that of man. The tarsal bones, in all important circumstances of number, disposition, and form, resemble those of man. The metatarsals and digits, on the other hand, are proportionally longer and more slender, while the great toe is not only proportionally shorter and weaker, but its metatarsal bone is united by a more moveable joint with the tarsus. At the same time, the foot is set more obliquely upon the leg than in man. (126)

Hardly any part of the bodily frame ... could be found better calculated to illustrate the truth that the structural differences between Man and the highest Ape are of less value than those between the highest and the lower Apes, than the hand or the foot, and yet, perhaps, there is one organ the study of which enforces the same conclusion in a still more striking manner—and that is the Brain. (130)

As if to demonstrate, by a striking example, the impossibility of erecting any cerebral barrier between man and the apes, Nature has provided us, in the lower animals, with an almost complete series of gradations from brains little higher than that of a Rodent, to brains little lower than that of Man. And it is a remarkable circumstance, that though, so far as our present knowledge extends, there *is* one true structural break in the series of forms of Simian brains, this hiatus does not lie between Man and the man-like apes, but between the lower and the lowest Simians; or, in other words, between the ... apes and monkeys, and the Lemurs. (134)

The surface of the brain of a monkey exhibits a sort of skeleton map of man's, and in the man-like apes the details become more and more filled in, until it is only in minor characters, such as the greater excavation of the anterior lobes, the constant presence of fissures usually absent in man, and the different disposition and proportions of some convolutions, that the Chimpanzee's or the Orang's brain can be structurally distinguished from Man's.... [T]he difference in weight of brain between the highest and lowest men is far greater, both relatively and absolutely, than that between the lowest man and the highest ape. (139–43)

Perhaps no order of mammals presents us with so extraordinary a series of gradations as this—leading us insensibly from the crown and summit of the animal creation down to creatures, from which there is but one step, as it seems, to the lowest, smallest, and least intelligent of the placental Mammalia. It is as if nature herself had foreseen the arrogance of man, and with Roman severity had provided that his intellect, by its very triumphs, should call into prominence the slaves, admonishing the conqueror that he is but dust. (146)

But if Man be separated by no greater structural barrier from the brutes than they are from one another—then it seems to follow that if any process of physical causation çan be discovered by which the genera and families of ordinary animals have been produced, that process of causation is amply sufficient to account for the origin of Man.... At the present moment, but one such process of physical causation has any evidence in its favour; or, in other words, there is but one hypothesis regarding the origin of species of animals in general which has any scientific existence—that propounded by Mr. Darwin. (147)

But desiring, as I do, to reach the wider circle of the intelligent public, it would be unworthy cowardice were I to ignore the repugnance with which the majority of my readers are likely to meet the conclusions to which the most careful and conscientious study I have been able to give to this matter, has led me.

On all sides I shall hear the cry—"We are men and women, and not a mere better sort of apes, a little longer in the leg, more compact in the foot, and bigger in brain than your brutal Chimpanzees and Gorillas. The power of knowledge—the conscience of good and evil—the pitiful tenderness of human affections, raise us out of all real fellowship with the brutes, however closely they may seem to approximate us."

To this I can only reply that the exclamation would be most just and would have my own entire sympathy, if it were only relevant. But it is not I who seek to base man's dignity upon his great toe, or insinuate that we are lost if an Ape has a hippocampus minor. On the contrary, I have done my best to sweep away this vanity. I have endeavoured to show that no absolute structural line of demarcation, wider than that between the animals which immediately succeed us in the scale, can be drawn between the animal world and ourselves; and I may add the expression of my belief that the attempt to draw a physical distinction is equally futile, and that even the highest faculties of feeling and of intellect begin to germinate in lower forms of life....

We are indeed told by those who assume authority in these matters, that ... the belief in the unity of origin of man and brutes involves the brutalization and degradation of the former. But is this really so? Could not a sensible child confute by obvious arguments, the shallow rhetoricians who would force this conclusion upon us? Is it, indeed, true, that the Poet, or the Philosopher, or the Artist whose genius is the glory of his age, is degraded from his high estate by the undoubted historical probability, not to say certainty, that he is the direct descendant of some naked and bestial savage, whose intelligence was just sufficient to make him a little more cunning than the Fox, and by so much more dangerous than the Tiger? Or is he bound to howl and grovel on all fours because of the wholly unquestionable fact, that he was once an egg, which no ordinary power of discrimination could distinguish from that of a Dog? Or is the philanthropist, or the saint, to give up his endeavours to lead a noble life, because the simplest study of man's nature reveals, at its foundations, all the selfish passions, and fierce appetites of the merest quadruped? Is mother-love vile because a hen shows it, or fidelity because dogs possess it? (151-53)

4. From Charles Darwin, *The Descent of Man and Selection in Relation to Sex* [1871]. New York: D. Appleton, 1896

[Eight years after Huxley had familiarized the public with the argument for the animal descent of the human species, Darwin published his own comprehensive book on the subject, *The Descent of Man*. Here Darwin provides the same anatomical argument as Huxley, emphasizes "sexual selection" as a principle of evolution separate from natural selection, and discusses in detail affinities between animal and human behaviour, along with the customs of "savages" or "barbarians" supposedly at the earliest stages of human development. The selections provided here illustrate Darwin's speculations about affinities between animal and human consciousness. The "Fuegians" described in the concluding selections are the aboriginal inhabitants of Tierra del Fuego at the southern tip of South America, which Darwin visited in his youth. He gives a more detailed account of them in chapter ten of *The Voyage of the Beagle* (1839).]

My object ... is to show that there is no fundamental difference between man and the higher mammals in their mental faculties. (66; ch. III)

Most of the more complex emotions are common to the higher animals and ourselves. Every one has seen how jealous a dog is of his master's affection, if lavished on any other creature; and I have observed the fact with monkeys. This shows that animals not only love, but have desire to be loved. Animals manifestly feel emulation.[1] They love approbation or praise; and a dog carrying a basket for his master exhibits in a high degree self-complacency or pride.... Dogs show what may be fairly called a sense of humour, as distinguished from mere play.... (71; ch. III)

As dogs, cats, horses, and probably all the higher animals, even birds have vivid dreams, and this is shown by their movements and the sounds uttered, we must admit that they possess some power of imagination. There must be something special, which causes dogs to howl in the night, and especially during moonlight, in that remarkable and melancholy manner called baying.... Houzeau thinks that their imaginations are disturbed by the vague outlines of the surrounding objects, and conjure up before them fantastic images: if this be so, their feelings may almost be called superstitious.

---

1   Imitation with intent to equal or surpass someone; a feeling of rivalry. This could be the attitude of the Ape Man towards Prendick.

Of all the faculties of the human mind, it will, I presume, be admitted that *Reason* stands at the summit. Only a few persons now dispute that animals possess some power of reasoning. Animals may constantly be seen to pause, deliberate, and resolve. It is a significant fact, that the more the habits of any particular animal are studied by a naturalist, the more he attributes to reason and the less to unlearnt instincts. (74-75; ch. III)

It has, I think, now been shown that man and the higher animals, especially the Primates, have some few instincts in common. All have the same senses, intuitions, and sensations,—similar passions, affections, and emotions, even the more complex ones, such as jealousy, suspicion, emulation, gratitude, and magnanimity; they practise deceit and are revengeful; they are sometimes susceptible to ridicule, and even have a sense of humour; they feel wonder and curiosity; they possess the same faculties of imitation, attention, deliberation, choice, memory, imagination, the association of ideas, and reason, though in very different degrees. (79; ch. III)

[The faculty of language] has justly been considered as one of the chief distinctions between man and the lower animals. But man, as a highly competent judge, Archbishop Whately remarks, "is not the only animal that can make use of language to express what is passing in his mind, and can understand, more or less, what is expressed by another." ... Although barking is a new art [learned by domesticated dogs], no doubt the wild parent species of the dog expressed their feelings by cries of various kinds. With the domesticated dog we have the bark of eagerness, as in the chase; that of anger, as well as growling; the yelp or howl of despair, as when shut up; the baying at night; the bark of joy, as when starting on a walk with his master; and the very distinct one of demand or supplication, as when wishing for a door or window to be opened....

The habitual use of articulate language is, however, peculiar to man; but he uses, in common with the lower animals, inarticulate cries to express his meaning, aided by gestures and the movements of the muscles of the face. This especially holds good with the more simple and vivid feelings, which are but little connected with our higher intelligence. Our cries of pain, fear, surprise, anger, together with their appropriate actions, and the murmur of a mother to her beloved child, are more expressive than any words.... It is not the mere articulation which is our distinguishing character....The lower animals differ from man solely in his almost infinitely larger power of associating together the most diversified sounds and ideas; and this obviously depends on the high development of his mental powers. (84-86; ch. III)

The feeling of religious devotion is a highly complex one, consisting of love, complete submission to an exalted and mysterious superior, a strong sense of dependence, fear, reverence, gratitude, hope for the future, and perhaps other elements. No being could experience so complex an emotion until advanced in his intellectual and moral faculties to at least a moderately high level. Nevertheless, we see some distant approach to this state of mind in the deep love of a dog for his master, associated with complete submission, some fear, and perhaps other feelings.... Professor Braubach goes so far as to maintain that a dog looks on his master as on a god (95-96; ch. III).

The following proposition seems to me to a high degree probable—namely, that any animal whatever, endowed with well-marked social instincts ... would inevitably acquire a moral sense or conscience, as soon as its intellectual powers had become as well, or nearly as well developed, as in man. (98; ch. III)

Besides love and sympathy, animals exhibit other qualities connected with the social instincts, which in us would be called moral; ... dogs possess something very like a conscience.

Dogs possess some power of self-command, and this does not appear to be wholly the result of fear.... They have long been accepted as the very type of fidelity and obedience. (103; ch. IV)

It is no argument against savage man being a social animal, that the tribes inhabiting adjacent districts are almost always at war with each other; for the social instincts never extend to all the individuals of the same species. Judging from the analogy of the majority of the Quadrumana [apes], it is probable that the early ape-like progenitors of man were likewise social.... Although man, as he now exists, has few special instincts ... this is no reason why he should not have retained from an extremely remote period some degree of instinctive love and sympathy for his fellows.... Instinctive sympathy would also cause him to value highly the approbation of his fellows.... Thus the social instincts, which must have been acquired by man in a very rude state, and probably even by his early ape-like progenitors, still give the impulse to some of his best actions; but his actions are in a higher degree determined by the expressed wishes and judgment of his fellow-men, and unfortunately very often by his own strong selfish desires. (108-09; ch. IV)

[E]very one who admits the principle of evolution, must see that the mental powers of the higher animals, which are of the same kind with those of man, though so different in degree, are capable of advancement. (609; ch. XXI)

The main conclusion arrived at in this work, namely that man is descended from some lowly organized form, will, I regret to think, be highly distasteful to many. But there can hardly be a doubt that we are descended from barbarians. The astonishment which I felt on first seeing a party of Fuegians on a wild and broken shore will never be forgotten by me, for the reflection at once rushed into my mind—such were our ancestors. These men were absolutely naked and bedaubed with paint, their long hair was tangled, their mouths frothed with excitement, and their expression was wild, startled, and distrustful. They possessed hardly any arts, and like wild animals lived on what they could catch; they had no government, and were merciless to everyone not of their own small tribe. He who has seen a savage in his native land will not feel much shame, if forced to acknowledge that the blood of some more humble creature flows in his veins. For my own part I would as soon be descended from that heroic little monkey, who braved his dreaded enemy in order to save the life of his keeper, or from that old baboon, who descended from the mountains, carried away in triumph his young comrade from a crowd of astonished dogs[1]—as from a savage who delights to torture his enemies, offers up bloody sacrifices, practises infanticide without remorse, treats his wives like slaves, knows no decency, and is haunted by the grossest superstitions.

Man may be excused for feeling some pride at having risen, though not through his own exertions, to the very summit of the organic scale; and the fact of having thus risen, instead of having been aboriginally placed there, may give him hope for a still higher destiny in the distant future. But we are not here concerned with hopes or fears, only with the truth as far as our reason permits us to discover it; and I have given the evidence to the best of my ability. We must, however, acknowledge, as it seems to me, that man with all his noble qualities, with sympathy which feels for the most debased, with benevolence which extends not only to other men but to the humblest living creature, with his god-like intellect which has penetrated into the movements and constitution of the solar system—with all these exalted powers—Man still bears in his bodily frame the indelible stamp of his lowly origin. (618-19; ch. XXI)

5. From Charles Darwin, *The Expression of the Emotions in Man and Animals* [1872]. New York: D. Appleton, 1896

[A discussion of facial expressions in animals and humans that Darwin had originally intended for *The Descent of Man* grew into a separate book which he published a year later. The selections are from chapter ten, "Hatred and Anger." Here Darwin passes from an argument that human facial expressions may originate with animal ancestors to the assertion of Dr. Henry Maudsley that mental illness is caused by regression to an animal inheritance in hu-

---

1 Darwin describes these instances of self-sacrificing courage and sympathy on the part of monkeys in chapter four, pp. 101 and 103.

man nature. This idea partakes of the theme of "degeneration" explored in Appendix F.]

The lips are sometimes protruded during rage in a manner, the meaning of which I do not understand, unless it depends on our descent from some ape-like animal. Instances have been observed, not only with Europeans, but with Australians and Hindoos. The lips, however, are much more commonly retracted, the grinning or clenched teeth being thus exposed. This has been noticed by almost everyone who has written on expression. The appearance is as if the teeth were uncovered, ready for seizing or tearing an enemy, though there may be no intention of acting in this manner.... Dickens, in speaking of an atrocious murderer who had just been caught, and was surrounded by a furious mob, describes "the people as jumping up one behind another, snarling with their teeth, and making at him like wild beasts."[1] Everyone who has had much to do with young children must have seen how naturally they take to biting, when in a passion. It seems as instinctive in them as in young crocodiles, who snap their little jaws as soon as they emerge from the egg... (243)

This retraction of the lips and uncovering of the teeth during paroxysms of rage, as if to bite the offender, is so remarkable, considering how seldom the teeth are used by men in fighting, that I enquired from Dr. J. Crichton Browne whether the habit was common in the insane whose passions are unbridled. He informs me that he has repeatedly observed it both with the insane and idiotic.... (244)

Dr. Maudsley, after detailing some strange animal-like traits in idiots, asks whether these are not due to the reappearance of primitive instincts—"a faint echo from a far-distant past, testifying to a kinship which man has almost outgrown." He adds, that as every human brain passes, in the course of its development, through the same stages as those occurring in the lower vertebrate animals, and as the brain of an idiot is in arrested condition, we may presume that it "will manifest its most primitive functions, and no higher functions." Dr. Maudsley thinks that the same view may be extended to the brain in its degenerated condition in some insane patients: and asks, whence come "the savage snarl, the destructive disposition, the obscene language, the wild howl, the offensive habits, displayed by some of the insane? Why should a human being, deprived of his reason, ever become so brutal in character, as some do, unless he has the brute nature within him?"[2] The question must, it would appear, be answered in the affirmative. (245-46)

---

1   *Oliver Twist*, the arrest of Fagin, chapter 50.

2   Henry Maudsley, *Body and Mind*, 1870. This provides an example of the view, common at the time, that mental illness is a form of degeneracy.

6. From H.G. Wells, *Text-Book of Biology* [University Correspondence College Tutorial Series]. 2 vols. Intro. G.B. Howes. London: W.B. Clive & Co., University Correspondence College Press, 1893

[This textbook grew out of Wells's "cramming" course intended to prepare undergraduates for the graduating examination in Biology at the University of London. The selections here are from the conclusion to his brief chapter on the theory of evolution.]

It would ... be beyond the design of this book to carry our demonstration of the credibility of common ancestry of animals still further back. But we may point out here that it is not a theory, based merely upon one set of facts, but one singularly rich in confirmation....

It is in the demonstration of this wonderful unity in life, only the more confirmed the more exhaustive our analysis becomes, that the educational value and human interest of biology chiefly lies. In the place of disconnected species of animals, arbitrarily created, ... the student finds an enlightening realization of uniform and active causes beneath an apparent diversity. And the world is not made and dead like a cardboard model or a child's toy, but a living equilibrium; and every day and every hour, every living thing is being weighed in the balance and found sufficient or wanting.

Our little book is the merest beginning in zoology.... The great things of the science of Darwin, Huxley, Wallace,[1] and Balfour[2] remain mainly untold. In the book of nature there are written, for instance, the triumphs of survival, the tragedy of death and extinction, the tragi-comedy of degradation and inheritance, the gruesome lesson of parasitism, and the political satire of colonial organisms. Zoology is, indeed, a philosophy and a literature to those who can read its symbols. (131)

7. From H.G. Wells, "The Rediscovery of the Unique." *Fortnightly Review*, n.s. 50 (1891): 106–11

[This essay launches the series of essays on scientific themes that Wells published in the 1890s. It consists largely of a tongue-in-cheek argument that the author's discovery of the uniqueness of all things must invalidate universal scientific laws, but concludes more seriously in suggesting that the unique-

---

1 Alfred Russel Wallace (1823-1913) developed a theory of natural selection independent of Darwin and continued to make contributions to evolutionary theory.

2 Presumably a reference to embryologist Francis Maitland Balfour (1851-82), as Wells lists his book, *Embryology*, among suggestions for further reading for this chapter (132).

ness and diversity of "living things" revealed by Darwin's theory invalidates the "trim clockwork thought" of the Enlightenment. Wells ends with the striking image of science as a lighted match, which offers a very limited view of the universe instead of the Temple of Nature that the observer expected to see.]

The work of Darwin and Wallace was the clear assertion of the uniqueness of living things....We are on the eve of man's final emancipation from rigid reasonableness, from the last trace of the trim clockwork thought of the seventeenth and eighteenth centuries....

Science is a match that man has just got alight. He thought he was in a room—in moments of devotion, a temple—and that his light would be reflected from and display walls inscribed with wonderful secrets and pillars carved with philosophical systems wrought into harmony. It is a curious sensation, now that the preliminary splutter is over and the flame burns up clear, to see his hands lit and just a glimpse of himself and the patch he stands on visible, and around him, in place of all that human comfort and beauty he anticipated—darkness still. (110-11)

8. From H.G. Wells, "The Mind in Animals," a review of *An Introduction to Comparative Psychology* by C. Lloyd Morgan. *The Saturday Review of Politics, Literature, Science and Art* 78 (22 December 1894): 683-84

[This review, focusing on the relation between animal and human consciousness, was published when Wells was writing his first version of *Moreau*. Conwy Lloyd Morgan (1852-1936) studied zoology under Huxley and became Professor of Geology and Zoology and later of Psychology and Education at the University of Bristol. He was deeply interested in the borderline between animal instinct and the human capacity for reason, and did much to establish the study of animal behaviour as a scientific discipline. In his pioneering study of animal behaviour in *An Introduction to Comparative Psychology* (1894) he finds no evidence of true human intelligence in animals and argues against Darwin's concept of an unbroken continuity between human consciousness and the mental processes of the higher animals. In his review of Morgan's book, Wells wants to give animals more credit for intelligence than Morgan allows, and suggests that the thought processes of the ordinary human may be far removed from Morgan's rather academic concept of reason. Steven McLean's article "Animals, Language and Degeneration in H.G. Wells's *The Island of Doctor Moreau*" provides an informative discussion of the relation of Wells's portrayal of the Beast People to the late-Victorian controversy, reflected in this review, over whether or not some animals, especially apes, possess a primitive form of speech and the intelligence to use language.

Wells suggests that because animals perceive the world through sensory modes different from ours, their intelligence may take a different form. This idea anticipates important developments in animal psychology, especially the concept put forward by Jacob von Uexküll (1864-1944) that the subjective world of an animal is created by its particular way of perceiving its environment.

All emphases below are those of the author.]

Though an out-and-out evolutionist, Professor Lloyd Morgan is disposed to establish a broad distinction between the human mind and that of the highest of other living creatures. He denies even the most rudimentary reason below the human level, and systematically criticizes many alleged cases of ratiocination[1] in animals, with singular clearness and convincingness. The well-authenticated stories of small dogs obtaining the assistance of larger friends to avenge their own defeats, for instance; latch-raising dogs;[2] Professor Sully's case of "canine conscience" (a dog that stole a piece of meat, and then evidently repented and took it to the feet of his mistress) ... are subtly analyzed, and shown to be explicable without supposing any rational process—using the term "rational" with scientific strictness. But Professor Lloyd Morgan lays himself open to criticisms in this use of "rational" as a definite distinction between man and animal. He tells us "That being alone is rational who is able to focus the *therefore*"; but, savages apart, does even such a highly finished product of civilization as a Wessex yokel "focus the *therefore*"? does he syllogize?[3] One may reasonably doubt whether syllogistic thinking is a common human property, is not rather an educational product—even a rare one; and it would, we believe, be at least as easy to dispose of any cases of apparently rational thought, using that term in its narrower sense, among quite illiterate people, as it has been with the animal anecdotes considered in this book.

Then in his experimental observations to test the perception of relations Professor Lloyd Morgan does not seem to give proper weight to the dif-

1   The process of logical reasoning.

2   Morgan observed how his terrier gradually discovered a method for opening the garden gate through simple trial-and-error learning.

3   The syllogism is a highly-structured form of logic containing two propositions which lead to a conclusion; the conclusion is always introduced by the word "therefore." A classic example of a syllogism is the following: "Socrates is a man; All men are mortal; Therefore Socrates is mortal." In making the word "therefore" the hallmark of reason, Morgan implies that all true human thought must partake of the syllogism.

ference in mental operations that must exist, due to the difference of sense basis. With man the whole mental structure rests upon touch impressions and visual images, his mental fabric is fundamentally spatial; almost all his prepositions, for instance, primarily express relative position; and consequently it seems to him that the very simplest test one can offer a dog is such an exercise upon spatial relations as to give it a walking-stick to carry through railings. That test Professor Lloyd Morgan used. But the dominant sense of a dog is olfactory,[1] and the series of delicate space perceptions that are the primary constituents of our thought, and which we obtain originally through our ten fingers, can scarcely have a place in its mental fabric. Nevertheless the dog, possessing, as it evidently does, a power of olfactory discrimination infinitely beyond our own, may have on that basis a something not strictly "rational" perhaps, but higher than mere association and analogous to and parallel with the rational. It may even be that Professor Lloyd Morgan's dog, experimenting on Professor Lloyd Morgan with a dead rat or a bone to develop some point bearing upon olfactory relationships, would arrive at a very low estimate indeed of the powers of the human mind.

---

1   Pertaining to the sense of smell.

Appendix E: Evolution and Struggle II: Later Huxley and Wells

1. From Thomas H. Huxley, "The Struggle for Existence in Human Society." First published in *Nineteenth Century* 23 (February 1888): 61–80. Published in Vol. 9 of *Collected Essays*, (*Evolution and Ethics and Other Essays*). New York: D. Appleton and Co., 1902. 196–236

[In the beginning of this essay Huxley clearly lays out a new development in his later thought. Six years later, in "Evolution and Ethics" he continues the argument stated here that human civilization develops in opposition to evolutionary process.]

From the point of view of the moralist the animal world is on about the same level as a gladiator's show. The creatures are fairly well treated, and set to fight—whereby the strongest, the swiftest, and the cunningest live to fight another day. The spectator has no need to turn his thumbs down, as no quarter is given. He must admit that the skill and training displayed are wonderful. But he must shut his eyes if he would not see that more or less enduring suffering is the meed[1] both of vanquished and victor. And ... the great game is going on in every corner of the world, thousands of times a minute.... (199–200)

In the strict sense of the word "nature," it denotes the sum of the phenomenal world, of that which has been, and is, and will be; and society, like art, is therefore a part of nature. But it is convenient to distinguish those parts of nature in which man plays the part of immediate cause, as something apart; and, therefore, society, like art, is usefully to be considered as distinct from nature. It is the more desirable, and even necessary, to make this distinction, since society differs from nature in having a definite moral object; whence it comes about that the course shaped by the ethical man—the member of society or citizen—necessarily runs counter to that which the non-ethical man—the primitive savage, or man as a mere member of the animal kingdom—tends to adopt. The latter fights out the struggle for existence to the bitter end, like any other animal; the former devotes his best energies to the object of setting limits to the struggle.[2]

---

1   Reward.

2   [Huxley's note:] The reader will observe that this is the argument of the Romanes Lecture ["Evolution and Ethics"] in brief.—1894.

In the cycle of phenomena presented by the life of man, the animal, no more moral end is discernable than in that presented by the lives of the wolf and the deer. However imperfect the relics of prehistoric men may be, the evidence which they accord clearly tends to the conclusion that, for thousands and thousands of years, before the origin of the oldest known civilizations, men were savages of a very low type. They strove with their enemies and their competitors; they preyed upon things weaker or less cunning than themselves; they were born, multiplied without stint, and died, for thousands of generations alongside the mammoth, the urus,[1] the lion, and the hyaena, whose lives were spent in the same way; and they were no more to be praised or blamed, on moral grounds, than their less erect and more hairy compatriots.

As among these, so among primitive men, the weakest and stupidest went to the wall, while the toughest and shrewdest, those who were best fitted to cope with their circumstances, but not the best in any other sense, survived. Life was a continual free fight, and beyond the limited and temporary relations of the family, the ... war of each against all was the normal state of existence. The human species, like others, plashed and floundered amid the general stream of evolution, keeping its head above water as it best might, and thinking neither of whence nor whither.

The history of civilization—that is, of society—on the other hand, is the record of the attempts which the human race has made to escape from this position.... The primitive savage ... appropriated whatever took his fancy, and killed whomsoever opposed him, if he could. On the contrary, the ideal of the ethical man is to limit his freedom of action to a sphere in which he does not interfere with the freedom of others; he seeks the common weal as much as his own; and, indeed, as an essential part of his own welfare. Peace is both an end and means with him; and he founds his life on a more or less complete self-restraint, which is the negation of the unlimited struggle for existence. He tries to escape from his place in the animal kingdom, founded on the free development of the principle of non-moral evolution, and to establish a kingdom of Man, governed upon the principle of moral evolution. For society not only has a moral end, but in its perfection, social life, is embodied morality.

But the effort of ethical man to work towards a moral end by no means abolished, perhaps has hardly modified, the deep-seated organic impulses which impel the natural man to follow his non-moral course. (202–205)

---

1 Wild ox.

2. From Thomas H. Huxley, "An Apologetic Irenicon."[1]
Fortnightly Review 52 (November 1892), 557-71

[This essay has remained relatively unknown. It was not included in Huxley's collected works, perhaps because of its narrow focus. Most of it consists of an attack on forms of disbelief milder and more optimistic than Huxley's Darwinism, especially the Positivist movement based on the philosophy of Auguste Compte. In the conclusion to the essay, Huxley makes another clear statement of his opposition between nature and human society. He sees nature as having the advantage in the struggle between animal inheritance and civilized values: the primitive energy of evolutionary struggle—the "cosmic process"—is a mighty river that threatens to sweep away the individual, while the civilized ethical tendency seems a "mere rill"[2] by comparison. He says that humanity pays a psychological price for civilization by replacing "the happy singleness of aim of the brute" with a divided mind and an inevitable sense of guilt. Huxley also makes a remarkable endorsement of a set of theological propositions unmistakably derived from Calvinistic Puritanism, presenting these as the best comment religion has made on the human condition. Wells too had Puritanism in his background.]

I hear much of the "ethics of evolution." I apprehend that, in the broadest sense of the term "evolution," there neither is, nor can be, any such thing. The notion that the doctrine of evolution can furnish a foundation for morals seems to me an illusion, which has arisen from the unfortunate ambiguity of the term "fittest" in the formula, "survival of the fittest."[3] We commonly use "fittest" in a good sense, with an understood connotation of "best;" and "best" we are apt to take in its ethical sense. But the "fittest" which survives in the struggle for existence may be, and often is, the ethically worst.

So far as I am able to interpret the evidence which bears upon the evolution of man as it now stands, there was a stage in that process when, if I may speak figuratively, the "Welt-geist"[4] repented him that he had made mankind no better than the brutes, and resolved upon a largely new departure.[5] Up to

---

1 An Irenicon is an attempt to promote peace and reconciliation between churches, but Huxley is rather uncompromising here.

2 Rivulet or small stream.

3 Huxley here makes an explicit attack on Herbert Spencer's phrase "survival of the fittest," which Darwin adopted in the second edition of *The Origin of Species*. Huxley especially objected to the implication in this phrase that progress would best be served by unrestrained competition in human society.

4 World Spirit.

5 Here Huxley uses the concept of a "World Spirit" (in which he did not believe) as a humourous way of referring to a new ethical consciousness that arose entirely from within human society.

that time, the struggle for existence had dominated the way of life of the human, as of the other, higher brutes; since that time, men have been impelled, with gentle but steady pressure, to help one another, instead of treading one another mercilessly under foot; to restrain their lusts, instead of seeking, with all their strength and cunning, to gratify them; to sacrifice themselves for the sake of the ordered commonwealth, through which alone the ethical ideal of manhood can be attained, instead of exploiting social existence for their individual ends. Since that time, as the price of the high distinction of his changed destiny, man has lost the happy singleness of aim of the brute; and, from cradle to grave, that which he would not he does, because the cosmic process carries him away; and that which he would he does not, because the ethical stream of tendency is but a rill.

It is the secret of the superiority of the best theological teachers to the majority of their opponents, that they substantially recognize these realities of things, however strange the forms in which they clothe their conceptions. The doctrines of predestination; of original sin; of the innate depravity of man and the evil fate[1] of the greater part of the race; of the primacy of Satan in this world; of the essential vileness of matter;... faulty as they are, appear to me vastly nearer the truth than the "liberal" popular illusions that babies are all born good and that the example of a corrupt society is responsible for their failure to remain so; that it is given to everybody to reach the ethical ideal if he will only try; that all partial evil is universal good; and other optimistic figments, such as that which represents "Providence" under the guise of a paternal philanthropist, and bids us believe that everything will come right (according to our notions) at last.

3. From Thomas H. Huxley, "Evolution and Ethics." [1893, 1894].[2] *Collected Essays.* Vol. 9. D. Appleton and Co., 1902

[This essay presents the fullest exposition of Huxley's later world-view; it has become the best-known of all his writings. Huxley's repudiation of "the gladiatorial theory of existence" is intended as an attack on Herbert Spencer's ideal of a society based on free competition. By emphasizing a communal concept of civilization, Huxley also gets beyond the darkness of his earlier essay, "The Struggle for Existence in Human Society." In "Evolution and Ethics" the phrase "cosmic process" means both the process of evolution itself and the animal energy that drives it—also manifested in human nature. As a central metaphor, Huxley makes the maintenance of a garden and the

---

1 I.e., damnation.

2 Huxley delivered the original text at Oxford as the Romanes Lecture in 1893 and published it in the same year. It was published again, with the "Prolegomena," a long preface to the lecture, in 1894.

exclusion of the natural world from it stand for the civilizing process. Here, selections from his fable of an all-powerful colonial administrator who could exercise eugenic control of the human species are placed after the selections on struggle and cosmic process.]

[I]n the living world, one of the most characteristic features of this cosmic process is the struggle for existence, the competition of each with all, the result of which is the selection, that is to say, the survival of those forms which, on the whole, are best adapted to the conditions which at any period obtain; and which are, therefore, in that respect, and only in that respect, the fittest. (4)

The garden is in the same position as every other work of man's art; it is a result of the cosmic process working through and by human energy and intelligence; and, as is the case with every other artificial thing set up in the state of nature, the influences of the latter[1] are constantly tending to break it down and destroy it....

Thus, it is not only true that the cosmic energy, working through man upon a portion of the plant world, opposes the same energy as it works through the state of nature, but a similar antagonism is everywhere manifest between the artificial and the natural....

Not only is the state of nature hostile to the state of art of the garden; but the principle of the horticultural process, by which the latter is created and maintained, is antithetic to the cosmic process. The characteristic feature of the latter [the cosmic process] is the intense and unceasing competition of the struggle for existence. The characteristic of the former [the garden] is the elimination of that struggle, by the removal of the conditions which give rise to it. (12-13)

[W]ith all their enormous differences in natural endowment, men agree in one thing, and that is their innate desire to enjoy the pleasures and to escape the pains of life; and, in short, to do nothing but what it pleases them to do, without the least reference to the welfare of the society into which they are born. That is their inheritance (the reality at the bottom of the doctrine of original sin) from the long series of ancestors, human and semi-human and brutal, in whom the strength of this innate tendency to self-assertion was the condition of victory in the struggle for existence. That is the reason of the *aviditas vitae*—the insatiable hunger for enjoyment—of all mankind, which is one of the essential conditions of success in the war with the state of nature outside; and yet the sure agent of the destruction of society if allowed free play within. (27)

---

1 I.e., nature.

[Through the moral education of the individual,] associations, as indissoluble as those of language, are formed between certain acts and the feelings of approbation or disapprobation. It becomes impossible to imagine certain acts without disapprobation....We come to think in the acquired dialect of morals. An artificial personality ... is built up beside the natural personality. He is the watchman of society, charged to restrain the anti-social tendencies of the natural man within the limits required by social welfare. (29–30)

[U]nless man's inheritance from the ancestors who fought a good fight in the state of nature, their dose of original sin, is rooted out by some method at present unrevealed, at any rate to disbelievers in supernaturalism, every child born into the world will still bring with him the instinct of unlimited self-assertion. He will have to learn the lesson of self-restraint and renunciation. But the practice of self-restraint and renunciation is not happiness, though it may be something much better.

That man, as a "political animal," is susceptible of a vast amount of improvement, by education, by instruction, and by the application of his intelligence to the adaptation of the conditions of life to his higher needs, I entertain not the slightest doubt. But so long as he remains liable to error, intellectual or moral; so long as he is compelled to be perpetually on guard against the cosmic forces, whose ends are not his ends, without and within himself; so long as he is haunted by inexpugnable memories and hopeless aspirations; so long as the recognition of his intellectual limitations forces him to acknowledge his incapacity to penetrate the mystery of existence; the prospect of attaining untroubled happiness, or of a state which can, even remotely, deserve the title of perfection, appears to me as misleading an illusion as was ever dangled before the eyes of poor humanity. And there have been many of them.

That which lies before the human race is a constant struggle to maintain and improve, in opposition to the State of Nature, the State of Art of an organized polity.... (43–45)

And the more we learn of the nature of things, the more evident is it that what we call rest is only unperceived activity; that seeming peace is silent but strenuous battle. In every part, at every moment, the state of the cosmos is the expression of a transitory adjustment of contending forces; a scene of strife, in which all the combatants fall in turn. (49)

But there is another aspect of the cosmic process....Where the cosmopoietic[1] energy works through sentient beings, there arises, among its other manifestations, that which we call pain or suffering. This baleful product of evolution increases in quantity and in intensity, with advancing grades of animal or-

---

1   World-creating (refers here to the energy of evolution).

ganization, until it attains its highest level in man. Further, the consummation [of pain] is not reached in man, the mere animal; nor in man, the whole or half savage; but only in man, the member of an organized polity. And it is a necessary consequence of his attempt to live in this way; that is, under those conditions which are essential to the full development of his noblest powers.

Man, the animal, in fact, has worked his way to the headship of the sentient world, and has become the superb animal which he is, in virtue of his success in the struggle for existence.... In the case of mankind, the self-assertion, the unscrupulous seizing upon all that can be grasped, the tenacious holding of all that can be kept, which constitute the essence of the struggle for existence, have answered. For in his successful progress, throughout the savage state, man has been largely indebted to those qualities which he shares with the ape and the tiger; his exceptional physical organization; his cunning, his sociability, his curiosity, and his imitativeness; his ruthless and ferocious destructiveness when his anger is roused by opposition.

But, in proportion as men have passed from anarchy to social organization, and in proportion as civilization has grown in worth, these deeply ingrained serviceable qualities have become defects. After the manner of successful persons, civilized man would gladly kick down the ladder by which he has climbed. He would be only too pleased to see "the ape and tiger die."[1] But they decline to suit his convenience; and the unwelcome intrusion of these boon companions of his hot youth into the ranged existence of civil life adds pains and griefs, innumerable and immeasurably great, to those which the cosmic process necessarily brings on the mere animal. In fact, civilized man brands all these ape and tiger promptings with the name of sins; he punishes many of the acts which flow from them as crimes; and, in extreme cases, he does his best to put an end to the survival of the fittest of former days by axe and rope. (50-52)

[C]osmic nature is no school of virtue, but the headquarters of the enemy of ethical nature.... [T]he cosmos works through the lower nature of man, not for righteousness, but against it.... (75-76)

Social progress means the checking of the cosmic process at every step and the substitution for it of another, which may be called the ethical process; the end of which is not the survival of those who happen to be the fittest, in respect of the whole of the conditions which obtain, but of those who are ethically the best.

---

1 Huxley here refers critically to section 118 of Tennyson's *In Memoriam* (Appendix D1), especially the last stanza, which exhorts the human species to "Let the ape and tiger die" through moral evolution. Huxley argues that this is biologically impossible, and hence the "ape" and "tiger" will remain permanent aspects of human nature.

As I have already urged, the practice of that which is ethically best—what we call goodness or virtue—involves a course of conduct which, in all respects, is opposed to that which leads to success in the cosmic struggle for existence. In place of ruthless self-assertion it demands self-restraint; in place of thrusting aside, or treading down, all competitors, it requires that the individual shall not merely respect, but shall help his fellows; its influence is directed, not so much to the survival of the fittest, as to the fitting of as many as possible to survive. It repudiates the gladiatorial theory of existence.... Laws and moral precepts are directed to the end of curbing the cosmic process and reminding the individual of his duty to the community, to the protection and influence of which he owes, if not existence itself, at least the life of something better than a brutal savage....

Let us understand, once for all, that the ethical progress of society depends, not on imitating the cosmic process, still less in running away from it, but in combating it....

The history of civilization details the steps by which men have succeeded in building up an artificial world within the cosmos. (81-83)

The theory of evolution encourages no millennial anticipations. If, for millions of years, our globe has taken the upward road, yet, some time, the summit will be reached and the downward route will be commenced....

Moreover, the cosmic nature born with us and, to a large extent, necessary for our maintenance, is the outcome of millions of years of severe training, and it would be folly to imagine that a few centuries will suffice to subdue its masterfulness to purely ethical ends. Ethical nature may count upon having to reckon with a tenacious and powerful enemy as long as the world lasts. But, on the other hand, I see no limit to the extent to which intelligence and will, guided by sound principles of investigation, and organized in common effort, may modify the conditions of existence, for a period longer than that now covered by history. And much may be done to change the nature of man himself. The intelligence which has converted the brother of the wolf into the faithful guardian of the flock ought to be able to do something towards curbing the instincts of savagery in civilized men.... I deem it an essential condition of the realization of that hope that we should cast aside the notion that the escape from pain and sorrow is the proper object of life. (85-86)

★ ★ ★

[Huxley's fable of the colonial administrator who intervenes in human evolution is intended as a critique of Francis Galton's new "science" of eugenics. Galton argued that it would be beneficial to the human species for a future government to improve on natural selection by arranging for selective breeding of superior individuals, while preventing the defective from reproducing. This idea became widely popular and led to concepts of racial purity—see James Paradis's introduction to *Evolution and Ethics* (1989), 47-48. Here Huxley acknowledges the usefulness of such a practice, but firmly rejects it because it would undermine human sympathy. Huxley's administrator could be seen as a prototype of Moreau, who relies on surgery rather than selective breeding—see David Y. Hughes, "The Garden in Wells's Early Science Fiction," 63-64.]

The process of colonization presents analogies to the formation of a garden which are highly instructive. Suppose a shipload of English colonists sent to form a settlement, in such a country as Tasmania was in the middle of the last century. On landing, they find themselves in the midst of a state of nature....

Let us now imagine that some administrative authority, as far superior in power and intelligence to men, as men are to their cattle, is set over the colony, charged to deal with its human elements in such a manner as to assure the victory of the settlement over the antagonistic influences of the state of nature in which it is set down. (16-17)

When the colony reached the limit of possible expansion, the surplus population must be disposed of somehow; or the fierce struggle for existence must recommence and destroy that peace, which is the fundamental condition of the maintenance of the state of art against the state of nature.

Supposing the administrator to be guided by purely scientific considerations, he would, like the gardener, meet this most serious difficulty by systematic extirpation, or exclusion, of the superfluous. The hopelessly diseased, the infirm aged, the weak or deformed in body or in mind, the excess of infants born, would be put away, as the gardener pulls up defective or superfluous plants, or the breeder destroys undesirable cattle. Only the strong and healthy, carefully matched, with a view to the progeny best adapted to the purposes of the administrator, would be permitted to perpetuate their kind.

Of the more thoroughgoing of the multitudinous attempts to apply the principles of cosmic evolution, or what are supposed to be such, to social and political problems, which have appeared of late years, a considerable proportion appear to me to be based upon the notion that human society is competent to furnish, from its own resources, an administrator of the kind I have imagined. The pigeons, in short, are to be their own Sir John Sebright.[1] A despotic government, whether individual or collective, is to be endowed with the preternatural intelligence, and with what, I am afraid, many will

---

1   John Sebright, a famous British breeder especially known for improvement of poultry. In the first chapter of the first edition of *The Origin of Species*, Darwin quotes Sebright's boast that he could redesign a pigeon within three to six years—see Appendix D2.

consider the preternatural ruthlessness, required for the purpose of carrying out the principle of improvement by selection, with the somewhat drastic thoroughness upon which the success of the method depends....

I have ... reasons for fearing that this logical ideal of evolutionary regimentation—this pigeon fanciers' polity—is unattainable. In the absence of any such severely scientific administration as we have been dreaming of, human society is kept together by bonds of such a singular character, that the attempt to perfect society after his [the administrator's] fashion would run serious risk of loosening them.... (21-24)

Every forward step of social progress brings men into closer relations with their fellows, and increases the importance of the pleasures and pains derived from sympathy. (29-30)

I have ... shown cause for the belief that direct selection, after the fashion of the horticulturist and the breeder, neither has played, nor can play, any important part in the evolution of society; apart from other reasons, because I do not see how such selection could be practised without a serious weakening, it may be the destruction, of the bonds which hold society together. It strikes me that men who are accustomed to contemplate the active or passive extirpation of the weak, the unfortunate, and the superfluous; who justify that conduct on the ground that it has the sanction of the cosmic process, and is the only way of ensuring the progress of the race; ... whose whole lives, therefore, are an education in the noble art of suppressing natural affection and sympathy, are not likely to have any large stock of those commodities left. But, without them, there is no conscience, nor any restraint on the conduct of men, except the calculation of self-interest, the balancing of certain present gratifications against doubtful future pains; and experience tells us how much that is worth. (36-37)

4. From H.G. Wells, "Bio-Optimism," *Nature* 52 (29 August 1895): 410-11

[Wells is here reviewing with much disapproval a journal published by the biological school of St. Andrews University which contains essays hostile to the Darwinian concept of evolution. The authors selected for particular attention argue that love, not struggle or natural selection, is the essence of nature and that the social virtues of the human community are supported by a vaguely-defined "Symbiosis" in nature. Wells coins the phrase "bio-optimism" to represent such high-minded views of evolution.

This review provides the first decisive indication of Wells's abandonment of belief in the inheritance of acquired characteristics and, as a result, his taking a grimmer view of the implications of Darwinian theory, especially for the human species, which now has no biological way of shedding its animal inheritance.[1] This review was published in late August 1895, when Wells had completed all revisions on *Moreau*, but there is evidence that he had rejected the inheritance of acquired characteristics earlier in 1895, when he was giving shape to the final version of *Moreau* (*Early Writings*, 10, note 27).]

Now there is absolutely no justification for these sweeping assertions, this frantic hopefulness, this attempt to belittle the giants of the Natural Selection period of biological history.[2] There is nothing in Symbiosis or any other group of phenomena to warrant the statement that the representation of all life as a Struggle for Existence is a libel on Nature.... Has anything arisen to show that the seed of the unfit need not perish, that a species may wheel into line with new conditions without the generous assistance of Death, that where the life and breeding of every individual in a species is about equally secure, a degenerative process must not inevitably supervene? As a matter of fact Natural Selection grips us more grimly than it ever did, because the doubts thrown upon the inheritance of acquired characteristics have deprived us of our trust in education as a means of redemption for decadent families.[3] In our hearts we all wish that the case was not so, we all hate Death and his handiwork; but the business of science is not to keep up the courage of men, but to tell the truth.... The names of the sculptor who carves out the new forms of life are, and so far as human science goes at present they must ever be, Pain and Death.[4] And the phenomena of degeneration rob one of any confidence that the new forms will be in any case or in a majority of cases "higher" (by any standard except present adaptation to circumstances) than the old....[5]

[Wells describes the various contents of the journal, including poetry and "amateurish short stories about spring."] In this manner is the banner of ... "Bio-optimism" unfurled by these industrious investigators in biology. It will not appeal to science students, but to that large and important class of

---

1 See discussion on this subject in the section on Huxley and Wells, Introduction, pp. 32–33.

2 The period when Darwin and scientific thinkers who supported his ideas were establishing the basic tenets of the theory of evolution, especially "natural selection" as the explanation for change in species.

3 For Wells, education remained the most important means of improving society. Here he gives up only the idea that education might improve human biological inheritance. Of course, it remains true that education of parents would likely benefit children by providing them with an improved social environment.

4 Moreau could also be seen as a "sculptor" who inflicts pain to carve out new forms of life.

5 Huxley and Wells both argue that evolution means simply adaptation to existing circumstances and thus does not necessarily mean a move towards greater complexity of the organism. Parasites "degenerate" by losing complexity in their dependence on a host.

the community which trims its convictions to its amiable sentiments, it may appear as a very desirable mitigation of the rigour of, what Mr. Buchanan[1] has very aptly called, the Calvinism of science.

5. From H.G. Wells, "Human Evolution, an Artificial Process." *Fortnightly Review*, n.s. 60 (October 1896): 590-95

[This is an important essay for understanding the young Wells's view of the social implications of evolution. Although Wells does not mention Huxley in this essay, he constructs an opposition between biological evolution and civilization very like Huxley's position in "Evolution and Ethics" and, like Huxley, insists on the artificial nature of the civilized individual and also locates the sense of sin in the animality of the "natural man," presenting his recently published *Island of Doctor Moreau* as the expression of this idea. Wells published this essay after *Moreau*, but Philmus finds evidence that he was working on a draft of it while writing the final version of *Moreau* (variorum *Moreau*, 188).

Wells uses various terms to refer to prehistoric periods. The "Palaeolithic period," the "Stone Age," and the "stage of unpolished flint instruments" all refer to the long period when humans and, earlier, proto-humans, chipped rocks to make primitive stone tools and followed a nomadic life of hunting and gathering. Wells argues that the biological nature of the human species developed as an adaptation to the constant struggle with nature during this period, and hasn't changed since. The "age of polished stone," usually known as the Neolithic period, initiated development towards ever more sophisticated tools of stone and bone, pottery, agriculture, and, ultimately, civilization. Wells points out that this period began at most ten thousand years ago, much too short a time for evolution to have brought about any change in human nature. Thus, according to Wells our essential nature must be permanently at odds with the needs of civilization. All emphases are those of the author.]

There is an idea abroad that the average man is improving by virtue of the same impetus that raised him above the apes, an idea that finds its expression in such works, for instance, as Mr. Kidd's *Social Evolution*.[2] If I read that

---

1 Robert Williams Buchanan (1841–1901), a Scottish poet, novelist and dramatist. He uses the phrase in a philosophical dialogue entitled "The Coming Terror" (9), published in 1891.

2 Benjamin Kidd, a popular Social Darwinist, argues that the process of evolution in nature also results in the moral development of society. *Social Evolution* was published in 1894.

very suggestive author aright, he believes that "Natural Selection" is "steadily evolving" the intrinsic moral qualities of man (p. 286). It is, however, possible that Natural Selection is not the agent at work here. For Natural Selection is selection by Death. It may help to clarify an important question, to point out what is certainly not very clearly understood at present, that the evolutionary process now operating in the social body is one essentially different from that which has differentiated species in the past and raised man to his ascendency among the animals. It is a process new in this world's history. Assuming the truth of the Theory of Natural Selection, and having regard to Professor Weismann's destructive criticisms of the evidence for the inheritance of acquired characters,[1] there are satisfactory grounds for believing that man (allowing for racial blendings) is still mentally, morally, and physically, what he was during the later Palaeolithic period, that we are, and that the race is likely to remain, for (humanly speaking) a vast period of time, at the level of the Stone Age. The only considerable evolution that has occurred since then, so far as man is concerned, has been, it is here asserted, a different sort of evolution altogether, an evolution of suggestions and ideas....

The fact which has so far been insufficiently considered in this relation is the slowness with which the human animal breeds.... (590) [Wells then argues that species such as rabbits, with a high rate of reproduction and mortality, will change through Natural Selection more rapidly than humans.]

Taking all these points together, and assuming four generations of men to the century—a generous allowance—and ten thousand years as the period of time that has elapsed since man entered upon the age of polished stone, it can scarcely be an exaggeration to say that he has had time only to undergo as much specific modification as the rabbit could get through in a century.... (591)

The fecund rabbit has been taken because it throws the factors of human stagnation (so far as Natural Selection goes) into effective contrast. In a lesser, though still considerable degree, the truth holds between man and all the higher animals. He breeds later and more sparingly than any other creature.... In view of which facts, *it appears to me impossible to believe that man has undergone anything but an infinitesimal alteration in his intrinsic nature since the age of unpolished stone.*

Even if we suppose that he has undergone such an alteration, it cannot be proceeding in the present civilized state. The most striking feature of our civilization is its careful preservation of all the human lives that are born

---

1   A reference to August Weismann's *The Germ Plasm, a Theory of Heredity*, published in English translation in 1893.

to it—the halt, the blind, the deaf and dumb, the ferocious, the atavistic;[1] the wheat and tares[2] not only grow together, but are impartially sheltered from destruction. These grow to maturity and pair under such complex and artificial circumstances that even a determinate Sexual Selection can scarcely be operating. Holding the generally-accepted views of variation, we must suppose as many human beings are born below the average in any particular as above it, and that, therefore, until our civilization changes fundamentally, the intrinsic average man will remain the same.

This completes the opening proposition of the argument, the *a priori*[3] case for the permanence of man's inherent nature; but before proceeding, it may be well to glance at another line of thought, which, followed out, would lead to practically the same conclusion, that the average man of our society is now intrinsically what he was in Palaeolithic times. Regard his psychology, and particularly his disposition to rages and controversy, his love of hunting and violent exercise, and his powerful sexual desires. At present normally a man's worldly interests, his welfare, and that of his family, necessitate a constant conflict to keep these dispositions under. A decent citizen is always controlling and disciplining the impulses of anger, forcing himself to monotonous work, and resisting the seductions of the sporting instinct and a wayward imagination. I believe it is a fact that most men find monogamy at least so far "unnatural" as to be a restraint. Yet to anyone believing in the Theory of Natural Selection it is incredible that a moral disposition, any more than an anatomical one, can have come into being when it was—as are these desires and dispositions just mentioned in civilized man—directly prejudicial to the interests of the species in which it was developed. And, on the other hand, it marches with all our knowledge to suppose that in a state of complete savagery the rapid physical concentration, the intense self-forgetfulness of the anger-burst, the urgency of sexual passion in the healthy male, the love of killing which has been for ages such a puzzle in his own nature to man, would have subserved with exactitude the interests of the species. Here, again, is at least a plausible case for the belief that the natural man is still what he was in the stage of unpolished flint instruments—a stage

---

1 The word "atavism"—reversion to animal ancestry—was popularized by Cesare Lombroso, who saw it as a major cause of crime. An atavistic individual would supposedly display mental and physical characteristics of animals, and would transmit them to offspring. See Appendix F4.

2 Noxious weeds. Wells refers here to Jesus's Parable of the Wheat and Tares (Matthew 13:24-30) in which a farmer tells his workers to allow wheat and weeds to grow in the field together until harvest time because in pulling up the weeds they might also pull up the young wheat.

3 Essential.

which certainly lasted one hundred thousand years, and very probably many hundreds of thousands of years, which covered many thousands of generations, which rose probably with extreme slowness from the simian level, and in which he might conceivably have become very completely adapted to the necessities of his life.

Coming now to the second proposition of this argument, we must admit that it is indisputable that civilized man is in some manner different from the Stone Age savage. But that difference, it is submitted, is in no degree inherited. That, however, is a thing impossible to prove in its entirety, and it is stated here merely as an opinion arising out of the considerations just advanced. The cases of Wolf-Boys that have arisen show with sufficient clearness, at any rate, that the greater part of the difference is not inherited.[1] If the child of a civilized man, by some conjuring with time, could be transferred, at the moment of its birth, to the arms of some Palaeolithic mother, it is conceivable that it would grow up a savage in no way superior, by any standards, to the true-born Palaeolithic savage. The main difference is extrinsic,[2] it is a difference in the scope and nature of the circle of thought, and it arose, one may conceive, as a result of the development of *speech*. Slowly during the vast age of unpolished stone, this new and wonderful instrument of intellectual enlargement and moral suggestion, replaced inarticulate sounds and gestures. Out of speech, by no process of natural selection, but as a necessary consequence, arose tradition. With true articulate speech came the possibilities of more complex co-operations and instructions than had hitherto been possible, more complex industries than hunting and the chipping of flints, and, at last, after a few thousand years, came writing, and therewith a tremendous acceleration in the expansion of that body of knowledge and ideals which is the reality of the civilized state. It is a pure hypothesis, but it seems plausible

---

1   The phrase "Wolf-Boy" originates with folk tales of children raised by animals, but here it refers to a real phenomenon also known as the "feral child," the "wild child," or "*l'enfant sauvage*," meaning children who have grown up in isolation and have not learned language or social behaviour. The most famous descriptions of such a child were provided by Jean Itard in the early nineteenth century. Study of such cases has revealed that if language is not acquired in childhood, it cannot be learned later, or only with great difficulty. Although evolution provides us with the physical ability for speech, language itself is a social acquirement. For Wells, the bleak depictions of such children provided by Itard and others represent the mere human animal without the civilizing influence of a social environment, especially language.

2   "Extrinsic" here means the influence of the social environment as opposed to the internal and inherited "intrinsic moral qualities of man" mentioned in the first paragraph. Since Wells, like Huxley, came to believe that the "intrinsic" nature of human beings was fixed and remained at an animal level, he sees social education as the hope of civilization—see *Early Writings*, 185–86.

to suggest, that only with writing could the directly personal governments coalesce to form an ampler type of State. All this was, from the point of view of the evolutionist, to whom a thousand years are but a day, a rapid and inevitable development of speech, just as the flooding of a vast country in the space of a few hours would be the rapid and inevitable consequence of the gradual sapping of a dam that fended off the sea. In his reference to this background of the wider state, and in its effect upon his growth, in moral suggestions and in knowledge, lies, I believe, the essential difference between Civilized and Palaeolithic man.

This completes the statement of the view I would advance.... That in civilized man we have (1) an inherited factor, the natural man, who is the product of natural selection, the culminating ape, and a type of animal more obstinately unchangeable than any other living creature; and (2) an acquired factor, the artificial man, the highly plastic[1] creature of tradition, suggestion, and reasoned thought. In the artificial man we have all that makes the comforts and securities of civilization a possibility. That factor and civilization have developed, and will develop together. And in this view, what we call Morality becomes the padding of suggested emotional habits necessary to keep the round Palaeolithic savage in the square hole of the civilized state. And Sin is the conflict of the two factors—as I have tried to convey in my *Island of Dr. Moreau.*

If this new view is acceptable it provides a novel definition of Education, which obviously should be the careful and systematic manufacture of the artificial factor in man.

The artificial factor in man is made and modified by two chief influences. The greatest of these is *suggestion*, and particularly the suggestion of example. With this tradition is inseparably interwoven. The second is his reasoned conclusions from additions to his individual knowledge, either through instruction or experience. The artificial factor in a man, therefore, may evidently be deliberately affected by a sufficiently intelligent exterior agent in a number of ways: by example deliberately set; by the fictitious example of the stage and novel; by sound or unsound presentations of facts, or sound or fallacious arguments derived from facts, even, it may be, by emotionally propounded precepts. The artificial factor of mankind—and that is the one reality of civilization—grows, therefore, through the agency of eccentric and innovating people, playwrights, novelists, preachers, poets, journalists, and political reasoners and speakers, the modern equivalent of the prophets who struggled against the priests—against the social order that is of the barbaric stage. And though from the wider view our most capricious acts are predestinate, yet, at any rate, these developmental influences are exercised as

---

1 Flexible and easily shaped, in this case by social environment.

deliberately, are as much a matter of design and choice, as any human act can be. In other words, in a rude and undisciplined way indeed, in an amorphous chaotic way we might say, humanity is even now consciously steering itself against the currents and winds of the universe in which it finds itself. In the future, it is at least conceivable, that men with a trained reason and a sounder science, both of matter and psychology, may conduct this operation far more intelligently, unanimously, and effectively, and work towards, and at last attain and preserve, a social organization so cunningly balanced against exterior necessities on the one hand, and the artificial factor in the individual on the other, that the life of every human being, and, indeed, through man, of every sentient creature on earth, may be generally happy. To me, at least, that is no dream, but a possibility to be lost or won by men, as they may have or may not have the greatness of heart to consciously shape their moral conceptions and their lives to such an end.

This view, in fact, reconciles a scientific faith in evolution with optimism. The attainment of an unstable and transitory perfection only through innumerable generations of suffering and "elimination" is not necessarily the destiny of humanity. If what is here advanced is true, in Education lies the possible salvation of mankind from misery and sin. We may hope to come out of the valley of Death, become emancipated from the Calanistic deity of Natural Selection, before the end of the pilgrimage.[1] We need not clamour for the Systematic Massacre of the Unfit, nor fear that degeneration is the inevitable consequence of security. (592-95)

6. From H.G. Wells, "The Acquired Factor." (A Review of *Habit and Instinct* by C. Lloyd Morgan.) *The Academy*. 51 (9 January 1897): 37

[Wells also reviewed Morgan's *Introduction to Comparative Psychology*—see Appendix D8. Here he entirely approves of Morgan's argument.]

[T]he main thesis [of Morgan's book] is ... sufficiently evident and sufficiently novel and far-reaching in its implications to make this one of the most important biological works, for the man of general culture at least, that

---

1   The mysterious word "Calanistic" is likely a misprint for "Calvinistic." Both Huxley and Wells saw an affinity between evolution and the world-view of Calvinistic Puritanism in the emphasis of Darwinian science on strict cause and effect, the unrelenting judgment passed on the shortcomings of all species by natural selection, and the sense of sin generated by the animality of the "natural man." In his essay "Bio-Optimism," published a year before "Human Evolution," Wells speaks approvingly of "the Calvinism of science" (Appendix E4).

last year has produced. It is a direct outcome of the important work of Prof. Weismann, work which has finally established the conviction that in the evolution of the larger and more complex animals, at any rate, the part played by the inheritance of modifications acquired by the parent is practically infinitesimal—if it operates at all. This work of Weismann, and the implications of it, necessarily affected systems of ethics and anticipations of man's material future based on biological generalization very profoundly; among others it seriously undermines many of the propositions of Mr. Herbert Spencer.[1] The bearing upon social work that was most immediately recognized was the discouragement with which Weismannism threatened efforts towards social amelioration. However you turn and safeguard your criminal and your weakling—though by good fortune or good example he altogether escapes the curse of his heredity and lives a decent life to the very end—the criminal tendencies go on to his descendants as unimpaired as though he lived criminal and vicious all his days. The new teaching, indeed, seems at first glance to present the social reformer as Sisyphus.[2] But the undeniable fact of the secular advancement of humanity is, on the face of it, antagonistic to pessimism....

[Morgan's book] shows with quite admirable conviction ... that the body of man and the instinct of man, at least of civilized man, are not at present undergoing evolution, that man is of all living things perhaps the most static, and that human evolution is a quite different process from that which has differentiated animal species, is instead the evolution of a mental environment. The development of the modern man by example, precept, subtle suggestion, the advantage of an ancient and growing tradition of living, is his real, perhaps his only difference, from his ancestor of the Age of Stone.

7. From H.G. Wells, "Morals and Civilization." *Fortnightly Review*, n.s. 61 (February 1897): 263–68

[This essay is a sequel to "Human Evolution, An Artificial Process," summarizing the conclusions of that essay and applying them to ideas about the development of society, a subject to which Wells turns to overcome the impasse presented by evolution in nature. In referring to the earlier essay as "The Artificial Factor in Man," Wells must have misremembered its title; his

---

1 Wells refers to Spencer's contention that evolution in nature also results in social progress, especially through unrestricted competition. Huxley vigorously attacks this idea in *Evolution and Ethics*.

2 In ancient Greek mythology, Sisyphus was punished in Hades by forever having to roll a stone up a hill, only to see the stone forever roll down again. Hence his name has come to stand for any hopeless task.

inclusion of passages taken from the essay makes clear that he is referring to "Human Evolution, An Artificial Process." Wells goes on to develop a contrast between active and static (decadent) civilizations (relevant to *The Time Machine*) and concludes that with reform of present concepts of property and sexuality a rational society might be achieved.]

In the *Fortnightly Review* for October, there was published a short paper entitled, "The Artificial Factor in Man," in which the view was advanced that the inherent possibilities of the modern human child at birth could differ in no material respect from those of the ancestral child at the end of the Age of Unpolished Stone. And the difference between the civilized man of today and the later Palaeolithic savage, his ancestor, was presented as an artificial factor developed in him after birth by example and precept, by the complicated influences of the civilized body into which he was born a member. The conflict between his innate Palaeolithic disposition and this artificial factor imposed thereon, was suggested as a new phrasing for the mortal conflict, and the discordance was pointed to as expressing an evolutionary view of Sin....

This conception of a civilized man as composed of these two factors, will be found, if it is accepted and its consequences followed up, a remarkably far-reaching one.... Indeed, ... the whole form of the social organization, the shape of our civilization, is nothing more nor less than the ... sum of the artificial factors of its constituent individuals—a fabric of ideas and habits. Civilization is not material. If, in a night, this artificial, this impalpable mental factor of every human being in the world could be destroyed, the day thereafter would dawn, indeed, upon our cities, our railways, our mighty weapons of warfare, and on our factories and machinery, but it would dawn no more upon a civilized world. And one has instead a grotesque picture of the suddenly barbaric people wandering out into the streets, in their nightgear, their evening dress, or what not, as chance may have left them at the coming of the change, esurient[1] and pugnacious, turning their attention to such recondite weapons as a modern city affords—all for the loss of a few ideas and a subtle trick of thinking.

Now, it is scarcely necessary to say that, in accordance with this view, there is no morality in the absolute. It is relative to the state, the civilization, the corporate existence to which the man beast has become adapted on the one hand, and to the inherent possibilities of the man on the other.... [W]hat was eminent virtue in the tribal savage may ultimately become sin in the civilized man. (263-64)

---

1 Greedy.

8. From H.G. Wells, "Human Evolution: Mr. Wells Replies." *Natural Science: A Monthly Review of Scientific Progress*, No. 62, Vol. 10 (April 1897): 242-44

[F.H. Perry Coste, an occasional writer on science and philosophy, published a letter in *Natural Science* (March 1897) arguing against Wells's view expressed in his article, "Human Evolution, an Artificial Process," that the human species has not changed physically since the Old Stone Age. In reply, Wells reaffirms his belief in the fixity of inherited human nature.]

Mr. Coste makes some illuminating criticisms of my sketch of a theory of human progress[1] and, I must admit, forces a certain modification of phrase upon me. But it does not appear to me that his objections justify his description of them as "fatal." My argument was that, save for culture, for the developing artificial factor, "man is still, mentally, morally, and physically, what he was during the later Palaeolithic Period." For the effective development of a subsidiary argument I have already restated that conclusion in an aggravated form.[2] And I see no reason to abandon it.... (217)

My article was in no sense an "alarmist" one, but the implications of my view are very far-reaching, as I have tried to indicate in my second *Fortnightly* article. The tendency of a belief in natural selection as the main factor of human progress, is, in the moral field, towards the glorification of a sort of rampant egotism—of blackguardism in fact,—as the New Gospel. You get that in the Gospel of Nietzsche.[3] But from the standpoint of my article the obvious gospel for the future is the gospel of discipline and education.... I feel no doubt whatever that the adequate discussion of this fundamental question is (if I may use a battered but expressive phrase) one of the crying needs of the age. After Darwin it has become inevitable that the moral conceptions should be systematically restated in terms of our new conception of the material destiny of man. (244)

---

1   [Wells's note] "The Artificial Factor in Man." *Fortnightly Review.* Oct., 1896. [Here Wells misremembers the title of "Human Evolution, an Artificial Process," from which the ensuing quote has been taken.]

2   [Wells's note] "Morals and Civilization." *Fortnightly Review.* Feb., 1897.

3   Here Wells must be thinking of Nietzsche's concept of the "Superman" presented in *Thus Spake Zarathustra* (1885), but he refers equally to Herbert Spencer's belief that social progress will be achieved through unbridled competition, as exemplified in the process of evolution.

Appendix F: Degeneration and Madness

1. From Charles Darwin, *The Descent of Man and Selection in Relation to Sex* [1871]. New York: D. Appleton, 1896

[These selections show how sympathetic Darwin had become, by the time he composed *The Descent of Man*, to the concept of selective breeding of humans put forward by the new science of "eugenics" founded by his cousin James Galton. Such anxiety about the degeneration of the human species in civilised circumstances underlines the need felt in late-Victorian Darwinism for human intervention in the process of evolution. Darwin's warning, however, that in refusing aid to the unfit we would be repudiating sympathy and the social instincts, shows that he was still ambivalent towards eugenicism. This passage might have inspired Huxley's attack on eugenicism in "Evolution and Ethics," and both might lie behind Doctor Moreau's explicit rejection of sympathy in his project to improve on evolution.]

With savages, the weak in body or mind are soon eliminated; and those that survive commonly exhibit a vigorous state of health. We civilized men, on the other hand, do our utmost to check the process of elimination; we build asylums for the imbecile, the maimed, and the sick; we institute poor-laws; and our medical men exert their utmost skill to save the life of every one to the last moment. There is reason to believe the vaccination has preserved thousands, who from a weak constitution would formerly have succumbed to small-pox. Thus the weak members of civilized society propagate their kind. No one who has attended to the breeding of domestic animals will doubt that this must be highly injurious to the race of man. It is surprising how soon a want of care, or care wrongly directed, leads to the degeneration of a domestic race;[1] but excepting in the case of man himself, hardly anyone is so ignorant as to allow his worst animals to breed.

The aid which we feel impelled to give the helpless is mainly an incidental result of the instinct of sympathy, which was originally acquired as part of the social instincts but subsequently rendered ... more tender and more widely diffused. Nor could we check our sympathy, even at the urging of hard reason, without deterioration in the noblest part of our nature. (133–34; ch. V)

---

1   A group of domestic animals created by selective breeding.

A most important obstacle in civilized countries to an increase in the number of men of a superior class has been strongly insisted on by ... Mr. Galton, namely, the fact that the very poor and reckless, who are often degraded by vice, almost invariably marry early, whilst the careful and frugal, who are generally otherwise virtuous, marry late in life, so that they may be able to support themselves and their children in comfort. Those who marry early produce within a given period not only a greater number of generations, but ... they produce many more children. The children, moreover, that are born by mothers during the prime of life are heavier and larger, and therefore probably more vigorous, than those born at other periods. Thus the reckless, degraded, and often vicious members of society, tend to increase at a quicker rate than the provident and generally virtuous members. (138; ch.V)

2. From H.G. Wells, "The Problem of the Birth Supply [1903]." *The Works of H.G. Wells* (Atlantic Edition). Vol. 4. New York: Scribner's, 1924. 305-37

[This article is from a collection of sociological essays, *Mankind in the Making*, that Wells published in 1903. It provides a detailed critique of Francis Galton's "science" of eugenics. The selections given here illustrate Wells's objections to the eugenicist ideal of attempting to breed an ideal type of human. As we see in the last selection, he is more sympathetic to the possibility of breeding out undesirable traits, though the rest of the essay warns of the problems of attempting this as well. When Wells refers to what "theoretical breeders of humanity" want, he means what in his opinion they should want in order to effectively benefit the human species.]

The first difficulty these theorists [such as Francis Galton] ignore is this: we are, as a matter of fact, not a bit clear what points to breed for and what points to breed out.

The analogy with the breeder of cattle is a very misleading one. He has a very simple ideal, to which he directs the entire pairing of his stock. He breeds for beef, he breeds for calves and milk, he breeds for a homogeneous docile herd. Towards that ideal he goes simply and directly, slaughtering and sparing, regardless of any divergent variation that may arise beneath his control. A young calf with an incipient sense of humour, with a bright and inquiring disposition, with a gift of athleticism or a quaintly marked hide, has no sort of chance with him at all on that account. He can throw these proffered gifts of nature aside without hesitation. Which is just what our theoretical breeders of humanity cannot venture to do. They do not want a homogeneous race in the future at all. They want a rich interplay of free, strong, and varied personalities, and that alters the nature of the problem absolutely. (310-11)

Our utmost practice here must be empirical. We do not know the elements of what we have, the human characteristics we are working upon to get that end. The sentimentalized affinities of young persons in their spring are just as likely to result in the improvement of the race in this respect as the whole science of anthropology in its present state of evolution. (315)

I believe that long before humanity has hammered out the question of what is pre-eminently desirable in inheritance, a certain number of things will have been isolated and defined as pre-eminently undesirable. (321)

3. From H.G. Wells, *A Modern Utopia* [1905]. *The Works of H.G. Wells* (Atlantic Edition). Vol. 9. New York: Scribners, 1925

[These selections are from chapter five, "Failure in a Modern Utopia." They illustrate a relatively mild way of dealing with traits that are "pre-eminently undesirable." In Wells's ideal world a self-denying elite called the Samurai will exercise a benevolent rule over the World State with the ultimate goal of enhancing both the life of the individual and the quality of the human species. Central to the goal of improving the species will be a program of "negative" eugenics that will prevent the physically and socially unfit from breeding, supposedly without interfering with their enjoyment of life. No attempt will be made to implement the "positive" side of Galton's eugenic program: selective breeding to produce an ideal type of human. Wells feels that evolution requires a wide variety of human types.

In *A Modern Utopia* Wells attempts to reconcile the practice of a limited eugenics with the universal benevolence of a Utopian government, and thus to avoid the undermining of human sympathy that both Darwin and Huxley warn could be a possible outcome of eugenics as a social policy. Here Wells presents a more considered and humane view on denying reproduction to the unfit than that proposed in *Anticipations* (1901), his first work of futurology. For a detailed discussion of Wells's shifting ideas about eugenics in relation to the development of his political ideas, see John S. Partington's two articles published in *Utopian Studies* and the third chapter of his book *Building Cosmopolis: The Political Thought of H.G. Wells.*]

The old Utopias—save for the breeding schemes of Plato and Campanella—ignored that reproductive competition among individualities which is the substance of life, and dealt essentially with its incidentals. The endless variety of men, their endless gradation of quality, over which the hand of selection plays, and to which we owe the unmanageable complication of real life, is tacitly set aside. The real world is a vast disorder of accidents and incalculable forces in which men survive or fail. A modern Utopia, unlike its predecessors, dare not pretend to change the last condition: it may order and humanize the conflict, but men must still survive or fail.

Most Utopias present themselves as going concerns, as happiness in being; they make it an essential condition that a happy land can have no history, and all the citizens one is permitted to see are well looking and upright and mentally and morally in tune. But we are under the dominion of a logic that obliges us to take over the actual population of the world with only such moral and mental and physical improvements as lie within their inherent possibilities, and it is our business to ask what Utopia will do with its congenital invalids, its idiots and madmen, its drunkards and men of vicious mind, its cruel and furtive souls, its stupid people, too stupid to be of use to the community, its lumpish, unteachable and unimaginative people? And what will it do with the man who is "poor" all round, the rather spiritless, rather incompetent low-grade man who on earth sits in the den of the sweater,[1] tramps the streets under the banner of the unemployed,[2] or trembles—in another man's cast-off clothing, and with an infinity of hat-touching—on the verge of rural employment?

These people will have to be in the descendent phase, the species must be engaged in eliminating them; there is no escape from that, and conversely the people of exceptional quality must be ascendant. The better sort of people, so far as they can be distinguished, must have the fullest freedom of public service, and the fullest opportunity of parentage. And it must be open to every man to approve himself worthy of ascendency.

The way of Nature in this process is to kill the weaker and the sillier, to crush them, to starve them, to overwhelm them, using the stronger and more cunning as her weapon. But man is the unnatural animal, the rebel child of Nature, and more and more does he turn himself against the harsh and fitful hand that reared him. He sees with a growing resentment the multitude of suffering ineffectual lives over which his species tramples in its ascent. In the Modern Utopia he will have to set himself to change the ancient law. No longer will it be that failures must suffer and perish lest their breed increase, but the breed of failure must not increase, lest they suffer and perish, and the race with them.... (122-23)

And if it can be so contrived that every human being shall live in a state of reasonable physical and mental comfort, without the reproduction of in-

---

1   An exploitative employer who operates a "sweatshop," where the workers are forced to work long hours for inadequate pay under unsanitary conditions.

2   I.e., in a public demonstration against unemployment.

ferior types, there is no reason whatever why that should not be secured. But there must be a competition in life of some sort to determine who are to be pushed to the edge, and who are to prevail and multiply.... A Utopia planned upon modern lines ... will insist upon every citizen being properly housed, well nourished, and in good health, reasonably clean and clothed healthily, and upon that insistence its labour laws will be founded. In a phrasing that will be familiar to everyone interested in social reform, it will maintain a standard of life.... (124-25)

The State would provide these things for its citizen as though it was his right to require them.... But on the other hand it will require that the citizen who renders the minimum of service for these concessions shall not become a parent until he is established in work at a rate above the minimum, and free of any debt he may have incurred.[1] The State will never press for its debt, nor put a limit to its accumulation so long as a man or woman remains childless.... By such obvious devices it will achieve the maximum elimination of its feeble and spiritless folk in every generation with the minimum of suffering and public disorder.

But the mildly incompetent, the spiritless and dull, the poorer sort who are ill, do not exhaust our Utopian problem. There remain idiots and lunatics, there remain perverse and incompetent persons, there are people of weak character who become drunkards, drug takers, and the like. Then there are persons tainted with certain foul and transmissible diseases. All these people spoil the world for others. They may become parents, and with most of them there is manifestly nothing to be done but to seclude them from the great body of the population. You must resort to a kind of social surgery. You cannot have social freedom in your public ways, your children cannot speak to whom they will, your girls and gentlewomen cannot go abroad while some sorts of people go free. And there are violent people, and those who will not respect the property of others, thieves and cheats; they, too, so soon as their nature is confirmed, must pass out of the free life of our ordered world. So soon as there can be no doubt of the disease or baseness of the individual, so soon as the insanity or other disease is assured, or the crime repeated a third time, or the drunkenness or misdemeanour past its seventh occasion (let us say), so soon must he or she pass out of the common ways of men.

The dreadfulness of all such proposals as this lies in the possibility of their execution falling into the hands of hard, dull, and cruel administrators. But in the case of a Utopia one assumes the best possible government, a government as merciful and deliberate as it is powerful and decisive. You must not too hastily imagine these things being done—as they would be done on

---

1   I.e., the State will provide work for all at a minimum wage, but workers who remain in this category will not be allowed to reproduce.

earth at present—by a number of zealous half-educated people in a state of panic at a quite imaginary "Rapid Multiplication of the Unfit...." (127-28)

I doubt even if there will be jails. No men are wise enough, good enough and cheap enough to staff jails as a jail ought to be staffed. Perhaps islands will be chosen, islands lying apart from the highways of the sea, and to these the State will send its exiles, most of them thanking Heaven, no doubt, to be quit of a world of prigs.[1] The State will, of course, secure itself against any children from these people, that is the primary object of their seclusion, and perhaps it may even be necessary to make these island prisons a system of island monasteries and island nunneries....

About such islands patrol boats will go, there will be no freedoms of boat building, and it may be necessary to have armed guards at the creeks and quays. Beyond that the State will give these segregated failures just as full a liberty as they can have. (130)

4. From Gina Lombroso-Ferrero, *Criminal Man According to the Classification of Cesare Lombroso* [1911]. Montclair, NJ: Patterson Smith, 1972

[One of the most accessible presentations of Lombroso's work available today, this volume consists of a translation of selections from his comprehensive *Criminal Man*, the first volume of which he published in 1876 and the second in 1887. Lombroso's concept of criminal atavism was widely influential in the late nineteenth century. In his opening account of his response to the skull of the bandit Vilella, Lombroso tells how he came to conceive of his science of "criminal anthropology."]

I ... began to study criminals in the Italian prisons, and, amongst others, I made the acquaintance of the famous brigand Vilella. This man possessed such extraordinary agility, that he had been known to scale steep mountain heights bearing a sheep on his shoulders. His cynical effrontery was such that he openly boasted of his crimes. On his death one cold grey November morning, I was deputed to make the *post-mortem*, and on laying open the skull I found on the occipital[2] part, exactly on the spot where a spine is found in the normal skull, a distinct depression which I named *median occipital fossa*, because of its situation precisely in the middle of the occiput as in

---

1   Aldous Huxley makes satiric use of the idea of sending social misfits to islands in his well-known dystopia *Brave New World*. In his study of Wells's influence on the dystopian tradition, Mark Hillegas notes that later dystopian writers tend to use the satiric methods they learned from Wells to satirize his utopias.

2   Back part of the skull.

inferior animals, especially rodents. This depression, as in the case of animals, was correlated with the hypertrophy of the *vermis*, known in birds as the middle cerebellum.

And this was not merely an idea, but a revelation. At the sight of that skull, I seemed to see all of a sudden, lighted up as a vast plain under a flaming sky, the problem of the nature of the criminal—an atavistic being who reproduces in his person the ferocious instincts of primitive humanity and the inferior animals. Thus were explained anatomically the enormous jaws, high cheekbones, prominent supercilliary arches, solitary lines in the palms, extreme size of the orbits, handle-shaped or sessile[1] found in criminals, savages, and apes, insensibility to pain, extremely acute sight, tattooing, excessive idleness, love of orgies, and the irresistible craving for evil for its own sake, the desire not only to extinguish life in the victim, but to mutilate the corpse, tear its flesh, and drink its blood.

I was further encouraged in this bold hypothesis by the results of my studies on Verzeni, a criminal convicted of sadism and rape, who showed the cannibalistic instincts of primitive anthropophagists[2] and the ferocity of beasts of prey.... (xxiv-xxv)

Physical Anomalies of the Born Criminal

The Face. In striking contrast to the narrow forehead and low vault of the skull, the face of the criminal, like those of most animals, is of disproportionate size, a phenomenon intimately connected with the greater development of the senses as compared with that of the nervous centres. Prognathism, the projection of the lower portion of the face beyond the forehead, is found in 45.7% of criminals. Progeneismus, the projection of the lower teeth and jaw beyond the upper, is found in 38%, whereas among normal persons the proportion is barely 28%. As a natural consequence of this predominance of the lower portion of the face ... the size of the jaws is naturally increased ... Among criminals 29% have voluminous jaws....

Asymmetry is a common characteristic of the criminal physiognomy. The eyes and ears are frequently situated at different levels and are of unequal size, the nose slants towards one side, etc. This asymmetry ... is connected with marked irregularities in the senses and functions.

The Eye. This window, through which the mind opens to the outer world, is naturally the centre of many anomalies of a psychic character, hard expression, shifty glance....

---

1   Leaf-shaped.
2   Eaters of human flesh.

The Ear. The external ear is often of large size; occasionally also it is smaller than the ears of normal individuals. Twenty-eight per cent. of criminals have handle-shaped ears standing out from the face as in the chimpanzee; in other cases they are placed at different levels. Frequently, too, we find misshapen, flattened ears ... a relic of the pointed ear characteristic of apes. Anomalies are also found in the lobe, which in some cases adheres too closely to the face, or is of huge size as in the ancient Egyptians; in other cases, the lobe is entirely absent, or is atrophied till the ear assumes a form like that common to apes.

The Nose. This is frequently twisted, up-turned, or of a flattened, negroid character in thieves; in murderers, on the contrary, it is often aquiline like the beak of a bird of prey. Not infrequently we meet with the trilobate nose, its tip rising like an isolated peak from the swollen nostrils, a form found among the Akkas, a tribe of pygmies of Central Africa....

The Mouth. This part shows perhaps a greater number of anomalies than any other facial organ. We have already alluded to the excessive development of the jaws in criminals. They are sometimes the seat of other abnormal characters—the lemurine apophysis, a bony elevation of the angle of the jaw, which may easily be recognized externally by passing the hand over the skin; and the canine fossa, a depression of the upper jaw for the attachment of the canine muscle. This muscle, which is strongly developed in the dog, serves when contracted to draw back the lip leaving the canines exposed.

The lips of violators of women and murderers are fleshy, swollen and protruding, as in negroes. Swindlers have thin, straight lips. Harelip is more common in criminals than in normal persons....

The Teeth. These are specially important, for criminals rarely have normal dentition. The incisors show the greatest number of anomalies. Sometimes both the lateral incisors are absent and the middle ones are of excessive size, a peculiarity which recalls the incisors of rodents.... In 4% the canines are very strongly developed, long, sharp, and curving inwardly as in carnivores. (12-17)

The criminal is an atavistic being, a relic of a vanished race. This is by no means an uncommon occurrence in nature. Atavism, the reversion to a former state, is the first feeble indication of the reaction opposed by nature to the perturbing causes which seek to alter her delicate mechanism....

This tendency to alter under special conditions is common to human beings, in whom hunger, syphilis, trauma, and, still more frequently, morbid conditions inherited from insane, criminal, or diseased progenitors, or the abuse of nerve poisons, such as alcohol, tobacco, or morphine, cause various alterations, of which criminality—that is, a return to the characteristics peculiar to primitive savages—is in reality the least serious, because it represents a less advanced stage than other forms of cerebral alteration.

The aetiology of crime, therefore, mingles with that of all kinds of degeneration: rickets, deafness, monstrosity, hairiness, and cretinism, of which crime is only a variation. (135-36)

5. From Cesare Lombroso, *Crime: Its Causes and Remedies* [1899]. Trans. Henry P. Horton. 1911. Montclair, NJ: Patterson Smith, 1968

[Much of the material in this volume was originally published earlier than 1899. In the passage below Lombroso lists identical vices supposedly found in criminals and "savages." The following passage could be relevant to the ecstatic dance of the Pig People in chapter nine of *Moreau*.]

At times ... impulsiveness, rather than sluggishness, seems to ally itself with a ceaseless need of movement, which asserts itself in savage peoples in a life of incessant vagabondage.... This attitude seems to be the result of a passage between physiopsychic inertia and an intermittent need of violent and unrestrained physical and moral excitation, which always goes with inertia and impulsiveness. Thus it is that those peoples who are normally most lazy and indolent have the most unrestrained and noisy dances, which they carry on until they get into a kind of delirium, and fall down utterly exhausted.... "The negroes of Africa," writes Du Chaillu, "dance madly when they hear the sound of the tom-tom, and lose all command of themselves." "It is," says Letourneau, "real dancing madness, which makes them forget their troubles, public or private." (367)

6. From William James, *Psychology: The Briefer Course.* (1892) New York: Henry Holt, 1910

[William James (1842-1910), older brother of the novelist Henry James, was an influential psychologist and philosopher in the late nineteenth and early twentieth centuries, and remains well known today, especially for *The Varieties of Religious Experience* (1902). His comprehensive survey of the psychological ideas of his time, *The Principles of Psychology* (1890), was widely accepted as authoritative. The passage below is from the popular condensation of the *Principles* for a textbook, published in 1892.

James suggests that psychological reversion could explain some irrational aspects of fear: we inherit a tendency to fear certain objects and situations that were more dangerous in prehistoric life than they are today. (Here James seems to agree with the position he ascribes to the "cock-sure evolutionist.") This idea could be relevant to the continuance of Prendick's dread and anxiety after his return to Britain. His traumatic experience among the Beast People could be the trigger that aroused inherited fears.]

[James discusses the basic fears of childhood—fear of strange people and animals, of high places, and of dark places such as caves.] The ordinary cocksure evolutionist ought to have no difficulty in explaining these terrors, and the scenery that provokes them, as relapses into the consciousness of the cave-men, a consciousness usually overlaid in us by experiences of a more recent date.

There are certain other pathological fears and certain peculiarities in the expression of ordinary fear, which might receive an explanatory light from ancestral conditions, even infra-human ones.... [T]ake the strange symptom which has been described of late years by the rather absurd name of *agoraphobia*. The patient is seized by palpitation and terror at the sight of any open place or broad street which he has to cross alone. He trembles, his knees bend, he may even faint at the idea. Where he has sufficient self-command he sometimes accomplishes the object by keeping safe under the lee of a vehicle going across, or joining himself to a knot of other people. But usually he slinks around the sides of the square, hugging the houses as closely as he can. This emotion has no utility in a civilized men, but when we notice the chronic agoraphobia of our domestic cats, and we see the tenacious way in which many wild animals, especially rodents, cling to cover, and only venture on a dash across the open as a desperate measure—even then making for every stone or bunch of weeds which may give a momentary shelter—when we see this we are strongly tempted to ask whether such an odd kind of fear in us be not due to the accidental resurrection, through disease, of a sort of instinct which may in some of our remote ancestors have had a permanent and on the whole a useful part to play?

7. From Jacques-Joseph Moreau (de Tours), *La Psychologie Morbide*. Paris: Victor Masson, 1859 (Translated by the editor)

[Several critics have seen Jacques-Joseph Moreau (1804-84), a French psychiatrist, as a likely source for the name of Wells's Doctor Moreau and also as providing a diagnosis for Doctor Moreau's state of mind. J.-J. Moreau was known for his innovative ideas; most of his professional life was spent working with severely disturbed patients at the Bicêtre mental hospital for men. He is known today for his book, *Hashish and Mental Illness* (1845), comparing drug-induced visions with psychotic hallucinations, but in the nineteenth century he was probably best known for *Morbid Psychology*, his book on affinities between genius and mental imbalance, which he considered his most important publication.

In this book J.-J. Moreau concludes that a pathological outcome from the overstimulation that might result from the accelerated mental activities of genius could take two forms: mania, a rapid and disordered flow of thoughts where attention cannot be fixed on any one idea; and an opposite state, monomania, in which a circle of obsessive thoughts is knitted so tightly together that the monomaniac comes to live in a self-enclosed mental world. Wells's character, Doctor Moreau, would fall into the second category.

In the nineteenth century J.-J. Moreau was considered an important psychologist. Wells would likely have become acquainted with his ideas, especially considering that he wrote a paper on psychology as part of his work for a diploma from the College of Preceptors—*Experiment in Autobiography*, 275.] (Except for quotes in French, all emphases in the text are those of J.-J. Moreau.)

"Argument"[1]

The mental characteristics which enable a man to distinguish himself from others by the originality of his thoughts and conceptions, by his eccentricity or the energy of his feelings, or by the superiority of his intellect, arise from the same organic conditions as the various mental disturbances which are most fully expressed in madness and idiocy.

No individual, surely, has developed within himself, by his own will, the various manifestations of the process of thought.... Nor is it his choice that his inclinations, his instincts, should be more or less energetic and compelling, his imagination more or less lively, his memory more or less reliable, his conceptions, his ideas more or less elevated. Does the writer, the poet, the musician, provide for himself, by his own will, the inspiration, the sacred fire that consumes him? Ask all scholars worthy of that name, if their work is not for them a real pleasure, a relaxation, more than that a real need, almost a necessity, as it is for an infant to move its limbs....

Such tendencies, such passions, such abilities, are born with the individual, ... develop with him, and finally go beyond their goal when an accidental cause, most often insignificant, suddenly or gradually distorts or even breaks down the activity of the organs of thought by intensifying it beyond its normal bounds. (128-29)

A new horizon now opens before us. Our subject will open up and offer us a completely new perspective. We will go beyond limits which up to now have seemed impenetrable, we will link together two modes of the intellectual faculty which, taken separately, seem to negate one another and to be

---

1   Summary of the book's theme, in this case printed on an unnumbered first page.

mutually exclusive. We will show the connections ... between the two most extreme conditions of the human spirit: madness and the highest abilities of the intelligence.... We now understand that there is no contradiction in affirming that ... delirium and genius have common roots....

Let us repeat it again, because this truth is the cornerstone of our work: madness arises from excessive mental activity, and from this sometimes will follow the disintegration and incoherence of ideas (*the manic state*) or the abnormal cohesion of ideas (*monomania*): it is in lessening this excessive activity, in breaking this cohesion, that one succeeds in reconstructing reason, and giving back to the patient his *self-power*....[1]

It becomes clear that the organic conditions most favourable to the development of the mental faculties are precisely those which give birth to delirium.

From the unusual accumulation of vital forces in an organ, two consequences are equally possible: more energy in the functions of that organ, but also more chances of aberration and deviation in those same functions.

One of the most conclusive proofs of what we have been arguing is this: the mental state in which intellectual power reaches its highest point throws off such brilliant beams of light that ancient philosophy explained it as possession by a divine being. The state of *inspiration* is precisely what offers the closest analogy with real madness. Here madness and genius become almost the same thing by dint of converging and mingling together. (385-87)

What is genius, that is to say the highest, the most essential aspect of intellectual activity, but a neurosis? Why not? One can very well, it seems to us, accept that definition ... in making [the word neurosis] simply stand for a highly stimulated state [*l'exaltation*] (we do not say disturbance or disruption) of the intellectual faculties.... The word neurosis expresses simply a special state of the brain corresponding to that disposition of intellectual power which we have just described and which is called genius. In other words, genius, like all aspects of the processes of thought, necessarily has its material basis; this basis is a semi-morbid state of the brain, a real excitation of the nerves.... (464-65)

Indeed, if the normal state of the organism is generally in accord with the regular action of the intellectual faculty, never, in such a case, or only by exception, does one see the intelligence raise itself above what one might call an honest mediocrity, in the realm of feelings as well as intellect.

Under these conditions, a person will be endowed with moral sense, a judgment more or less reliable, a certain degree of imagination; his pas-

---

[1] This phrase is given in English in the original.

sions will be moderate; always master of himself, he will practise better than anyone the doctrine of enlightened self-interest; he will never be a great criminal, but neither will he be a person who makes great contributions to humanity; he will never suffer from that *mental malady* which one calls genius; in no case, to put it briefly, will he ever rise to the rank of privileged beings. (468)

In summary, it seems to us sufficiently established that the organic basis for the preeminence of the intellectual faculties is a special unhealthy state of the nervous system.

This morbid condition, which, by the way, only rarely compromises the other mental functions, at least not in an obvious manner (with the exception of idiocy), is nothing other than a nervous excitability or irritability of which the essential nature is to push incessantly the activity of the mental faculties to extremes, and which by the same token constitutes a strong predisposition to cerebral disorders of all kinds, and to a chronic delirium which includes all these disorders and is the most complete expression of them. (481)

Is it not evident, after all that we have said, that it is precisely in the brains so magnificent, so powerfully organized, that the true origin of high intellectual faculties must reveal itself by some recognizable sign, by some fact decisively indicating a pathological condition? (490)

All the ways in which exceptional men deviate from the common path require a more searching investigation on our part....

We have said that [their mental processes including their leisure activities] are the result of an excessive concentration of the mind on a habitual subject of study: this is evident, and we would not know how to give a better explanation. But we hasten to add that when this concentration is carried to a certain degree, it comes close to being a symptom of illness....

We should not forget that what distinguishes the insane person from other men is that, at least in the circle of his delirious convictions, he lives entirely in himself, stranger to all the things of the external world, deaf to all the impressions that come to him from it. Is he not in a continuous state of distraction, this insane person for whom no voice, no reasoning, can capture his attention or move his feelings, with whom it is also impossible to enter into communication, at least on any subject foreign to his fixed ideas, as though one were addressing a man who speaks while dreaming?

This concentration which isolates an individual so completely from his fellow humans ... is it not the sign of *fixed ideas*?... In mania or general delirium, impressions are so fugitive and numerous, ideas are so abundant, that the manic person cannot fix his attention on particular objects or ideas; with the monomaniac, attention is so *concentrated that it can no longer focus on objects in the outside world, or on ideas not directly related to his obsessions.*

Now, is not this what happens in the mental state one calls distraction; is it not evident that this temporary absence, this failure of the mind of the distracted person to be present, is at least somewhat related to the fixity of ideas which characterizes the monomaniac? (500-02)

Human intelligence is never closer to failure than when it raises itself to the greatest heights. The causes of its decadence are also those of its grandeur. (576)

8. From Gustave Le Bon, *The Crowd: A Study of the Popular Mind*. Ernest Benn: London, 1896. Originally published as *Psychologie des foules*, 1895. Name of translator not given

[Gustave Le Bon (1841-1931), French psychologist and sociologist, is regarded as one of the founders of social psychology. He is best known today as the author of *Psychologie des foules*, a study of mob psychology. When it was published in 1895 this book quickly became a best-seller, attracting wide attention and commentary across Europe. Whether or not Le Bon's ideas were available to Wells in time to influence the composition of *Moreau*, most of which seems to have been completed in the first three months of 1895, his book represents a general interest in mob psychology in the late nineteenth century which continued into the twentieth. Freud used extensive quotations from Le Bon's book to launch his own study of the subject, *Group Psychology and the Analysis of the Ego* (1921).

In *Moreau* there are two scenes in which the Beast People become a mob: the hunting of Prendick in chapter 11; and, described in detail, the hunting of the Leopard Man, led by Moreau, in which Prendick participates in chapter 16. Also, Moreau himself was "howled out of the country" by an enraged public (94; ch. 7).]

We see, then, that the disappearance of the conscious personality, the predominance of the unconscious personality, the turning by means of suggestion and contagion of feelings and ideas in an identical direction, the tendency to immediately transform the suggested ideas into acts; these we see, are the principal characteristics of the individual forming part of a crowd. He is no longer himself, but has become an automaton who has ceased to be guided by his will.

Moreover, by the mere fact that he forms part of an organized crowd, a man descends several rungs in the ladder of civilization. Isolated, he may be a cultivated individual; in a crowd, he is a barbarian—that is, a creature acting by instinct. He possesses the spontaneity, the violence, the ferocity, and also the enthusiasm and heroism of primitive beings, whom he further tends to resemble by the facility with which he allows himself to be impressed by words and images—which would be entirely without action on each of the isolated individuals composing the crowd—and to be induced to commit acts contrary to his most obvious interests and his best-known habits. An individual in a crowd is a grain of sand amid other grains of sand, which the wind stirs up at will.... (33-36; ch. 1)

It will be remarked that among the special characteristics of crowds there are several—such as impulsiveness, irritability, incapacity to reason, the absence of judgment and of the critical spirit, the exaggerations of the sentiments, and others besides—which are almost always observed in beings belonging to inferior forms of evolution—in women, savages, and children, for instance....

When studying the fundamental characteristics of a crowd we stated that it is guided almost exclusively by unconscious motives. Its acts are far more under the influence of the spinal cord than of the brain. In this respect a crowd is closely akin to quite primitive beings. (40; ch. 2.1)

We have shown that crowds do not reason, that they accept or reject ideas as a whole, that they tolerate neither discussion nor contradiction, and that the suggestions brought to bear on them invade the entire field of their understanding and tend at once to transform themselves into acts....

When these convictions are closely examined, whether at epochs marked by fervent religious faith, or by great political upheavals such as those of the last century, it is apparent that they always assume a peculiar form which I cannot better define than by giving it the name of a religious sentiment.

This sentiment has very simple characteristics, such as worship of a being supposed superior, fear of the power with which the being is credited, blind submission to its commands, inability to discuss its dogmas, the desire to spread them, and a tendency to consider as enemies all by whom they are not accepted.... The hero acclaimed by a crowd is a veritable god for that crowd.... The crowd demands a god before everything else. (81-85; ch. 4)

Reason and arguments are incapable of combating certain words and formulas. They are uttered with solemnity in the presence of crowds, and as soon as they have been pronounced an expression of respect is visible on every countenance, and all heads are bowed. By many they are considered as natural forces, as supernatural powers. They evoke grandiose and vague images in men's minds, but this very vagueness that wraps them in obscurity augments their mysterious power. They are the mysterious divinities hidden behind the tabernacle, which the devout only approach in fear and trembling. (117-18; Bk. II, ch. 2)

9. From H.G. Wells, *The Croquet Player* [1936]. New York: The Viking Press, 1937

[Wells never lost his touch for fantasy and the macabre. Late in his career he produced this Gothic novella focusing on the animal inheritance of the human species as the central problem of civilization. The tale is presented as a ghost story, but is meant to have wide implications, dramatizing the worst possible outcome of the Darwinian problems explored over forty years earlier in *Moreau* and "Human Evolution, an Artificial Process." It projects on a large scale the fear expressed by Prendick in the last chapter of *Moreau* that the animal in human nature might be "surging up" in ordinary people and that "presently the degradation of the Islanders will be played over again on a larger scale" (173; ch. 22).

The apocalyptic mood of *The Croquet Player* was provoked by ominous international developments in the late 1930s, especially the atrocities of the Spanish Civil War and the approach of World War II, which Wells foresaw more clearly than most of his contemporaries. The reference to children killed by air-raids refers to the bombing of civilians by the German air force in Spain.

One of the characters, Dr. Finchatton, convalescing in an asylum, tells the Croquet Player (the frame-narrator) of the experiences that led to his nervous breakdown. He took up a medical practice in a remote, marshy area called "Cainsmarsh" where he became increasingly troubled by fear of shadows and open spaces and by nightmares of violent struggle. He comes to suspect that his patients are suffering from the same state of mind. A fanatical local clergyman provides a supernatural explanation; he insists that archaeological exploration in the area is unearthing an ancient evil, thus reviving "the punishment of Cain" for murdering his brother Abel (43). Finchatton visits the local museum where the scientific-minded curator explains that the bones being dug up are those of the Neanderthal people and shows him a nearly-intact skull. When Finchatton asks for advice about his strange anxieties, the curator becomes philosophical and even suggests that there might be some point in the idea of a haunting. Finchatton narrates the following sequence.]

"[The curator] embarked upon quite a history of the region. 'It must have been inhabited,' I said, 'for thousands of years.'

"'Hundreds of thousands,' he told me. 'There were Neanderthalers[1] and—But let me show you our special glory!'

"He led me to a locked glass cupboard in which was a thick lowering beetle-browed skull, that still seemed to scowl from its empty sockets. Beside it was its under jaw. This dirty rusty-brown treasure, he said, was the completest specimen of its kind in the world.... The little curator watched me as I surveyed his prize specimen and marked the snarling grin of its upper jaw and the shadowy vitality that still lurked in the caverns whence its eyes had once glared upon the world.

"'That might, I suppose, be our ancestor?' I said.

"'More probable than not.'

"'That in our blood!' I said.

"I turned half round and looked at the monster askance and, when I spoke again, I spoke as if he also might be listening. I asked a score of amateurish questions. There had been countless generations of him and his kind, I learnt. His sort had slouched and snarled over the marshes for a hundred times the length of all recorded history. In comparison with *his* overlordship our later human rule was a thing of yesterday. Millions of these brutish lives had come and passed, leaving fragments, implements, stones they had chipped or reddened by their fires, bones they had gnawed. Not a pebble in the marsh, not an inch of ground, their feet had not pressed or their hands gripped a myriad times....

"'The marshes have got hold of me,' I said. 'And if I do not do something about it, they will drive me mad.... Tell my why it is one dreams there so dismally, why one is haunted by fear in the daylight and horrible fears in the night?...You don't think an ugly beast like that could really leave a ghost?' I asked.

"'It's left its bones,' he said. 'Do you think it had anything you could call a spirit? Something that might still be urgent to hurt and torment and frighten? Something profoundly suspicious and easily angered?.... [I]n the last century or so ... [w]e have poked into the past, unearthing age after age, and we peer more and more forward into the future. And that's what's the matter with us.'

"'In the Marsh?' said I.

"'Everywhere.... Sometimes it's nearer the surface in the Marsh—but it's everywhere. We have broken the frame of the present and the past, the long black past of fear and hate that our grandfathers never knew of, never sus-

---

1 In a combination of essay and short story entitled "The Grisly Folk" (1921), set in the Old Stone Age, Wells casts the Neanderthals as a lurking cannibalistic threat to the fully-human Cro-Magnon people. William Golding reverses this situation in *The Inheritors* (1955) by making the Neanderthals morally superior to the Cro-Magnons.

pected, is pouring back upon us. And the future opens like a gulf to swallow us up. The animal fears again and the animal rages again and the old faiths no longer restrain it. The cave man, the ancestral ape, the ancestral brute, have returned. So it is. I can assure you I am talking realities to you. It is going on now everywhere. You have been in the Marsh. You have felt them in the Marsh, but I tell you these resurrected savageries are breathing now and thrusting everywhere. The world is full of menace—not only here.'" (58–64)

[After his talk with the curator, Finchatton has a dream of the Neanderthal skull.]

"More and more did the threat of that primordial Adamite dominate me. I could not banish that eyeless stare and that triumphant grin from my mind, sleeping or waking. Waking I saw it as it was in the museum, as if it were a living presence that had set us a riddle and was amused to hear our inadequate attempts at a solution. Sleeping I saw it released from all rational proportions. It became gigantic. It became as vast as a cliff, a mountainous skull in which the orbits and hollows of the jaw were huge caves. He had an effect—it is hard to convey these dream effects—as if he were continually rising and yet always towering there. In the foreground I saw his innumerable descendants, swarming like ants, swarms of human beings hurrying to and fro, making helpless gestures of submission or deference, resisting an overpowering impulse to throw themselves under his all-devouring shadow. Presently these swarms began to fall into lines and columns, were clad in uniforms, formed up and began marching and trotting towards the black shadows under those worn and rust-stained teeth. From which darkness there presently oozed something—something winding and trickling, and something that manifestly tasted very agreeably to him. Blood." (70)

[The story ends with Dr. Finchatton's psychiatrist, a figure in whom Wells presents a satire of himself trying to re-shape society, lecturing the Croquet Player on the need to strengthen civilization in the face of the coming resurgence of primitive savagery. Although here these ideas are presented by a rather overbearing character, Wells wanted them to be taken seriously.]

Appendix G: The Vivisection Controversy

1. From Claude Bernard, *Report on the Progress and Development of General Physiology in France* [1867]. Quoted by John Vyvyan, 32

[Dr. Claude Bernard (1813-1878) is probably the leading physiologist of the nineteenth century. He is also the most notorious vivisector of the period, partly because of his ruthless use of animals in research and partly because of his outspoken defence of vivisection.]

Twenty-five years ago, when I began my career in experimental physiology, I found myself in those difficulties that are reserved for experimenters.... As soon as an experimental physiologist was discovered, he was denounced; he was given over to the reproaches of his neighbours, and subjected to annoyances by the police. At the beginning of my experimental studies, I ran into such difficulties many times.

2. From Michael Foster, *Claude Bernard*. London: Unwin, 1899

[An account of Bernard's surgical skill and passion for research by a friend and biographer.]

Without haste and without hesitation, taking step after step swiftly and in due order, he would with exact strokes lay bare and isolate a delicate structure by disentangling it, with the utmost neatness, from its perplexing surroundings, and would complete a difficult operation in time needed by others for mere preliminary preparation. It is told of him that sometimes, urged by the pressing need to get an immediate answer to some question with which his mind was stirred, he would come suddenly into the laboratory, call for an animal, and then and there, without so much as removing his hat, perform an experiment, it may be of no little difficulty. (236)

3. From Claude Bernard, *An Introduction to the Study of Experimental Medicine*. Paris [1865]. Trans. Henry Copley Green. New York: Dover, 1957

[Selected passages defending the vivisection of animals from Bernard's most famous book, *An Introduction to the Study of Experimental Medicine*. All emphases are those of the author.]

If a comparison were required to express my idea of the science of life, I should say that it is a superb and dazzlingly lighted hall which may be reached only by passing through a long and ghastly kitchen. (15)

[I]f the subject is entirely dark and unexplored, physiologists should not be afraid even to act somewhat at random, so as to try,—permit me the common expression,—fishing in troubled waters. This amounts to saying that, in the midst of the functional disturbances which they produce, they may hope to see some unexpected phenomena emerge which give direction to their research. Such groping experiments, which are very common in physiology and therapeutics because of the complex and backward state of these sciences, may be called *experiments to see*, because they are intended to make a first observation emerge, unforseen and undetermined in advance, but whose appearance may suggest an experimental idea and open a path for research. (20-21)

Now, a living organism is nothing but a wonderful machine endowed with the most marvellous properties and set going by means of the most complex and delicate mechanism.... To succeed in solving these various problems, we must, as it were, analyze the organism, as we take apart a machine to review and study all of its works. (63, 65)

We have succeeded in discovering the laws of inorganic matter only by penetrating into inanimate bodies and machines; similarly we shall succeed in learning the laws and properties of living matter only by displacing living organs in order to get into their inner environment. After dissecting cadavers, then, we must necessarily dissect living beings, to uncover the inner or hidden parts of the organisms and see them work; to this sort of operation we give the name of vivisection, and without this mode of investigation, neither physiology nor scientific medicine is possible; to learn how man and animals live, we cannot avoid seeing great numbers of them die, because the mechanisms of life can be unveiled and proved only by knowledge of the mechanisms of death.

Men have felt this truth in all ages; and in medicine, from the earliest times, men have performed not only therapeutic experiments but even vivisection.... In our time ... vivisection has entered physiology and medicine once and for all, as an habitual and indispensable method of study.

The prejudices clinging to respect for corpses long halted the progress of anatomy. In the same way, vivisection in all ages has met with prejudices and detractors. We cannot aspire to destroy all the prejudices in the world; neither shall we allow ourselves here to answer the arguments of detractors of vivisection; since they thereby deny experimental medicine, i.e., scientific medicine. However, we shall consider a few general questions, and then we shall set up the scientific goal which vivisection has in view.... (99-101)

Another question presents itself. Have we the right to make experiments on animals and vivisect them? As for me, I think we have this right, wholly and absolutely. It would be strange indeed if we recognized man's right to make use of animals in every walk of life, for domestic service, for food, and then forbade him to make use of them for his own instruction in one of the sciences most useful to humanity. No hesitation is possible; the science of life can be established only through experiment, and we can save living beings from death only after sacrificing others. Experiments must be made either on man or on animals. Now I think that physicians already make too many dangerous experiments on man, before carefully studying them on animals. I do not admit that it is moral to try more or less dangerous or active remedies on patients in hospitals, without first experimenting with them on dogs; for I shall prove, further on, that results obtained on animals may all be conclusive for man when we know how to experiment properly. If it is immoral, then, to make an experiment on man when it is dangerous to him, even though the result may be useful to others, it is essentially moral to make experiments on an animal, even though painful and dangerous to him, if it may be useful to man.

After all this, should we let ourselves be moved by the sensitive cries of people of fashion or by the objections of men unfamiliar with scientific ideas? All feelings deserve respect, and I shall be very careful never to offend anyone's. I easily explain them to myself, and that is why they cannot stop me.... I ... understand perfectly how people of fashion, moved by ideas wholly different from those that animate physiologists, judge vivisection quite differently. It cannot be otherwise.... (102-03)

A physiologist is not a man of fashion, he is a man of science, absorbed by the scientific idea which he pursues: he no longer hears the cry of animals, he no longer sees the blood that flows, he sees only his idea and perceives only organisms concealing problems which he intends to solve. Similarly, no surgeon is stopped by the most moving cries and sobs, because he sees only his idea and the purpose of his operation.[1] Similarly again, no anatomist feels himself in a horrible slaughter house; under the influence of a scientific idea, he delightedly follows a nervous filament through stinking livid flesh, which to any other man would be an object of disgust and horror. After what has gone before we shall deem all discussion of vivisection futile or absurd. It is impossible for men, judging facts by such different

---

1 Here Bernard is thinking of the old-fashioned practice of conducting operations on human patients without anaesthesia.

ideas, ever to agree; and as it is impossible to satisfy everybody, a man of science should attend only to the opinions of men of science who understand him, and should derive rules of conduct only from his own conscience. (103)

The scientific principle of vivisection is easy, moreover, to grasp. It is always a question of separating or altering certain parts of the living machine, so as to study them and thus to decide how they function and for what. Vivisection, considered as an analytic method of investigation of the living, includes many successive steps, for we may need to act either on organic apparatus, or on organs, or on tissue, or on the histological[1] units themselves. In extemporized[2] or other vivisections, we produce mutilations whose results we study by preserving the animals. At other times, vivisection is only an autopsy on the living, or a study of properties of tissues immediately after death. The various processes of analytic study of the mechanisms of life in living animals are indispensable ... to physiology, to pathology and to therapeutics.... (103-04)

But when we reach the limits of vivisection we have other means of going deeper and dealing with the elementary parts of organisms where the elementary properties of vital phenomena have their seat. We may introduce poisons into the circulation, which carry their specific action to one or another histological unit. Localized poisonings ... are valuable means of physiological analysis. Poisons are veritable reagents of life, extremely delicate instruments which dissect vital units. I believe myself the first to consider the study of poisons from this point of view, for I am of the opinion that studious attention to agents which alter the histological units should form the common foundation of general physiology, pathology and therapeutics.[3] We must always, indeed, go back to the organs to find the simplest explanations of life.

To sum up, dissection is a displacing of a living organism by means of instruments and methods capable of isolating its different parts. It is easy to understand that such dissection of the living presupposes dissection of the dead. (104-05)

---

1   Microscopic; histology is the study of the organization of cells in the tissues of plants and animals.

2   Experimental operations done to see what effect they will have on the animal over a period or time.

3   Through his study of the effect of poisons on animals Bernard made important discoveries, such as the nature of carbon monoxide poisoning and the use of curare as a medicine.

[Primacy of the laboratory in research]

As we see, experimental medicine does not exclude clinical medicine; on the contrary, it comes after it. But it is a higher science, and necessarily more vast and general.... [F]or a man of science there is no separate science of medicine or physiology, there is only a science of life.... I consider hospitals only as the entrance to scientific medicine ... the true sanctuary of medical science is a laboratory; only there can [the physician] seek explanations of life in the normal and pathological states by means of experimental analysis.... In leaving the hospital, a physician, jealous of the title in its scientific sense, must go into his laboratory; and there, by experiments on animals, he will seek to account for what he has observed in his patients, whether about the action of drugs or about the origin of morbid lesions in organs or tissues. There, in a word, he will achieve true medical science. (146-47)

4. From Dr. George Hoggan (and R.H. Hutton). Letter, *Spectator*, Vol. 48 (1875), London, 177

[Dr. George Hoggan's letter to the editor, first published in *The Morning Post*, 2 February 1875, was probably the single most influential public statement against vivisection in Victorian Britain. After retiring from a career as a naval officer, Hoggan took a medical degree from Edinburgh University and then spent four months in the laboratory of Claude Bernard in Paris. Although Hoggan does not mention him by name, it was widely known that Bernard was the person referred to in the letter as "one of the greatest living experimental physiologists." Included here is a prefatory paragraph provided by the editor of *The Spectator*, R.H. Hutton, when the letter was reprinted in that journal on 6 February 1875. Hutton was the most influential of the anti-vivisection members of the Royal Commission established in June 1875 to investigate vivisection, partly in response to the public furor aroused by Hoggan's letter.]

(We republish with much reluctance the following painful letter to the Editor of Monday's *Morning Post*, as showing what the practice of Vivisection, when applied at least to the higher kinds of animals, really means. It has been conjectured, probably enough, that the laboratory referred to is not an English one. But whatever slight shades of difference the personal humanity of the physiologist who presides in such laboratories may make, the main characteristics of these vivisections, when performed on the higher orders of animals, like dogs and cats, cannot greatly differ, since they depend on the permanent conditions of the case. Let no one read the letter who has already made up his mind that the practice must be rigidly restricted or put an end to. For such a one it would be needless suffering.—Ed. [R.H. Hutton] *Spectator*.)

Sir,—If the Society for the Prevention of Cruelty to Animals intend to give effect to the Memorial[1] presented to it on Monday, and do its utmost to put down the monstrous abuses which have sprung of late years in the practice of Vivisection, it will probably find that the greatest obstacle to success lies in the secrecy with which such experiments are conducted; and it is to the destruction of that secrecy that its best efforts should be directed, in the Legislature or elsewhere. It matters little what criminality the law may clearly attach to such practices. So long as the present privacy be maintained in regard to them, it will be found impossible to convict, from want of evidence. No student can be expected to come forward as a witness when he knows that he would be hooted, mobbed, and expelled from among his fellows for doing so, and any rising medical man would only achieve professional ruin by following a similar course. The result is that although hundreds of such abuses are being constantly perpetrated amongst us, the public knows no more about them than what the distant echo reflected from some handbook for the laboratory affords....[2] As nothing will be likely to succeed so well as example in drawing forth the information on these points from those capable but hesitating to give it, I venture to record a little of my own experience in the matter, part of which was gained as an assistant in the laboratory of one of the greatest living experimental physiologists. In that laboratory we sacrificed daily from one to three dogs, besides rabbits and other animals, and after four month's experience, I am of opinion that not one of those experiments on animals was justified or necessary. The idea of the good of humanity was simply out of the question, and would have been laughed at, the great aim being to keep up with, or get ahead of, one's contemporaries in science, even at the price of an incalculable amount of torture needlessly and iniquitously inflicted on the poor animals. During three [military] campaigns I have witnessed many harsh sights, but I think the saddest sight I ever witnessed was when the dogs were brought up from the cellar to the laboratory for

---

1   A petition drawn up by Frances Power Cobbe, the dominant personality of the anti-vivisection movement, urging the RSPCA to take action in restricting vivisection.

2   The most notorious of these was the lavishly illustrated *Handbook for the Physiological Laboratory*, published in 1873, compiled by eminent British researchers as a practical guide to the growing number of British medical students and doctors who were interested in conducting research through vivisection. The *Handbook* aroused a hostile public response quite unexpected by its authors.

sacrifice. Instead of appearing pleased with the change from darkness to light, they seemed seized with horror as soon as they smelt the air of the place, divining apparently their approaching fate. They would make friendly advances to each of the three or four persons present, and as far as eyes, ears, and tail could make a mute appeal for mercy eloquent, they tried it in vain. Even when roughly grasped and thrown on the torture-trough, a low, complaining whine at such treatment would be all the protest made, and they would continue to lick the hand which bound them till their mouths were fixed in the gag, and they could only flap their tail in the trough as their last means of exciting compassion. Often when convulsed by the pain of their torture this would be renewed, and they would be soothed instantly on receiving a few gentle pats. It was all the aid or comfort I could give them, and I gave it often. They seemed to take it as an earnest of fellow feeling that would cause their torture to come to an end—an end only brought by death.

Were the feelings of experimental physiologists not blunted, they could not long continue the practice of vivisection. They are always ready to repudiate any implied want of tender feeling, but I must say they seldom show much pity; on the contrary, in practice they frequently show the reverse. Hundreds of times I have seen when an animal writhed with pain, and thereby deranged the tissues, during a delicate dissection, instead of being soothed, it would receive a slap and an angry order to be quiet and behave itself. At other times, when an animal had endured great pain for hours without struggling or giving more than an occasional low whine, instead of letting the poor mangled wretch loose to crawl painfully about the place in reserve for another day's torture, it would receive pity so far that it would be said to have behaved well enough to merit death, and as a reward would be killed at once by breaking up the medulla with a needle, or "pithing," as this operation is called. I have often heard the professor say, when one side of an animal had been so mangled, and the tissues so obscured by clotted blood, that it was difficult to find the part searched for, "Why don't you begin on the other side?" or, "Why don't you take another dog? What is the use of being so economical?" One of the most revolting features in the laboratory was the custom of giving an animal on which the professor had completed his experiment, and which still had some life left, to the assistants to practise the finding of arteries, nerves, &c., in the living animal, or for performing what are called fundamental experiments upon it,—in other words, repeating those which are recommended in the laboratory handbooks. I am inclined to look on anaesthetics as the greatest curse to vivisectable animals. They alter too much the normal conditions of life to give accurate results, and they are therefore little depended upon.

They indeed prove far more efficacious in lulling public feeling towards the vivisectors than pain in the vivisected....[1]

To this recital I need hardly add that, having drunk the cup to the dregs, I cry off, and am prepared to see not only science, but even mankind, perish rather than have recourse to such means of saving it. I hope that we shall soon have a government inquiry into the subject, in which experimental physiologists shall only be witnesses, not judges. Let all private vivisection be made criminal, and all experiments be placed under Government inspection, and we may have the same clearing-away of abuses that the Anatomy Act caused under similar circumstances.[2]

5. From R.H. Hutton's Testimony, *Report of the Royal Commission on the Practice of Subjecting Live Animals to Experiments for Scientific Purposes, with Minutes of Evidence and Appendix*. London: HMSO, 1876

[Hutton led the opposition to vivisection on the Royal Commission. He especially opposed the use of vivisection for pure research—to investigate scientific problems rather than to provide an obvious medical benefit.]

Modern civilization seems to be set upon acquiring, almost universally, what is called biological knowledge; and one of the consequences of that is, that whereas medical men are constantly engaged in the study of anatomy and physiology for a human purpose,—that is, for the purpose of doing immediate good to mankind,—there are a number of persons who are now engaged in the pursuit of these subjects for the purpose of acquiring abstract knowledge. This is quite a different thing. I am not at all sure that the mere acquisition of knowledge is not a thing having some dangerous and mischievous tendencies in it.... I am not at all prepared to say that the mere desire to attain so much more knowledge is a good condition of mind for a man ... now it has become a profession to discover; and I have often met persons who think that a man who is engaged in original research for the sake of adding to knowledge is therefore a far superior being to a practising physician who is simply trying to do good with his knowledge.... (*Question 944*)

---

1   Anaesthesia had been available since the late 1840s, but it is difficult to get a clear picture as to how much it was used in vivisection in the late nineteenth century. Those who supported vivisection as a method of research claimed that it was used whenever possible, while those who opposed vivisection claimed that it was rarely used, or failed to mention it as an alternative to pain.

2   The Anatomy Act of 1832 regulated the use of cadavers for dissection in medical schools. It was intended to put an end to such gruesome practices as robbing graves or even murder to provide corpses that could be sold to medical schools.

6. From Dr. Emanuel Klein's Testimony, *Report of the Royal Commission on the Practice of Subjecting Live Animals to Experiments for Scientific Purposes* (1876)

[Dr. Claude Bernard was not the only defender of vivisection to gain public notoriety. The brutally frank testimony of Dr. Emanuel Klein (1844-1925) before the Royal Commission may also have contributed to Wells's portrayal of Moreau. To Huxley's dismay, Klein arrogantly insisted on his complete indifference to animal suffering. Members of the Commission repeatedly raised the question of using anaesthesia.

An Austrian doctor and bacteriologist who had been trained in Vienna, Klein came to Britain in 1871 to pursue a career in research. He contributed to an illustrated handbook on vivisection in the laboratory that aroused public hostility. He also became deputy-director of an institute for animal welfare, endowed by charity. When published in the *Report* his testimony caused public uproar. Huxley said that Klein had done more damage to the cause of scientific research than any of the opponents of vivisection.]

Answer to *Question 3538*: "What is your own practice with regard to the use of anaesthetics in experiments that are otherwise painful?"

"Except for teaching purposes, for demonstration, I never use anaesthetics, where it is not necessary for convenience...."

3539. "When you say that you only use them for convenience sake, do you mean that you have no regard at all for the suffering of the animals?"

"No regard at all."

3540. "You are prepared to establish that as a principle of which you approve?"

"I think with regard to an experimenter, a man who conducts special research, he has no time, so to speak, for thinking what the animal will feel or suffer. His only purpose is to perform the experiment, to learn as much from it as possible, and to do it as quickly as possible."

3541. "Then for your own purposes you disregard entirely the question of the suffering of the animal in performing a painful experiment?"

"I do."...

3739. "And you think that the view of scientific men on the Continent is your view, that animal suffering is so entirely unimportant compared with scientific research that it should not be taken into account at all?"

"Yes, except for convenience sake."

[The Commission may have been thinking partly of Klein's testimony when it made the following comment in the preface to its *Report*.]

It is manifest that the practice [of vivisection] is from its very nature liable to great abuse; and that since it is impossible for society to entertain the idea of putting an end to it, it ought to be subjected to due regulation and control. Those who are least favourable to interference assume ... that interference would be directed against the skilful, the humane, and the experienced. But it is not for them that law is made, but for persons of the opposite character. It is not to be doubted that inhumanity may be found in persons of very high position as physiologists. (xvii)

7. From Frances Power Cobbe, *Life of Frances Power Cobbe. By Herself.* Vol. 2. London: Richard Bentley & Son, 1894

[Frances Power Cobbe (1838-1904) was an influential journalist and philanthropist with a wide range of interests. She campaigned for legal and voting rights for women, and for their right to higher education. Today, she is often seen as an early feminist. She also wrote on liberal developments in religion, and supported education for children of the poor. In 1875 she joined forces with George Hoggan to found a society for opposing vivisection and became the leader of the anti-vivisection movement in Britain through the late nineteenth century, resolutely demanding the total abolition of vivisection. Showalter says that a number of sympathizers with the women's movement "saw a clear connection between feminism and anti-vivisection" ("Apocalyptic Fables" 79-80).

The following selections are from chapter 20—"The Rights of Brutes"— of Cobbe's autobiography, which provides a full account of her campaign against vivisection. Cobbe felt betrayed by the inadequacies of the Cruelty to Animals Act, passed by Parliament in 1876 in response to the report of the Royal Commission, and inspired the anti-vivisection movement to increase activity in response. French says that the practice (described in the first selection below) of reproducing gruesome illustrations from handbooks on laboratory methods for vivisection may actually have alienated a good part of the British public (French, 260; 267). The second selection sums up the basis for Cobbe's view that vivisection is a threat to public morality. All emphases are those of the author.]

In February, 1877, the Committee [of the Society for the Protection of Animals], to my satisfaction, unanimously agreed to support Mr. Holt's Bill for total prohibition; and in aid thereof exhibited on the hoardings of London 1,700 handbills and 300 posters, which were enlarged reproductions of the illustrations of vivisection from the Physiological Hand-books. These posters certainly were more effective than as many thousands of speeches and pamphlets; and the indignation of the scientific party sufficiently proved that such was the case. (283)

[W]hen we found that the compromise which we proposed had failed, and that our Bill providing the *minimum* of protection for animals at all acceptable by their friends, was twisted into a Bill protecting their tormentors, we were driven to raise our demands to the total prohibition of the practice, and to determine to work upon that basis for any number of years till public opinion be ripe for our measure.

This was one aspect of our position; but there was another. We had in truth gone into this crusade almost as our forefathers had set off for the Holy Land, with scarcely any knowledge of the Power which we were invading. We knew that dreadful cruelties had been done; but we fondly imagined they were abuses which were *separable* from the *practice* of experimenting on living animals. We accepted blindly the representation of Vivisection by its advocates as a rare resource of baffled surgeons and physicians, intent on some discovery for the immediate benefit of humanity or the solution of some pressing and important physiological problem; and we thought that with due and well considered restrictions and safeguards on these occasional experiments, we might effectually shut out cruelty. By slow, very slow degrees, we learned that nothing was much further from the truth than these fancy[1] pictures of ideal Vivisection, and that real Vivisection is *not* the occasional and regretfully-adopted resource of a few, but the *daily employment* ... of hundreds of men and students, devoted to it as completely and professionally as butchers cutting up carcasses. Finally we found that to extend protection by any conceivable Act of Parliament to animals once delivered to the physiologist in the laboratories, was chimerical.[2] Vivisection, we recognized at last to be a *Method* of *Research* which may be either sanctioned or prohibited as a Method, but which cannot be restricted efficiently by rules founded on humane considerations wholly irrelevant to the scientific inquiry.

On the moral side also, we became profoundly impressed with the truth of the principle to which Canon Liddon refers ... that the Anti-Vivisection cause is "of even greater importance to human character than to the physical comfort of our fellow creatures[3] who are most immediately concerned." As I wrote of it, about this time in *Bernard's Martyrs*:[4]

"We stand face to face with a *New Vice*, new, at least in its vast modern development and the passion with which it is pursued—the Vice of Scientific Cruelty. It is not the old vice of *Cruelty for Cruelty's sake....* It is not like most

---

1   I.e., fanciful.

2   Illusory.

3   I.e., animals.

4   Cobbe quotes from her own recently-published essay; the title refers to Dr. Claude Bernard.

other human vices, hot and thoughtless. The man possessed by it is calm, cool, deliberate; perfectly cognizant of what he is doing; understanding, as no other man understands, the full meaning and extent of the waves and spasms of agony he deliberately creates. It does not seize the ignorant or hunger-driven or brutalized classes; but the cultivated, the well-fed, the well-dressed, the civilized, and (it is said) the otherwise kindly-disposed and genial men of science, forming part of the most intellectual circles in Europe. Sometimes it would appear as we read of these horrors,—the baking alive of dogs, the slow dissecting out of quivering nerves, and so on,—that it would be a relief to picture the doer of such deeds as some unhappy, half-witted wretch, hideous and filthy in mien or stupefied by drink, so that the full responsibility of a rational and educated human being should not belong to him, and that we might say of him, 'He scarcely understands what he does.' But, alas! this *New Vice* has no such palliations; and is exhibited not by such unhappy outcasts, but by some of the very foremost men of our time; men who would think scornfully of being asked to share the butcher's honest trade: men addicted to high speculation on all the mysteries of the universe; men who hope to found the Religion of the Future, and to leave the impress of their minds upon their age, and upon generations yet to be born.[1]

Regarding the matter from this point of view,—as our leaders, the most eminent philanthropists of their generation, Lord Shaftesbury, Lord Mount-Temple, Samuel Morley, and Cardinal Manning, emphatically did,—the reasons for calling for the total Prohibition of Vivisection rather than for its Restriction became actually clearer in our eyes on the side of the human moral interests than on that of the physical interests of the poor brutes. We felt that so long as the practice should be sanctioned at all, so long the Vice of Scientific Cruelty would spring up in the fresh minds of students, and be kept alive everywhere. It was therefore absolutely needful to reach the germ of the disease, and not merely to endeavour to allay the worst symptoms and outbreaks. It is the *passion itself* which needs to be sternly suppressed; and this can only be done by stopping altogether the practice which is its outcome, and on which it feeds and grows.

But (say our opponents), "Are you prepared to relinquish all the benefits which this practice brings to humanity at large?"

Our answer to them, of course, is, that we question the reality of those benefits, but that, placing them at their highest estimation, they are of no appreciable weight compared to the certain moral injury done to the com-

---

1   This sounds like Huxley's scientific rationalism, which Cobbe regards as a coldly objective world-view which will tend to undermine human sympathy.

munity by the sanction of cruelty. The discovery of the *Elixir Vitae*[1] itself would be too dearly purchased if the hearts of men were to be rendered one degree more callous and selfish than they are now. And that the practice of vivisection by a body of men at the intellectual summit of our social system, whose influence must dribble down through every stratum of society, would infallibly tend to increase such callousness, there can exist no reasonable doubt. (289-92)

8. From H.G. Wells, *Text-Book of Biology* [University Correspondence College Tutorial Series]. 2 vols. Intro. G.B. Howes. London: W.B. Clive & Co., University Correspondence College Press, 1893

[In his textbook Wells does not discuss the methods or morality of vivisection: his students were engaged in the dissection of dead animals only. In the passage excerpted below, however, he theorizes that animals which depend largely on unconscious reflex action in their movements may not possess a lively sense of pain and that therefore much of the criticism of vivisection may be misdirected. The last sentence of the last paragraph given below seems clearly hostile to the "enemies of vivisection." All emphases are those of the author.]

From section VI, "Muscle and Nerve."

The simplest example of the action of the nervous system is *reflex action....* A vast amount of our activities are reflex....There appears to be a direct relation between sensation and motion. For instance, the shrieks and other instinctive violent motions produced by pain, "shunt off" a certain amount of nervous impression that would otherwise *register* itself as additional painful sensation. Similarly, most women and children understand the comfort of a "good cry," and its benefit in shifting off a disagreeable mental state.

Voluntary actions may, by constant repetition, become *quasi-reflex* in character....

This fluctuating scope of mind should be remembered, more especially when we are considering the probable mental states of the lower animals. An habitual or reflex action may have all the outward appearance of deliberate adjustment. We cannot tell in any particular case how far the mental comes in, or whether it comes in at all. Seeing that in our own case consciousness does not enter into our commonest and most necessary actions, into breathing and digestion, for instance, and scarcely at all into the *details* of such

---

1   Elixir of eternal youth.

acts as walking and talking, we might infer that nature was economical in its use, and that in the case of such an animal as the Rabbit, which follows a very limited routine, and in which scarcely any versatility in emergencies is evident, it must be relatively inconsiderable. Perhaps, after all, pain is not scattered so needlessly and lavishly throughout the world as the enemies of the vivisectionist would have us believe. (I:43-44)

9. From H.G. Wells, "Popular Feeling and the Advancement of Science. Anti-Vivisection." *The Way the World Is Going: Guesses and Forecasts of the Years Ahead*. London: Ernest Benn, 1928. 221-30

[In this essay, published more than twenty years after *Moreau*, Wells strongly defends vivisection, especially its use for pure research. Wells begins by defining three issues that "really serve to classify men's minds": religious affiliation; attitudes towards birth control; and attitudes towards vivisection. The last is the main subject of the essay.]

What is vivisection? It is a clumsy and misleading name for experimentation on animals for the sake of the knowledge to be gained thereby. It is clumsy and misleading because it means literally cutting up alive and trails with it to most uninstructed minds a suggestion of highly sensitive creatures, bound and helpless, being slowly anatomized to death. This is an idea naturally repulsive to gentle and kindly spirits, and it puts an imputation of extreme cruelty on vivisection which warps the discussion from the outset. But the larger bulk of experiments upon animals for scientific purposes involve no cutting about and very little pain. Many cause discomfort rather than actual pain. There may be the prick of an injection and a subsequent illness.[1] Where there is actual cutting it is nearly always performed under anaesthetics, and in a considerable proportion of such cases there is no need for the animal to recover consciousness and it does not recover consciousness.

Still, a residue of cases remains in which real suffering is inflicted. Far more pain, terror, and distress is inflicted on the first day of pheasant shooting every year, for no purpose at all except the satisfaction of the guns, upon the wounded and mutilated birds which escape, than is inflicted by all the scientific investigators in the world vivisecting for a year. The lives of "fancy" dogs, again, invalid and grotesque deformations of the canine type, must make an aggregation of prolonged discomfort beyond all comparison greater than that of the creatures inoculated by the physiologist. But such considerations

---

1 Beginning in the 1890s, anti-vivisectionists directed increasing protests against the growing use of animals for experiments in vaccination to serve the new science of immunology.

do not release us from the straight question whether it is right and permissible to cut even a single animal about, or indeed to hurt any living creature at all, for the sake of knowledge.

That is what the scientific experimentalist claims to be free to do and which the anti-vivisectionists labour strenuously to prevent. There is no denial on the part of the scientific experimentalist that a certain number of experiments are painful and have to be painful, and that they are of a sort that have to be performed upon animals of an order of intelligence that leaves one in no doubt of the reality of the suffering inflicted. The large majority of experiments involve no inconvenience to the creatures tested, but there is this residuum of admittedly painful cases. It is an amount of suffering infinitesimal in comparison with the gross aggregate of pain inflicted day by day upon sentient creatures by mankind, but it occurs.

The anti-vivisectionist wants legislation to prevent all experiment upon living things for the sake of knowledge. Failing that he wants to prevent experiment upon dogs in particular, even when the experiment involves no pain whatever to the subject. But you will find that the typical anti-vivisectionist is incapable of believing that an experiment can be painless; his imagination is too vivid for any assurance to the contrary. The idea of living substance cut while it quivers and feels is too powerful for him. When the arguments and imaginative appeals to his agitation are scrutinized it will be found that his objection is to real or imagined pain, inflicted in cold blood to no matter what beneficial end.

That is what he wants to stop. His propaganda literature is filled with assertions that no knowledge of any value has ever been gained by biological experimentation, but these preposterous denials of widely known facts are the natural and habitual exaggerations of controversial literature. The sound anti-vivisectionist would not rest his case on any such proposition, for, even if it were true, a single wonderful discovery tomorrow would upset it again. Pushed into a corner he will admit that he does not care whether the knowledge gained is worth while or no. He will not have knowledge gained in this fashion.

It would be easy to convict the anti-vivisectionist movement of many manifest inconsistencies, but my object here is rather to disentangle a fundamental idea than to exhibit confusions of thought. I want to disentangle what is at the root of the feelings of the anti-vivisectionist, and not to score controversial points.... His or her—it is more commonly her—intention is to prevent and forbid the infliction in cold blood and for a scientific end of anything that looks like pain on any animal that can be imagined to suffer.

The hatred is not against pain as such; it is against pain inflicted for knowledge. The medical profession is massively in support of vivisection, and its testimony is that knowledge derived from vivisection has made possible the successful treatment of many cases of human suffering. So far as we can measure one pain against another, or the pain of this creature against the pain of that, vivisection has diminished the pain of the world very considerably. But the anti-vivisectionists will hear nothing of that. They will hear nothing of that because it is not material to their conception of the case.

The peculiar animus of the anti-vivisectionist is clearly against the deliberation and the scientific aim and not against the pain itself. The general subjugation of animals to human ends is not questioned. Many anti-vivisectionists are, like their pets, carnivorous. They will leave the abattoir to go on when they have closed the laboratory; they will recognize the right and duty of the owner of a big dog to beat his fortunate possession into good behaviour and keep it short of food to tame it. They would be indignant if they were refused the freedom of giving their pets anything to eat they fancied—provided always that no scientific knowledge ensued from its subsequent reactions. It is the quiet determination of the clean-handed man with the scalpel that they cannot endure.

It is not that he is cruel, because manifestly he is not cruel—if he had a lust for cruelty the richly emotional nature of the anti-vivisectionists would probably understand him better—it is because he is not driven by his feelings or cravings to do what he does, but by a will for abstract lucidity, that he arouses the antagonism, the violent sense of difference, in his "antis."[1] Vivisection is only occasionally and incidentally the infliction of pain, and anti-vivisection is not really a campaign against pain at all. The real campaign is against the thrusting of a scientific probe into mysteries and hidden things which it is felt should either be approached in a state of awe, tenderness, excitement, or passion, or else avoided. It is, we begin to realize, a campaign to protect a world of fantasy against science, a cherished and necessary world of fantasy. It is a counter-attack upon a treatment of animals that gives the lie to a delightful and elaborated mythology in which these poor limited creatures are humanized and have thrust upon them responses, loyalties, and sympathetic understandings of which they are, in reality, scarcely more capable than plants. The curious, materialistic, shameless, and intelligent monkey lends itself far less easily than the dog to such mythological interpretation, and so gets far less consideration from anti-vivisectionists. It pulls everything to pieces, including pleasant fantasies about itself. But you can tell a dog that it thinks and feels anything you like, however noble and complex, and it watches you hopefully and wags its tail. And so it is about the dog that the controversy centres, and the passions of the dispute rage most obstinately.

To the question we have posed, whether it is justifiable to inflict pain upon animals if need be for the sake of knowledge, the supporter of vivisec-

---

1 Opponents.

tion says "Yes." He says "Yes" because he regards the whole animal creation as existing not merely for its present sensations, but as a contributing part of a continuing and developing reality which increases in knowledge and power. His disposition is to see things plainly and to accept the subservience of beast to man in man's increasing effort to understand and control. He regards animals as limited and simplified cognates of our own infinitely more complex and important beings, illuminating inferiors, and he can conceive no better and more profitable use for their lives than to serve the ends of mental growth. What otherwise are their lives? A play of desires and fears, that ends in being devoured by other creatures great and small.[1] To this mentality that of the natural anti-vivisectionist is in the completest contrast. The world that the pro-vivisectionist is by his nature impelled to strip bare, the anti-vivisectionist clothes in rich swathings of feeling and self-projection. He imagines souls in birds and beasts, long memories and intricate criticism. He can imagine dogs and cats pressed by forebodings, a prey to anxiety, vexed and thwarted. He does not clearly separate them from humanity. Often he will compare these dream-enriched animals of his with mankind to the disadvantage of the latter. He enriches reality but at the same time he distorts and conceals it by these ornamentations. He is afraid of bare reality as a child is afraid of a skeleton.

The biological experimenter experiments because he wants to know. He is neither dismayed by pain nor does he desire that pain should enter into his experiments. He avoids it when possible. I doubt if his work is largely determined by practical ends, or whether it would have much value if he undertook it directly for the sake of curing disease, benefiting humanity or anything of that sort. Sentimental aims mean loose, sentimental, ineffective work. He wants knowledge because he wants knowledge; it is his characteristic good. Practical applications follow unsought. He is a type of humanity that may or may not be increasing in the world. Most of us do not stand up to knowledge like that. We want to keep our illusions. We do not want knowledge for ourselves or others very much, we prefer to be happy in our imaginations, and the rescue of animals from the "clutches" of the vivisectionists appeals to our deep instinctive self-protection quite as much as it does to the widely diffused desire to champion the weak against the strong. (222-30)

---

[1] I.e., the Darwinian fate of wild animals in nature, without the protection of human civilization.

Appendix H: Wells Explains: Two Essays Relating to Moreau's Argument

I. From H.G. Wells, "The Province of Pain." *Science and Art* 8 (February 1894): 58-59

[The parallels between two of Wells's early essays and Moreau's explanation to Prendick in chapter 14 show that Wells and Moreau had some ideas in common. The first essay, "The Province of Pain," published several months before Wells composed the first draft of *Moreau*, provides a background to Moreau's assertion of superiority to pain. In response to Prendick's question, "Where is your justification for inflicting all this pain?", Moreau gives a condensed version of Wells's argument in this essay, but frames it with some philosophical ideas of his own (126-27).]

In spite of the activity of the Society for the Prevention of Cruelty to Animals in our midst, and of the zealous enemies of the British Institute of Preventive Medicine, there have been those who have doubted whether animals—or, at least, very many animals—feel pain at all.[1] This doubt is impregnable, so far as absolute disproof goes. No scientific observer has, as yet, crept into the animal mind; no reminiscences of metempsychosis[2] come to the aid of the humane. We can only reason that there is evidence of pain from analogy, a method of proof too apt to display a wayward fancy to be a sure guide. This alone, however, does not prevent us discussing the question—rather the reverse, for there is, at least, the charm of uncertainty about any inquiries how animals may feel pain. It is speculation almost at its purest.

Many people regard the presence of nerves as indicative of the possible presence of pain. If the surmise is correct, then every kind of animal, from

---

1   The opening paragraphs of this essay appear hostile to the anti-vivisection movement. The British Institute for Preventive Medicine, modelled on the Pasteur Institute in Paris, was dedicated to the study of vaccination to prevent disease, especially rabies. Because it experimented with vaccines on animals, it was an important target for anti-vivisectionists (French 274). In a later essay, "Popular Feeling and the Advancement of Science: Anti-Vivisection," Wells strongly approves of the use of animals for experiments in vaccination (Appendix G9). On the question of how much animals may feel pain, see also Appendix G8.

2   A wry reference to the doctrine of the "transmigration of souls," holding that the soul is reborn in a different body in each generation and hence we can recapture memories from past ages. In this case the memory would be of a previous existence as an animal.

the jellyfish up to man, suffers. Some will even go further, and make plants feel, and figure the whole living creation as groaning and travailing together. But the probabilities are that neither is life nor nervous structure inseparably tinted by the possibility of pain. Among the considerations that point to this conclusion is the fact that many of the nervous impressions of our own bodies have no relation either to pleasure or pain. Most of the impressions of sight are devoid of any decided flavour of the kind, and most sounds, and all those many nervous impressions that never awaken consciousness; those that maintain the tonic contraction of arteries, for instance, are, it goes without saying, painless. Then the little ganglia and nerve-threads that lie in the substance of the heart and keep it beating have nothing to do with pain. The nerves retain their irritability, too, in many cases, after death; and a frog's hind leg may be set moving after being cut off from the body. Here, again, is nerve, but no one will believe there can be pain in an amputated limb. From considerations such as these, one is forced to conclude that the quality of pain becomes affixed to an impression, not in the nerves that conduct, but in the brain that receives it.

Again, we may have pain without receiving nervous impressions—or, at least, we may have pain not simply and immediately arising from nervous impressions. The emotions of fear, jealousy, and even anger, for instance, have all their painful hue. Pain independent of sensation is possible, but so is sensation without pain. Pain without thought is possible, but so is thought without pain. Pain, then, though a prominent feature of our mental scheme, is not a necessary companion either to any living thing or nervous thread, on the one hand, or to any mental existence, on the other.

The end of pain, so far as we can see its end, is protection. There seems to be little or no absolutely needless or unreasonable pain in the world, though disconsolate individuals might easily be found who see no good in gout or toothache. But these, indeed, may be blessings in a still impenetrable disguise. The man in the story, at any rate, whose wish was granted, and who was released from pain, burnt first one hand and then had the other arm mortify, and was happily saved from dying of starvation through indifference by getting himself scalded to death. Pain, rightly seen, is, in fact, a true guardian angel, watching over the field of our activities, and, with harsh tenderness, turning us back from death. In our own bodies it is certainly only located where it is needed.

The whole surface of man's body has painful possibilities, and nerve-ends are everywhere on the watch against injury, but deeper the sense is not so easily awakened. In proof of this it is a common trick among medical students to thrust a pin into the thigh. There these nerve-ends are thinly scattered over the skin, and these once passed the muscle is penetrated with scarcely a pang. Again, as most people have read, the brain has often been cut in operations after injury to the head without causing pain. Internal pains are always less acute, and less definitely seated than external ones. Many grave internal disorders and injuries may manifest themselves merely as a general feverishness and restlessness, or even go on for long as quite unsuspected. The province of pain, then, in man, so far as detailed government is concerned, is merely the surface of his body, with 'spheres of influence,' rather than proper possessions in the interior, and the centre seat of pain is in the mind. Many an operation which to describe gives an unpleasant thrill to the imagination—slicing away the brain, for instance, or washing away the brain with a jet of water—is, as a matter of fact, absolutely painless.

The relation of physical pain to the imagination and the emotions is worthy of consideration. There seems to be a direct relation between emotional and physical sensibility, the one varying inversely, to borrow a convenient technicality, as the other. Professor Lombroso recently raised all the militant feminine by asserting that women felt physical pain less acutely than men.[1] He hardly deserved the severely sarcastic retorts that appeared in the ladies' papers. His critics, from want of practice or other causes, failed to observe the compliment he was paying them. But a man must have been singularly unobservant if he has failed to notice that, while women are more sensitive to fear and to such imaginary terrors as reside in the cockroach and the toad, they can, when physical pain has secured its grasp upon them, display a silent fortitude quite impossible to ordinary men. Their pains are more intense mentally, but less so physically. This is quite in accordance with the view that needless pain does not exist; where the quickness of imagination guards against danger there is evidently a lessened need for the actual physical smart.

Emotional states are anaesthetic. A furious man feels neither fear nor bodily pain, and there is even the clearest antagonism of pain and calm mental occupation. Do not let your mind dwell upon it is the advice of common sense.... This is not the only way in which men can avoid the goad. In the use of anaesthetics we have men anticipating and meeting the warning. So far as physical pain goes, civilized people not only probably do not need it so much, but probably do not feel it so much, or, at any rate, so often as savages. Moreover, the civilized man evidently feels the spur of passion far less acutely than his less advanced brother. In view of the wise economy of nature, it is not immaterial to ask whether this does not open a probability of man's eventual release from pain. May he not so grow morally and intellectually as to get at last beyond the need of corporal chastisement, and foresight take the place of pain, as science ousts instinct? First, he may avoid pain, and then the

---

1 Cesare Lombroso published an article entitled "Physical Sensibility in Woman" in the *Fortnightly Review* 51 (March 1892): 354–57. (For this reference I am indebted to *Early Writings* 196.) Here Wells approves of Lombroso's ideas.

alarm-bell may rust away from disuse. On the other hand, there is a quantitative relation between feeling and acting. Sit still, inhibit every movement, your sensations are at a maximum. So you behave when you would hear low music, and lose nothing. Struggle violently, the great wave of nervous energy flowing out neutralizes the inward flow of feeling. A man when his 'blood is up,' when he is pouring out energy at every point, will fail to notice the infliction of a wound, which, if he were at rest, would be intensely painful. The struggles and outcries of animals being wounded have their merciful use—they shut off so much energy that would register as pain. So the acts of sobbing and weeping are the proper channels of escape from a pressure that would otherwise be intolerable. Probably a great proportion of the impressions that would register as pain in man are immediately transmitted into impulses of movement in animals, and therefore cause no pain. With the development of the intelligence in animals there is, however, a diminution of the promptness with which an animal reacts to stimuli. The higher animals, like man, look before they act; with the distinction of approaching man in being less automatic and more intelligent, it seems credible that they also approach him in feeling pain. Probably, since their emotions are less subtle and their memories less distinct, the actual immediate smart of pain may be keener while it lasts than in man. Man being more intelligent, needs less severity, we may infer, from the hands of his great teacher, Nature, just as the woman needs less than the man.

Hence we may very well suppose that we have, as it were, a series among living things with respect to pain. In such an animal as the dog we may conceive that there is a fairly well-developed moral and intellectual rule, and a keen sense of pain. Going downwards, the mental factor diminishes, the smart of the pain becomes greater and greater in amount, but less and less enduring, until at last the mental disappears and the impression that would be pain is a momentary shock, translated into action before it is felt. On the other hand, as we ascend from the dog to the more complex human, we find physical pain becoming increasingly subordinate to the moral and intellectual. In the place of pains there come mental aversions that are scarcely painful, and an intellectual order replaces the war of physical motives. The lower animals, we may reasonably hold, do not feel pain because they have no intelligence to utilize the warning; the coming man[1] will not feel pain, because the warning will not be needed.

Such considerations as these point to the conclusion that the province of pain is after all a limited and transitory one; a phase through which life must

---

1   I.e., the next stage of human evolution, a subject in which Wells had a perennial interest. In popular Evangelical discourse this phrase also means the appearance of Christ at the Second Coming, to which Wells here makes a playful allusion.

pass on its evolution from the automatic to the spiritual; and, so far as we can tell, among all the hosts of space, pain is found only on the surface of this little planet.

2. From, H.G. Wells "The Limits of Individual Plasticity." *Saturday Review of Politics, Literature, Science and Art* 79 (19 January 1895): 89-90

[Passages that parallel this essay in Moreau's explanation to Prendick in chapter 14 provide much of the basis for the scientific and psychological concepts behind Moreau's project. This essay was intimately involved in the composition of *Moreau*. A short version of Moreau's explanation appears in the manuscript draft of *Moreau* Wells was working on in December, 1894. Just as he gave up on his first draft and started on the second, Wells used the manuscript version of Moreau's explanation as the basis for the essay given here, published early in 1895. In the essay Wells leaves out the dialogue and expands on the scientific aspects of transforming animals through vivisection. Wells then created the final version of this part of Moreau's explanation by working much of the essay back into the dramatic format provided by the manuscript version—see Philmus, variorum *Moreau*, 131-32; 149-52; 188.

In publishing this essay, Wells did not hesitate to present as his own some important ideas that he had originally given to Moreau. Also, in framing the essay in his own ideas he seems to be taking a sympathetic view of a possible aspect of Moreau's motivation. In the first paragraph Wells presents surgical restructuring as a way in which human intervention can escape from the determinism of evolution and heredity. If Wells seems to be making fun here of the eugenicists' attempt to improve the human species through selective breeding, he also seems to speculate that a radical surgery like Moreau's might provide an alternative to eugenics.

Some of the allusions in this essay are footnoted in chapter 14 of this edition.]

The generalizations of heredity may be pushed to extremes, to an almost fanatical fatalism. There are excellent people who have elevated systematic breeding into a creed, and adorned it with a propaganda. The hereditary tendency plays, in modern romance, the part of the malignant fairy, and its victims drive through life blighted from the very beginning. It often seems to be tacitly assumed that a living thing is at the utmost nothing more than the complete realization of its birth possibilities, and so heredity becomes confused with theological predestination. But, after all, the birth tendencies are only one set of factors in the making of the living creature. We overlook only too often the fact that a living being may also be regarded as raw material, as something plastic, something that may be shaped and altered, that this, possibly, may be added and that eliminated, and the organism as a whole developed far beyond its apparent possibilities. We overlook this collateral factor, and so too much of our modern morality becomes mere subservience to natural selection, and we find it not only the discreetest but the wisest course to drive before the wind.

Now the suggestion this little article would advance is this: that there is in science, and perhaps even more so in history, some sanction for the belief that a living thing might be taken in hand and so moulded and modified that at best it would retain scarcely anything of its inherent form and disposition; that the thread of life might be preserved unimpaired while shape and mental superstructure were so extensively recast as even to justify our regarding the result as a new variety of being. This proposition is purposely stated here in its barest and most startling form. It is not asserted that the changes effected would change in any way the offspring of such a creature, but only that the creature itself as an individual is capable of such recasting.... (89-90)

Now first, how far may the inherently bodily form of an animal be operated upon? There are several obvious ways: amputation, tongue-cutting, the surgical removal of a squint, and the excision of organs will occur to the mind at once. In many cases excisions result in extensive secondary changes, pigmentary disturbances, increase in the secretion of fatty tissue, and a multitude of correlative changes. Then there is a kind of surgical operation of which the making of a false nose, in cases where that feature has been destroyed, is the most familiar example. A flap of skin is cut from the forehead, turned down on the nose, and heals in the new position. This is a new kind of grafting of part of an animal upon itself in a new position. Grafting of freshly obtained material from another animal is also possible, has been done in the case of teeth, for example. Still more significant are the graftings of skin and bone— cases where the surgeon, despairing of natural healing, places in the middle of the wound pieces of skin snipped from another individual, fragments of bone from a fresh-killed animal; and the medical student will at once recall Hunter's cock-spur flourishing on the bull's neck. So much for the form.

The physiology, the chemical rhythm of the creature, may also be made to undergo an enduring modification, of which vaccination and other methods of inoculation with living or dead matter are examples. A similar operation is the transfusion of blood, although in this case the results are more dubious. These are all familiar cases. Less familiar and probably far more extensive were the operations of those abominable medieval practitioners who made dwarfs and show monsters, and some vestiges of whose art still remain in the preliminary manipulation of the young mountebank or contortionist. Victor Hugo gives us an account of them, dark and stormy, after his wont, in *L'homme qui rit*. But enough has been said to remind the reader that it is a possible thing to transplant tissue from one part of an animal to another, or from one animal to another, to alter its chemical reactions and methods of growth, to modify the articulation of its limbs, and indeed to change it in its most intimate structure. And yet this has never been sought as an end and systematically by investigators. Some of such things have been hit upon in the last resort of surgery; most of the kindred evidence that will recur to the reader's mind has been demonstrated as it were by accident—by tyrants, by criminals, by the breeders of horses and dogs, by all kinds of untrained men working for their own immediate ends. It is impossible to believe that the last word, or anything near it, of individual modification has been reached. If we concede the justifications of vivisection, we may imagine as possible in the future, operators, armed with antiseptic surgery and a growing perfection in the knowledge of the laws of growth, taking living creatures and moulding them into the most amazing forms; it may be, even reviving the monsters of mythology, realizing the fantasies of the taxidermist, his mermaids and what-not, in flesh and blood.

The thing does not stop at a mere physical metamorphosis. In our growing science of hypnotism we find the promise of a possibility of replacing old inherent instincts by new suggestions, grafting upon or replacing the inherited fixed ideas. Very much indeed of what we call moral education is such an artificial modification and perversion of instinct; pugnacity is trained into courageous self-sacrifice and suppressed sexuality into pseudo-religious emotion.

We have said enough to develop this curious proposition. It may be the set limits of structure and psychical capacity are narrower than is here supposed. But as the case stands this artistic treatment of living things, this moulding of the commonplace individual into the beautiful or the grotesque, certainly seems so far credible as to merit a place in our minds among the things that may some day be. (90-91)

Appendix I: "The Terrible Medusa Case": An Historical Source for Prendick's Shipwreck

From J.B. Savigny and Alexander Corréard, _Narrative of a Voyage to Senegal in 1816_. First published in English translation in 1818. Reprinted by Dawsons of Pall Mall, London, 1968

[Narratives of shipwrecks were among the favourite reading of the Victorian public. The nineteenth century was an age of wide maritime commerce and travel; shipwrecks were frequent and often involved terrible suffering for the survivors, sometimes with incidents of cannibalism and throwing passengers overboard from overcrowded lifeboats. The most famous of these for its horrors, its political significance, and above all its representation in a famous painting, was the wreck of the _Medusa_ off the coast of Africa in 1816. When Prendick compares the wreck of the _Lady Vain_ to "the far more horrible _Medusa_ case" (73) he evokes a well-known disaster of which his own sufferings at sea could be taken as a miniature version. Prendick's ill-provisioned boat, his involvement in at least intended cannibalism, the homicidal violence with which the other two castaways kill each other, and his abandonment by the drunken captain of the _Ipecacuanha_ all find echoes in the story of the _Medusa_.

On 17 June 1816, the French frigate _Medusa_, with 240 passengers and 160 crew, set sail for St. Louis, capital of the French colony of Senegal. Through the incompetence of the captain (a political appointee) the ship ran aground on a reef about 100 miles off the coast of Senegal and began to break up. The three life boats could not take all of those on board. The boats were filled first with the senior officers and the richest and most important of the passengers, including the captain, and a raft was hastily constructed out of spars and boards for the rest. With the weight of its human cargo of 150 the raft began to sink beneath the surface, so most of the provisions had to be thrown overboard. The raft was supposed to be towed by all three boats, but the ropes were soon cut by officers in the boats. The boats then sailed away and left the raft on its own. After the boats reached land no effort was made to initiate a search for the raft. When it was accidentally discovered thirteen days later, only fifteen were left alive and five of these soon died. This incident fuelled an already widespread resentment in France against the reactionary government imposed by the restoration of the Bourbon monarchy after the defeat of Napoleon. The narrative of the ordeal, published by two survivors from the _Medusa_'s crew, quickly became a best-seller and was translated into English and other languages.

In 1819 Théodore Géricault, a French painter, exhibited a large and very dramatic painting entitled *The Raft of the Medusa*, depicting the survivors on the raft in the last stage of their suffering. This soon became one of the most famous paintings in Europe. The art critic Auguste Jal proclaimed, "it is our entire society that is embarked on the *Medusa's* raft" (quoted by Brown, 114). When the painting was exhibited in London, over 50,000 people paid to see it (Koch 39).]

If the preceding night had been terrible, this was still more horrible. Mountains of water covered us every moment, and broke, with violence, in the midst of us; very happily we had the wind behind us, and the fury of the waves was a little checked by the rapidity of our progress; we drove towards the land. From the violence of the sea, the men passed rapidly from the back to the front of the raft, [and] we were obliged to keep in the centre, the most solid part of the raft; those who could not get there, almost all perished. Before and behind the waves dashed with fury, and carried off the men in spite of all their resistance. At the centre, the crowd was such that some poor men were stifled by the weight of their comrades, who fell upon them every moment.... (83)

The soldiers and sailors, terrified by the presence of an almost inevitable danger, gave themselves up for lost. Firmly believing that they were going to be swallowed up, they resolved to soothe their last moments by drinking till they lost the use of their reason; we had not strength to oppose this disorder; they fell upon a cask which was at the middle of the raft....

The fumes of wine soon disordered their brains, already affected by the presence of danger and want of food. Thus inflamed, these men, become deaf to the voice of reason, desired to implicate, in one common destruction, their companions in misfortune; they openly expressed their intention to rid themselves of the officers, who they said, wished to oppose their design, and then to destroy the raft by cutting the ropes which united the different parts that composed it.... Exasperated by so many cruelties, we no longer kept any measures, and charged them furiously. With our sabres drawn we traversed the lines which the soldiers formed, and many atoned with their lives for a moment of delusion.... (84-87)

Thinking that order was restored, we had returned to our post at the centre of the raft, only we took the precaution to retain our arms. It was nearly midnight: after an hour's apparent tranquillity, the soldiers rose again: their senses were entirely deranged; they rushed upon us like madmen, with their knives or sabres in their hands. As they were in full possession of their bodily strength, and were also armed, we were forced again to put ourselves on our defence. Their revolt was the more dangerous, as in their delirium they were entirely deaf to the cries of reason. They attacked us; we charged them in our turn, and soon the raft was covered with their dead bodies. Those among our adversaries who had no arms, attempted to tear us with their teeth; several of us were cruelly bitten.... (96-97)

In the midst of this general madness, some unfortunate wretches were seen to rush upon their comrades with their sabres drawn, demanding the *wing of a chicken*, or *bread* to appease the hunger which devoured them.... Many fancied themselves still on board the *Medusa*, surrounded with the same objects which they saw there every day. Some saw ships, and called them to their assistance, or a harbour, in the back ground of which there was a magnificent city.... We were really seized with a fever on the brain, the consequence of a mental exaltation carried to the extreme....

For forty-eight hours we had taken nothing, and had been obliged to struggle incessantly against a stormy sea.... [A]n extreme resource was necessary to preserve our wretched existence. We tremble with horror at being obliged to mention what we made use of!... Reader, we beseech you, do not feel indignation towards men who are already too unfortunate; but have compassion on them, and shed some tears of pity on their unhappy fate.

Those whom death had spared in the disastrous night which we have just described, fell upon the dead bodies with which the raft was covered, and cut off pieces, which some instantly devoured. Many did not touch them; almost all the officers were of this number. Seeing that this horrid nourishment had given strength to those who made use of it, it was proposed to dry it, in order to render it a little less disgusting.... (107-08)

The fourth morning's sun, after our departure, at length rose on our disaster, and shewed us ten or twelve of our companions extended lifeless on the raft. This sight affected us the more as it announced to us that our bodies, deprived of existence, would soon be stretched on the same place. We gave their bodies to the sea for a grave; reserving only one, destined to feed those who, the day before, had clasped his trembling hands, vowing him an eternal friendship.... (109-10)

We dressed[1] some fish, which we devoured with extreme avidity; but our hunger was so great and our portion of fish so small, that we added to it some human flesh, which dressing rendered less disgusting; it was this which the officers touched, for the first time. From this day we continued to use it; but we could not dress it any more, as we were entirely deprived of the means; our barrel[2] catching fire we extinguished it without being able to

---

1   Cooked.
2   An improvised stove.

save anything whereby to light it again next day....This repast gave us all fresh strength to bear new fatigues.... (111)

We were now only twenty-seven remaining [on the seventh day]; of this number but fifteen seemed likely to live some days: all the rest, covered with large wounds, had almost entirely lost their reason; yet they had a share in the distribution of provisions, and might, before their death, consume thirty or forty bottles of wine, which were of inestimable value to us.[1] We deliberated thus: to put the sick on half allowance would have been killing them by inches. So after a debate, at which the most dreadful despair presided, it was resolved to throw them into the sea. This measure, however repugnant it was to ourselves, procured the survivors wine for six days; when the decision was made, who would dare to execute it? The habit of seeing death ready to pounce upon us as his prey, the certainty of our infallible destruction without this fatal expedient, every thing in a word, had hardened our hearts, and rendered them callous to all feeling except that of self-preservation. Three sailors and a soldier took on themselves this cruel execution; we turned our faces aside, and wept tears of blood over the fate of these unhappy men.... (118-19)

This dreadful expedient saved the fifteen who remained; for, when we were found by the *Argus*, we had very little wine left, and it was the sixth day after the cruel sacrifice which we have just described: the victims, we repeat it, had not above forty-eight hours to live, and by keeping them on the raft, we should absolutely have been destitute of the means of existence two days before we were found. Weak as we were, we considered it certain that it would have been impossible for us to hold out, even twenty-four hours, without taking some food.... (120)

[When discovered by the *Argus*, the raft had been at sea for thirteen days. The captain of the *Argus* reported that "Those whom I rescued had been feeding themselves on human flesh for several days and, when I found them, the ropes (that held the raft together) were covered with human meat set out to dry" (quoted by Alhadeff, 17).]

---

1   "Inestimable" because they had no water.

Appendix J: Wells's first draft of Moreau

From H.G. Wells, "The First *Moreau*." *The Island of Doctor Moreau: A Variorum Text*. Edited by Robert M. Philmus. Appendix I, 100-40. Athens, Georgia: U of Georgia P, 1993

[Wells's original draft of *Moreau* has been published for the first time by Robert M. Philmus in his variorum edition of *Moreau*. I am grateful for his permission to publish excerpts from it here. Philmus shows that Wells likely finished this version by Christmas of 1894, then changed his mind and was well into the second and final version in the first two months of the new year (xviii; xl-xli, note 34). Philmus provides a detailed comparison of the two versions (xvii-xxvi). Despite a similarity in plot, they are quite different in spirit. Study of the changes Wells made in reaching the final version provides a fascinating glimpse into the way the story developed in his imagination.

In the first version of *Moreau*, Wells follows a conventional Victorian mode of mildly satiric whimsy. Moreau is provided with a comfortable domesticity. Despite being built of lava blocks his house is pleasantly English. Above all, he is accompanied by a Mrs. Moreau who presides over his domestic interior. Her alienation from his practice of vivisection hints at a future alliance with Prendick, who sympathizes with her evident distress at the crying of the puma. Making an effort to tell Mrs. Moreau about literature published since she left England, Prendick begins an account of Stevenson's immensely popular *Doctor Jekyll and Mr. Hyde*. It would seem that Wells wanted to highlight a Gothic predecessor of his story. The Moreaus have a son, and Montgomery is incorporated into family life as his tutor. The village of the animal people has an English country appearance.

In the village, a drunken local offers to take Prendick to a secret place where one can engage in comically animal activities. They are overheard and a mob of villagers threatens them with real violence, pursuing morality with an animal ferocity—in the published version, the hunt of the Leopard Man provides a grimmer statement of this theme. Here, however, the village police intervene to take the miscreants before an animal-person magistrate, where they are subjected to a parody of court procedure.

This version ends with a confidential conversation between Prendick and Montgomery, who seems a clearer-thinking person than in the final version and shows no sign of alcoholic tendencies. In the final version Wells strips the story of domesticity, reduces the animal people to a very primitive way of life, and gives them the cult of the Law, rather than police and judicial procedure, as a means of enforcing morality on animal nature.

While a few excerpts are provided here, the entire narrative should be read to appreciate the full significance of the changes.Wells made in the published version. Some of the spelling is normalized and Philmus's indications of minor clarifying changes are omitted. All emphases are those of Wells.]

[Leaving Moreau's house to visit the village of the animal-people, Prendick hears the crying of the puma, but retains his composure in order not to embarrass Mrs. Moreau.]

As I turned dropping the revolver into my pocket there suddenly arose such a cry of pain, such an intense expression of maddening suffering in sound, that—but for her—I would have thrust my fingers into my ears, & run headlong from that accursed house. But knowing that this woman had to suffer as much or more than I suffered, & furthermore had the shame of her husband's cruelty upon her, I made as though I did not hear, but whistling idly & trying to keep my hearing intent upon my tune, strolled slowly away from the house. (116)

[The houses in the village of the animal people] were of one storey built of lava & thatched—in no sense barbaric, but indeed with a certain agreeable appearance of finish, strange in the tropics. I advanced towards them, with a certain queer & extremely agreeable feeling, half curiosity, I fancy, half fear. I passed an individual working in a garden.... The general appearance of the place was an odd blending of an English country town with altogether tropical scenery & materials.... I turned & saw the most piggish looking man that I have ever beheld, small eyes, fat heavy cheeks, flat nose & tusky underjaw exactly like a hog. He walked unsteadily.

"Stranger!" he said as he saw my face. "New 'rival. Find me ... Drunk. Don't 'pologize I'm sure. How *are* you?" And then he added with the air of a desperate man; "*How's your scars?*"

He laughed. "*I* don't care!" He staggered towards me & caught my arm. He was in the maudlin stage of drunkenness....

"You're the right sort I can see," said he. "A brother. None of your infernal logicians. Can't stand 'em. Higher humanity—all the rest of it ... hogwash.You come on the spree with me. I'll show you life. I know a thing or two."

He hesitated. He hiccuped & then bringing his greasy face close to mine whispered; "I know a place—*where they let you drink out of saucers!*"

He seemed disappointed at my calmness. "*Where you can go on all fours,*" he said still more mysteriously.

"I'm hanged," said I aloud & angrily with the idea of being rid of him, "if I see anything attractive in that. It seems to me that you will have to go on all fours in a minute here."

"Sssh!" he said. "Not so loud!"... Passers-by stopped, others came hurrying up & in a minute we four were in the centre of a little crowd of people....

I looked at the faces about me & suddenly that horror of these people that had affected me on the beach came back again with redoubled force. They were all men, with an elvish bright-eyed child or so; & yet there was that odd indefinable touch in their faces. What was it? Even then I did not perceive, though one looked at me with the dull stare of bovine anger, & the glance of another was sidelong & furtive & hateful. At back was another with a calm leonine face, tawny hair & vertical pupils....

"This individual"—I pointed to the drunkard—"asked me to come to a place where one could lap up ..."

I did not finish my sentence. A yell of execration went up from the crowd—with just a touch of cruel derision—& I will confess that moment as the most fearful in my life. "Beast, Beast!" they cried. I was struck on the back of the head and again in the side. "Kill them," said a voice. I never saw a crowd so possessed by animal rage before.... Then I was collared on either side by the men in yellow,[1] & amidst a babel of noises ... I was hustled along towards the market place. I dream even now of those faces, lit by a strange lust of cruelty, surging & grimacing about me, of the threatening hands, some with stumpy unwieldy fingers & some with lank talons; & their eyes blazing with a strange light behind them.

I and the hog-faced man were thrust by the men in yellow up the steps of a house.... Other yellow clad men emerged to assist them & the mob was left to howl outside & gibber at the windows. I stood, bruised, panting, muddy & torn, & not a little dismayed at my reception by these people....

There suddenly entered the man with vertical pupils [the magistrate] whom I had first noticed on the beach, & with him the person called Sturmins[2].... "What is this?" [the magistrate] said to the nearest man in yellow. "And who is this stranger?"

"A case of grossly indecent language, my lord."

He looked grave, went & glared for a moment out of the window, & I noticed the populace shrunk back, & then seated himself at a small table in the centre of the room. We two malefactors stood up before him, the hoggish man unsteady but almost scared back into sobriety.... Then I noticed that the great man's hand, which lay carelessly on the table, was deformed by the loss of a thumb.

He looked at us darkly for a moment. "*This*," said he, pointing to my companion: "is a familiar face. Last time—let me see—it was grubbing up roots & eating them raw. A most disgusting thing."

---

1   The village police.
2   A prototype of the Ape-Man.

"Pardon, m'lord," said the criminal; "last time it was drinking wrong. Rooting, time before."

"Doesn't matter," said his lordship testily. "The thing is you're an obstinate beast. Nothing seems enough, no punishment, no warning, to eradicate these animal traits in you. It almost makes me despair. You & the like of you with your swinish desires & gratifications make this place a pandemonium." ...

Then the two men in yellow gave their evidence in that stiff concise manner that distinguishes the police officer all the world over....

[The magistrate addresses Prendick.] "You came down into the village," said his lordship changing the line of this examination "& fell in with the other defendant."

I said I had & in answer to further questions testified to those singular remarks about the scars, drinking & going on all fours. My evidence was received with considerable emotion. Sturmins held his hands up & repeated "Wretched Man!—Wretch-ed man!" several times. His lordship fidgetted uneasily, & the men in yellow regarded my companion with something between envious amazement and virtuous disgust.

"Have you anything to say to this?" said his lordship in a stern voice.

"I was drunk, my lord; I was drunk!" said the defendant with a piggish squeal & forthwith began to weep bitterly. At that sound the crowd outside howled derision.

"We *must* stamp out this kind of thing," said his lordship gloomily. "I will purify this place if I have to send every other citizen to prison. And *you*," said he addressing me: "surely you knew the bestial wickedness of his conversation? Yet you continued that conversation!"

"I am sorry, my lord," said I: "You must remember I am a newcomer. My moral standards are imperfect I fear.... I have ... never had a properly intense sense of the vileness of going on all fours or lapping one's drink—such as you evidently possess. It's true they seem silly unnatural things to do."

"They are," groaned his lordship, "*most* unnatural, *most* unnatural. But temptation is often very sore. Don't speak of them so lightly." ...

His lordship then proceeded to pardon me. His sentence on the drunken man was as mad as the rest of these fantastic occurrences & I had the hardest task to believe I was awake. Solitary confinement it was, until he had got one play by Shakespeare & one book of the Bible by heart. "We mean to humanize you somehow," said his lordship, "& for that give me Shakespeare and the Bible," & thereupon the poor wretch was led away whimpering. (117-22)

[Montgomery speaks privately to Prendick.]
"I daresay [Moreau's project] seems amazing to you. To me it's lost all that long ago.... It made me sick at first when I found out what he was up to, but afterwards I got interested in a kind of way. But not like he is. This research

is only a sane kind of mania. It's irresistible. He's driven to make these things, can't help it any more than an avalanche that's got to fall can help smashing a tourist that's walking underneath. After they're made he likes them for a little & then he gets restless & starts another.... He doesn't care what becomes of them, provided they don't interfere with him. Of course he has all his own way here, but sometimes I think.... The plain fact of it is, I can't stand up to him & he does what he likes." (136)

Select Bibliography

[This bibliography lists all works cited plus some criticism on *The Island of Doctor Moreau*, as well as some other works by Wells that have been useful but are not cited. It does not attempt to be comprehensive.]

I. Works by H.G. Wells, in Chronological Order

"The Rediscovery of the Unique." *Fortnightly Review*, n.s. 50 (1891): 106-11.

Text-Book of Biology [University Correspondence College Tutorial Series]. 2 Vols. Intro. G.B. Howes. London: W.B. Clive & Co., University Correspondence College Press, 1893.

"The Province of Pain." *Science and Art* 8 (February 1894): 58-59.

"The Mind in Animals." *Saturday Review of Politics, Literature, Science and Art* 78 (22 December 1894): 683-84.

The Time Machine. London: William Heinemann, 1895. Reprinted, ed. Nicholas Ruddick. Peterborough, Ont.: Broadview, 2001.

"The Limits of Individual Plasticity." *Saturday Review* 79 (19 January 1895): 89-90.

"Bio-Optimism." *Nature* 52 (29 August 1895): 410-11.

The Island of Doctor Moreau. London: William Heinemann, 1896. (The text used here is from the first American edition, published by Stone and Kimball, 1896.)

"Human Evolution, an Artificial Process." *Fortnightly Review*, n.s. 60 (October 1896): 590-95.

Letter. *Saturday Review*. (1 November 1896).

"The Acquired Factor." (A review of *Habit and Instinct* by C. Lloyd Morgan.) *The Academy*, 51 (January 1897): 37.

"Morals and Civilization." *Fortnightly Review*, n.s. 61 (February 1897): 263-68.

"Human Evolution: Mr. Wells Replies." *Natural Science: A Monthly Review of Scientific Progress*. No 62, Vol. 10 (April 1897): 242-44.

"The Romance of the Scientist: An Interview with Mr. H.G. Wells." Arthur H. Lawrence. *The Young Man*, No. 128 (August 1897): 254-57.

"The Problem of the Birth Supply." 1903. *The Works of H.G. Wells* (Atlantic Edition). Vol. 4. New York: Scribner's, 1924. 305-37.

A Modern Utopia. 1905. *The Works of H.G. Wells* (Atlantic Edition). Vol. 9. New York: Scribner's, 1925.

"Preface" [1924]. *The Works of H.G. Wells*. Vol. 2. (Atlantic Edition). New York: Scribner's, 1924. ix-xiii.

"Popular Feeling and the Advancement of Science. Anti-Vivisection." *The Way the World Is Going: Guesses and Forecasts of the Years Ahead*. London: Ernest Benn, 1928. 221-30.

"Preface" [1933]. *The Scientific Romances of H.G. Wells*. London: Gollancz, 1933. vii–x.

Experiment in Autobiography: Discoveries and Conclusions of a Very Ordinary Brain. 2 Vols. London: Gollancz and Cresset Press, 1934.

The Croquet Player. New York: The Viking Press, 1937.

H.G. Wells: Early Writings in Science and Science Fiction. Ed. Robert M. Philmus and David Y. Hughes. Berkeley: U of California P, 1975.

II. Criticism on *The Island of Doctor Moreau* and Wells's Science Fiction in General

Anon. Rev. of *The Island of Doctor Moreau*. *Manchester Guardian*, 14 April 1896: 4.

Anon. Rev. of *The Island of Doctor Moreau*. *The Guardian*, 3 June 1896: 871.

Asker, D.B.D. *The Modern Bestiary—Animals in English Fiction 1880-1945*. Queenston, ON: The Edwin Mellen Press, 1996.

Beauchamp, Gorman. "*The Island of Dr. Moreau* as Theological Grotesque." *Papers on Language and Literature* 15 (1979): 408-17.

Bergonzi, Bernard. *The Early H.G. Wells: A Study of the Scientific Romances*. Manchester: Manchester UP, 1961.

Bowen, Roger. "Science, Myth, and Fiction in H.G. Wells's *Island of Doctor Moreau*." *Studies in the Novel* 8 (1976): 318-35.

Bozzetto, Roger. "Moreau's Tragi-Farcical Island." Trans. Robert M. Philmus and Russell Taylor. Ed. Robert M. Philmus. *Science-Fiction Studies* 20 (1993): 34-44.

Ferguson, Christine. *Language, Science and Popular Fiction in the Victorian 'Fin-de-Siècle.'* Aldershot, UK: Ashgate, 2006. (See also article by Ferguson in Section III.)

Fried, Michael. "Impressionist Monsters: H.G. Wells's *The Island of Dr Moreau*." *'Frankenstein': Creation and Monstrosity*. Ed. Stephen Bann. London: Reaktion Books, 1994.

Glendening, John. "'Green Confusion': Evolution and Entanglement in H.G. Wells's *The Island of Doctor Moreau*." *Victorian Literature and Culture* (2002): 571-97.

Gold, Barri J. "Reproducing Empire: *Moreau* and Others." *Nineteenth Century Studies* 14 (2000): 173-98.

Gomel, Elena. "From Dr. Moreau to Dr. Mengele: The Biological Sublime." *Poetics Today* 21 (2000): 393-421.

Hamilton, Craig A. "'The World Was a Confusion': Imagining the Hybrids of H.G. Wells's *The Island of Dr. Moreau*. *The Undying Fire* 2 (2003): 28-36.

Hammond, J.R. "*The Island of Doctor Moreau*: A Swiftian Parable." *The Wellsian* 16 (1993): 30-41.

——. *An H.G. Wells Chronology*. London: Macmillan, 1999.

——. *A Preface to H.G. Wells*. London: Longman, 2001.

Harris, Mason. "Vivisection, the Culture of Science, and Intellectual Uncertainty in *The Island of Doctor Moreau*." *Gothic Studies* 4 (2002): 99-115.

Haynes, R.D. "Wells's Debt to Huxley and the Myth of Dr. Moreau." *Cahiers Victoriens et Edourdiens* 13 (1981): 31-41.

——. "The Unholy Alliance of Science in *The Island of Doctor Moreau*." *The Wellsian* 11 (1988): 13-24.

Hendershot, Cyndy. "The Animal Without: Masculinity and Imperialism in *The Island of Doctor Moreau* and 'The Adventure of the Speckled Band.'" *Nineteenth Century Studies* 10 (1996): 1-32.

Hillegas, Mark R. *The Future as Nightmare: H.G. Wells and the Anti-Utopians*. New York: Oxford UP, 1967.

Hughes, David Y. "The Garden in Wells's Early Science Fiction." *H.G. Wells and Modern Science Fiction*. Ed. Darko Suvin and Robert M. Philmus. London: Associated UP, 1977.

Huntington, John. *The Logic of Fantasy: H.G. Wells and Science Fiction*. New York: Columbia UP, 1982.

Hurley, Kelly. *The Gothic Body: Sexuality, Materialism, and Degeneration at the "Fin de Siècle."* Cambridge: Cambridge UP, 1996.

Hutton, R.H. Rev. of *The Island of Doctor Moreau*, by H.G. Wells. *Spectator* 76 (11 April 1886): 519-20.

Jackson, Kimberly. "Vivisected Language in H.G. Wells's *The Island of Doctor Moreau*. *The Wellsian* 29 (2006): 20-35.

Kirby, David A. "Are We Not Men? The Horror of Eugenics in *The Island of Dr. Moreau*." *Horror*. Ed. Steffen Hantke. Vashon Island, Washington: Paradoxa, 2002.

Krumm, Pascale. "*The Island of Doctor Moreau*, or the Case of Devolution." *Foundation* 75 (Spring 1999): 51-62.

Lehman, Steven. "The Motherless Child in Science Fiction: *Frankenstein* and *Moreau*." *Science-Fiction Studies* 18 (March 1992): 49-57.

Mackerness, E.D. "Nathan Benjulia, a Prototype of Dr Moreau?" *The Wellsian* 2 (1978): 1-5.

McCarthy, Patrick A. "*Heart of Darkness* and the Early Novels of H.G. Wells: Evolution, Anarchy, Entropy." *Journal of Modern Literature* 13 (1986): 37-60.

McConnell, Frank. *The Science Fiction of H.G. Wells*. New York: Oxford UP, 1981.

McLean, Steven. "Animals, Language and Degeneration in H.G. Wells's *The Island of Doctor Moreau*." *The Undying Fire* 1 (2002): 43-50.

Mitchell, Chalmers. Rev. of *The Island of Doctor Moreau*, by H.G. Wells. *Saturday Review* 81 (11 April 1896): 368-69.

Parrinder, Patrick, ed. *H.G. Wells: The Critical Heritage*. London: Routledge and Keegan Paul, 1972.

——. *Shadows of the Future: H.G. Wells, Science Fiction and Prophecy*. Liverpool: Liverpool UP, 1995.

Philmus, Robert M. "The Satiric Ambivalence of *The Island of Doctor Moreau.*" *Science-Fiction Studies* 8 (1981): 2-11.

———. "Introducing Moreau." *The Island of Doctor Moreau: A Variorum Text.* By H.G. Wells. Ed. Robert M. Philmus. Athens and London: U of Georgia P, 1993.

Platzner, Robert L. "H.G. Wells's 'Jungle Book': The Influence of Kipling on *The Island of Dr. Moreau.*" *Victorian Newsletter* 36 (Fall 1969): 16-22.

Punter, David. *The Literature of Terror: A History of Gothic Fictions from 1765 to the Present Day.* London and New York: Longman, 1980.

"Recent Novels." Rev. of *The Island of Doctor Moreau. The Times,* 17 June 1896: 17.

Redfern, Nick. "Abjection and Evolution in *The Island of Doctor Moreau.*" *The Wellsian* 27 (2004): 37-47.

Reed, John R. "The Vanity of Law in *The Island of Doctor Moreau.*" *H.G. Wells under Revision.* Ed. Patrick Parrinder and Robert M. Philmus. London: Associated UP, 1986.

Roberts, Ian F. "Maupertuis: Doppelganger of Doctor Moreau." *Science Fiction Studies* 23 (2001): 261-74.

Showalter, Elaine. *Sexual Anarchy: Gender and Culture at the Fin de Siècle.* New York: Penguin, 1990.

———. "The Apocalyptic Fables of H.G. Wells." *'Fin de Siècle / Fin de Globe': Fears and Fantasies of the Late Nineteenth Century.* Ed. John Stokes. New York: St. Martin's, 1992. 69-83.

Steffen-Fluhr, Nancy. "Paper Tiger: Women and H.G. Wells." *Science-Fiction Studies* 12 (1985): 311-29.

Stover, Leon, ed. *The Island of Doctor Moreau. A Critical Text of the 1896 London First Edition, with an Introduction and Appendices.* Jefferson, NC and London: McFarland, 1996.

Vallorani, Nicoletta. "Hybridizing Science: The 'Patchwork Biology' of Dr. Moreau." *Cahiers Victoriens et Edourdiens* 46 (1997): 245-61.

Weeks, Robert P. "Disentanglement as a Theme in H.G. Wells's Fiction." *Papers of the Michigan Academy of Science, Arts, and Letters* 39 (1954): 439-44. Reprinted in *H.G. Wells: A Collection of Critical Essays.* [Twentieth-Century Views.] Ed. Bernard Bergonzi. Englewood Cliffs, NJ: Prentice-Hall, 1976. 25-31.

III. Background

Alhadeff, Albert. *The Raft of the Medusa: Géricault, Art, and Race.* New York: Prestel, 2002.

Atwood, Margaret. *Oryx and Crake.* Toronto: Seal Books (Random House of Canada Limited), 2004.

Bernard, Claude. *An Introduction to the Study of Experimental Science.* 1857. Trans. Henry Copley Green. New York: Dover, 1957.

Brown, David Blaney. *Romanticism*. New York: Phaidon Press, 2001.

Browne, Janet. *Charles Darwin: The Power of Place*. Princeton, NJ: Princeton UP, 2002.

Buchanan, Robert Williams. *The Coming Terror and Other Essays and Letters*. London: W. Heineman, 1891.

Cobbe, Frances Power. *Life of Frances Power Cobbe. By Herself*. London: Richard Bentley & Son, 1894.

Darwin, Charles. *On the Origin of Species by Means of Natural Selection*. 1859, 1872 (Sixth Edition). New York: D. Appleton, 1898.

———. *The Descent of Man and Selection in Relation to Sex*. 1871. New York: D. Appleton, 1896.

———. *The Expression of the Emotions in Man and Animals*. 1872. New York: Appleton, 1896.

Desmond, Adrian. *Huxley: From Devil's Disciple to Evolution's High Priest*. London: Penguin, 1998.

Drinka, George Frederick. *The Birth of Neurosis: Myth, Malady and the Victorians*. New York: Simon and Schuster, 1984.

Ferguson, Christine. "Decadence as Scientific Fulfilment." *PMLA* 117, No. 3 (May 2002): 465-78. (See also book by Ferguson in Section II.)

French, Richard D. *Antivivisection and Medical Science in Victorian Society*. Princeton, NJ: Princeton UP, 1975.

Freud, Sigmund. *Civilization and Its Discontents*. Trans. James Strachey. New York: W.W. Norton, 1989.

Gould, Stephen Jay. *The Mismeasure of Man*. New York: Norton, 1981.

Great Britain. Royal Commission. *Report of the Royal Commission on the Practice of Subjecting Live Animals to Experiments for Scientific Purposes, with Minutes of Evidence and Appendix*. London: HMSO, 1876.

Hoggan, George. Letter. *Morning Post*, 2 February 1875. Reprinted in *Spectator* 47 (6 February 1875): 177-78.

Huxley, Thomas H. *Man's Place in Nature*. 1863. Published as vol. 7 of *Collected Essays*. New York: D. Appleton, 1902. Reprinted, New York: Greenwood Press, 1968.

———. "The Struggle for Existence in Human Society." *Nineteenth Century* 23 (February 1888): 61-80. Published in vol. 9 of *Collected Essays*. Reprinted, New York: Greenwood Press, 1968.

———. "An Apologetic Irenicon." *Fortnightly Review* 52 (November 1892): 557-71.

———. "Evolution and Ethics." 1893. *Evolution and Ethics and Other Essays*. Published in vol. 9 of *Collected Works*. Reprinted, New York: Greenwood Press, 1968.

James, William. *Psychology: The Briefer Course*. 1892. New York: Henry Holt, 1910.

Jones, Ernest. *The Life and Work of Sigmund Freud*. 3 vols. 1953. New York: Basic Books, 1957.

Koch, Tom. *The Wreck of the William Brown: A True Tale of Overcrowded Lifeboats and Murder at Sea.* Vancouver, BC: Douglas & McIntyre, 2003.

Leakey, Richard. *The Origin of Mankind*. New York: Basic Books, 1994.

Lombroso, Cesare. *Crime: Its Causes and Remedies*. Trans. Henry P. Horton. 1911. Montclair, NJ: Patterson Smith, 1868. (Originally published as Volume III of *Criminal Man*.)

Lombroso-Ferrero, Gina. *Criminal Man According to the Classification of Cesare Lombroso*. 1911. Montclair, N.J.: Patterson Smith, 1972. (Excerpts from Lombroso's *Criminal Man*, first published in 1876.)

MacKenzie, Norman and Jeanne MacKenzie. *H.G. Wells: A Biography*. New York; Simon and Schuster, 1973.

Moreau, Jacques-Joseph (de Tours). *Hashish and Mental Illness*. Ed. Helene Peters and Gabriel Nahas. Trans. Gordon J. Barnett. New York: Raven Press, 1973.

——. *La Psychologie Morbide*. Paris: Victor Masson, 1859.

Olmsted, J.M.D. *Claude Bernard: Physiologist*. New York: Harper, 1938.

Paradis, James G. *T.H. Huxley: Man's Place in Nature*. Lincoln and London: Nebraska UP, 1978.

——. "*Evolution and Ethics* in Its Victorian Context." *T.H. Huxley's "Evolution and Ethics."* Ed. James Paradis and George C. Williams. Princeton, NJ: Princeton UP, 1989.

Partington, John S. "The Death of the Static: H.G. Wells and the Kinetic Utopia." *Utopian Studies* 11, No. 2 (2000): 96-111.

——. *Building Cosmopolis: The Political Thought of H.G. Wells*. Aldershot, UK: Ashgate, 2003.

——. "H.G. Wells's Eugenic Thinking of the 1930s and 1940s." *Utopian Studies* 14, No. 1 (2004): 74-81.

Savigny, J.B. and Alexander Corréard. *Narrative of a Voyage to Senegal in 1816*. 1818. London: Dawsons of Pall Mall, 1968.

Smith, David C. *H.G. Wells: Desperately Mortal*. New Haven: Yale UP, 1986.

Shelley, Mary. *Frankenstein*. (1818 text.) Ed. Marilyn Butler. New York: Oxford UP, 1994.

Swift, Jonathan. *Gulliver's Travels*. 1735. Ed. Claude Rawson. Notes by Ian Higgins. New York: Oxford UP, 2005.

Tarshis, Jerome. *Claude Bernard: Father of Experimental Medicine*. New York: The Dial Press, 1968.

Vyvyan, John. *In Pity and in Anger: A Study of the Use of Animals in Science*. London: Michael Joseph, 1969.

West, Geoffrey. *H.G. Wells*. New York: Norton, 1930.

From the Publisher

A name never says it all, but the word "Broadview" expresses a good deal of the philosophy behind our company. We are open to a broad range of academic approaches and political viewpoints. We pay attention to the broad impact book publishing and book printing has in the wider world; for some years now we have used 100% recycled paper for most titles. Our publishing program is internationally oriented and broad-ranging. Our individual titles often appeal to a broad reader-ship too; many are of interest as much to general readers as to academics and students.

Founded in 1985, Broadview remains a fully independent company owned by its shareholders—not an imprint or subsidiary of a larger multinational.

For the most accurate information on our books (including information on pricing, editions, and formats) please visit our website at www.broadviewpress.com. Our print books and ebooks are also available for sale on our site.

broadview press
www.broadviewpress.com

This book is made of paper from well-managed FSC® - certified
forests, recycled materials, and other controlled sources.